ALEX SELKY ... AGED SIX ... MISSING ...

'Alex isn't home yet and, I was wondering, would you just ask Justine if she remembers did he stay to play ball in the yard or anything, or did he say anything about stopping somewhere?...'

'Alex isn't *home* yet?'

That was a bad moment. The moment when you have to admit to another parent that you don't know where your child is.

'Hold on a sec,' said Jocelyn. Susan could hear her calling Justine.

It took a long time. It took such a long time that while she was holding on, Susan died and went to hell and came back a soul in torment. It took such a long time that before Jocelyn picked up the phone again, Susan already knew. 'Susan ... Justine says Alex wasn't in school today at all.'

He didn't go home with a friend? Didn't stop to read comics? She was still reaching for reasons for him not being home yet. She couldn't begin to grasp the idea of him not getting to school at all.

'Susan,' said Jocelyn, 'I'm coming over. Call the police.'

Call the police.

Call the police.

Still Missing

BETH GUTCHEON

SPHERE BOOKS LIMITED
30–32 Gray's Inn Road, London WC1X 8JL

First published in Great Britain by
Michael Joseph Ltd 1981
Copyright © 1981 by Beth Gutcheon
Published by Sphere Books Ltd 1982
Reprinted 1982

Set in Times

Printed and bound in Great Britain by
Cox & Wyman Ltd, Reading

Author's Note

As usual, I'm indebted to the kindness of friends. Without Susan Bagg Todd, this would have been a different book. Susan Isaacs, Jesse Kornbluth, Nancy Rhey and George Semler each gave me their time at moments that mattered much more to me than to them, and more important, each gave me the kind of specific and informed responses to the material that only another writer could. Sol Slotnik and Michael Taylor with great and offhand generosity tracked down for me technical information and material that was exactly what I needed when I needed it. I thank you all. And I thank Tina Nides and especially my editor, Diane Reverand, and my agent, Wendy Weil, for the intelligence, composure and kindness with which they seem inexhaustibly supplied. And to J and D—this time, most of all, thank you. This book is of you, and for you.

For my sister Gray

Deep with the first dead lies London's daughter
Robed in the long friends,
The grains beyond age, the dark veins of her
    mother
Secret by the unmourning water
Of the riding Thames.
After the first death, there is no other.

—Dylan Thomas, *A Refusal to Mourn the Death, by Fire, of a Child in London*

YOU COULD HARDLY get to age thirty-four without learning something about loss. By thirty-four you're bound to have lost your Swiss Army knife, your best friend from fourth grade, your chance to be center forward on the starting team, your hope of the Latin prize, quite a few of your illusions, and certainly, somewhere along the line, some significant love. Susan Selky had in fact recently lost an old battle, for her marriage to the man she was in love with, and with it, many ancillary dreams of more babies, and of holding his hand in the dark when they were old.

It may be that one loss helps to prepare you for the next, at least in developing a certain rueful sense of humor about things you're too old to cry about. There's plenty of blather, some of it true, about turning pain into growth, using one blow to teach you resilience and to make you ready for the shock of the next one. But the greater truth is that life is not something you can go into training for. There was nothing in life that Susan Selky could have done to prepare for the breathtaking impact of losing her son.

Susan Selky, bright, loyal, stubborn, shy. If you knew her professionally, you probably wouldn't have guessed that whatever accomplished forays she made daily outside, she thought with relief of her narrow brick house on Fremont Street as if it were a shell. Inside, dumb and unguarded as a mollusk, was the heart of life, her private days and nights with Alex.

Alexander Graham Selky, Jr., age 6¾, a freelance spaceman. A small, sturdy child with a two-hundred-watt smile and a giggle like falling water, a child who saw *Star Wars* once with Mommy, twice with Daddy, and once again with TJ. Owner-trainer of Taxi, an oversized Shetland sheepdog.

Taxi was a near-total loss in the training department. He had only managed to learn to start barking with joy when Alex got home from school, a full minute before any human could have heard his feet on the step, and to smuggle himself soundlessly onto Alex's bed at night against orders. Most evenings when she went to kiss Alex one more time on her own way to bed, Susan found Taxi burrowed against her sleeping boy with his nose in his armpit, still as a statue except for the wistful eyes that tracked her approach and begged, "Pretend you don't see me."

"He thinks he's my brother," said Alex. "He thinks he's a fur person."

Alex Selky, going on seven, so eager to grow up, kissed his mother good-bye on their front steps on the hot bright morning of May 15, 1980, and marched himself down the street on his way to the New Boston School of Back Bay, two blocks from his corner. He never arrived at school, and from the moment he turned the corner, he apparently disappeared from the face of the earth.

IT WAS, after all, only 2:50 in the afternoon when Susan jogged down Fremont Street. She'd been held up after her seminar by a chatty student, and she worried that she wouldn't get home before Alex. The entryway downstairs was dark; the tenant of her ground-floor apartment was, of course, at work. Alex's bike lay against the wall by the door that led upstairs to the two floors they occupied. As she unlocked this inner door, she could hear Taxi flinging himself against it on the other side, squeaking in his attempts not to howl with delight that one of his people had come back.

"Yes, good dog," said Susan fondly, bending over the ecstatic Taxi. "Yes, lovely Taxi. No, hush. Can't learn not to bark my ears off, can you, poor Taxi, you dumbbell?" Taxi was bouncing up the stairs between her feet all the while she was talking to him.

She put away her groceries, found her morning *Globe*, as yet unopened, and went to settle herself in the deep chair by the window. Sunlight flooded this front room in the afternoons, slanting in in wide shafts between the curtains that framed the windows floor to ceiling. Sunlight glowed in patches across the ash-blue chairs and sofa, the fading Persian carpet, and the wide dark polished boards of the old hardwood floor. What a pleasure it was to have the room in ticking silence for a minute or two.

It was almost 3:30 before some stirring in the house, some creaking so soft that it reminded her nothing human was moving, caused her to look at her watch. That was the moment it began. It was thirty minutes since school let out. It took seven minutes to walk from the schoolyard home. Where was Alex?

She went to the window and leaned out over the sidewalk. She looked to north and south. The street lay silent in the sunlight. She watched for a moment or two, knowing that if she refused anything as dramatic as that quiver of fear starting under her rib cage, Alex would sprint around the corner bouncing his Spiderman backpack.

"I won't dawdle," he had said manfully when he asked permission to walk himself home from school. "You can *count* on me," in a voice that sounded so like his father's.

"Okay," she said. "I will." She had reached across the supper table to shake on it. Alex shook, seriously, and with his elbow, overturned his milk.

Susan kept her eyes on the corner, trying to make Alex appear. She felt she could do it by force of will. Just do it. Just come around the corner, panting, with your cheeks flushed and your bright hair flying and your totally plausible six-year-old's explanation. (Almost seven. He'll be seven in two months. My good little man.) Just show up right now, before I allow this feeling to have a name, and panic, and make an ass of myself. (Yes, I know I said he was missing and must have been murdered, officer, but you see he was actually at his friend's house reading Batman comics. . . . Yes, I know the entire department is on its way over here in squad cars—yes, he *is* here now, he just . . . But you see, he promised he wouldn't dawdle. . . . Seven. Well, almost seven. But he's a very responsible. . . . Well, I'm *sorry*. Yes, I know I inconvenienced you. . . . No, I'm not a hysterical woman, I'm a tenured professor of American literature. . . . I *said* I was sorry. . . .)

The street was so strangely still that she suddenly noticed something moving around under the lid of the Berlins' garbage can next door. She flashed cold. A rat? She watched for a long minute, then another. At last the plastic lid was nudged a definitive inch to one side, and out slid Tom Berlin's pet ferret, looking furtive. It slunk away toward the backyard, with its sly waddle and distinctive smell, perceptible even from Susan's window.

Enough, she said to herself. Please. I think I just almost had a heart attack. She went to the phone and called Jocelyn, just to be paranoid.

"Hey," said Susan. "It's me."

"Hey. I'm glad you called. I'm really having a swell day, let me tell you. I waited four hours this morning for the damn lumberyard to deliver my plywood, and when they finally got here I practically had to suck their toes to get them to carry it up the stairs. Ten four-by-eight sheets of five-ply . . . What good was it to me on the sidewalk? It's not like it was a puny order. Do you know what that stuff costs?"

"You should work in something light, like paper."

Jocelyn's current works were huge bas-relief wooden wall sculptures of nuts and bolts and gear wheels, painted in matte-finish pastels. Before she discovered Art, she'd run a health-food catering service, and before that she wrote publicity for a publishing company, and before that she was a model. She'd dyed her hair blond and worked for Filene's until the vogue died out for girls who look like Twiggy.

"Forget paper," said Jocelyn. "Paper was last year. Paper is craft. You can't work in paper without a penis. They want women to deal with the biggest, heaviest, most macho shit they can find. . . . That damn lumberyard. I was late to pick up Justine and everything."

"Oh, Justine's home?" asked Susan.

"Oh, yes. Finally. I had to stop and feed her on the way, though, because she traded her lunch at school for a Cat-woman doll. She's in her room putting Hulk costumes on it."

"Oh, good, okay. Actually, Alex isn't home yet, and I was wondering, would you just ask Justine if she remembers did he stay to play ball in the yard or anything, or did he say anything about stopping somewhere? . . ."

"Alex isn't *home* yet?"

That was a bad moment. The moment when you have to admit to another parent that you don't know where your child is. It takes about one millisecond for that thought to pierce through a mother's sheen of selfishness, her minor annoyance with the demands of caring for a small child, to strike a core of exquisite terror. Susan felt that quiver run through Jocelyn.

"Hold on a sec," said Jocelyn. Susan could hear her calling Justine.

It took a long time. It took such a long time that while she was holding on, Susan died and went to hell and came back a soul in torment. It took such a long time that before Jocelyn picked up the phone again, Susan already knew. "Susan . . . Justine says Alex wasn't in school today at all."

Later Susan actually remembered hearing a crash at that moment. She remembered the words accompanied by a noise as if a giant tree were being shattered by lightning. There was a bright lurid flash, too, like the kind of frightening light you get in a thunder squall just at twilight.

He didn't go home with a friend? He didn't stop to read comics? She was still reaching for reasons for him not being home yet. She couldn't begin to grasp the idea of him not getting to school at all.

"Susan," said Jocelyn, "I'm coming over. Call the police."

Call the police.

Call the police.

In the quiet room, in the sunlight, Susan felt herself sink into a well of horror so great that it was all colors, all light and all darkness, scalding heat and killing cold. It was miles deep and glassy-sided. The sensation was beyond anything you could feel and not be seared along every nerve and cell, altered forever.

By the time she picked up the phone again, she had passed through the first shock. You couldn't feel that way long without it stopping your heart. Everything blurred and tingled slightly; she went numb. She was certainly not a hysterical woman as she called the police.

Susan knew what to expect. She had read the stories in the newspapers. Your son disappears, you call the police, and they tell you your boy ran away. They tell you you have to wait

13

forty-eight hours before he's a Missing Person. And by then it's too late, and then five months later they find out that some pervert creep has been killing small boys and eating them. He's got an attic full of little bones.

Susan didn't know what precinct she lived in. She called 911. "Yes, it's an emergency. My son has disappeared. . . ."

"What address?"

"What? . . . Fremont Street. Back Bay."

"That's the Fourth District. I'll connect you."

The phone was answered on the first ring. "Fourth District."

"Yes. Hello. I want to report a missing child."

"Juvenile. Hold on." The line went numb, then came alive again. Another voice said, "Detective Menetti."

It shook her to have to begin a third time: Yes, I want to report . . . This is Mrs. . . . My son is missing. He's six years old.

"Name," said the toneless voice on the other end.

"My name is Susan Selky, his name is Alex. . . . Is that what you meant? Alexander. I saw him—"

"Your address, Mrs. Selky?"

"Sixty-three Fremont Street. Between Marlborough and Beacon."

"You last saw your son . . . when?"

"At 8:50 this morning. I kissed him good-bye and watched him to the corner. He walks himself to school. It's only two more blocks."

"He was last seen at 8:50 *this morning*? Why did you wait so long to call us?"

"Oh, please . . ." she said very softly.

"Never mind. I'll be right there." Lieutenant Menetti hung up.

The doorbell rang: Jocelyn and Justine. Taxi greeted them fervently, but was a little surprised. *They* weren't Alex. He did his best to welcome them anyway. Justine, wearing a white leotard and a red peasant skirt, looked grave and held her mother's hand.

"He never *came* to school today," she started explaining to Susan while still climbing the stairs. "I waited outside for him until the bell rang. He has my red pencil."

Jocelyn silently put her hands on Susan's shoulders and looked intently into her eyes. Far in the distance, Susan thought, then knew, she heard a siren. It whined quickly louder and louder through the streets toward them until at last it pulled up with a threatening wail in front of Susan's door. Jocelyn held Susan's hand as they listened to the footsteps on the stairs.

Susan felt weirdly calm. She felt as if she were outside her body altogether, picturing this scene. There she was, standing at the top of the stairs, holding the door open. She was slim, tall, with fine dark hair and unusually light blue eyes. There she was in her bare feet; her sandals were by the chair where she curled up with the paper an hour ago. There was Jocelyn, with her fashionably wild brown hair streaked with gray, looking bony in her ancient blue jeans and workshirt, but, as always, carefully made-up. Here were the two detectives. This one is big, dark, fifty, with a flushed face and creases around his mouth and eyes so deep that folds of flesh nearly cover his upper eyelids. Detective Menetti. This other one is younger. Pale. Heavy.

Detective Menetti sized up the house. He sized up Susan. He introduced himself to Jocelyn and Justine, and registered their names. Susan told him again what she'd told him on the phone. "He never got to school at *all*," Justine kept piping up. "I waited for him, I waited and waited."

"Often we meet him on Beacon Street as we come across Exeter," added Jocelyn in her slow Texas drawl. "Susan saw him turn the corner, but we never saw him after that." Menetti looked quickly at Susan. Her eyes were steady. Her skin was fine and deadly pale; a vein was twitching along one side of her throat. "I kissed him good-bye, and I watched from the steps till he turned the corner. I had to go the other way, you see, to get the T to Cambridge. My honors students are finishing their theses this week. He's very responsible, he's almost seven. It's only two blocks up Beacon Street. He only has to cross one street. He . . ."

"Tell me a little more about him, Mrs. Selky."

She paused for a minute. How can you tell a little about your whole child? "He's unusually dependable," she said again. To one side, the second detective was watching her.

15

"Can you let me have a more complete description?" Menetti asked. He had his pad out and his pen poised.

"Oh. Yes. He's, um, he's almost seven years old, he has dark brown hair, straight, about this length." She gestured with her hand. "He's very friendly and happy, and he loves soccer . . . and riddles . . ."

"How tall is he, Mrs. Selky?"

"How . . . well . . . he comes to right here on me . . ." Her arms curved outward, as if to embrace her missing boy.

"He's exactly Justine's height," said Jocelyn softly, moving to stand very close to Susan.

Justine stood up straight, and Menetti looked at her, and wrote on his pad. "I have a seven-year-old myself," he said to Justine. "He's just about your size. I bet you weigh, what, fifty-five pounds?"

"Fifty-seven," said Jocelyn.

"And would that be about the same as the boy?" asked Menetti.

"A pound or two lighter," said Jocelyn. "She's got a little potbelly." About fifty-five pounds, wrote Menetti.

"Wearing?" They looked at Susan.

She took a deep breath. "Wearing. Blue jeans, red-and-white T-shirt, and blue running shoes. He was carrying his Spiderman knapsack, with his lunch in it."

"Okay, got that. Mrs. Selky, was Alex the kind of kid who talked to strangers?"

Susan shuddered. She shook her head. "We went over and over that when we decided he could walk to school by himself. We talked about strangers and what they might say, and all the ways Alex could handle it."

"Okay. Now, you say *we* decided—you mean you and Mr. Selky?"

"I mean Alex and me. Graham and I are separated . . ." A look passed between the two detectives. "I did discuss it with Graham, of course, but Alex and I decided."

"Uh-huh. And how long have you been separated, Mrs. Selky?"

"Three months."

"Uh-huh. And where is Mr. Selky living now?"

"In Cambridge. Do you want to know with whom?" she

asked tartly.

"It was a painful separation, then? Still pretty raw?"

"Painful? Of course it was painful—may I ask why this is important? Couldn't we be doing something? Couldn't we . . . ?"

"In just a second. Just a second. You had a custody fight, did you, over Alex, when you separated?"

She shook her head impatiently and brushed the air vaguely with her hand. "No, nothing like that. Graham wouldn't do that to me. We didn't separate to hurt each other, we were trying to *stop* hurting each other."

"I see. Mr. Selky sees Alex when he wants to, then?"

"All the time. They adore each other—Graham's a wonderful father." Her voice was starting to tremble.

"Could we have that address, please, then, Mrs. Selky? Your husband's address."

She recited it, and both detectives wrote it down.

"Good. Got it." Menetti snapped his pad shut. "Okay, Mrs. Selky. Now, listen. I'll lay you any odds you want we'll have Alex back here by bedtime. I know you're feeling anxious right now, and I don't blame you. Now, I'm going to radio from my car for some help, and we're going to cover the neighborhood here. I have seven kids of my own, Mrs. Selky, and I'm going to have your rascal back here for you by bedtime."

He smiled at Susan, a warm genuine smile, and she felt a sudden thaw of hope. Could he be right? Of course he could. By bedtime she could have Alex in her arms, astonished and shivering from his big adventure.

"We'll canvass the neighborhood," Menetti went on. "There must have been plenty of people going to work that time of day who saw him. He must be a pretty familiar sight along these three blocks, right?" She nodded. "Okay. We'll find everyone who saw him, we'll find out who he talked to, and we'll find out who saw him last down there. You and Mrs. Norris here can help out, if you would."

"Anything," said Jocelyn. "You name it."

"You can start phoning the parents of Alex's classmates, anyone he usually plays with, anyone he meets when he walks to and from school. Find out if any of them saw him, tell them that he's missing, and tell them what he was wearing. Ask them to pass it on.''

''You got it,'' said Jocelyn. ''Can I use the phone in the kitchen, honey?'' Susan, mute, just touched her on the arm. The two women exchanged a long look, then Jocelyn went out.

''I'm going down to my radio,'' Menetti said to Susan. ''Do you mind if Detective Sachs looks over the house now?'' Susan shook her head. ''Good. Thanks. Now, remember: kids do *not* disappear into thin air. Sometimes we can't *find* them for a while . . .'' He smiled paternally.

''Not mine,'' said Susan.

''But they do not just disappear. Can you remember that? Keep calm.'' Menetti went on downstairs.

Detective Sachs put away his pad and came forward. ''Before we go over the house, Mrs. Selky, do you have a good picture of Alex you can let us have?''

Susan put her hand to her mouth nervously, caught herself, dropped it. ''I have one—the most recent is . . . six months old. . . . Children change so fast. Maybe Graham has more recent ones. Oh, God, I've got to tell him.'' She started for the phone.

''Mrs. Selky, I'm going to ask you to hold off doing that for a while.''

''Doing what?''

''Calling your husband. Or your relatives. No need to alarm them yet, and it would just make our job easier if you leave that alone for a while.''

''Really? But you told us to call our friends.''

''I know, but we prefer to do it this way.''

''Oh,'' Susan said vaguely. She felt taut as a harp string, one quivering thread of gut, and she was easily distracted. There was a tightness in her chest, and she couldn't seem to take a deep enough breath to fill her lungs. She sat down. Stood up. Said, ''I'll get the pictures.''

Detective Sachs followed her out of the room. He was a man about Susan's age. He had narrow shoulders and wore a large drooping sandy mustache. He went methodically from room to room, showing particular interest in the bathrooms. He opened the hamper in Susan's bathroom and took everything out, socks, towels, and underwear. In Alex's bathroom across the hall, he did the same thing. He opened doors, checked in

18

closets. He studied the pictures on the mantelpiece in Susan's bedroom. "This your husband?" he asked, pointing to a family group smiling on a lawn before a large white-brick house.

"No," said Susan, "that's his brother Robert. The blond one is Graham. They're twins, but you'd never know it. Fraternal."

"Good-looking guy," said Detective Sachs. "Your husband."

"Yes," said Susan, snatching snapshots from the other mirror frame. "These are Alex." She brought them and laid them on the mantelpiece beside the large framed picture of Alex at five, his head thrown back in the sunlight, laughing. There were snaps of Alex in his Camp Woonsocket T-shirt that he tie-dyed with boysenberry juice in crafts class. Alex naked in the backyard at his first-birthday party, solemnly studying a balloon. Alex at three with Graham and Graham's father, all looking alike except for Mr. Selky's little gray brush mustache. Alex on Graham's shoulders on Boston Common, Alex at four on an airplane sleeping in Susan's arms.

"Please don't cry, Mrs. Selky," said Detective Sachs.

"Oh. No. No, okay."

"Does this work?" he asked, tapping the mantel with his hand.

"What?"

"The fireplace, does it work?"

"Oh. Yes."

"Must be nice, a fire in the bedroom." He crouched down and peered up into the chimney. He moved the lever to open the flue and closed it again. Then he stood and asked, "Do you have a laundry?"

"Yes. In the basement. It's this way."

They trooped downstairs. As they passed the living room, Susan could hear Jocelyn saying efficiently, "Blue jeans, a red-and-white T-shirt, and blue jogging shoes. And a Spiderman backpack. . . . Nothing. We don't know. Yes, please ask Colin, and let me know. . . ."

On the next floor Sachs asked about the tenant in the ground-floor apartment.

"I don't know her that well," said Susan. "She's a widow,

19

her name is Margaret Mayo. She moved down here when her husband died, and she works at the library at MIT."

"She have children?"

"Two. Grown up. They live in California, I think, but I met one girl when she helped Margaret move in. They seem very close—they laughed a lot."

"I'd like to look around her apartment if I may."

Susan looked surprised. But there was something reassuring about Detective Sachs. He had a big soft body that he carried wearily, moving with methodical composure. Method and composure seemed to Susan precisely what were needed to find Alex, and precisely what she didn't have. So she nodded and said, "I'll get the key."

He went all through Margaret Mayo's apartment, opening closets, checking under the beds, riffling through paperwork on the desk, looking into the refrigerator and the oven. The apartment was tidy, but full of life. There were books in mid-reading, a sweater in progress sitting in a basket of heathery skeins of wool on top of the television. There was a Crock Pot burbling on the counter in the kitchen, cooking Margaret's dinner. Sachs opened the pot and stirred it thoroughly, bringing up chunks of meat and carrots. "Lamb stew," he said, replacing the top.

They turned off the lights, locked the door, and went on down the stairs to the cellar. Susan followed him patiently, feeling hopeful and curious. She didn't ask herself what he was doing. She simply clung to the simplicity of minutes passing and somebody doing something. He was very thorough in the basement. He looked in the washer and the dryer. He took out his flashlight and checked behind the machines, around the boiler and hot-water heater, under the sheet keeping dust from the baby carriage and crib, which Susan had stored hopefully when Alex outgrew them. Sachs opened cartons of which Susan had forgotten the contents. In one corner he opened a large storage crate full of place mats, cheese boards, and fondue pots still in gift boxes. Sachs took out two layers from the top and set the things in a row. He looked deeper into the box and then straightened, saying, "You have a lot of fondue pots."

"It was the year of the fondue pot, the year I got married."

"My wife loves fondue pots," said Sachs. "She enjoys eating things with those little forks."

Susan smiled. If the world was ending, if her son were gone, would detectives talk of eating with little forks?

"I bet your wife feels safer having you work in Juvenile than on the Bomb Squad or something," she offered.

"Oh, I'm not on Juvenile," Sachs said. "I'm on Homicide."

AS THE AFTERNOON light began to deepen into evening in the corners of the living room, so did Susan's horror. It was past Alex's suppertime. His package of chicken breasts lay in the refrigerator, the layers of plastic wrap filmed with thin blood. Jocelyn had been sent home to continue telephoning. Detective Menetti had decided by six that they should keep Susan's line clear in case of a ransom call. So far, no one had seen Alex from the moment he turned the corner onto Beacon Street. It was as if he walked out of sight and out of this life.

Thank God for Jocelyn. Jocelyn was obviously the person for spreading the word. She'd been wielding the phone like a tailor with a pair of scissors, deftly slicing the oblivious cities of Boston and Cambridge into pockets of people who would care, or at least know, about Alex. She reached family after family, she explained the situation, she asked her questions, noted the answers, and moved on. She took about one minute for each call. Susan had taken this in with mute gratitude, because she was having a great deal of trouble speaking. She sat in her chair by the window, very still on the outside, flooded with intolerable feeling.

With Jocelyn sent home, the phone silenced, Susan wanted Graham. In three months, she had only called him at the department office, never at his girlfriend's. But there were times when she had imagined some emergency that would require her to call. To say to the girlfriend: "This is Graham's wife, this is an emergency, please let me talk to him." To let the girl know that whatever she had with Graham was nothing

21

compared to the years and the love and the hurt and the passion and the boy that united Graham and Susan. Why, Susan wondered, were there so many folk tales, or horror stories, about people whose wishes are granted, but slightly changed in some unforeseen, frightening way? What are those stories about? About not knowing to be satisfied with what life means you to have?

As she was trying to make herself get up and go to the phone and dial the number, to say to a girl on the other end, "This is Susan, this is Graham's wife," the phone rang. It was very loud, and Susan jumped. Detective Menetti, standing by the window, put his finger to his lips to order silence to two officers talking in the kitchen. Then he gestured Susan to answer. Upstairs, she knew, another detective would silently pick up the extension.

Susan's mind went blank. Menetti had explained to her in detail how to talk to a kidnapper, but she had forgotten. She just picked up the phone and said, "Hello," and started praying.

"Susan?" said the woman's voice, very young and low and tense. "This is . . . Naomi, this is Graham's friend."

Susan stopped praying. It took her a moment or two to whisper, "Oh."

"The police were just here, looking for Graham. They searched the apartment and they kept asking me questions about Alex. I'm sorry if I . . . They didn't want to answer any questions, but I suddenly felt so afraid for you. Susan . . . are you all right? Is there any way I can help you?"

Oh, please, Susan chanted silently inside, don't let me cry.

She said, "Alex has disappeared, Naomi. We don't know anything. He hasn't been seen since nine o'clock this morning. You can help me by getting me Graham."

"That's what the police wanted too. But he . . . he told me he was having dinner with TJ, but I called there, and he isn't." Naomi paused. Susan felt something in her heart go out to this younger woman.

Oh, Graham, she thought hopelessly. Oh, Graham, you shit. Can't you stop it, *can't* you stop it? Was there ever a moment when she thought this would give her satisfaction? No. She always knew it wasn't a girl that was taking Graham away from her, it was that bitter strain of whatever it was in Graham himself.

"I would find him for you if I could," said Naomi simply. "I don't know what to say."

"It's all right. I know." Oh, I do know.

"Susan, could I tell you something?"

"Yes."

"I always wanted to tell you that . . . I wanted you to know that . . . because I read your study of Willa Cather . . . That's how I first introduced myself to Graham . . . I wanted him to tell you how very much I admire your work. . . ." When Susan didn't answer her, Naomi paused, uncertain. Susan's throat at that moment was aching with anger. She tried twice to speak again, but found she couldn't. After looking at the floor for a minute and trying once more, she just hung up.

Almost immediately, the phone rang again. The kidnappers? Or Naomi again? Menetti had to signal her twice to pick up the receiver.

"Susan. TJ. Look, did you know the police were looking for Graham?" His voice was big and deep. Susan pictured him, his tall long-waisted body, in Levi's with a hole nearly through his back pocket where he carried his keys. He would be leaning against the doorjamb to his kitchen, one arm stretched up the wall to the ceiling. She began to cry.

"TJ. They're not looking for Graham, they're looking for Alex. He never got to school this morning but I didn't know it and he's been gone all this time and I didn't know it. TJ, can you help me?"

"I'm on my way," he said, and the phone clicked down. TJ had been Graham's closest friend, since graduate school, and he was Alex's godfather. He was smart and wry and laconic and absolutely true. If you were facing the longest night of your life, TJ was the one you'd want to face it with.

By the clock, it was less than eight minutes between the time she hung up and the moment she heard TJ's ancient Porsche rocket down Fremont Street and screech to a stop in front of her house. He used his own front-door key and took the stairs three at a time with his little plump girlfriend, Annie, scampering behind him. Annie had to stand on the stair waiting while TJ wrapped Susan in a long speechless embrace. He wasn't a man to hug or kiss anyone lightly. Susan kept a tight grip on his hand even as she hugged and kissed Annie. With them in the room the blue glow of the last light outside the window seemed less evil.

After introductions, Detective Menetti questioned both TJ and Annie about Graham. TJ had no idea where he was.

"If I did," said TJ, "I'd . . . he'd be here."

"You've known the Selkys for . . . ?"

"Fifteen years. I've known Graham for twenty years, but at this moment I'd like to give him a kick in the butt."

"Really?" asked Menetti. "Why?"

"Because where the hell is he? . . . This is going to take him apart. He thinks Alex makes the sun rise."

"Can you help me find Graham, Mr. French?"

"Dr. French," said Susan.

"TJ," said TJ. "Sure I can help find Graham, but I'd rather find Alex. What can we do?"

"Okay," said Menetti, "here's the drill. I've got men in the streets all along the route the boy usually takes to school in the morning. They're questioning everyone they meet walking, and they're knocking on every door to see if the people who live along there saw anything. Tomorrow morning—I mean, if he's still missing tomorrow morning—I'll have a lot more men out there and we'll find every parent and student and dog-walker who was on the street yesterday between eight and ten A.M., and we'll find someone who saw what happened."

"Have you got any leads at all yet?"

Menetti and Sachs exchanged a glance.

"We've got a lot of people who recognize the boy, all right."

The police on the street were now carrying Xerox copies of the photograph of Alex in his boysenberry shirt.

"We've got a dozen who know they see him most mornings, and we've got a couple who think they saw him today."

"What does that mean, they *think*?"

"Well, in a case like this, it's human nature to want to help. Everyone and his Uncle Harry wants to turn in the big clue. Pretty soon they're positive they saw him this morning, only it turns out to be they saw him last week, on a morning when the weather was like today."

"In other words, you don't have anyone who definitely saw him after he left Susan?"

"Not at this moment, no. No one who really can say for sure. But we'll check out every lead we get. Don't worry about that, we will trace down every single story."

Susan looked at him with envy. It would be so good to have something to do, even something that sounded so fruitless. To have routine and process to follow instead of having to sit here and *think* about what exactly they were trying to do. Trying to find out what happened when a fifty-five-pound flesh-and-blood child, full of humor and courage and dreams, vanished without any trace. When he could be dead in an alley right under their noses, he could be in the river, he could be bound and gagged in a closet, he could be lost, having somehow wandered off farther and farther. He could have asked the one wrong person in the world for help, he could be hurt now, he could be crying for her.

"Susan," whispered Annie, at her elbow, "here." Annie handed her a mug of steaming coffee laced with rum. Susan shook her head.

"Drink, Susan," said TJ. She took the cup. Annie went back to the kitchen for a glass of wine for herself and a snifter of neat rum for TJ. "I suppose you don't drink on duty?" TJ asked Menetti.

"Look, I've got a seven-year-old kid myself. I wouldn't say no to a shot of whatever you've got there." Silence followed this speech. It seeped through the room all the time TJ was pouring the rum. He took the glass to Menetti, who stood looking down from the window.

"So," Susan managed to say finally. "You have children?"

"Seven," Menetti said, and smiled. "All hellions." Susan smiled back. Menetti looked out the window again. He looked tense, and he had a nervous habit of methodically searching through his pockets, like a man who has recently stopped smoking and keeps forgetting, wondering where he put his cigarettes. He'd reach his left hand into his jacket and stretch out his fingers inside the pockets, shaking to dislodge whatever was in the folds. Then he'd try his breast pocket; in a few moments, distracted, he'd begin again. Almost as if talking to himself, Menetti said, "He could have wandered off and fallen down, and gotten hurt and kind of taken a while to come to and remember what to do next. Or he could have had an accident and be in a hospital, and sooner or later he'll identify himself. If he doesn't, we'll see the report, an unidentified patient. Or he could be embarrassed or afraid you'd be mad at him for getting lost, so he doesn't want to come home . . ."

Both TJ and Susan stirred and started to speak.

"I know, I know." Menetti held up a hand to stop them. "He isn't that kind of a kid. He wouldn't be afraid of you. I know you told me that, and from everything I've heard about him, you're right, but you'd be surprised, that's all. Besides, things could be worse than we'll find him crying in a doorway on Mass Ave, not wanting anyone to know he got himself lost when his mommy was counting on him."

Susan absorbed this picture. It seemed that every picture she could form of Alex at this moment threatened to crush her slowly from the inside out, but at the same time she could admit that however wrenching the thought was, it was something to hope for. That her sweet good boy, trying so hard to help, somehow (but how? *How*? Don't think about it. . . .), somehow did in fact take a wrong turn trying to walk up Beacon Street to school, and that he didn't ask for directions because he'd been told not to talk to strangers, and that he felt more and more bewildered and embarrassed, until finally he was so lost that he just sat down somewhere and decided to wait for help to find him. It could be worse . . . there could be worse things . . . than to have him out there, alone in the city in the dark . . . with no food and the air turning cold. . . .

"And if he's not lost?" asked TJ.

"Yes," said Menetti. "If he's not . . . Well, then, you've got some other possibilities. One is kidnapping. For money. Mrs. Selky tells me that her father is comfortable and that Mr. Selky's parents are fairly wealthy. In other words, she could raise a ransom if she had to . . ."

"Yeah, but if someone were going to take a risk like kidnapping, wouldn't they go for some Rockefeller kid or something?"

"Listen," said Menetti, "people don't usually go into kidnapping because they got tired being nuclear physicists. An enormous number of brains may not exactly be part of the package, okay? Kidnapping isn't a crime for pros. Unless they're terrorists and political, your kidnapper is probably on his maiden voyage, and he may do plenty of things that you and I would consider stupid. Like picking a kid whose family doesn't have money. You don't know—there are plenty of people who would look at this house and this street, and to them, that's big money. Kid in private school. Both parents professors. They might not even know that much. They might just have hung around and figured out that here was a pretty small kid who always walked the same two blocks at the same time of morning, and just picked him because it would be easy."

Susan put her head in her hands. TJ went over and knelt in front of her chair and lifted her arms around his neck. "Don't think it," he said, holding her with both arms. "He *is* old enough to walk two blocks by himself. You didn't risk him; you gave him room to grow up, by trusting him."

"Room to grow up?" she wept, so softly that only TJ could hear. "This is very hard . . ."

"Don't cry yet," TJ whispered back. "It's not time for that. It's time to have faith, and be ready . . ." He held her tight and felt her quiet herself. "Good girl," he said. He went back to his place at the window.

Menetti was plunging into his pockets again. "I'm finding it pretty hard to figure out how a kid could disappear so fast or completely. . . . On a normal morning we'd have found half a dozen people who saw him walk down that block . . . let alone if there was a struggle. It's hard to see how it could happen unless he was taken into a building right there . . . or into a car . . ."

The phone rang. Susan ran for it. It was Alex's teacher, distraught because she hadn't called Susan immediately when she learned that the school nurse hadn't had a sick call to explain Alex's absence. "I just never *thought* . . ." the woman sobbed. "Parents forget to call us all the time when they keep a child home. . . ."

"It's all right," Susan kept murmuring to her, "it's all right. It's not your fault." What am I talking about? her head said while her mouth spoke. It's not all right; it is certainly *not* all right.

When she came back to the living room, Menetti was saying, "Something that happens more often than you think is a kid getting stolen by someone who actually wants a kid. As a matter of fact, we've seen an increase in those cases since the abortion law passed, whenever it was, ten years ago. There are less babies around to adopt, and some people really want babies."

"Jesus," said TJ. "What kind of person *does* that?"

"You name it . . . any shape, size, or color. Can be a lonely woman . . . or man . . . can be a frustrated grandparent, somebody older who doesn't have anyone to live for. . . . They sit around the park, they watch the kids, they hear the mothers complain. They start telling themselves young people aren't taking proper care of the kids, and the next thing you know, they've adopted one, as a public service."

TJ and Susan looked at each other.

"Then we had a case last year of a teenage boy . . . He stole a little two-year-old he'd been baby-sitting for. We picked them up in Texas after almost a month . . . got really lucky, some businessman saw a news story in a New York paper at the airport. When he checked into his hotel in Dallas that night, there was this runaway kid working as a night porter. The kid seemed truly amazed that anyone was mad at him. He said he just felt like hitting the road, and he wanted a traveling companion.

"See, with that kind of situation, they just want this kid; they don't really think about what it's going to be like once they got one . . . how long you have to hide him, how you do it, where you go, what a kid needs. The kid may get away, he may be recognized—they may get feeling guilty, especially if the kid gets very depressed or gets sick or something and they don't know how to handle it. You can keep a kid quiet for a week, maybe, but it's pretty hard to keep one hidden forever. And when you do take him out, you have to explain where he came from all of a sudden." TJ and Susan looked at each other, and TJ could almost hear her thinking. It sounded all too likely. It sounded to her much more likely than some amateur ransom job—the idea that someone, some lonely person, could look at her lovely, jaunty little boy and just want him so badly, she took him.

"Of course," said Menetti, "it's a long shot that we're ever going to seriously face that kind of possibility."

"Why do you say that?" TJ asked.

Menetti frowned. "Look, you gotta understand. What is it, sixty percent of murderers know their victims? Same thing with rape . . . crimes of passion. Now, nine times out of ten, when a child disappears, you've got your runaway or you've got custodial interference. You know."

"I *don't* know," said Susan, staring at him.

"Look," said Menetti, "you just separated from your husband, right? You're still pretty ticked off at him, right? . . . And he's pretty ticked off at you. I know you say, 'Not my husband, *he'd* never do a thing like this,' but you want to know how many times I've heard that before?"

"Now *wait* . . ." said Susan sharply.

"Mrs. Selky . . . calm down, Mrs. Selky. . . . I'm telling you the truth . . . nine times out of ten, when a kid disappears, the person you look for first is the other parent. Or a grandparent or—"

"I am not 'ticked off' at Graham! And he is not 'ticked off' at me. Oh, *Jesus*! You *can't* be doing all you can to find out what really happened, if you're seriously wasting men on looking for Graham. Oh . . . no . . . I thought you were trying to tell him—I thought you just wanted to ask him things, for his help. . . ."

For the first time, TJ too showed signs of his own slow but serious anger. "Look, sir, you are way off the mark now—" The phone rang again. Everyone in the room froze. Graham? The kidnapper? Susan stared at TJ. She picked up the phone.

"Hello?"

"Hello," said a woman's smooth voice. "Mrs. Selky? Is this Mrs. Selky?"

"Yes . . . this is she." Susan had to push to make her voice come out at normal volume. Who are you? Do you have my son?

"Mrs. Selky, this is Maureen Laugherty, with the Channel Eleven news team, and we understand that your little six-year-old boy has vanished into thin air."

"Oh!" Susan wailed in frustration and disappointment. "It's some woman from the news . . ." Menetti took the phone from her. "This is Detective Menetti—who is it, please?"

The woman on the other end went into her spiel again.

"The situation at this point," said Menetti, "is that the child is missing and we have no more information whatsoever. There will be no more comment at this time."

Susan could hear the voice saying, "Is it true that Mrs. Selky is a professor at—" when the receiver hit the cradle.

"Dammit," said Menetti. He went quickly downstairs to talk to the men in the radio car, then jogged back up to Susan's landing. He called up the stairs to the officer assigned to listen on the extension, that every time a phone call came from the press, the officer was to cut in with the word that there is no comment at this time and that police orders are to keep the line clear.

"Okay," Menetti said to Susan, "now we're going to be in for it. I'm surprised we stayed clear this long, with my men in the neighborhood and your Mrs. Norris calling everyone in the city. I just ordered a cordon in the street so no one can get closer to the house than we want them to. We'll try to keep them off the phone here, but we can't keep them from camping all up and down the block or from interviewing your neighbors. I'm afraid that with you and your husband both college professors and Alex such an appealing kid, you're going to look like awfully good copy."

Susan looked at TJ and then at Annie. The phone rang again. She picked it up, but before she even spoke, the voice said, "This is Newscenter 5 calling. Is Mrs. Selky there, please?" and she heard the officer upstairs take it, so she hung up.

Alex hungry and frightened. Alex out there in the dark, crying. Alex in a hospital unconscious, no identification for them to notify her. Alex bruised, broken, bloody, dead. Alex threatened by criminal fools suddenly frightened by lights and cables and a crowd of reporters. She looked at TJ and at Annie where they stood, their arms around each other, looking mutely back at her.

"I want to know where he is," she said to Menetti. "Whatever it is, wherever he is, I want everyone who can see me to know that I love him and that I just want to know . . ."

Menetti looked surprised. "Are you sure?" he asked. "We could try to hold them off at least until morning, you know. We could try to keep things quiet through the night in case somebody's trying to set up a ransom. . . . You don't want to scare them off. . . . Do you know what it's going to be like? It's not Walter Cronkite out there. It's some very ruthless garbage hounds, believe me . . ."

Menetti could see that she wasn't listening. She shrugged. "Doesn't matter. Couldn't hurt anymore. It's one thing I can do—the one thing I can do."

The phone rang again. Again, the caller introduced herself; it was Vivienne Grant with Channel 5 News. She wanted to know, if she brought a mini-cam down to Fremont Street, could she do a live interview with Susan, in the missing boy's bedroom. "Yes," said Susan. "Yes, you can."

The phone rang again. It was Jocelyn. "How are you, baby?" she murmured. "Is there anything new at all?" Susan said not. "Well, I've got Katherine Abbot and Martina calling too now. I think we've reached every parent from Beacon Hill to Porter Square. People are absolutely shitting about this, praying for you. I've got a whole army out here ready to help you, if there's anything they can do."

"Thank you, Jocelyn—thanks for what you've done already. Did you . . . I guess you haven't found anyone who saw anything."

"I don't think so, honey. One guy who remembers Alex from when he used to come over to play-group on Commonwealth Ave thinks he saw him at noon with some freak at the Star Market. I wrote it all down, and I'll tell it to the detective. But just a minute . . . Do you have a policeman listening in to your calls?"

Susan pictured the sluggish young officer in uniform, patiently sitting upstairs on the edge of her bed.

"Yes," said Susan. "In case of ransom calls."

"Well, I thought you might. I was just wondering if you want me to bring you any . . . salad. . . . I know you don't keep any greens in the house." Susan almost smiled, wondering if her monitor had just found himself in a quandary. Salad —greens—grass—pot. "Thanks," she said, "but we're not very hungry."

"You sure? It might make you feel better."

"I'm sure. Can I put Menetti on, so you can tell him what you got?"

She listened to Menetti saying, "Yes? . . . Yes . . . name . . . phone number . . . good. Could help . . . you never know. By the way, I'd rather you didn't discuss with anyone anything that you get. Oh, you did . . . good for you.

"No. There's nothing more you can do tonight. Mrs. Selky wants to go public . . . the eleven-o'clock news. It may be that we'll flush something out pretty quickly. If it doesn't, if you've really got some volunteers lined up, let's say we'll have a meeting of volunteers right here at ten tomorrow morning. Can you get that word out? Okay. Okay. Yes. Good job. Yes, she's all right, she has some friends here. No, we're still looking for him. Yes. Good-bye."

As he hung up, Annie went to answer a light tapping at the door, and came back, followed by Margaret Mayo, Susan's tenant. She was a graceful woman with straight iron-gray hair and brilliant eyes and one of the world's readiest smiles. She always paused a moment before she answered a question, as if aware that there is plenty of time in this life and no point in speaking if you don't plan to say what you mean. She was so often humorous without ever being light-minded that she made Susan feel, with longing, the difference in depth between thirty and sixty.

Margaret somehow introduced herself to everyone in the room while moving straight to Susan. She took her hand, and gave her her strong steady gaze. "Well, the police have been questioning me," she said, "and I've been questioning them. Now I want to know how I can help you." Her grip was deliberate and firm.

"Margaret. Thank you. I don't know. There doesn't seem to be anything we can do."

"Well, I can't believe that. Let me see, have you eaten anything?"

"No." Susan shook her head. "No."

"Well," said Margaret, "I agree with you. I couldn't eat a thing. Tell me this, have you called your father?"

Susan paused for a moment, then looked at her.

"You were hoping any moment Alex would be found, and

then you could let them know you'd had a scare.''

Susan nodded.

''Well, you can't just let him hear it on the news,'' said Margaret. ''Why don't I call him for you? I'll call Graham's parents, too—where are the numbers?''

Susan pointed to the list in felt-tip pen on the wall above the telephone. ''Margaret . . . thank you.'' It was all in her voice —she so much didn't want to have to make those calls that she would have left them unmade.

''You're welcome,'' said Margaret. ''First, would you like a big hug?'' Susan actually smiled for the first time in hours. Margaret's hug was warm and firm and deliberate, like her handshake. Susan suddenly wondered if she'd felt that peculiar and irreplaceable brand of comfort since her mother died.

Menetti thanked Margaret too, and asked her to make the calls downstairs, from her own phone. ''Certainly,'' said Margaret. ''In fact, why don't you always use my phone for making calls out, and that way you can keep this number free.''

''I was just going to ask if you would let us do that.'' Margaret waved over her shoulder as she hurried off.

The phone rang twenty-two times in the next hour. It was getting on toward eleven. Some of the callers were friends wanting news. Interestingly, few were close friends. Those seemed to have reasoned by themselves that they could help best by staying off the line. Or perhaps they'd all been reached by Jocelyn's message network. In a very far-off corner of her mind, Susan wondered if her reactions were skewed by fear, or if there was not a slightly lascivious quality to the anxious quest for news, the expression of terrible sympathy.

The rest of the calls were from news personnel. Outside in the street, the reporters and camera crews gathered. Presently an officer in charge of the press would choose a small group with lights and mini-cameras to come upstairs for a live interview with Susan. The rest would send their stories from downstairs, giving information bulletins as they received them from the police. Huge lights were being set up to illuminate the facade of the house. Their intense pure white blaze made the street seem unreal. The sidewalk became a snake's nest of cables from lights and microphones. Technicians tested connections, the lighting men ran up and down the steps with gray cards. TV reporters patted their hair and clipped their lavaliere microphones to their lapels. In between, they wrote their copy and clamored at anyone going in or out for details, for human interest, for news.

Upstairs, Susan felt numb. She could hardly think of Alex. There was so much noise and confusion that she was finding it hard to recapture some concrete detail of him. The smell of his hair warm from the sun. The perfect roundness of his head, how it fit the curve of her palm when she stroked it. Some woman from the network with a large black case kept opening it and asking her something; she had trouble understanding what the woman was talking about. Finally, Margaret intervened. "No, she doesn't want any makeup," she said gently, shooing the woman away. "She feels like hell, and she might as well look that way."

Vivienne Grant wanted Susan sitting on Alex's bed, holding something that belonged to him. "Get the dog in the shot, get the dog," the cameraman kept urging. *Taxi*, thought Susan with a stab of worry—had anyone fed him this evening? Taxi came into the bedroom with her, apparently thinking each one of Susan's movements was bound to lead to Alex. He lay down by her feet, looking bewildered, but got up and ran out of the room as they switched on the brilliant lights. "Damn," said the cameraman. "Can you call him back?"

"No," Susan said, "it's too bright."

"Well, could you hold something of the boy's, then? How about a teddy bear?" Susan looked at the threadbare plush rabbit that Alex had had since he was in his crib. It was lying as always on Alex's pillow.

"No," she said, "I think not."

Vivienne Grant and the cameraman exchanged a look. Susan felt weirdly calm. Now Alex's room was a movie set. Alex was nowhere. Alex had been gone for years. There had never been a real Alex.

The lights went off for a moment and the room seemed very dark. White spots with blue edges bobbled in Susan's eyes. The lights went back on again. Vivienne Grant touched her hair, dabbed expertly at her lip gloss one more time. She stood poised, looking intently into the camera. Susan realized she was listening to a black slice of plastic that was transmitting into her ear from her studio, where the nightly news was in progress. Suddenly she began to speak.

"Thank you, Bob. We're here on Fremont Street at the home of Mrs. Susan Selky, where today, tragedy struck. Mrs. Selky's little son Alex, whom you see in this photograph, left for school this morning at 8:50 as usual. Although the boy is only six, we're told he was an unusually responsible child, and for several months now he has been allowed to walk to school by himself. But this morning, somewhere between the corner of Beacon and Fremont streets and the New Boston School two blocks away, little Alex . . . disappeared. Mrs. Selky, could you tell us please, in your own words, exactly what happened?" She stepped slightly sideways so the camera could move in on Susan. While she questioned, and Susan talked, she took a small mirror from her pocket, checked her makeup, and then put the mirror away.

Susan's voice was clear and calm. "Alex left the house at exactly 8:50 this morning. He was wearing blue jeans, a red-and-white striped shirt, and blue jogging shoes; he was carrying a Spiderman knapsack. I watched him walk to the corner, and he turned and waved to me." He waved to me! I forgot that, until this second! "Then he turned the corner," her calm voice continued, "and disappeared. There were mothers at the next corner who keep an eye out for him every morning, but none of them saw him today, and he never reached school."

"I see," said Vivienne Grant. "Now, I understand that police have mounted a thorough search in this neighborhood, looking for someone who might have seen something. So far there are no leads. Tell me, Mrs. Selky, would Alex have been on his guard against strangers?" Of course Alex was on his guard against strangers. Of *course* he understood that there were people in the world not to trust or talk to. And don't say again that he was "only six"—he's known since he was two that traffic could kill him, and he certainly knew not to wander off with a pervert offering lollipops.

"He is friendly but wise," she said, "and he was very proud of being trusted to walk himself. He doesn't dawdle and he doesn't wander. I would like to appeal to your audience . . .

35

Somewhere, someone out there has seen something that will help us find him. Please," she said straight to the camera, "if you have any information about Alex, whether or not it seems important to you, please get in touch with the police."

Vivienne Grant stepped back into the shot. "In Boston tonight . . . a mother's nightmare. Alex Selky, missing tonight at age six. His mother, a professor of literature at Harvard, showing a great deal of courage at this moment. The boy's father, Graham Selky, still has not been located. Mr. Selky teaches English at Boston University; he has been separated from his wife for the past three months. Police are looking for Mr. Selky, but they say that, as of this moment, he is not officially a suspect. This is Vivienne Grant, in Back Bay."

Susan shot up from where she was sitting, the moment the shot was over. "You did *fine*," said Vivienne Grant sympathetically. Susan remembered that later; as if stage fright were something on her mind at that moment. But right then, she mumbled, "Thank you . . . excuse me . . ." and made her way through the equipment back to Menetti.

He was on the phone, confirming a special police information number for viewers to call, to be broadcast before the end of the program. He was beginning to look haggard, and the thought occurred to Susan that he wasn't just doing a job—he really cared about Alex.

"Detective Menetti . . ." she said, touching his arm.

He held up his hand, said, "Right—got it," into the phone, then hung up. "Look, why don't you call me Al?" he said to her wearily.

"Al, you're just plain wrong about Graham. I'm asking you now and I'll beg if it will help—I know you don't have all the men in the world. Will you *please, please* not waste time chasing Graham. We may have had problems, but this isn't a crazy family. We're straight normal people, and some lunatic has done . . . something . . . to our . . ." She could feel the hysteria welling up through her chest. Al Menetti looked terribly strained.

"I know how you feel," he began.

"No, you don't. Excuse me, but you don't. You cannot possibly know, at this moment how I . . ." The phone rang.

Graham? Kidnappers? Alex? A lead? How many ideas

could the brain hold simultaneously? All of these burned in her at one instant every time she heard the phone.

"Susan?" said the anxious voice. "This is Robert."

"Robert! Is there something on the news about Alex in New York?" Graham's brother? Detective Menetti asked her soundlessly. She nodded yes.

"I'm in Boston. I just saw you on the news. Jesus Christ, Susan, is there anything I can do?"

"But you're never in Boston. What are you doing here?"

"I came up last night. Look, why don't I come over there? Have you talked to Mom and Dad? I can't believe this is happening. Let me talk to Graham."

"He isn't here yet, Robert, we don't know where he is, really. Does he know you're here? We've *got* to find him. . . ."

"I'm coming over there," said Robert. "I'll be there in twenty minutes."

"Oh, okay," said Susan. She hung up.

"Robert's in Boston?" asked TJ. "That's weird."

"It *is* weird," said Susan.

"Robert's one of those types who brags about never stepping in the provinces except to change planes," TJ explained to Annie.

"I'm not sure if I really want him here," said Susan. "He's not the most centered person . . ."

There was some kind of commotion downstairs.

There was an increasing murmur of raised voices, some from police, some from the reporters who were waiting around on the steps. Then out of the confusion one voice soared to desperate volume: "Just get the hell out of my way, *I want my wife!*"

"Graham!" TJ and Susan cried at the same time.

Menetti threw open the window and yelled down angrily, "Let him come!"

In another moment Graham was on the stairs. Menetti was yelling down from the window not to let the reporters follow him in, when he burst through the door. The expression on his face was something Susan felt she'd never forget for the rest of her life. She ran to him and held him as hard as she could, knowing that the first shock was burning through his mind and heart like acid, as if it would literally kill him.

"I was in a taxi on my way home," he said into her hair. "The driver had the news on the radio." His voice sounded as if he were strangling. In the first private shock of grief, Susan knew it didn't make sense to him that the room was full of people. He seemed to duck his head, bending into her as if the only way he could fend off the pain was by closing out sight and sound, feeling only her body with his. Susan could feel the anguish working in his chest, as he tried not to cry.

TJ was beside them. He put his hand on Graham's shoulder, then more decisively wrapped an arm around him and clasped him hard. His other arm held Susan.

Finally Graham straightened and gave TJ his hand. "Thank you for being here, man," he said. "Annie"—over TJ's shoulder—"thank you for coming." The two men stood looking at each other, as if they could exchange with their eyes the love and empathy that women expressed more easily with words and touches. They looked very alike, both muscular, long-waisted, and tall, except that Graham was clean-shaven with thick honey-blond hair. He wore a dark blue shirt and a tweed jacket, and looked almost exactly the same as when Susan fell in love with him. Except that he was twelve years older now. Except that his eyes no longer glowed with that generous joy that he had back when he was young and thought he couldn't lose. With some years and with seeping disappointment in himself, he grew capable of a closed-off, crafty look. But it didn't stop Susan from feeling a surprised burst of love at the swing of his hips and the tilt of his head every time she caught sight of him, for a moment, as if it were the first time.

Tonight he looked totally whipped. His eyes were dull with fear. She could feel him staring around, as she had for hours, unable to believe that Alex wasn't in the next room, having to contain himself to keep from going to look. Taxi was leaping at him with joy, and Graham bent to let his face be licked and to pat the bewildered furry head. Soon he would feel the numbness begin. Soon he would be with her in the unreality.

He wanted to ask questions. He wanted to know everything that had happened, what was being done, what he could do. He wanted to bolt out into the street again with Taxi and TJ and start searching.

"But, Mr. Selky," said Menetti firmly, "could you please tell me where exactly you have been for the last six hours?"

Graham made a face as if he couldn't answer. "All this time," he said, and his arms went around Susan, "all this time, and I could have been here and *done* something . . ."

"Mr. Selky? This is not idle curiosity. I really must know."

"I was visiting a friend." He didn't even look at Menetti when he said it, and consequently he had to repeat it to be heard.

"Mr. Selky," said Menetti, "I have had police officers who could have been otherwise occupied looking for you for six hours, and I want to know *exactly*—"

"I was in Charlestown fucking a nurse!" Graham yelled, turning. "Do you want to talk to her? You'll find it delightful, she's got a vocabulary of at least forty words." Then he did begin to cry, and Susan, stricken for him, held his bowed head against her cheek and began to cry too. Holding him for the first time in so many months, her mouth against his hair, filled her with piercing memory.

"Yes," said Menetti. "I'm sorry, but I'm afraid I do want to talk to her."

"Shit," said Graham. He shook Susan off and covered his face with his hands, furiously stripping away the tears. Then he began searching his pockets. Graham's pockets, she knew, were always an owl's nest of receipts, deposit slips, and scraps of paper with phone numbers but no names, or names and no phone numbers. "Shit," he said again suddenly, throwing it all on the floor. "I don't have her damn number. I wasn't going to call her. I don't even know her last name. What the hell does it matter? *Where is my son?*"

"Hey, Graham . . ." TJ was close to him again. "Cool down, he's trying to do his job."

"So why isn't he out doing it?"

"I know you're angry, man, but be angry at God, not the rest of us. He's asking you where you were because they thought you might have taken Alex."

"Oh, Christ . . . they thought what?"

"Look," said TJ, "they don't know you. The important thing is you're here, and you've got to let them check out your story so they'll believe you."

"Oh, God," Graham groaned. "I met her on a bus. Her name was Claire. That's all I know."

"You've been gone six hours, man, you must have said more than, 'Hi, do you want to get laid?' Where does she work? What kind of nursing? Surgical? Pediatric? What?"

"I don't know. Oh, wait—Mount Auburn Hospital."

"That's it?"

"That's it. That's all I know."

TJ stared at him. "If I didn't feel so fucking frightened for you right now, I'd kick your butt in, man."

"Please," said Graham. "Please."

"Now call Naomi," said TJ.

Graham looked at Susan.

"She called me," said Susan. She had dried her eyes. "The police were at her apartment looking for you—and for Alex. She called TJ looking for you."

Graham looked miserable.

"She was very worried, Graham."

"Okay, okay. I'll call."

"You can use Mrs. Mayo's phone downstairs," said Menetti. "We're keeping this line clear, in case."

Graham looked at him, as if he suddenly remembered again what the fear and shame were about. "Kidnappers, you think? Have you heard something?"

"Nothing. By the way, did you know your brother is in town?"

"Robert? In Boston?"

"Yeah. He's on his way here, as a matter of fact."

"Robert? That's weird. Well . . . good, I guess."

"None of you seem very enthusiastic about Robert," said Menetti.

"No—Robert's okay," said Graham vaguely. "I'll go call."

"I'll go with you," said Margaret, standing up suddenly from the chair in the corner where she'd been waiting to see if Susan was going to need her.

"Margaret . . . I didn't even see you. Okay, thank you. Thank you very much for being here and letting us . . . and everything." Margaret took his arm and walked him quietly out. They were followed by a uniformed patrolman.

"They're not very close, then?" Menetti asked Susan.
She looked up, distracted.

"Graham and Robert," he prompted.

"Oh . . . they don't have much in common."

"Didn't you tell Detective Sachs that they were twins?"

"Fraternal. They're very different."

"But twins are usually close."

"Or else they aren't," she said.

"Hey," TJ asked, "don't you have any relatives you think are creeps?"

Menetti snorted. "Doesn't everybody?"

WHILE GRAHAM WAS downstairs, Robert arrived. Menetti watched him closely as he greeted Susan and TJ and was introduced to Annie. Smaller, darker, with something soft about him, as if he had only cartilage, no real bones, he looked nothing like his brother, and yet he had a kind of presence. Perhaps it was the quality of his self-absorption, Menetti thought; but there was indeed something about him that seemed not precisely restful.

"Susan, it's *unreal*," he kept saying. He was right about that, so Susan nodded. "Graham!" he cried. "Graham, I can't believe it!" He and Graham shook hands.

"Robert. It's strange to see you here."

"Well, it seems like malicious Fates. It was last-minute, someone got sick, and they asked me to fill in up here at a conference on public broadcasting. God, my first time here in three years or something, and it has to be today!"

No one had anything to say in reply to this. Graham seemed to have already tuned him out in mid-sentence. When Robert stopped talking, he said to Menetti, "There must be something we can do besides standing here. I don't mean you—I understand that you should be here. But Susan can handle the phone —couldn't TJ and I take the dog or something and go out there?"

"I had a team of trained men on the street for as long as we

41

had light," said Menetti. "There just isn't anything to see. If I thought we could do any good in the dark, I'd have kept my men out there all night."

"I want to help. I want to do something."

"I think you're going to have to help each other get through tonight," said Menetti.

"Are you going to stay?" asked Susan. She realized she was beginning to have problems with time; she wasn't sure if it was midnight or four in the morning.

"Yeah," said Menetti. "I guess I'd have to say the odds are with ransom now. If we're going to hear from the kidnappers, my guess is the first contact will come in the next six hours."

"How about hospitals?" Graham asked suddenly. "Did you think of that? Supposing he's hurt and unconscious and . . ."

"We've checked them all," said Menetti.

"Oh," said Graham.

"Only one unidentified male child admitted to a hospital tonight anywhere in Boston. He's black; he's got three long scars from old wounds or burns."

"The only scar Alex has is on his toe," said Graham.

"I know. Mrs. Selky told me."

"He's never been hurt before," said Graham.

"Just that one time, he had stitches in his toe."

Into the silence that followed this remark, Robert said, "Graham, try not to dwell." Graham turned and looked at him.

"Graham," said TJ, rising suddenly, "let's walk the dog."

"What?"

"Come on, man. Let's go out and walk around. Let's take Taxi out—it's time, anyway."

They went out for about twenty minutes, again escorted at a distance by a policeman. On the way back, they jogged the last few blocks, which Susan knew because she could hear Taxi's fervent barking. She saw by the red in Graham's eyes when the two of them came upstairs that TJ had deemed it wise to get Graham good and stoned.

For the first two hours after the news broadcast, the phone seemed to ring every time it touched the cradle. Susan's father called; Graham's parents called. Students and colleagues of

Graham's and Susan's called; total strangers called, offering help. Others called to offer psychic information and tips from God. An old bachelor professor of Jacobean drama whom Graham used to make fun of for his stutter called to offer five thousand dollars for a reward. A woman called to tell Susan to confess that she had murdered her son herself and then reported him missing.

Margaret took all the calls, while an officer listened in upstairs. Menetti thought it would be best, psychologically, for a woman to answer a ransom call. Susan's frantic jittery feeling had worn off, and she felt instead muffled and numb. She just wanted to sit still and try to make her mind remember what had happened. The major fact kept escaping her, like a dream in which you know you're in prison for life but can't remember why. She found she couldn't recall any sense memory of Alex at all. She knew she had a son. She could imagine a crime done to a child and feel great anger. But she couldn't hold in her mind the two ideas at once. Her own boy, and a crime, an act causing pain, an act of evil.

Then she would suddenly, as if sliced through the brain with a knife, have a vivid picture of Alex still and white. An arm broken and bent the wrong way. Dry brown blood at his nose and mouth. His eyes were open, glazed forever, holding the expression of horror, the first knowledge of terror, coming into his life at the moment his life ended. Then blank. Then she thought: Well, I see. This is why people don't actually die of horror, because there's a circuit breaker. You can't feel it for more than a second at a time. Then you drop all the strings, and it takes you all that time to gather them up again.

TJ was watching her sitting in her chair across the room from him. Her skin, which was always milk pale, now had almost a bluish cast, as if it were translucent. There were dark blue smudges like bruises under her eyes. Otherwise, she looked still and composed, as if she were waiting for tea. He thought she looked like someone who is freezing, who gets beyond pain and feels finally sleepy and warm, and lies down to die.

After three A.M. the phone calls began to taper off. A last call from Jocelyn; Susan shook her head, she couldn't speak. Margaret went in to make a pot of coffee, and Susan suddenly got up and went to the kitchen too, to feed Taxi, but when she got there, she saw by the kibbles left in his dish that she'd already done it.

For Graham's benefit and Robert's, Menetti went over the possibilities again. Alex might be lost (out there . . . in the dark, alone . . .), but if that were the case, nothing could be done until light. He could have somehow wandered off in some wrong direction, and for some reason been afraid or ashamed to ask for help.

"But he knows to look for policemen," said Graham. "And he knows his phone number, and he always carries a dime." Oh, no, thought Susan—did he have his dime? He had called her from school to ask to play with Justine on Monday. . . . Had she given him another one?

No one even discussed how it was possible to take a wrong turn when walking two blocks you've walked thirty times before.

"There was no one home to answer the phone," Al pointed out.

"How would he reach a phone in a phone booth?" asked Robert. No one answered. "Really—a little kid, he couldn't reach the dial."

"He would ask someone to lift him up," said Susan. "Or to dial for him." But she was picturing big hands picking Alex up. Big hands gripping his rib cage, lifting him, as she lifted him to hug him. Hands grasping and crushing.

"He could have asked the wrong person for help," said Robert. "We've got to face it."

We? thought Susan. Suddenly she wished Robert would go away. She wished they would all go away. She wished, in fact, she could stand up and howl like a cornered animal, that they could all take their fatuous sympathy, and get the hell out of her house. She just wanted them all the hell *out*—except Graham. And except TJ. And except Margaret . . . She started to cry.

Quite a while passed in silence.

"I think we have to say the odds are with kidnapping," said Menetti aloud, finally, although he had said the same thing before. "The next few hours will tell the tale. Now that the phone's free, and they've had time to think it over and make a plan, I think we'll be hearing something.''

Some more time passed. Annie, sitting with TJ in one big chair, settled her head on his shoulder and fell asleep. Graham and Susan sat side by side on the couch. Graham held Susan's hand. Margaret sat at the table by the telephone, playing solitaire. Sequence, pattern, order from chaos, she shuffled and dealt and gathered the cards up and shuffled again. Menetti, sitting in a chair by the window, slept sitting bolt upright. Robert got up eventually and went up the stairs. From the creaking of his feet crossing the floor above, Susan knew he'd gone into Alex's room and stretched out on the bed.

"Margaret," said Susan, "you have to work tomorrow. Don't you want to go down and get some sleep?"

"I don't believe so," said Margaret. Susan nodded. Menetti woke up, got up, and walked around. Then he sat down again, staring intently at the phone. Graham got up and went into the kitchen; he came back with two snifters of brandy and gave one to Susan. He offered one to Menetti, who shook his head.

"I believe I will," said Margaret. Graham went back for a third glass for himself. TJ had fallen asleep.

In the darkest hours of the night, Susan thought once or twice of things she might say. Graham was there beside her. They sat, hands and thighs touching, each utterly alone. She considered some words, as if from a great distance, but she always found it was too much trouble to form them with her mouth, to open her throat and make a noise. There was, then, actually such a thing as unspeakable.

If it's kidnap, she would think, if it's ransom, then he's not dead. If he's not dead, then the phone will ring. I would like to be dead now. I would like to die now, rather than live through the next five minutes. But what I must do is make the phone ring. It could ring at any time. It could ring in the next second. You can make things happen, the mind-control people say, by making an image of it happening. You can make a taxi come by methodically picturing it coming around the corner and stopping in front of you. You can win contests by picturing yourself being notified that you have won. There are whole societies of people who enter contests full-time. Jocelyn told me about one woman who kept picturing herself winning a color TV, who won seven black-and-whites before she got it right.

I am picturing the phone ringing, right now. I am hearing the voice on the other end.

"Hello, Mrs. Selky?"

or

"Hello . . . Mommy?"

I am picturing the phone ringing, right now.

I am picturing the phone ringing. In the next second, it is going to ring. I can feel it, you sometimes hear it a second before it actually starts to ring. Like thinking of someone you haven't seen for years, and meeting them on the street the next day.

I am picturing the phone beginning to ring.

They sat in that room like stones, until the black sky diluted with the gray of morning light. It leaked into the room like the death of hope.

TJ and Annie woke up. Menetti went into the kitchen to make himself instant coffee. Margaret put away her cards and folded her hands in her lap.

Graham stretched and stood up and began to pace around the room. Annie shook herself, looked bleary, then went briskly into the kitchen, where Susan heard her grinding coffee beans.

"Well, good," said Menetti. "We've got the light back. Now we can do something."

"What?" asked Graham.

"We can get out there as the street starts to wake up, and we can find every human being who was on the street yesterday morning.

"And we can also hope that a meteor falls on Philadelphia or something pretty soon, or the media's going to be hell down here."

"Oh, I don't wish that," said Susan.

Menetti and Graham both looked at her.

"It's not going to be ransom. They'd have called by now if it was that. He's either been taken by someone who wants him, or he's been killed. Either way, I want to know."

"Or he's lost," said Graham, "or hurt . . ."

Susan shrugged. "Or he's lost, or hurt, or he's fallen down a manhole and he's dead one block away from us. I just want to know. Somewhere, somebody out there knows what happened, or saw something . . . or did something. . . . If I can reach them, I'm going to."

Menetti said, "I really don't think you know how weird people can be. . . . Not just the reporters, but the people who get your number, and your address. There are people who get off on other people's trouble . . . there are people who just get off on whatever they see on television."

"I don't care."

"Okay," Menetti said. "I'll do what I can to keep it from getting too crazy for you."

Robert came downstairs, with his hair rumpled and sleepers in his eyes. He grunted hello at everyone and went into the kitchen to help himself to Annie's coffee. Everyone seemed reluctant to talk; they milled in and out of the kitchen getting things for themselves, rather than offering milk or sugar around as they normally would. Menetti stood staring down at the street. Suddenly he turned to Graham and said, "Well, I'll tell you this. One is, a kid cannot disappear into thin air. It doesn't happen. Especially not at 8:50 in the morning. Two is, it's easier to hide a live kid than a dead one."

Susan came up behind them. "What did you say?"

"I said it's easier to hide a live kid than a dead one. A body is a real problem, especially in hot weather. In a way, the longer we don't turn anything up, it could be a good sign."

"He has a very small body," said Susan.

Menetti looked at the street. "I don't really think I'm a morning person," he said. "I don't know what it is, low blood sugar or something. Early morning's just not the best time for me."

Graham put down his coffeecup, took Susan's from her and set it on the windowsill, and put his arms around her. She leaned against him and closed her eyes. Everything went away for her except touch and sound. Warm dark. Shirt against her cheek. Smell of sweat and scent of his skin. Sound of someone —Robert—going up the stairs, feet going across into Alex's room. Silence. Footsteps. Faint hiss. The shower.

It was 6:10 A.M. when, for the first time that day, the phone rang.

IT WAS HARDLY past first light when the phone rang in Jocelyn's darkened bedroom on Marlborough Street. It hurt to put the receiver to her ear; she'd been on the phone so long last night. She rolled over in the tangle of bedclothes and tried to catch it before the second ring, so it wouldn't wake Justine.

"Hi, it's Martina—I'm sorry, did I wake you?"

"God, who could sleep," Jocelyn answered groggily.

"I couldn't," said Martina. "I got up and went running along the river. I couldn't stay inside, I kept thinking he's *out* there. Of course, once you get outside you realize he could be in ten million places a foot away from you and you'd never know it. But when you're in your house, you feel, Christ, why aren't I out there *doing* something? I just wondered if you'd heard anything."

Jocelyn had managed to turn over to a position from which she could see her bedside clock. 6:20. She turned on the light. "Not since about 3:30 last night. Susan was too wrecked to come to the phone, but that lady, Margaret, said they hadn't heard a thing."

"Did you see Susan on the news? She was incredible."

"No, I didn't, I heard about it. I was still on the phone, but Chris said she was totally calm."

"She was incredible. Just very dignified and collected. 'My little boy has been stolen and he's probably been raped and murdered, and I'm not going to fall apart as long as there's a single thing I can do to help him.' It was like that. If it were me, I'd have been on there *screaming*. 'They've got my kid, you fat fuckers, put down your beer cans and get out there and *help me!*' "

"No, you wouldn't," said Jocelyn. "You think you would, but when it's happening to you . . . You'd deal with it. Chris said she was sort of weirdly cool, anyway."

"Not weirdly. She had dignity—unless Chris thinks that's weird. She was like that all through that mess with Graham, too. So in love with him and so angry and sad, but she was always fair. She just kept saying, you know, that it had been hard for Graham to feel stalled and sterile after that book he's been trying to write and to have people make such a fuss about *her* book. She said he was such a star when she met him, when she was still a graduate student, and it was very hard for him when things shifted. It wasn't anybody's fault. It was just sad."

"Sad, my foot," said Jocelyn. "I think she was a fool to carry a torch for that prick."

"You *do?* God. And she'd never even admit that her book is *great*, she just said, oh, it was a political thing, all the feminists taking it up, and that really it was Graham who had a gift. Have you read her book?"

"No," said Jocelyn. "Between work and Justine, I wake up in the morning with the light burning and a novel on my chest."

"It's a *great* book," said Martina.

"Did you hear they couldn't even find Graham until 11:30 last night?"

"I know. It must have been killing her. Where do you think he was? Did you find out?"

"He was probably in the supermarket, fucking the frozen ducks," said Jocelyn. "I hope we don't all have to go around again with him because of this other thing."

"Oh . . . ? I was thinking that at least that might be some good that could come out of it, if he came back."

"Look, having a guy like that back isn't going to do her any good."

"Why?" Martina said. "I can't believe they couldn't make it together if he really wanted to come back. He's not the first guy to have an affair with a student and then be sorry."

"If Susan thinks he stops at his students," said Jocelyn scornfully, "she's more naive than I thought."

"What do you mean?"

"What do you think I mean?" There was a smug silence. "Jocelyn!"

"Oh, come on. What's the big deal? I just meant, don't get

so wrapped up with Susan that you think Graham's the heavy-weight she says he is. For one thing, he wasn't that great."

"I can't imagine what she's going through," said Martina after a long pause.

"I ought to call her soon, actually. I'm sure they're up."

"Yes. Look, call me back if there's anything, and if I don't hear from you, then what? I assume that the meeting is on for ten o'clock?"

"Right. Get the word around, and I'll see you there."

"It was good of you to do all that phoning yesterday," said Martina.

"Oh, hey—the telephone is my format. And it's not just about Alex, you know. If there's a pervert kid killer out there, it's about all of us."

"I know," said Martina.

IT HAD BEEN a slow news day, the day before. Meteors had not fallen; no new wars had broken out. When the first editions of the Boston *Globe* and the *Record American* hit the morning streets, they carried the story of Alex's disappearance on page one. The *Record American* ran a front-page picture of his laughing face. The three networks carried the story on their national morning-news broadcast. For about eighteen million people the story of Alex's disappearance became part of breakfast.

When Al Menetti walked into his kitchen in Saugus, his wife had the *Today* show going on the Sony portable on the kitchen counter. Eugene, Eileen and Roberta were sitting around the table watching while they ate their soft-boiled eggs. Marco, who was sixteen, was sitting in the living room drinking a cup of coffee and reading the *Record American*. "Hey, hi, Dad," they all mumbled.

Al's wife kissed him hello. Her face smelled of her skin cleanser. She noticed his ashen face and gave him a look, but he turned to give his small children a hug and a kiss each in turn. Then he went upstairs to shower, shave, and change. From the upstairs bathroom window, he watched his four children leave the house to walk to the corner where they picked up the school bus. Eugene lagged far behind the others, swinging his book bag against his thigh as he walked. Al could tell from the swinging arm and the little skips he took now and then that Eugene was singing to himself.

His wife had poured him a cup of coffee when he came downstairs. "Any breakfast?" she asked him.

He shook his head, then said, "Yeah . . . toast." She made it and brought it to him, then sat down with him with a cup of coffee for herself. She leaned on her elbows and held the steaming cup close under her face and watched him. He knew, when she did that, she was giving herself a little facial sauna. She'd read about doing that for your complexion in one of the magazines. He liked to see the gleam of moisture on her chin— it seemed very intimate and struck him funny.

"See the news?" he asked her.

She nodded. "They had a picture of the little boy on."

"He's about a few months younger than Eugene," said Al. "I saw these drawings he did, all Scotch-taped to his wall. They look just like Eugene's." He took a deep breath and stared into his coffee cup.

"How's the mother?" Pat Menetti asked. She was wearing stretch blue jeans and one of her husband's shirts with the tail out. He had a very pure moment of seeing her suddenly, not as the woman who kept serving frozen codfish cakes and who fell asleep in the movies, but as the very pretty girl with amazing boobs who met him when he was seventeen and never knew she would raise his seven children.

"The mother's good," he said thoughtfully. "She's amazingly good." He stared into space for a while, and then, feeling overwhelmingly tired, added, "Jesus . . . this is murder."

"You think he was murdered?" asked his wife. Sometimes he couldn't tell if she was not as bright as she used to be or if maybe she'd had a hearing loss. Or, did he think it was murder?

"No," he said. "I mean . . . I frankly don't know. I made a mistake last night. I put a lot of men on finding the separated father. Should have been able to tell from the mother that it wasn't a custody thing. She told me it wasn't, and it wasn't. I should have had bloodhounds on it right away. There's not much point now. They can't do much after eight hours. I don't even know if state police would have given me the blood-hounds with the father out, the way it looked. But what else

51

could I have done? I don't know."

"The thing I wonder," said his wife, "is, if you only have one, and something happens to him, it must be the worst thing in the world. But then, when you have seven, don't you just worry for them seven times as much?"

"If you don't know, who does?"

"*I* don't know," said Pat. "But I don't see how she went on the television like that. If it was me, I couldn't have done that."

"Yeah, you could," he said, looking at her. "If you believe you could help Eugene, I bet you could."

"Are you sure there's nothing . . . funny about her?" his wife asked.

"What do you mean?"

"She was so cool," said Pat. Uh-huh, thought Menetti. Now it starts. It can't happen to me. It happened to her, she lost her kid, but if there's something funny about her, then there's a reason it could happen to her but it couldn't happen to me. Now starts the drawing away, the pulling aside, the setting the Selkys apart.

"There's nothing funny about her." He finished his coffee and stood up regretfully. Jesus, he was tired. His wife stood too, and she came around the table to give him a real kiss.

"Any idea of your schedule?" she asked.

He shook his head. "I have to be back in the city at ten. They've got a couple of volunteers, neighborhood parents and friends, coming in to see what they can do. I guess I'll start them putting the pictures of the kid around—I can use the extra hand or two. After that, looks like I'll just have to see what breaks." He looked at her. Then he sighed and added softly, "Jesus, I hoped all last night it was going to be a ransom thing. I sure as hell hope I don't have a nice wacko kid killer here. That's what I really don't want." His wife nodded. "If anything's moving, I'll stay. Otherwise, I'll come home for dinner."

"Roberta's having her slumber party tonight," Pat said.

"Good," he said wearily, "we can all sit around the TV with curlers in our hair."

WHEN SUSAN was growing up in Quaker Village, Ohio, a middle-class suburb of Cleveland, she thought of Boston as a place where people lived wider, richer lives than in Ohio. She knew the Boston of Henry James and William Dean Howells, when it was known as the Athens of America. She could still remember vividly sitting cross-legged on the floor in the front hall of her father's house, with her sneakers tucked under her and a streak of sunlight slanting from the door across her open book, trying feverishly to finish *The Bostonians* before the car pool arrived to take her to her tennis lesson. The Boston of her mind's eye with its Public Gardens and the elegant sweep of Commonwealth Avenue seemed like a European capital. It was a place for people of character and wit, people who "had conversation." In Henry James' Boston, people asked moral questions. They acted on principle. They took risks.

By the time Susan and Graham actually moved to Boston, the flavor and charm of the city neighborhoods had changed, and so had the people who were charmed. Boston's first families had gradually sifted out of Beacon Hill and Back Bay to the rural comfort of the suburbs. Vast mansions along Commonwealth and Beacon had been converted to offices and seemingly countless schools. When Susan and Graham found their narrow town house on Fremont Street, it had been badly used by generations of students from the scattered institutions that Graham called collectively Unknown Junior College. It had taken them seven years to fix the house up again, and it still had two unconverted rooms in the attic and was a little short on furniture. But for neighbors the Selkys had a Chinese scholar who had been born in Peking, a poet who worked for the *Atlantic Monthly*, and a curator from the Boston Museum of Fine Arts who lived with his male lover. (What Susan's little classmates in Ohio called queers. No one in Quaker Village admitted to being one or even having seen one, but all the children knew what it meant if someone chose to wear green and yellow on a Thursday. ("Ooo, look what Larry's wearing! Larry is a queer! Larry is a queer! Trying to tell us something, Larry?") Discreet and sophisticated, Boston is a more congenial place to be gay than Quaker Village, Ohio, and the number who choose to be gay there contributes to the urbane quality of the city's life.

With one of the highest per capita student populations in the world, Boston seems simultaneously very young and very old, a city full of diversity, experiment, tradition, and transience. And to Susan, it felt like a feast. There was a high-caste Hindu teaching assistant in her department, and a Boston Brahmin in Alex's play group, and her kitchen shelves were built by a carpenter from the South End who had a Ph.D. in philosophy. The South End, just across Copley Square from Back Bay, was a neighborhood in the midst of what Boston called "gentrification." Streets full of row houses falling into ruin and left to the angry poor were being restored to their pre-Civil War fineness. The streets rang with the sound of power saws and sand blasting and were suddenly home again to a mixture of young professionals, academics, and artists. The angry poor had been eased sideways into the already restless black ghetto of Roxbury. The Fourth District police headquarters was on one seedy edge of the South End.

Menetti, driving in from Saugus, had to remind himself that it takes all kinds. He'd worked his butt off to move away from the ghetto and raise his kids someplace where everybody tried hard to stay married and keep the lawn cut. If he'd been to Harvard, he was pretty damn sure he wouldn't choose to live in the South End, next door to a slum, on a street with no big trees, in a neighborhood with no good schools. Even over where the Selkys lived, instead of clean sheets and the PTA, it looked to him like what people thought about was abortions and yoga and eating out in restaurants. His feeling was that there was no there, there. No center. People moving in all the time, other people moving out. And none of them seemed to stop and think that they were basically living in a zoo. A city wasn't a place for people, especially kids. It was more like a big zoo with concrete floors and all the cage doors left open. He was extremely surprised, in fact, when he trudged up the stairs to Susan's living room for his briefing of the handful of volunteers and found that more than a hundred people had passed up their yoga classes and were crowded into the room, quietly waiting for him.

SUSAN COULDN'T TELL if she was surprised or not at the number of people who came to the meeting. She was dazed to have so many people in the house at all. Watching them come up the steps, people from Harvard, parents of kids with whom Alex had gone to day-care, parents of children in his class at NBS, she thought to herself that if this had happened to any of their kids, she'd be there for them. She wondered if they knew that. She wondered if she should say so. No, of course they knew it, and that was why they were here. Besides, they weren't here for her; they were here for themselves and their children. As long as nobody knew what had happened to Alex, no one knew whose child might be next.

When Menetti arrived, Susan rose from the chair where she had perched on the arm, leaning on Jocelyn. She couldn't seem to light anywhere for long; she had felt terribly restless and bereft while Menetti was gone. She hadn't wanted to leave the house for fear of missing a phone call, but so far the phone had brought her either the press or this sort of thing:

"Hello, let me speak to the boy's mother."

"This is Mrs. Selky."

"Please! The boy's mother! I have vital information but I'm . . ." (The voice drops to a whisper.) "Please. Get me the mother, I don't have much time."

"Yes, this is she . . ." Susan had looked up and seen one of the policemen watching her expression.

"Oh, okay, I'll talk fast. Can you hear me?"

Susan said yes, although she hardly could.

"Okay, listen. Okay, can you hear me, I don't want them to hear. Across the street, the house at 211, there have been lights in there for weeks, late at night. White ones, and now green ones. They don't know I'm up, but I have pain at night, I get up and sit at the window. I know they can see in the dark, but they got bad information, they thought everyone on the street was asleep. But last night they sensed me. I could feel them all around me in the dark, like they were smelling me all over, but from way over there, if you waved your arms you couldn't—"

"Excuse me, could I have your name and address?"

"Wait," the voice whispered urgently. "Listen! So last night there was a commotion, a struggle, the lights bobbing all around in the windows, and there were purple ones. I heard a child cry out, and then the lights, they all seemed to come together, they sort of all swam together in a rush, and they made this disk, so bright you couldn't *look* at it, on the lawn, and then there was a noise like wind, but real loud and high, and then that's when they suddenly realized a human was watching, because I was all surrounded with this feeling of them sniffing and smelling me, because it's forbidden to see, and they *knew* I knew what they were doing, and then . . . ."

The policeman had taken the phone from Susan and listened for a moment. Then he said, "Is that you, Mrs. Bonesteel? . . . Uh-huh . . . I understand. Yes . . . we'll get in touch with Saturn, then. They didn't hurt you, did they? . . . Fine. Good-bye, Mrs. Bonesteel." He hung up. The phone rang again almost immediately. Susan, wide-eyed and slightly nauseous, had let the police answer it. She went to sit at the window. Since eight in the morning the streets had been filled with policemen. She had a grim feeling that they weren't terribly clear about what they were doing. They seemed to mill around and repeat each other's moves, in something of the self-important pattern children use when they're trying to imitate the rhythms of something grown-ups do, without understanding the logic behind it. (Alex and Graham and TJ playing cowboys and Indians in the living room, scrambling for cover behind chairs and sofas, bouncing up to shoot, making kkkkkkkkkkk gun noises in the roofs of their mouths. Alex always ducked way down behind the sofa, going kkkkkkk, then bounded up to make of himself a target like the side of a barn, while the others fired. . . . At least he had the motions right. He gurgled with triumph when Graham and TJ would crash to the floor and die their noisy deaths.) Could those officers keep taking their walkie-talkies out of their bulging back pockets and saying snappy things into them, without feeling that they were on television?

Just be calm, she told herself. Just hold on to it. Get through this hour, and then Menetti will be back and our friends will be here, and that will change things.

"They're being wonderful," Susan greeted Menetti hopefully, gesturing around the room jammed with volunteers.

Menetti surveyed the group. They didn't look like any group of concerned citizens he'd dealt with lately. Out in Saugus, you could probably muster a small crowd of professional joiners—the full-time moms, the Community Chest-type dads. His wife, Pat, would be there with her big heart and her straining slacks as long as the meeting were held between nine and 2:30. But this was a different sort of group. On the sofa before him, designed for two people, sat four slender women who balanced their oval heads on delicate necks as if they were eggs in the egg-and-spoon race; they had to be dancers. At the window, between two men who were clearly gay, was a small, Semitic-looking woman, very young, with black hair and porcelain skin, who was draped in layers and layers of Indian gauze, topped by what seemed to be a silk bathrobe. She emerged as the doyenne of the Space for Children day-care center, where many of these parents had met Susan and each other. There were women in overalls with GI haircuts that startlingly made you more aware of their eyes and lips and breasts than you would have been if they had hair. There were women in jeans with wild curly hair that stood out from their heads like pyramids of Brillo, what police slang called a Jewfro. There were several men among the women. One man dressed in natty oxford bags was a chef who lived in the South End with his lawyer wife. Another, who was wearing a graying ponytail and a denim jacket with the sleeves cut off, turned out to be not a Hell's Angel but a jazz clarinetist Menetti had admired since Police Academy days.

Graham came across the room to Susan. "You want to do this, or me?" he asked softly, bending over her.

"You, please."

He put his hand on her shoulder and she put her small one up to cover it, but didn't look at him. He straightened and faced the room, clearing his throat for attention.

"Lieutenant Menetti is here now. I guess we can start. I want to thank you all for coming today. It means a great deal to Susan and me to see you here. At this point, as I guess we've already told most of you as you came in, we just don't know anything. So . . . Susan, did you want to say anything?''

"Just . . . thank you,'' she said from her seat.

"I know you must have questions, so Lieutenant Menetti will try to answer them.'' Graham looked around for a place at the edge of the room to retire to, and Menetti stood up.

What people wanted to know was whether their own children were in danger, and that was what nobody knew. There was a darting, stricken look in the eyes of the mothers.

"Do you have any idea,'' one of the dancers asked first, "if this was a crime committed by somebody Alex knew?''

"Well, we don't know yet that a crime was committed at all,'' said Menetti. "The boy may be lost. He could have run away. There could be custodial interference . . .''

"What's 'custodial interference'?'' several voices asked.

"Are you saying that's what you think?'' asked another mother sharply.

"No, I'm not. I'm saying we don't know yet what's happened.'' A hundred attentive pairs of eyes were fixed on him. "We have leads. We're not in the dark . . . not at all. I don't want to be more specific, because of the press. But at this point, I do feel we have ample reason to hope for a speedy solution to this case. By the way, I want to make clear, our department has *never* had a case of a child this young disappearing without a trace.''

He said this with great firmness, and though some in the group stirred, as if objections or memories were disturbing something at the edges of their thoughts, no one said anything.

"And I want you to know that my office will not take this case lightly and we will not stop till we find out what happened to Alex. Whatever resources the police department has or can call on, that's what we'll use, until we find this little boy.''

A man who had come with Jocelyn, whom Susan didn't know, asked, "Lieutenant Menetti . . . are you considering seriously that Alex might have run away?'' For a moment, it seemed as if the reflexive lack of sympathy between this neighborhood and the police might precipitate into hostility.

Menetti stiffened. "Look, try to understand, I'm telling you what my position is. As long as we don't know anything, we have to consider everything possible. . . . But he's really just a baby . . ."

"Lieutenant Menetti," asked Susan's friend Martina, "if you were raising a young child in this neighborhood, what would you go home and tell him? How would you handle this?"

Menetti had been waiting for this question. Reluctantly he put his hands in his pockets and fished around, as if he might find a way not to answer. "Well," he said, "I wouldn't scare them. I mean, I'd have a little talk with them about strangers, if you haven't already. But I also would supervise them pretty carefully."

"Meaning?" "What do you mean?" "What does that mean?" a dozen voices asked.

"Well . . . Meaning, I don't think I'd let a young child out of the house without an adult, until we have some idea what's happened."

"What do you mean by young?"

"If it was me?" asked Menetti. "I'd say . . . under twelve."

There was something awful in hearing him say something so specific. What did he know? What was he thinking of? Why twelve? Why not eight? Why not twenty? No one asked. Instead, Graham said, "Lieutenant Menetti, a lot of us would feel better if we could help."

"Absolutely," said Menetti. "We didn't expect quite so many of you, so I don't know if we have enough of these. . . ." An officer who was waiting at the door of the room came forward now with a stack of handbills. Menetti took them, thanked him, and held one up.

It showed two snapshots of Alex, one of his smiling face and the boysenberry-dyed T-shirt, the other of him standing smiling on a patch of grass holding a baseball cap and his mitt. Under the pictures was a description of what Alex was wearing, his age, height, and weight, and the exact time and place of his disappearance. Across the top of the paper was the bold headline "MISSING." Menetti asked them all to take handbills everywhere they went in the next few days. To staple them onto trees, tape them onto lampposts. To get permission from every shop they could to post the handbills in the windows.

"A child cannot disappear into thin air," he said. "Some-where, somebody knows something. Somebody's seen some-thing. If anyone gives you information directly, please write it down, word for word if you can, and get the source's name and address. Call the number on the handbill with anything you get, day or night. And . . . I think it will help to move fast."

As they left, Susan thanked each one for coming. She stood at the door, as if it were a receiving line. Some kissed her, or shook her hand, or touched her cheek as they passed. "It's remarkable how kind people are, really," she said when they were gone. She mused on the strangeness of this, the sense of community. Then she drifted into trying to picture Alex. Try-ing to bring back a round, scented image of him, of his touch. All she could bring was a mental picture of his photograph on the poster. MISSING. Yes.

By sundown, it seemed that there were posters of Alex in every drugstore, butcher shop, luncheonette, and boutique from the Charles River to Boston harbor. The media followed the troop of volunteers everywhere, and the six-o'clock news on all stations carried interviews. "Mrs. Norris, you've been walking for two hours now, going into shops and getting per-mission to put up these handbills of the missing boy, little Alex Selky? Why are you doing that? . . . I see, and are you worried for your own child? . . . I see, and what would you say is the mood of the community here this evening? From Boston, the scene of a truly stirring volunteer effort to find little Alex Selky, missing now for thirty-three hours. Police say they have never seen anything like the way this community has turned out in response to this case, and the mood here among these parents tonight is hopeful—but there is also, certainly, fear. This is Vivienne Grant . . ."

There was an interview with Susan, too, taped early in the afternoon. "We're very grateful to the community for their help and support," she said calmly. "The police feel they have several promising leads, and my husband and I feel very hope-ful that something or someone will lead us to Alex very quickly."

"You believe, then, that your son is alive, Mrs. Selky?"

"Absolutely," she said to the camera.

Susan sat on her bed in the dusk, watching the broadcast,

and wondered: How could I? How did I ever stand so straight and speak like that? She felt so dull and tired and heavy, she wasn't sure she could move, let alone lie.

There was Menetti on the screen, looking exhausted. "Lieutenant Menetti," the reporter said, "there have been several cases in the last two years of children disappearing. There was quite a scandal just recently with the Gacy case in Illinois—where dozens of boys and young men over a long period disappeared, while nothing was done. Apparently you're determined that there will not be a repeat of that story here. Is that right?" Microphone to Menetti. What was he supposed to say? "Well, that's right . . ." said Menetti.

IN SAUGUS, Detective Menetti turned off the news and got up to refill his glass. Roberta and her friends were in the kitchen making fudge. Eugene was listening to his *Sesame Street Fever* record upstairs.

"You look like you've been worked over by Nick the Bouncer," said Pat, glancing up from her needlepoint.

"I hate this case," he said.

"You hate them all." Pat was pawing around in her bag for another color yarn.

"I don't hate them all. Sometimes it's like a good puzzle. This one's got me. I wish I was drunk."

"I can see that," said Pat. "What were you going to say, on the tube, when you turned yourself off?"

"You know. They write out their soap-opera questions so the question is the answer. All that's left is to say 'Yes' or 'No.' 'Do you have any leads?' 'Yes.' 'Can you tell us about them?' 'No.' 'Are you hopeful for an early break?' 'Yes.' "

"Do you think you're going to get an early break?" asked Pat.

"You should hear the kinds of leads we have. A neighbor near the school is *sure* he saw the boy yesterday afternoon, unless it was the day before. A woman claims she saw him alone at ten A.M. walking on Newbury Street. She can't explain why she didn't think anything about it, a kid that age during school hours wandering around by himself. But I still have to make four guys spend a morning on Newbury Street trying to find someone else who saw Alex too.

61

"I have a man living on Beacon Street who claims he saw a woman waiting in a car for about ten minutes the morning in question. He cannot describe the woman; he can sort of describe the car. He claims it's been there before. But he never saw Alex; he just saw this car, and when he finished shaving and went downstairs at nine o'clock, it was gone.

"Then I've got a guy who thinks he saw Alex in a Cambridge food store at noon. He thinks he was with a punk with bad skin and peroxide hair. Now, why would a smart little kid who knew not to talk to strangers be pricing Twinkies with some pimply shit instead of screaming his head off? Tell me the truth, would Eugene do that?"

Pat nodded over her needlepoint and went on working. It seemed a rhetorical question.

"I'm serious," said Menetti. "Is there anything some geek could say to Eugene that would get him to wander off shopping with him? Think about it? I want to know."

Pat thought about it. She shrugged. "Promise to take him to meet the real Batman?"

"I hope you're kidding."

"I don't know if I am or not."

"Well, Pat . . . well, what have you actually told him, about strangers?"

"I've told him not to talk to them, I've told him not to go anywhere with them, and I've told him not to believe anyone who says I sent them unless they know the code word."

"Really?"

"Really. If I ever sent someone he didn't know to pick him up at school or something, the person would say to him, 'Your mother sent me to get you and the code is 'Howdy Doody, Daddy.' "

Menetti grunted. "Well, that's original."

"You don't want to scare them to death, you know. They're just little kids. You can't bring them up to feel safe and unsafe every minute at the same time."

"Do all mothers have codes?"

"No, I thought it up four years ago, when we thought Nicole Cluny was kidnapped. Nicole Cluny was a spoiled little brat from Roberta's class who got mad at her mother and ran away to her aunt's for two days. No one ever explained why the aunt

62

hadn't let her sister know Nicole was safe. The mother seemed very happy to get Nicole back, but the neighborhood was so angry at the scare that many seemed to think kidnapping would do Nicole good.

"I don't suppose this boy is at his aunt's?" asked Pat.

"I don't suppose so, no. . . . Do you really think some guy could talk Eugene into going with him, even though you told him this code and everything?"

"Hey, Al . . . Eugene is seven years old. A seven-year-old is not a responsible person, no matter what you tell him. Not if he has to handle something that hasn't come up before. He's a good boy, he trusts people. Sure, I think a reasonably bright grown-up could talk him into anything. . . . Gee, why don't you have another drink?" said Pat with irritation, seeing him reach to pour.

"I'll tell you where he is," Menetti said. "That neighborhood is one block from the Esplanade, and these hot mornings the whole riverbanks is full of people from sunrise on. Drunks, creeps, joggers, kids necking, guys exposing themselves . . . the whole mixed grill. It could be the Emerald City, it's so full of fairies, for instance."

"I thought we don't let the children use that word."

"I happen to like them, frankly," he said. "Every group has its little quirks. We don't say it at work because we have to show how much hair we have on our chest, but if you want to give me a choice of what kind of loonies to work with, I like fruits. I've got one on my staff, in fact."

"Who?"

"Never mind. My point is, that strip there . . . anyone who can't see the odds here couldn't find his behind with a mirror."

"Meaning?"

"Meaning, he was a beautiful little boy. Real beautiful, with a great smile. If he's not dead by now. . . . It would probably be better if he was." As Menetti said that, tears came into his eyes.

Pat studied him from her chair, her hand over her mouth. "You drunk now?" she said at last.

"Yeah." He wiped his eyes.

"Going to want dinner?" The sounds from the kitchen suggested that Roberta and her friends had reached the pot-and-spoon-licking stage.

"No . . . bed," he said. He went upstairs, taking the bottle with him.

⸻❧ ☙⸻

AT MIDNIGHT, the street was gleaming with a slow, cold, steady rain. Susan stood at her bedroom window, looking down. From that height, you couldn't always tell if it was only wind, or wind with rain in it. Alex, are you out in this? Alex, my baby, I know it's May, but won't you take your jacket? Alex . . . The gooseflesh on your bare arms when you're cold . . . O Lord, deliver me. Christ, deliver me. Oh, God, help me . . . how do I bear unbearable loss?

At Lent in the church in which Susan was raised, there is a moment in the service when the choir rises and slowly marches down the center aisle, chanting. The rector walks behind them. He chants, *Oh, God the Son, Redeemer of the World,* and the choir and congregation respond, *Have Mercy Upon Us.* He chants, *From lightning and tempest; from plague and pestilence and famine; from battle and murder; and from sudden death . . .* and the people respond, *Good Lord, Deliver Us.* The choir and the rector slowly circle the entire congregation, like ancient priests in that dark winter season drawing a magic circle of protection around the church, chanting, *We beseech thee to hear us, Good Lord.* It is the Litany, the oldest chant in the prayer book, the first to be translated from the Latin, and tonight it reverberates in Susan, a primitive longing for ritual. She hadn't been to church since Alex was christened, but tonight she would resort to occult spells . . . she would wail aloud and tear her clothes . . .

Here is pain beyond sense, the inchoate anguish of an animal. . . . She once knew a dog whose grief was such, when she saw her last puppy killed by a car, that she howled all night and tried to bite off her own tail.

Downstairs in the living room, the ash-blue couch had been pushed against the wall to make room for a long table the police had brought in. There were now three telephones there,

Susan's and the special police number with two extensions. Three large uniformed officers sat there in a row, smoking cigarettes and drinking coffee from paper cups, logging in every telephone call. At eight o'clock, the shift changed and three new uniforms replaced the first ones. The constant noise and the number of people made the room a surreal imitation of the one she used to live in. She wandered vaguely around it as if she couldn't remember what she was doing there. The three phones seemed to ring incessantly—nearly four hundred calls between noon and midnight.

By midafternoon, Menetti had had over three hundred uniformed officers in the streets, searching every house and store and garage and warehouse. Helicopters cruised overhead, flying so low their noise and whir and threatening shadows seemed to fill the skies with clamor. They scanned rooftops and piers looking for a place a small boy could have ventured out and gotten stuck or trapped. In the streets, blue-and-white patrol cars drove slowly through the Italian North End, through Brighton, around the Fenway, through Chinatown, broadcasting through PA systems on car roofs. "We are looking for a white male child, age six, missing since yesterday. He is wearing a red-and-white striped T-shirt, blue jeans, and blue jogging shoes. His name is Alex. Anyone with information concerning this child, please call the police." Volunteers from the neighborhoods had come forward to translate the MISSING posters into Spanish, Italian, and Chinese.

Menetti was downstairs most of the time keeping in touch with searchers through a communications van parked in front of the house. People were stopping the officers in the streets and asking if they could help. Yes, of course—yes, please. Go everywhere, look at everything, as if you were a six-year-old. The newspapers were to announce with fervor that it was one of the biggest manhunts in living memory. Graham and TJ were out in the streets all day, going everywhere Alex would go, doing everything Alex did. Two blue-coated policemen followed them everywhere. They took notes, they asked questions, they reported to Menetti on walkie-talkies every ten minutes. Nothing so far. We're on Dartmouth Street, we're on Clarendon, we're on Berkeley—there's nothing yet. Nothing yet. Nothing.

Manhunt. Childhunt.

Sometime in midafternoon, Susan went to answer the door and found there, looking uncertain, a girl with wide eyes and high cheekbones, and soft straight hair. Even though the hair was redder and the girl was ten years younger than Susan, Susan knew without a mirror how much they looked alike. Oh, Graham, she thought, can't you find a faster way to break my heart? She said, "You're Naomi."

Naomi nodded. She looked at Susan as Susan looked at her. "Well," she said in the soft quick voice Susan recognized from the phone, "I can see why Graham's friends laugh at him when they meet me."

"I guess I should be flattered," said Susan.

"Is it all right that I came? I couldn't think of anything else —if there's anything I can do . . ."

Susan knew, without wanting to, that she was very pretty, and bright and decent. She finally said, "I'm glad you came. I thank you. But if you don't mind, I'd rather you didn't come in."

Naomi just nodded again. "I'm so sorry . . ." And then she put out her hand to Susan, who took it and shook it. Susan wondered if it was an odd thing to do, but she felt that they both understood it. Then Naomi went away.

It was surprising, at a time like this, how hard you had to work to keep people from pumping you full of drugs. By suppertime, Susan's bedroom was like a pharmacy. Downstairs, neighbors had dropped off homemade bread and casseroles, and Craig Collier, the costume designer who lived downstairs from Jocelyn and often baby-sat Alex and Justine, came over with a bowl of fresh flowers.

"Craig . . ." Susan was somehow especially touched by this. "You can't afford these . . ."

"Oh, it's all right," he said gallantly. "I stole them." He pulled away and crumpled behind his back the green florist's paper that protected the bowl.

Upstairs, Philippe, her cleaning person, had made a special trip to bring her a supply of Quaaludes.

"Don't give her 'ludes, man, that's the worst thing," Jocelyn was saying. Philippe looked sulky. "Honey, these are Elavils. Don't take more than four between now and bed, and

66

don't mix them with alcohol." Jocelyn poured tiny blue pills onto Susan's dresser. Another friend had wordlessly pressed on her a small carved wooden pipe and a tiny chunk of something wrapped in aluminum foil, which Susan had dropped into a pocket and forgotten. Two of her students had brought her what must have been their exam-period stash of cocaine, but she made them keep it. "I could get you some meth, I think, if you'd rather," one of them whispered.

Susan finally managed to convince Jocelyn and Philippe that she didn't want to take anything. She couldn't describe to them how numb and skewed she already felt, but she sometimes thought she must be shaking her head from time to time in an effort to clear it or to feel like the woman she remembered being, once.

Philippe pocketed his 'ludes, and looked disappointed. Susan wondered if she saw in Jocelyn's eyes a flicker of impatience. She wanted to help me, thought Susan, and if I'd taken her pills, she'd have felt better. How quickly a person in pain whom you can't help becomes a reproach. And then, no doubt, a thorn.

Margaret came up as soon as she came home from work. She brought her bright eyes and her warm strong smile. She looked tired. Her presence, as it had the night before, distracted Susan and took the edge from her absorption. Margaret seemed to have a gift for distance, as if she could simultaneously deeply feel and stand apart from her feelings.

"Do you know what's happening out there?" asked Margaret. "I noticed all the way home. An *unusual* number of people putting out garbage tonight."

Susan looked up.

"The police are searching house to house, and you'd be surprised how many people just remember that they have something they've been meaning to get rid of. Of course, the police knife open the bags; I watched them do one. Three radios, a tape deck, and a bag of little brown leaves. . . . Well, I wish I were a sanitation man."

For a moment Susan had a slapstick vision of petty thieves all over town trying to cram hot goods into Hefty bags, trying to remember if the clock radio was stolen or not . . .

"Well, I'm starved," said Margaret. "I brought up some of

this crab soup I keep in the freezer, and we'll have some toast with it. Up here, or will you come down?"

"Down," said Susan.

When she was called, she came and sat down at the table, which Margaret had set with candles and Craig's flowers. She tried as hard as she could to eat. The soup was rich and fragrant and Margaret had chopped fresh chives to sprinkle on the top. Susan felt nausea boil up in her.

"This is sickening," she said, laying down her spoon.

"Why, yes, it is," Margaret agreed. "I never can eat when I should."

"No, neither can I," said Susan.

"We'll try again later." Margaret cleared the supper away. The police were eating Big Macs at the table and continued to take phone calls while they chewed. The room seemed to be filled with racket. All evening the phones rang and rang, and it was torture. Then they began to ring less, and that was worse.

SUSAN HAD TO WAIT until very late that night before she could say to herself: I was wrong to let him walk by himself. I was wrong. He was so young . . . too young . . .

It was me.

There had been plenty of calls like that. The police didn't say so, but she knew. "A six-year-old child wandering down the street by himself? What do you expect?"

Going on seven . . . almost seven . . .

Such a bright, earnest six. Age doesn't mean anything. He *never* strayed.

No.

He was just a baby. He was *six*.

She sat in the darkness, feeling like an open wound.

She thought: It's days since I had any sleep. I should sleep, or else I'm going to hallucinate. This is much worse than last night. I can't even trace for myself what has happened, in a clear linear way.

Though, they say that time isn't linear. That the past and the future all exist at the same time. It's only the limitation of our brains that keeps us from being in all time, all the time. The way dogs see only in black and white. They never suspect that color is there. Maybe the past is all around us, waiting to be changed. Maybe I can be in the past again—I can be together in time with Alex, before . . .

Wishing to be out of your brain is the same thing as wishing for death. Not going to do that. Not even going to think that.

The phone might ring. It could ring at any time. Couldn't it?

It's been fifteen years since I went to church. I stopped going because religion was the opiate of the masses. Tonight, I see that it's the only drug that could do me any good, but it's too late.

In fact, faith isn't a drug. It's an active practice, an act of will. *Now* I see.

To have faith that Alex is alive—it has nothing to do with belief, or thought. Do I *think* so? Do I think he's alive? To *think* or to *know* has nothing to do with it. I commit myself to his being alive, as an act of will.

Lord, I believe; help thou mine unbelief.

I'm beginning to have longer stretches of my mind going blank. It's like being in a huge empty cavern, with just enough light, from an unclear source, to see that it's empty. I think I'm beginning to slow down.

I wonder if I could sleep.

SATURDAY MORNING, seven o'clock. It had been full light for over an hour. Hundreds of uniformed police went on with their house-to-house search across Back Bay. Menetti had been downstairs in the street since dawn, directing the operations by radio from the police van. Susan looked down at the street from the living-room window. It seemed to have taken her forever to get there. She felt when she moved as if she were an elderly bug, numbly and slowly crossing familiar distances that had somehow become vast. Her whole body felt bruised and sour.

". . . one of the largest manhunts in city history," said the morning news. "Police here indicate that they have never had a case of a child this young disappearing without a trace. They say they will keep up their exhaustive efforts until they find out exactly what happened to little Alex Selky, age six, missing now from his home in Boston for two days." Then the pictures, the phone numbers, the appeal for information.

Susan could hear the phones shrilling as she lowered herself like a brittle old woman into a tub full of steaming water. On the edge of the tub, by her foot, lay Alex's blue plastic dolphin that swam around by jerking its tail back and forth when you wound it up. Alex, flushed and wet and slippery in his bath, winding it over and over again. Alex's giggle. Alex learning to wash his own hair, his little blunt fingers clamped together, rubbing the lather on his head with his hands held as if they were paddles. His eyes and lips ferociously clamped together to keep out the soap as he hung his head back under the faucet to rinse. Alex eagerly combing his clean wet hair himself with a part that was nearly diagonal across his head. (Not quite tall enough to see himself in the mirror, not quite sure he could balance on his knees on the stool to see, and hold the comb at the same time.) The smell of Alex's clean soapy skin, his warm breath and his cold wet hair on her cheek as he kissed her good night.

At eight o'clock Al Menetti came up with two cardboard cups of coffee and two gelatinous Danish pastries wrapped in wax paper. He said to Susan, "Share this with me," and it sounded more like an order than an invitation. She obediently sat down and slowly managed to eat the whole sweet roll. He watched her carefully as she did it. She ate with small precise bites and somehow dropped no crumbs on her breast.

Once again there were dozens of policemen all over the house. One of the officers on the telephones this morning was a woman. She wore exactly the same uniform as the men, not like the lady traffic cops of Susan's youth in their blue skirts and sensible shoes.

"Could I speak to you for a minute, Lieutenant?" this officer called across the din in the room to them, and Menetti gestured to her to join them.

"Getting an awful lot of dreams, the last two hours," said Officer Hines, pulling up a chair to the dining table and leaning on her elbows. She was a tough, bottom-heavy woman, and she addressed herself to Menetti rather than to Susan.

"Adding up to anything?"

She shrugged. "Maybe half say they see him near a body of water. . . ."

"River? Lake? Ocean?"

She shook her head.

"Great," said Menetti. "How much of the earth is covered with water?"

Officer Hines shrugged again. "You ever work with Alison Busch?" she asked him.

"The woman in Providence?"

Officer Hines nodded. "She's not exactly batting four for four, but she hits it now and then."

"Isn't she the one they went to in the Patty Hearst case? She kept saying she was in a small dark place? There are lots of closets in California. . . ."

"Yeah, but I worked on one case she was in on, where a guy ran a small computer business, disappeared one night between work and home. A solid family guy and everything, but gone without a trace. With no physical evidence, we didn't know what to think except he must have done a bunk. Alison Busch kept seeing him *under* water. There was a place along his route home where the highway ran by a river, and, sure enough, we finally found a clump of trees she kept describing, and there were tire marks and there was the car, in about eight feet of water, with the guy in it. He'd had a heart attack at the wheel and apparently he just pulled the wheel to get the car out of traffic, just pulled it right off the road, but died before he could stop it. No water in the lungs."

Menetti looked at Susan. She looked sharply from one of them to the other.

"She won't work on just any case," said Officer Hines. "She doesn't claim she can see everything. She'll only get involved if she thinks she can actually help. I could give her a call for you." She finally looked directly at Susan.

"Do it. Yes . . . please do it," said Susan.

"Yes, I think we should," he said. "Thank you, Officer."

The woman said heartily, "No problem," and went back to her place at the telephones.

Susan and Menetti sat silently in their chairs for some

minutes listening to the phones ring. The officers took names, addresses, phone numbers. They copied down descriptions seen in dreams, they recorded messages from Ouija boards. They took down descriptions and details of supposed sightings of a little boy—it was so hard to get a sense of the living boy from the flat gray picture. People wanted to help so much. They kept seeing things.

"Lieutenant, I think I've got something," one of the telephone men called, with a tiny thread of excitement strung through his voice. "A third sighting of a boy who fits our description, on Newbury Street Thursday morning."

"Let's have it," said Menetti, crossing the floor in two steps. He scanned the name and address and the facts of the conversation; then he sprinted down the stairs to the communications van, with Susan at his heels. He dispatched a detective with a copy of Alex's picture to talk to the woman who called, and he called for a dozen men to get back to Newbury Street, to go into every store, to get names of every employee and every deliveryman who was on the street anywhere from Arlington Street to Hereford. He gave orders for men to stay on the street till noon, stopping everyone, looking for neighborhood people, until they found others who were there at ten on Thursday morning who might have seen Alex.

"Okay," he said with a smile, turning to Susan. "*Okay*. Now we're going to see some movement. I *told* you we'd start to get a handle on it today." He caught himself, as if he wanted to go on thinking out loud. "Okay," he said once more, with new energy.

"The next thing I want to do is, I want to get in a hypnotist, to talk to the people who reported these Newbury Street sightings—and why don't we have you go under hypnosis, too, and the guy on Beacon Street, to see what more you can remember about the street that morning?

"You know," he said as they walked back up the stairs, "a case like this is like dominoes. You get nothing, nothing, nothing, and you feel like you're looking at a brick wall, and then suddenly one brick falls, and in a second you've got them all tumbling one after another till the whole case falls into your lap. I can feel it.

"Officer Hines," he boomed as he walked into the room.

Taxi hurled himself first at Susan and then at Menetti. "Walk this dog for me, will you? Yes, Taxi, you're a nice guy, aren't you? Are you a full dog? Okay, pal, here's your friend to take you for a walk. That's a funny name, Taxi," he added to Susan.

"Graham named him. He thought it would be funny to be on the street calling, 'Oh, Taxi.' " Menetti's sudden optimism had given her a real flush of hope.

THE NEWBURY STREET sightings were a false alarm. Under hypnosis, the two people who claimed to have seen Alex gave completely divergent descriptions. The first man described a child of at least twelve; the woman could give no details that were not mentioned in the handbill, and in fact had almost surely seen nothing at all. Next Menetti had the man from around the corner put under hypnosis to see if he could remember anything more about the car he saw parked in the street, or if he could remember seeing Alex approach it. The man identified the car as a light blue Oldsmobile, vintage '63 or '64, with rust spots on both doors and one whitewall—the front-right tire. The car was parked across from him so that he couldn't see a license. He insisted he had seen the car parked in exactly the same place at least once, earlier in the week, but at no time had he seen Alex approach it. He hadn't seen Alex at all Thursday morning; he'd evidently gone back to shaving before Alex came around the corner.

The police hypnotist came to Susan next. They sat facing each other in two kitchen chairs that Menetti had carried up to Susan's bedroom, where it was relatively quiet.

"Just relax," said the young doctor. "Focus your eyes right here," and he tapped the bridge of his nose directly between his eyes. Susan looked. In a moment the spot seemed to glow brightly. She wondered if she was allowed to blink. They sat in silence. Menetti, behind her on the bed, was perfectly still.

When the doctor spoke again, his voice had a slight echo, as if he had moved away from her. "Now I'm going to count. With each number, your eyelids will grow heavier. When I reach ten, your eyes will close."

He began to count, and by the time he reached five, her eyelids dragged downward like lead. At ten, they irresistibly closed. She sat as if suspended. Every muscle in her body was hyperrelaxed.

"Can you hear me, Mrs. Selky?" asked the doctor's voice, simultaneously quite a distance away and apparently inside her head. She nodded.

"Your eyelids are very heavy now, and you cannot open your eyes," said the voice. Susan sat still.

"Try to open them," said the voice. She tried. They weighed a ton. "Good," said the voice. More stillness.

"Your arms are growing heavy," said the voice. "They are as heavy as lead now." Her arms hung at her sides, the hands in her lap. "You cannot lift your arms." More stillness.

"Try to lift your right arm." She tried. She could feel every muscle from shoulder to wrist flex and tense. The arm didn't move.

"Good," said the voice.

"Now," it said. "It's the morning of May 17. It's 8:45 in the morning. What are you doing?"

"I'm standing in the kitchen, putting my students' papers in my folder . . ."

"Good. Where is Alex?"

"He's beside me. He's putting an apple into his lunch bag." Alex brushed his forelock out of his eyes and picked up his knapsack. He put the brown lunch bag into his knapsack.

"You ready to go, honey?" asked Susan.

"Yep," he said.

"What about tying that shoe before you take a trip down the stairs?" Alex giggled. He put down his pack and dropped to his knee. Subduing the shoelace took almost a minute of struggle.

"Honey . . ." said Susan, a little impatient.

"I got it, I can do it," said Alex. He stood up.

The doctor's voice: "All right. You are leaving the kitchen. Now what do you do?"

"We go downstairs." Susan goes first. She listens to the careful beat of Alex bouncing down the stairs behind her; he is holding himself sideways on the narrow stairs. Ker-bump. Ker-bump. He does not step on a loose shoelace.

"Very good," said the doctor. "Now, you are outside. On the front steps." They are. The morning sun, suddenly bright and hot, warms her face and arms. She has to squint a little when she first opens the door and steps outside.

Alex is looking up at her, and the sun on his hair makes it gleam like polished wood. "Have a good day, sweet-heart," she says. "If you want to bring Justine home with you this afternoon, it's fine with me."

"Okay, Mommy. Bye." She bends down to kiss him, and he puts his right arm around her neck. His left holds his knap-sack. His cheek, cool as satin, is against her lips.

"Now, Mrs. Selky," said the doctor, "look down the street to your left. Tell me what you see." She turned her head inside her mind and saw the whole street, down to the corner. As she watched, a truck came around the corner. Two men in running clothes jogged up the street toward her. When she was done, he told her to turn to the right. She described every tree. Every door that opened. The three people who passed, dressed for work. It took nearly forty-five minutes to describe all that she could see. She did not see an old blue car; it must have passed her house and turned the corner. What she could see with stag-gering immediacy was every lilt of Alex's last steps as she watched him to the corner. The swing of his bare arms. The turning at the corner to see if she was still watching, the wave of his small right hand. She came out of the trance with a terrible sense of loss, and began to cry.

"It's all right," said Menetti. "The odds are that the car isn't important. If it is important, we'll find someone else who saw it." Susan didn't bother to explain that that wasn't what she was crying about.

Alison Busch, the psychic, arrived in the middle of the after-noon. Her hair was dyed an improbable jet black and she wore a jumper and soft black ballet slippers. Her large dark eyes were liquid with sympathy for Susan.

"Well, I hope I can help you, dear," she said to Susan, with-out waiting to be introduced. "I'm glad you called, you've been on my mind."

"Do you have an idea . . . do you think you know what's happened to Alex?"

"Don't know yet. I'll tell you one thing, though. I'm not one of these dames who thinks my dreams must have special meanings because I'm such a nice person. When I can see, I know it. When I can't, I say so.'' All the while Mrs. Busch was talking, Susan had the feeling that her eyes, with imperceptible flicking glances, were picking up minute invisible signals from all over the room. Her voice was rich and level. Although she spoke of lack of confidence, she gave the impression of being utterly secure in her powers.

She accepted a cup of coffee and sat down with it in the living room. Susan was glad to notice all the police treated her with deference. She felt a slight tremor of foolishness at the notion of a psychic—at herself rendered gullible by despair, like any rube with a storefront tarot reader. But there was nothing about the woman herself to make her feel foolish. On the contrary, she could all too easily imagine her in a more mystical age being taken very seriously indeed.

When she had finished her coffee, Mrs. Busch asked to be taken to Alex's room. Susan had been careful not to go in there more than once or twice since Alex disappeared, because each time she did a palpable sense of his presence pierced her like a lance. More and more she had only an abstract knowledge that something terrible had happened. She was saving his room, like a secret cache of something, to be felt with the greatest intensity only in deepest privacy. She didn't know how long she had before it would be used up.

Mrs. Busch led the way. She went straight to the bed and sat down on it, and remained very still a moment or two.

''There's been a great deal of loss in this house,'' she said pointedly to Susan. ''A great deal of pain in the little heart that slept here.''

''Alex's father and I separated three months ago. We'd been married nine years.''

''Um. Well, from the feel of things, I'd say you fought it hard.''

''We did,'' said Susan.

''You feel a great sense of failure.''

''Yes.''

''Could I have something Alex played with or used when he was happy, please?''

''What? Oh, yes . . . sure.'' Susan looked around, then scooped up Alex's soccer ball from beside his bookcase. Mrs. Busch took it between her plump, short-fingered hands and

76

said, "Good—he played with this with his father?"

"Yes."

Then she sat for a while in silence. Susan didn't know if she was meant to go or stay, but she didn't want to break the concentration by speaking, so she stood where she was, and watched the woman's face. Mrs. Busch closed her eyes, and sat for some time. Now and then Susan would see a certain flicker of strain cross her face, like someone trying again and again to fasten a difficult latch. At last she opened her eyes.

"I can see *him*," she said. "I can't see much else that's any use. He's standing by a window, and the window has cheap venetian blinds, and there's a large road or highway outside, so I'd say it's a motel room. That's really all I can see."

"You mean, that's what he's doing right this minute?"

"Yes."

"You mean you're sure . . . he's alive, and he's standing by a window? You can tell that didn't happen yesterday . . . or . . ."

"Yes," said Mrs Busch, "I can tell that much. I'm afraid it's not much help . . ."

"Oh, God, he's alive!" said Susan.

"Oh, yes," said Mrs. Busch, "of course he's alive. I wouldn't have bothered to come if I didn't know that."

Menetti thanked Mrs. Busch and asked if she'd be willing to come back to try again the next day. She said she would. Menetti was trying not to let Susan see how disappointed he was.

That night on the eleven-o'clock news, there was an interview with Susan, saying that they felt much more hopeful, now that they had definite word through psychic Alison Busch that Alex was alive and safe.

"Oh, Gawd," said Jocelyn to Martina as they watched the news together.

"What do you mean by that?"

"Nothing," said Jocelyn, getting up to turn off the set. "I just mean, oh, God."

In their kitchen on Charles Street, Annie and TJ sat on wooden ladder-back chairs and shared a nightcap which Annie had rolled from the dope she grew in the upstairs window box. Except for the rasping sound in inhalation, they had made no noise during the news. TJ never liked to talk much, and when he had something on his mind, he usually talked not at all.

"Graham and I came in just after she finished—Mrs. Busch," he said after a while, as if they'd been in the middle of a conversation. Annie paused and then nodded. "What did you think of her?"

"Think she's a witch," said TJ.

"Speaking as a doctor of science?"

"Yeah. I had the feeling she could sense 360 degrees around her, like a plant."

Annie thought about that for a while. She traced a pattern on the kitchen floor with her toe. When she felt like it, she went and got TJ's cello from the living room, and located her own recorder in its flannel case in the breadbox, and they settled down to play. TJ began a melody from Mozart, and Annie, after several bars, followed in measured improvisation.

Mozart was all they seemed to feel like playing, since Alex disappeared.

AT FREMONT STREET, the phones were still ringing as they had at midday, with competing psychics reporting their visions. One woman had called fifteen times to say that she knew for sure Alex had been taken by the elders of Zion; that was the bad news. The good news was that he was alive and well in Tel Aviv, and she could undertake to go to Israel and bring him back if someone would just pay for her ticket. Earlier in the evening they'd had an oddly upsetting disturbance. A fat woman with very greasy hair pulled back in a bun appeared downstairs and demanded to be allowed to see Susan. She had with her a little black-eyed girl in a filthy red dress. The fat woman had only a few teeth in her mouth, but her hands were covered with diamond rings. Susan could hear the shrill menacing tone of the woman's voice from the upstairs window, and she found it frightening. Lieutenant Menetti had to go downstairs himself and speak to her before she'd go away, and she didn't do so with much grace.

"Gypsies," he explained to Susan when he came back.

"You're kidding."

"I wish I was. They can steal the caps off your teeth while you're talking to them."

"What did she want?"

He shrugged. "To tell your fortune . . . to try to sell you the little girl. I don't know."

"But maybe she knows something." Susan went to the window to see if the woman and child were still in the street.

"She does; she knows a person in trouble is the perfect patsy. The nice little girl is a pickpocket—the kids go into restaurants in pairs, and while one is begging for a quarter for milk, the other one's lifting your wallet. . . . I know what I'm talking about."

But Susan was still scanning the street. Right, he thought. Big cynical cop knows shit, motherhood makes you all sisters. Don't you wish.

SUSAN TAUGHT GRAHAM to play Russian bank. She felt oddly energetic this night, full of a kind of conviction that she felt no need to examine. Graham sat across the table from her, sunken and still. It looked as if even shifting the direction of his gaze required a great effort. She had felt that way for two days, while Graham was out on the streets searching. Much as they wanted to help each other, they seemed permanently out of phase.

"You going to put out that seven of spades?" she asked. "Because if you don't, I'm going to get to unload this whole run here, up to the queen."

"What?" he said. She pointed to the play he was missing. "I'm cheating because I love it when you win," he said wearily.

"No, you hate me when I win."

"Yes . . . that's true." I hate you when you win. Too tired to lie. Too sad. No comfort.

ALL AFTERNOON and into the night, in different rooms, in the same room, side by side or back to back, Susan and Graham had been questioned over and over by Al Menetti, by Sergeant Bevan, by Lieutenant Smith, by a dozen others. They had to climb up into closets to get out old calendars and address books, until Susan managed to find names and numbers for virtually every person who ever baby-sat for Alex. They named all the friends they saw regularly, and then the ones not so regularly; they had to characterize the relationships.

"But why do you want to know?" Susan would ask at first. "We haven't seen them for years. Besides, they're perfectly nice . . ." The detectives just kept writing.

One name kept coming up through the afternoon, the father of a child named Bina whom Alex had played with in day-care. Bina's mother, Maeve, was a weaver, she said. She was very lovely, though she sometimes struck Susan as being a little loose in the head. On one or two occasions when Alex went to Bina's to play, Susan had called to pick him up and found that Maeve had "had to go out," and Bina's father, Richard, was there with the children instead. He seemed nice enough, and she never thought more about it, except to wish that Maeve would explain her plans beforehand, because small children liked to know in advance what was going to happen.

"You told her that you felt that way?"

Susan tried to remember if she had or if she'd just mentioned it to Graham. "I did tell her," she said at last. "I said I thought it made kids feel more secure to describe the day to them. At that age you have to keep reminding yourself that they can't tell time. I'd always say something like, 'Maeve will be here with you and Bina for two hours, and that's like watching *Sesame Street* twice, and then I'll be back.' "

"Did Maeve respond, when you told her that?"

"I *said* that sometimes Alex would be upset if we forgot to tell him that a baby-sitter was coming, or that Daddy wouldn't be home for dinner. . . ."

"But what did she say?"

"It didn't seem to register. That I can remember. It wasn't that important. I just would have preferred—"

At this point Menetti came up and interrupted. He said, "Susan, you're going to find that a community like this, where people are always coming and going and everyone's allowed to be slightly weird, is not just a nice place for people like you, who maybe want to be a little unconventional and have artistic friends." Susan bristled, but Menetti didn't notice. "Use your head—it's 'ask me no questions, I'll tell you no lies,' right? 'Do your own thing'? No references, no résumés. Use your head—if you'd been bouncing from one unsavory situation to another all your life, where would *you* go to start over and do your thing? Dune, Iowa? You'd come straight here, where all the neighbors are proud of not paying any attention to how off you are.

"Your nice friend Richard, for instance, he's supposed to be a carpenter, right? He's a junkie. He's been booked a dozen times for dealing cocaine and heroin, and twice for armed robbery. The last time, he did four years in prison in New Mexico. And he has a nineteen-year-old son in California who just went to prison for trying to hold up a gas station, wearing high heels and a shirtwaist dress."

Susan felt a clammy cramp of nausea in her intestines. She guessed she felt . . . shocked. It was a bewildering feeling to one who had indeed prided herself on her utter tolerance, who had made a life-style out of celebrating differences. But she was shocked now—and frightened. How could Maeve . . .? "But how could Richard have a son that old?" she asked irrelevantly. "He's only . . ."

"Forty-two," said Menetti.

Jesus, thought Susan. She remembered Richard in his overalls and ponytail patiently crawling around on the living-room floor to help Alex find a lost mitten. She remembered prompting Alex to say, "Good-bye and thank you . . ." And Richard's response, solemnly coaching Bina to say good-bye to Alex and Mrs. Selky. It came back to her that once Maeve had come to day-care to pick up Bina with a very pale, very pimply lank-haired kid of about sixteen in tow. Maeve had remarked vaguely that the kid was staying with her because Richard was out of town, and that it was a drag because he stole things.

Susan had passed her teenage years in distress at her step-mother, who greatly simplified her life by dismissing people who were not "our kind." Susan had thought this a very ungenerous and self-limiting way to be. It was chilling to come to understand there are many kinds of harm, and greater kinds of evil, than the narrow mind.

IT WAS SOMEWHERE around the middle of Saturday afternoon, when Graham decided to go home to his apartment for an hour to get some clean clothes and Menetti assigned a detective to go with him, that Susan realized that both she and Graham were essentially under house arrest. She hadn't left the house since Thursday evening. Graham and TJ had been out with the detectives, but always, she realized, escorted. She was too tired really to feel much of anything about that.

"I've ordered a lie-detector test for you," Menetti said.

She said, "Fine."

"We don't do them . . . you'll have to go up to state police at 1010 Commonwealth. Do you mind?"

"Of course not," she had said. But on Monday, when she was being escorted into the state police headquarters building, a chilling cube of beige metal that looked like a garage or factory, she felt that it was not after all exactly in the course of things to agree to this. She noticed the men in and out of uniform turn flat superior expressions to her as she passed them led by a detective. It was not a pleasing experience to be shown into the small tiled chamber, to be told to sit in the battered chair, to allow herself to be wired up to the black electrical apparatus at so many pulse points. She watched the face of the operator as he in turn watched the machine graphing her reactions to his questions.

"Is your name Susan Selky?"

"Yes."

"Is your address 63 Fremont Street?"

"Yes."

"How old are you?"

"Thirty-four."

"Have you ever stolen anything?"

"Yes."

"What did you steal?"

"An Esterbrook fountain pen from the school supply closet."

"When was that?"

"I was in the fourth grade."

"Is that the only thing you ever stole?"

"That's all I remember."

The man administering the test was plump and officious, with red hair, freckles, and eyelashes so blond they appeared to be transparent. He hunched intently forward on his elbows and grunted slightly when he shifted positions.

"Do you ever masturbate?" he asked.

Susan shot him a surprised look of resentment. He stared back blandly. "Yes," she said coldly.

"Is your husband's name Alexander Graham Selky?"

"Yes."

"Is that his real name?"

Susan hesitated. Why did he ask that? "Yes," she answered.

"How old is your husband?"

"Thirty-eight."

"Did you kill your son?"

"No."

"Do you know where your son is?"

"No."

"Did you see your son for the last time at 8:50 A.M. Thursday?"

"Yes."

"Do you know where he is now?"

"No."

The operator asked her a few more irrelevant questions; then he thanked her, and one by one disconnected her from the wires with their gauges that had measured her heart rate, breathing and perspiration. He made no attempt to chat or be civil during any of this, and she was reminded of the nurses in her gynecologist's office whose answer to any question other than "What time is it?" was, "Doctor will discuss that with you" or else a tight-lipped sour smile.

Menetti joined her. "Why did you hesitate when you were asked about your husband's name?"

Susan felt a strange guilty pang.

"Did I?"

"Yes," he said, "you did. I've checked, of course, and I know that's his name, so I'm just curious."

Caught, Susan. Guilty. The snob within is under arrest. "His grandfather's name was Selkowitz. His father changed it to Selky. I was uncertain if that meant it wasn't his real name."

"But it is his legal name?"

"Yes," she said. "And mine."

Graham and TJ both passed lie-detector tests, as did Margaret Mayo. Nevertheless, neither Graham nor Susan left the house without the persistent company of at least one policeman in blue. Throughout Saturday afternoon, Susan had developed a malaise of physical restlessness like a slight fever. She announced that she would go to the supermarket, in spite of a light rain that had begun to fall and several offers from friends and police to go for her. She had put on her raincoat and found her shopping bag on its hook in the closet. Then she went to the pad in the kitchen where the family wrote down items for the shopping list. The family rule was that when you used the last of something you threw away the package and wrote down that you needed more, a practice begun to keep Graham from returning empty cartons of milk to the refrigerator and then blaming Susan on Sunday morning when he went to make breakfast and found nothing to put on Alex's cereal.

She found the shopping list under a police-report sheet that was stained with rings from the bottom of Styrofoam coffee-cups. On the pad was written in Alex's fairly irregular printing:

Cheerios

banananas

Her expression didn't change. Her eyes filled and she stood very still, deep in tears, but she showed nothing, spilled nothing. Alex must have written that while she was having her shower Thursday morning. He must have copied the spelling from the Cheerios box—he usually spelled it with one "e."

Her policeman had on his coat and was standing watching her. She carefully tore off the shopping list and put it in her pocket, and they went out. Along every step of the route to the supermarket, she saw the streets honeycombed with basements and shafts and alleys and stairwells where a small body could fall or be thrown, hide or be hidden. This was a new horror, a great horror. To see the streets and sidewalks that had all her life been just the places that she lived, to see them now as sites of danger, scenes of crime. She felt like a fledgling owl, raised in a cage and coddled and fed, who suddenly wakes up blinking its dazed yellow eyes at night in the middle of a forest. Set free.

84

The wild things set free.

In the gray of the rainy afternoon, the market's yellow fluorescent glow gave the impression of shelter. Inside, the rain stopped falling on them, and that too added to the impression of haven, a condition improved. But pushing her cart down the aisle was no longer a familiar experience in any way. Now the shelves were filled with things that were for Alex, or else not for Alex. The Sugar Pops he could eat at Justine's but not at home, the snack packs of raisins she never kept enough of in the cupboard. Another jar of popcorn—they were out of that—and lemonade now that the hot weather had come. The aisles were also, weirdly, full of people who recognized her. Who felt the same indiscriminate thrill they would feel if she were an actress on a soap opera or a housewife who gave a product testimonial on a commercial. They had seen her on television, and now there she was, in the flesh, the woman who lost her little boy and was on with Vivienne Grant.

Many behaved as if she were still on television, as if they could see her but she couldn't see or hear them. Of course many were discreet, but a surprising number simply talked loudly to each other about her, or pointed, or stared. A total stranger came up to her and gently touched her arm and told her she was real sorry about Alex. That they were all praying for him. Then another and another and another spoke to her. She nodded to them one after the other. She thanked them calmly and heard with surprise that her voice was perfectly steady. "Thank you. No, we haven't heard anything. Yes, I feel terrible. Yes, please pray."

A small old woman in black with a face deeply grooved into lines of dissatisfaction pushed her cart close to Susan's and stared at her. Susan, heartsore, was absorbed in choosing bananas that were ripe enough to eat but not ready to rot. Alex tried not to complain, but he shuddered at the gushy parts. A bruised piece of fruit seemed to show him more than he wanted to know about nature. It took a little act of faith for him to eat the good parts even after the rot was cut away, as if in his heart he feared the pathology was systemic, that it spread invisibly cell by cell into the firm white fruit flesh, and would go on spreading inside his tummy.

Susan, actually, felt that way about chickens. She hated to

85

buy cut-up chickens in the market, knowing the agri-business packagers would butcher a chicken with a tumor in one breast, throw out the diseased part, and package and sell the rest. Eggs to market in six weeks. Chickens pumped full of hormones to make everything grow faster, wings, breasts, and cancers. Speedy hyped-up little cancer cells metastasizing through your dinner as fast as they could, till the moment of death. She looked at the groceries she'd chosen and saw injury and poison in the bag of plums, the loaf of bread, the crisp shining innocence of a green pepper, and thought seriously of leaving the cart in the aisle and going home.

The small woman with the angry face pushed closer to her and lit a cigarette. Smoking was illegal in supermarkets, and the smell made Susan's head ache. She turned. The woman was staring at her coldly. Although the day was muggy, she wore a droopy black cardigan over a mole-colored sweater. White ankle socks pushed into black shoes. The woman looked at the policeman at Susan's side, and far from being deterred in her stare, his presence seemed to confirm her intention.

"Think you're going to get away with it?" she asked suddenly in a loud voice. "How do you feel, that's what I'd like to know. You think you're so smart, you think you can kill your own little boy. How do you *feel* now, that's what I'd like to know." The woman's eyes were calm, sane, full of hate.

At first, Susan barely felt the words land. She just shrugged and moved quickly away, the policeman helping to hurry her cart toward the checkout. It was too peculiar to react to; it didn't fit anywhere in her frame of reference.

But as she walked home, the shock of the blow began to wear off and she found her knees and hands shaking. She remembered reading often of people wounded with knives or bullets who sometimes don't notice until minutes or hours afterward, and then only because they feel the wetness of their own blood. Jesus . . . Jesus. Was that what was going on in people's minds? Those people that you see on the street every day, those people who drop their litter on the ground and smoke in the checkout line, with their set resentful faces, is *that* what's going on in their minds? That anger, that twisted loathing? Is that what's all around us?

The officer took the bag of groceries from her despite the shaking of her head at his offer. What point pretending anything was normal? She let him take them, and they walked side by side back to her house in the drizzle, she with her hands deep in her pockets to hide their shaking.

PERHAPS THE WORST thing that happened to Susan in the two weeks that followed Alex's disappearance was that she gradually came to see the world as the police saw it. Of course, it would take many months more until she could assess the things she'd lost, the way she'd lost them. What she'd lost was far more than a child. Even though, at the time, she'd have said there *was* nothing more to lose than the child. Like a deranged hobbyist who has dropped her glue-and-toothpick model of the Parthenon, Susan felt surrounded by scattered pieces of a world view, a view that she came to recognize as pitiful, fabulous, undefended, and indefensible. If she ever tried to reconstruct it, she would find a lintel whole with its pillars gone, fractured chunks without supports, and the greatest pain was to recognize that after all that work, a lifetime of picky building, it was more trouble to reconstruct than it was worth.

There was the fatigue, of course. Her skin was gray with it. She had no idea of when she slept or how long, or if she was really asleep, and when she did sleep her dreams were so full of torture that it seemed to drain her more than staying awake. She often woke up clammy with sweat.

She had one persistent dream in which she and Alex were walking down a street and they saw Graham coming toward them, hands in pockets and whistling, wearing a pink cowboy shirt and an unfamiliar broad-brimmed Stetson hat. He had a wonderful swinging walk, and she watched him full of love, waiting for him to notice her and wave. But he did not. Instead he stopped at a house Susan had never seen before and let himself in with his own key. Susan followed him in and found there a woman bathing a baby in a bathinet, a portable bath made of oilcloth suspended from a collapsible wooden frame. The baby was Graham's and the woman was Graham's other wife.

She had dreams in which she lost her wallet, with all her money and cards, and could not afterward get home. She found that without proof of identity she was no longer who she was. She had dreams in which her car was stolen—a little blue Volkswagen she had had in graduate school, a present from her father when she made Phi Beta Kappa. She had dreams that she left Taxi tied outside the supermarket while she shopped, and when she came out he was gone. She had dreams about her mother, for the first time since her death. She had dreams that she had murdered Graham. She had dreams that she was in prison for the rest of her life and she hadn't done anything, but she knew she would never get out. She had moments of waking up heavy with dread and anger, unable to remember what she had dreamed. And whatever it was, the dreams were never as bad as the reality.

She lost weight. She didn't want people to nag her about it, so after the first week she refused to weigh herself. But she bathed every day and washed her hair, so her eyes and hair were always shining. Her cheeks were often flushed as May turned to June and the heat rose. Very hard to hide a body in the heat, because of the smell.

The constant din and the milling of scores of people in and out of the house were a true torture. She was a private person, very much a homebody, and she often had to fight panic at finding her home completely invaded, finding no room that was hers, no place ever to be alone. More than once, the police would wake her up in the middle of the night to get her to come downstairs and act out exactly what she had done the last morning she saw Alex. Perhaps they thought the shock of being awakened would help her remember something. Perhaps they just didn't think. It never occurred to her to protest; forms of torture had become the norm of her nights and days.

For the first two weeks, Graham was there every day from eight in the morning until late at night, when he went back to his own apartment to sleep. He looked gray and strained. He'd been good about insisting that his parents stay away. Graham's father was retired, and Alex was their only grandchild; if they came, he and Susan would have had to spend energy comforting them, and they couldn't afford it. The police had been up to West Hartford to question them twice, and Susan knew they had found it a horrible ordeal. They were conservative people, and the very presence of police in their lives, the possibility of crime other than the theft of jewelry from hotel rooms, severely unbalanced them. Still, they telephoned all the time. Alex's disappearance was the most shattering thing to have happened to them in their long, sheltered lives, and Susan had to remind herself that nobody owns grief. They had a right to their horror. In fact, a lot of people seemed to. Alex's disappearance touched deep wellsprings of unanalyzed sorrow in many people who were not even particularly close to her.

There was something about this terrible loss of a child, lost in this terrible way, that seemed to stand for many kinds of loss. Everywhere she looked, in the eyes of friends, acquaintances, and strangers, she saw the pain and pity. After a day or two she came to see, whether they understood it or not, that they were weeping for their own losses, and this too became a part of her normal day. It was sickening and bewildering. So many people have lost children. So many people have grown up in households where children have been lost. To have her house and her heart and her life held open, exposed to the public at this moment, to be robbed of the personal and private in tragedy, was particularly bitter.

And Graham was bitter, so angry and guilty. It was terrible for him not to be able to do anything to bring Alex back. He didn't have Susan's numbness. He'd get into fevers of activity, and activity would seem to give rise to hope, and he'd do this and do that, run here and there, call this one and that one, and be suddenly surprised by a great explosion of pain. It was the way he was wired up, like a toy train on a circular track with a little mine field rigged to go off each time the engine chugged around. That was what he'd always been like. Daily life, daily life, this okay, that okay, this day up, that day down, then BOOM. He even knew he needed the explosions, got edgy and tumescent building toward them, but, oh, Christ, they hurt when they came. Picking fights, leaving clues, pushing Susan till she fought with him. How could it be, after all the times she loved him back, that she could have finally said, "That's the last time"? "That's enough now, and too much," she'd finally said. "You need the release, but I don't need the pain. Take it somewhere else. I love you, but you hurt too much—take it somewhere else."

How could it be? It was bad enough to be the way he was; was it fair that he should lose so much more because of it?

Was it fair?

ONE DAY at the beginning of the second week, four different people, soi-disant psychics, called in to report a similar vision. The first saw Alex in the front seat of a car. The car was moving, and it was a light blue color, and Alex was eating raisins. The second caller saw Alex also in a light blue car, an old-model American sedan. The car was moving, but she had no picture of the locale except blue sky, nor did she get any picture of the driver. Alex was asleep in the backseat. Policemen were dispatched with pictures of automobiles from 1955 models on, to see if they could identify the make and year.

Fifteen minutes later a third caller described almost the identical scene. She had had a trance, she said, and she had just seen the missing boy lying on the backseat of a car. The car was moving and the driver was a woman, but she couldn't see her face in the vision. She could only see the scene as if from the backseat of this moving car. It was blue and it was a large four-door sedan. She wasn't sure if the boy were asleep or dead.

By that time the first and second callers, examining police photographs, had each identified the car as an American make from the early sixties. The second woman was sure it was a '62 Chevy, but even under hypnosis, neither could see the license plate nor describe the driver.

Late that afternoon they had a report from Alison Busch. She saw Alex asleep on the backseat of a four-door sedan, a blue or gray car about fifteen years old. The driver was a woman. Mrs. Busch could not see a license plate, but she could see the car approach, then pass under, a big green sign with white letters suspended overhead: Charter Oak Bridge, South, New York. Mrs. Busch had no idea where it was. She thought Canada was possible.

But Graham and Susan both knew immediately: "The

Charter Oak Bridge is the toll bridge right outside Hartford," Graham said. He wanted to get in a police car and go himself. He wanted to speed up and down the New England thruway all night and all day until he found the car himself. He flooded the room with energy and hope. If he were a beast, he would have roared.

Menetti checked with Connecticut highway police. Graham was right, of course. Highway police in Massachusetts, Connecticut, and New York received the urgent report by radio, and across three states a dragnet was ordered. On every highway, at every toll plaza from Boston to Bridgeport, police and highway personnel were on the alert for a light blue four-door sedan, American model, year '63 or '64, driven by a woman and carrying a little six-year-old boy. The picture of Alex was also sent by wire, but it wasn't needed. Every law-enforcement officer in the East had studied Alex's picture for the last eight days.

Since there was no proof that a crime had been committed, let alone that it involved crossing state lines, there was no official way for Menetti to call in the FBI. But FBI agents have kids too, and they can volunteer. That night, both Graham's parents in West Hartford and his brother Robert in New York were visited and relentlessly questioned by new investigators. These new investigators harped repeatedly on the coincidence of a sighting of the boy so close to the grandparents' home and they made a rather vicious second search of the elder Selkys' house. That night Graham's father was briefly hospitalized with what his doctor thought at first was a mild heart attack.

At home, Graham and Susan were sick with hope. They both paced up and down the living room, and spent much of the evening standing close behind the bank of telephones, listening to the officers taking the calls. Their eyes met often, speechless and prayerful. They gripped each other's hands.

By midnight, they were sagging. In the intervening hours they had learned to think of hope as a vicious tease, the enemy, for in all that time there had been absolutely nothing to confirm what the psychics saw. There was not a toll-taker who remembered such a car, or boy or driver, not a highway patrolman all day or evening who had seen them either. The odds seemed to Graham and Susan too cruel, that there had not

91

been even a sight of the *wrong* woman in a blue car with the wrong little boy—how on two hundred miles of highway, in eight hours, could there be not even one woman in an old blue car driving alone with a six-year-old boy? Susan felt more devastated than she had the night Alex disappeared.

Menetti, who was beginning to look haggard himself, went home about one in the morning, but Graham made no move to follow him. Instead, in tears, he and Susan climbed the stairs together. There were still lights blazing all over the house, with people talking, sometimes laughing, making coffee, and smoking cigarettes. The phones went on ringing in a desultory way, as they would for another few hours until daylight. They lay down together on the bed that had been theirs. Susan sobbed and Graham began to cry openly as well. They lay in the dark like that.

After a while, Graham whispered to Susan, and his voice sounded muffled, as if tears had swollen his lips and tongue. "Susan . . . let's have another baby." She held him in the dark, shaking her head vehemently, clenching trembling closed lips.

It was so familiar, so bitter, to be hugging his warmth in the dark, her lover, her enemy. She had a piercing headache from crying, and she could feel Graham's tears slip down the hollow of her neck and along her collarbone, as he cried against her shoulder.

Another baby, because Alex is dead. No, no, no, her head shook in the dark, and she went on crying. The thing she felt most was just how much she wanted it to stop.

They made love anyway, for the first time in many months. At first Susan felt nothing except that she wanted to stop crying, and then, like a sudden return of feeling when a frozen limb begins to thaw, she felt everything, and she had a vision in purple darkness that she was being split up the middle and that when he stopped holding her together and the shuddering was over she would fall neatly cloven in two halves. Her exposed inner surfaces would look like the cut insides of a pomegranate. They both cried and cried.

AND NEXT THERE was the relentless horror of losing her sense of the goodness of the world. It was a creeping awful wisdom, to learn so much more about her friends, her neighbors, the people who made up the fabric of her life, than anyone wants to know. In the first few days she had resisted the police in their refusal to exempt anyone from suspicion. She did not resist any longer.

There were the people next door, the Berlins. They had teenage children and had been kind to the Selkys when they arrived in the neighborhood, passing on good babysitters and including them in their larger holiday parties. They were not best friends, but they were casually intimate in the way people are who live in close proximity. They went in and out of each other's houses, lending eggs and salad oil and wine when such were needed, feeding each other's pets and watering plants when the other family was away. When Alex disappeared, Betty Berlin was the first at Susan's door with a casserole, and she arranged to have her son walk Taxi for Susan every afternoon. That was until the fourth day Alex was gone.

It was a Sunday, and the church where Dean Berlin was assistant minister made a point of appealing to the congregation for help in finding Alex. Similar appeals for active assistance and for prayers for his safety were being issued from pulpits all over the city. Dean stopped by on his way home from church to tell Susan that the Presbyterians were with her in strength.

By the next afternoon, it was Betty Berlin at her door, and she was angry. "What did you tell the police? What have we ever done to you? What do you expect the children to think, seeing their own mother and father treated like criminals. Deanie's in tears over there!"

Susan had been talking to Alison Busch on the phone. She'd

been trying herself to find in her mind some vision of Alex. If everyone, as Mrs. Busch said, was psychic to some degree, perhaps she could use the great fuel of her need to break through and see what no one else could. So it took her a moment to come back to the present. She stared at Betty and wondered what she was talking about. She took in the fact of her distress, but by the time she had risen and gone to her, Betty was angrily marching down the stairs.

Susan looked to Menetti, and her expression held question and irritation. Yeah, thought Menetti to himself, big cynical cops. You need to trust, lady. I need to know what the fuck's going on.

"I just ordered a lie-detector test for them," he said. "Don't worry—they passed."

"But why?" asked Susan. "Are you doing the whole neighborhood? . . . Why is she so upset?" Susan felt obscurely guilty, so strange a feeling was it to be suddenly blamed—for what? Especially now, when she needed support from her neighbors.

"The guy's got a record," said Menetti.

"Who? Dean? He's a minister!"

"He was arrested in Kansas City in 1959, and again in Pittsburgh in 1962. Since then his church has moved him to different parishes twice before they moved here in '69."

"Arrested?" Susan said after a pause. "For what?"

"Child molesting."

Susan felt her knees give way suddenly, and she sat down on her chair hard. She felt a wave of nausea, followed by a roar of blood to her face. Then it passed. It passed with cold quickness. So. Dean Berlin. So. Well . . . she didn't *know* them that well, the way you know someone you like or love. She just trusted them. She just accepted and trusted them casually, with her dog and her house and her keys and her kid and her life. She never thought too much about them except they were there and pleasant, and so was she, and that was life. So.

"He wasn't convicted either time—he was suddenly moved by his church, and the cases were dropped," Menetti added.

"Little boys?"

"Boys *and* girls."

God, thought Susan—how about little Deanie? Little blond

Deanie, living in the same house with him. But, did child molesting have anything to do with incest? Did being one kind of creep mean you were also another?

God, she thought again. If it was someone else's story, she'd have felt pity, knee-jerk pity, for Betty and even for Dean. How sad for him, to be a creep. But not now. She had changed in a moment. He was a creep who did things to children, and he lived right next door and went his way and lived his pleasant life, and now his wife was scared and mad, and his daughter was in tears. Well, that was too damn bad.

She stood up and went to the window and looked out, over to the Berlins' front steps. So, she thought once more to herself, and that was all she felt. The street was all changed for her now, all the streets she walked every day. All faces were changed. All people looked at her now with eyes capable of sly deceit.

She remembered that once when she was about ten, on a smoky winter afternoon, she'd been in the office of a city parking garage with her mother, waiting for the attendant to drive their car up the spiral ramp. Susan had been brought into town after school to have her hair cut—or was it to have something done to her braces? No, she wasn't old enough for braces then. Her mother was reading a magazine and didn't notice, but the man who stood at the other side of the office waiting for his car had quietly turned himself toward Susan and let his coat fall open. Beneath his belt buckle, at the top of his pants zipper, there was a mottled soft pink thing about the size of a Ping-Pong ball. It was tightly caught and looked pinched, like a head straining sideways from a noose.

The man didn't really look at her—she knew, because she checked to see if he knew she was staring. She thought actually that he'd made some mistake in dressing himself and the pink thing was some piece of men's clothing stuck in his zipper, but she finally realized after thoughtful deduction and more staring that it was much more likely to be the fleshy end of his penis.

When she realized that, she stared even more, partly because she had never seen a grown man's penis and partly because it was winter, and so cold in the little office that you could see your breath. She kept thinking that the pink thing must be

95

freezing and he must be awfully stupid not to notice it and zip himself up right. She tried not to stare anymore, because she knew it wasn't polite, but she felt also an impatient sense that if he was going to be that stupid, he might deserve to be stared at.

Eventually the man moved a package he was carrying around in front of him to hide the pink thing, but she was pretty sure he still hadn't fixed his zipper. The man's wife was standing beside him, staring into space, the whole time. Susan hadn't thought about that for years. It hadn't actually been very interesting. Just pathetic.

LEARNING TO SEE the world as the police did was slow and cumulative. The more Susan learned, the more she lost. Each new piece of information surprised less, and, in a subtle way, hurt her more, or at least changed her more. She probably minded the most about Jocelyn.

Jocelyn had invited Martina to have coffee after the second-week meeting of the Volunteers to Find Alex Selky. They each had a new stack of handbills, and new territories to cover with the MISSING posters. They were going to concentrate this week on getting posters taped inside the windows of people's cars, so Alex's face would be moving all over the city, in traffic, and so the message would go out onto the highways as people began leaving for vacation.

Jocelyn and Martina took their handbills and settled at a window table of a café on Newbury Street, where the sun streamed in and the ferns hanging from the ceiling barely cleared their heads.

"First," said Jocelyn, squeezing out her tea bag, "they had this guy hypnotize me, and it was *incredible*. I always wanted to be hypnotized. They asked me all about what I saw the last few blocks walking to school with Justine the morning Alex disappeared, and I talked for about an hour. It was *total* recall. I could remember this guy walking down the street, across the street; I watched him come toward us, and when he got close I could see the color of his tie, and describe the little anchors on it. Then I described all the traffic; there was some old gray car, and then a bakery delivery truck, and I could even see the license plate. I saw a woman walking her dog, and I remember her calling its name—Folly. They're looking for the woman now to see if *she* saw Alex. Then I remembered these two joggers, matching faggots in their color-coordinated sweat-suits, one blue and one green. They had white towel sweat-bands on, and matching mustaches. Did you ever think about those couples? They're the same height and same weight and same build and same haircut—they're so cute. Being in bed together must be like masturbating. So now the police are looking for them, and I might have to go down and look at mug shots to see if they're known for anything."

"But you didn't see Alex? In your trance?"

"I sure didn't. Zippo. Nothing. If he was ever anywhere on those last two blocks that morning, he was gone before I got there, because I saw everything, every step of the way. It was incredible. The guy could say, 'Okay, now tell me what you see on the far corner of the street,' and it would seem to be out of my sight, not a direction I had looked at all, but I could sort of turn inside the picture in my mind, like a camera, and then zoom in on all this stuff I didn't even know I'd seen. I thought it was incredible. The brain! You should try being hypnotized sometime. You won't believe it."

"The police asked me about Alex and all about any baby-sitters who had stayed with him and Jorge when Alex was at our house . . ." Martina began.

"Oh, yes, they asked me that too. They asked me all about that, and about the other kids he played with, although he really played with Justine by far the most. They asked me whether he was a happy kid, too. Did they ask you that? They wanted to know if *I* thought he would ever have run away."

"Yes, they did ask me . . ."

"I said, frankly, that I thought he had taken the separation very hard. That he was *basically* happy but he had taken the split a lot harder than it looked."

Martina stared at her.

"Well, that's what I think," said Jocelyn, lighting a ciga-rette. "I'm not saying I think he ran away or that he *would* run away, but they asked me if I thought he was happy at home, and I had to tell the truth."

"You know he didn't run away," said Martina.

Jocelyn leaned forward, exhaling smoke, and tapped with a long red fingernail on the table. "Listen, honey, we don't know *anything*. We don't know *anything* about this case, and neither do the police. And if I know what's good for Justine, and if you know what's good for Jorge, you'll think about it that way. The police don't know shit from Shinola about where he is, or what happened to him, or where the hell to look for him next, and as long as they're fishing, I'm not letting Justine out of my sight.''

Martina felt a flush of irritation at Jocelyn, not for the first time. Why, she wondered, does it always seem to me that no matter what this woman is talking about, she's talking about herself? And how come she's managed to put herself at the center of this situation, so all the rest of Susan's friends have to go through her to reach Susan? But then she pushed the thought aside. After all, helping Susan wasn't a contest. Martina knew herself to be often jealous and wanting to be the favorite; her shrink said that was common for a middle child in a big family who grew up with never quite enough attention. Of course she wanted to be Susan's best friend. She also wanted to get the most valentines in fifth grade.

''So tell me about the lie-detector test,'' Martina said.

''Okay, the lie-detector test,'' said Jocelyn. ''You go to the state police and they have this machine with all these needles and dials, and the guy who does the test is *real* cute. They spent most of the time asking about my sex life.'' She laughed. ''And we all got off on it.''

''I don't understand.''

''You don't understand getting off on it?'' Jocelyn smiled.

''No, I don't understand why they want to know.''

''Oh. Well, they have to ask you things that you'll lie about, so they'll have a reference . . .''

''I know.''

''But of course I didn't lie to them, so . . . they asked me an awful lot about when I slept with Graham. Maybe they thought that I had some kind of grudge against him, I don't know. If they want to start giving lie-detector tests to every honey Graham's slept with . . . I think they were just getting off on it.'' There was a brief silence.

''Or maybe not,'' Martina finally couldn't resist saying. She saw a brief dark flush on Jocelyn's cheeks.

''Hey,'' said Jocelyn, recovering quickly, ''I'm easy. I like easy, I forgive easy. It's no big thing. I've just been very close to the family and I can see they want to know everything—after all, they don't know what the fuck they're doing; they don't know where else to look. They got to do all this stuff because, otherwise, Susan will go bat-shit.''

It was at approximately that moment that Martina decided that the only thing she remotely liked about Jocelyn was her sense of chic, and that that wasn't nearly enough. She excused herself, left a bill for her coffee and share of the tip, and left. All the way home, Martina, who exercised not less than four hours a day at class or at the barre to make her body a reliable dancer's instrument, strong and true and hard, wondered how anyone could use the word "easy" about herself as anything but pejorative. She could think of a number of better synonyms, but the kindest one was "shallow."

She got Susan on the phone when she got home. "I stopped on the way home to have coffee with Jocelyn," she said. "She was great running the meeting this morning."

"Yes," said Susan listlessly. "She's been great. I suppose she's driving everyone crazy, but I don't know what I'd have done without her."

"She's been a really good friend," said Martina, fuming, and hoping Susan would contradict her.

"She has."

"Well . . . I really just wanted to check to see if there was anything I could do for you. I didn't get to talk to you this morning at all. Do you have anything new at all? Any new leads? Jocelyn was telling me about her hypnosis and her lie-detector test and everything."

"Well, Jocelyn saw a witness—a possible witness—we didn't know about before. The police are trying to find her, a woman with the dog named Folly. If she lives in the neighborhood, the Berlins next door would be the people who would know her, but they're really not speaking to me anymore since the police gave *them* lie-detector tests."

"Why? What happened?"

"Oh . . ." Susan decided she hadn't the energy to go into it. "Nothing, really. They just aren't into being very helpful anymore, and I guess I never noticed before how really helpful they always were. I have to go out now and walk the dog, because they won't let Tommy do it.''

"Susan, you sound absolutely wrecked."

There was a long silence. "Yeah," said Susan wearily.

"Are you sure I can't help somehow?"

"I don't see how," said Susan. They said their good-byes and then hung up. She went to the couch to where Al Menetti was talking intently with Graham. He had a list of parents of children in Alex's class in his hand, but he stopped in mid-sentence as Susan approached, and both men looked at her.

She sank down in a chair beside them, and Graham noticed her cover one eye with her fingers briefly, which often meant she felt the beginning of a headache. She seemed to forget for a minute why she had come over.

"Oh, yes," she began after a while. "Al. That was Martina Rolley on the phone, and she happened to mention you'd given Jocelyn a lie-detector test." Al made a sound that indicated that that was true. Susan looked to have lost her train of thought again for a second or two.

"Well, was that necessary?" she asked next. "Al, I need my friends. If you go around one by one and accuse them of kidnapping—"

"I guarantee you, she didn't mind the lie-detector test," said Al.

"Oh, that's not the point. The point is, I know you're trying everything you can think of, but use a little restraint, will you? I need Jocelyn. How can my friends be my friends if they all feel like suspects?"

Al could see that she was tired nearly beyond making sense, but he still felt annoyed. "I wouldn't have done it if I didn't think it was necessary," he said coldly.

"Oh, come on. Jocelyn? That was necessary?"

"I have to know all I can about anyone who might have a reason to want to hurt this family."

"And what—are you going to tell me Jocelyn has a record too?"

"No, not a police record, no. But we did find more than a couple of sources that indicate that she's quite . . . active, and not very restrained about who she sleeps with."

Susan felt the throb in her eye again. Goddammit! There was no hope. This wasn't an investigation; this was the Keystone Kops acting out their prejudices. First they waste all that time suspecting Graham because they don't have the brains to see that no matter what the manual says, Susan knew her husband; now they start looking for suspects based on their sex lives.

"That's ridiculous. Who cares how many people she sleeps with?" she said scornfully. "What does that have to do with anything?"

Al looked at her wan angry face, and spoke in spite of himself. "It's not how many she sleeps with, it's who," he retorted, and instantly regretted it. Inadvertently he glanced at Graham.

No matter how tired she was, Susan's intuition about information of that kind was all too keen. She looked at Graham, and back at Al's sorry face, and got the same message from both of them.

"Oh . . . shit," she whispered, and her face crumpled. She covered it with her hands. In tears, again. Al and Graham looked at each other. Al reached out to put his hand on her arm, and to his surprise, she reached up and covered it tightly with hers as she cried.

She soon stopped. She wiped her eyes and nose with a tissue and stood up, saying in a shaky voice to Al, "That was rude. I'm sorry."

He made a gesture with one hand, no apology necessary. He could hardly look at her.

"I take it Jocelyn passed the test?"

Al nodded.

"Well," said Susan. She tried a small smile. "I think I would be a more pleasant person if I weren't quite so tired, so I'm going up to see if I can sleep at all . . ." She left the room and went up the stairs.

GRAHAM STOOD at the door of the darkened room for a minute or two, looking at Susan lying prone and still, her face turned away from him. "You asleep?" he whispered. No response. He went over and sat on the edge of the bed, and when she still didn't stir at all, knew she was awake and holding still. He put a hand on her shoulder in the darkness. She didn't respond.

101

"Susan . . . honey? Philippe is downstairs . . ." It was Philippe's afternoon to clean. "Do you want him to stay?"

She took a long time to make up her mind to answer.

"Yes."

"I'm sorry . . .?"

"I said, *yes*, I want him to stay. Tell him I'll be down soon."

"Susan . . . I'm . . . sorry," he said again, this time meaning Jocelyn. To this she made no response.

"It was nearly two years ago . . . only a couple of times . . ." he whispered. "It was nothing."

"Two years ago!" She suddenly turned over. "Two years ago, Graham, what excuse did you have two years ago? We were talking about having another baby two years ago! That was supposed to be our *happy* time together, remember? Didn't I just sit through weeks of hearing you say how perfect things had been for two years, except that you just happened to meet Naomi?"

He hated that cold hurt voice. She *hated* when he came offering tenderness, and she met him with totting-up, trotting out dates and quotes like a fucking computer of all his (according to her) endless sins. He took his hand away from her as if she had burned him, and the muscles in his whole arm tensed, as if it might involuntarily hit her.

"Goddammit! Will you not be such a damn baby? It was only a couple of times . . ."

"How many is that? Two? Five?"

"It was only a couple of times," he repeated through clenched teeth, very deliberately, "and it meant *nothing!*"

She stared at him with such intensity that it took all his willpower to keep glaring back. How well he knew that quality in her, that emotion burning airlessly inside her, relentless, murderous. "Well, guess what," she pronounced, her voice level and furious. "It doesn't mean *nothing* to me!"

For several moments, while he cast for some view that made his act not a betrayal, not a shame, or this moment somehow not his fault, it was not clear to either of them if he would hit her or not. He didn't. He got up and left, slamming the door violently.

Menetti took in every detail of his physical rage as he came down the stairs, his face red, his eyes slightly bulging, his shoulders and arms tense as drum skins. Every officer in the room made a mental note of it.

Graham flopped into a chair in the corner of the room and glared at the wall, for once oblivious of the roomful of people. Within minutes his anger was over. "Stupid fucker," he said aloud, miserably. Menetti heard him, and looked over to where he sat with his hands over his mouth. He'd best find out who was supposed to be the stupid fucker, Graham or Susan.

SUSAN, LYING STILL and tearless in the dark, heard a tap on the door. Graham, she assumed with a sorrowful rush of ambivalence. How often, how often. To have snarled at him, filled with fury, and the minute he left the room want him back. She flopped her head toward the wall and stared at the crack of afternoon sunlight that beamed under the heavy curtains at the window.

"Suusan," a low voice murmured, "it's Philippe. Do you want me to come iin?" Philippe seemed to stretch and sing all the vowels in his words, as if trying to make language softer in his wide mouth. He pronounced his own name "Feeleepe," with a long French accent.

Philippe, Jesus. Although he'd been coming to her every other Tuesday for two years, Susan suddenly saw him as *Jocelyn's* Philippe, *Jocelyn's* "gay cleaning guy" who was easily worth six dollars an hour to Jocelyn because she dined out on merciless "Philippe" stories. He cleaned the stove as if it were a fetish. ("When I came home and found him unscrewing the knobs on the stove so he could clean that gunk that gets behind 'em, I asked him to *marry* me," Jocelyn would drawl to an amused audience.) She talked all her friends into trying him. Philippe also read palms and tarot cards and gave his clients a Christmas party every year. He was famous for his *bûche de Noël*.

"You're crazy not to use Philippe," Jocelyn had said several times to Susan, with a look around the kitchen that hinted she thought Susan's housekeeping could stand the improvement.

"If I can afford him, *you* can afford him. Why should you bring home half the money and do *all* of the picking up after Graham? If he won't help, at least let him pay for someone else to help you. I'll ask Philippe if he has a free afternoon. He's *touchy*." Jocelyn had given a nelly wave of her hand as she said the last, and rolled her eyes, making Susan laugh.

THAT WAS just about two years ago.

How did a woman like that get to be so much in her life? Do I like her? Susan wondered. Does she like me? If so, why? When Susan was in fourth grade, she knew who her best friends were, ranked in order of preference from one to seven, and she knew where she ranked with each of them. She had time for friendship then; it was a major avocation. Now she realized she didn't even know if she had friends, the way they used that word in grade school. Graham had TJ. And she had a profession and a child and a marriage that had been in trouble for years. In the time left over, she had the people she happened to see.

For instance now, because of her friend Jocelyn, she had Philippe.

Susan, can you, as the man says, try not to be *such* a baby? It's not Philippe's fault.

She had, in fact, found Philippe to be everything Jocelyn claimed—sweet, funny, silly, good company, and utterly honest and reliable. Philippe did, in fact, unscrew the handle on the lid of her Dutch oven to clean under it. At least he worked out better than Jocelyn's pet hairdresser whom she kept bragging about to her friends and who had given Susan the worst haircut of her life. "Oh . . ." said Jocelyn vaguely, "gee, he's great on curly hair . . ." Getting you to do what she did was one of Jocelyn's ways of affirming herself, and she gave unwanted and often unreliable advice with such disarming nerve that most people just took it as a price of being Jocelyn's friend.

And now Susan knew of another.

Tap tap tap. "Suuusan!" Philippe said again.

"I'm sorry . . . come in!" She sat up on the bed.

"I figured you weren't asleep after Graham slammed the door," he said, bustling in. "Ooomph, it's so daaark in here.

104

Do you mind if I open the curtains?'' The sunlight cut painfully across the room in a brilliant ribbon, and then, on the
second jerk of the cord, it flooded to all corners.

"Honey . . . you are a wreeeck! You look like my dead
aunt! Do you know what you should do? You should soak
cucumbers in milk and put them on your eyes for fifteen
minutes. It just takes down that swelling and takes the red *right
out*. Just very thin, paper-thin, slices of cucumber—do you
want me to do it for you?''

Susan smiled. Before she could even decide what to say, he
had bustled out of the room again and she heard him making
purposefully for the kitchen. Soon he was back with a tray,
bearing two cups of hot coffee, a glass plate with translucent
slices of peeled cucumber, and a bowl of milk. He darted into
the bathroom for a towel, which he spread over the pillow.

"Now, lie down flat, and this way the milk won't get on the
pillowcase.'' She closed her eyes and felt a wet slimy round
plop onto one eyelid, then the other. "Though I do know that
the milk has a tendency to run into your ears . . .''

He laid a damp washcloth across her eyes and forehead and
pressed lightly again on each eye. "I'll time you. This works
wonders. Of course, you know me, I'm so brave I *never* cry,
but my friends tell me that if you do, this is a wonder cure.
Your eyelids look like they've been through the wars.''

From under her wet bandage she could hear the clink of cup
on saucer as Philippe drank his coffee. "*Oh!* I'm just a
caffeine fiend,'' he said. He said that at least once every time
she saw him. "Do you want me to hold your cup for you? You
can sit up a little and drink, if you hold your cucumbers on.''

"No, thanks. You drink my cup, and I'll make some more
later.''

"Why, thank you,'' he said. She knew he had planned to
anyway.

"Okay, half done. Let me just refresh the milk bath here,''
and he deftly replaced her first cucumbers with two dripping
fresh slices, and put back the washcloth. She lay again in darkness with Philippe sitting carefully on the side of the bed.
"And he's so good-looking,'' she could hear Jocelyn saying.
"What a waste.''

"Only from your point of view,'' Susan had said. "I doubt

105

if his boyfriends think so.'' Jocelyn had seemed miffed. Philippe was short, solid, and muscular, with curly graying hair; he *was* Jocelyn's type.

"Now, Susan," he said. "What do you want me to do today? Your house smells like a smoker. Do you want me to do the living room? I don't want to get in their way."

Susan knew that police and Philippe were not likely to be the most comfortable social grouping. Philippe had told her once about being beaten up by a cabdriver in Washington, who, when Philippe pressed charges, proved to be an off-duty cop. "I mean, I could understand if we'd been in draaag or something, but all we did was get in and say, 'We want to go to the Kennedy Center.' " It was, actually, the only direct reference she remembered him making to his gayness, except to say naughtily, when Graham noticed he'd lost some weight, "Why, Graham, I didn't think you cared."

"Would you mind very much just dusting and washing the ashtrays in the living room? Don't bother to vacuum. Then do up here and the kitchen. Do spring cleaning on the refrigerator, if you have time."

"Okay. Do you want me to do anything in Alex's room?" She stiffened. "Just leave it."

"Okay. Time's up." He took off the cloth and scooped up the cucumbers. "There! Much better!"

"Really?"

"Of cooourse!"

She smiled and got up to look in the mirror. "Well, Philippe—I mean, I don't know what they looked like before, but . . ."

"*And*, you're smiling!"

"Yes . . . that's true. So you must be right."

"See?" he said proudly. He put the things back on his tray and went down again to the kitchen.

SUSAN FELT the kind of fatigue that leaves you too dragged down to do anything for yourself that might help. She thought that food might make her feel better, but the only foods she could think of were crackers and fruit and tomato juice. Each time she ran mentally through the process of going to the kitchen, opening the refrigerator or cupboard, getting out the food, putting it in her mouth and swallowing it, the whole thing seemed like more trouble than it was worth. She tried to read the newspaper the police had brought that morning, but her attention seemed to bounce off the lines of type.

Menetti questioned her over and over again, but it all seemed to be ground they'd covered before, and she found it numbingly boring. Graham was gone now, and she was glad. He called twice a day and talked to Menetti, but since the afternoon she found out about Jocelyn, he'd stayed out of her way. Graham took more energy than she had now to give.

"DEAR GEORGE AND MARIANNE," Susan wrote to Graham's parents, "as I said on the phone, I was disappointed not to get the copy of the sermon you sent me. There has been such a lot of mail—hundreds of letters a day—and the police go through all of it before any of it comes to me. I gather quite a lot of it is the kind of thing I'd rather not see. An amazing number of people write us about their dreams—nearly six hundred so far. And a lot of prayers and hopes for Alex. So many people have been kind. If prayers will help, we have them. Most of the mail is addressed to me and marked 'Personal,' like yours, so that's why yours got lost. The simplest thing will be if you just send any mail for me in care of Mrs. Margaret Mayo downstairs. Don't even address it to me—when she opens it she'll see it's from you and bring it up.

"There is so little privacy here and the phones are in use all the time for police business, I didn't want to tell you this morning—the police feel they have a real lead, as of two days ago. It is *very* important that the press not get wind of it because they think they may be able to locate the person quite soon, if nothing alarms him. . . . I just wanted you to know that things are not as hopeless as the paper makes them sound. I really can't tell you more."

She sent messages of love and urged her father-in-law to take very good care of himself. Then she sent a similar note to her father and stepmother.

The reason she gave for writing was a half-truth. The half that was true was that so many people were in and out of the house all day you couldn't even tell who most of them were unless they were in uniform. Susan had found to her pain that several things said to friends in her living room had turned up in the Boston papers. The half that was false was the implied hope that in hours or days her sweet gallant boy might be back in her arms, the same child that went away. She just wanted the comfort, however wishful, of saying to someone somewhere that there was good news. She was so weary of pity and pain and ambivalence, of having every source of hope and strength somehow compromised.

Her father used to say you should try to learn something new every day, and that would keep you young. Not what she was learning. What she had learned in the last two weeks had changed her to a weary old woman. The subject she'd been learning all day with Menetti was chicken porn.

There was, Menetti explained reluctantly, a loosely organized ring of men from Baltimore to Portsmouth, New Hampshire, who produced pornographic photographs and films of little boys. Little boys in seductive poses, little boys in apparent terror bound and gagged, about to be anally raped, groggy little boys with drugged smiles looking naked and willing, little boys dressed as little girls. Little boys doing things with other little boys, and especially little boys with men.

"There's really no need for you to hear this," Menetti said several times to Susan.

"Excuse me," she answered, "there is. If you're saying what I think you're saying , if Alex comes back from . . . I have to know where he's been."

"Look, we don't *know* . . ."

"It won't kill me to hear it. On the scale of what's possible, it won't even hurt me much."

Al really didn't want to go on.

"What are you protecting?" she asked. "My innocence?"

OF COURSE the men didn't kidnap all the little boys they used. They didn't have to. Often they were apparently normal men with wives and children who made friends with neighborhood kids one way or another—the Boy Scout troop, the weekend touch-football game. One guy was the town orthodontist. Sometimes the little boys were drugged or forced, but the men were rarely afraid to let them go on home afterward. It was not that difficult to convince five- or six- or seven-year-old children that they were profoundly bad and that if they ever told what they had done, they would be blamed. It was basically a piece of cake to persuade a six-year-old boy that you were telling the truth and that he, the boy, was wrong and in danger and guilty as sin. The little boys would go home and not say a word. They would even do it again and again, if they were told to.

ALEX WITH his Batman cape and his Superhero dolls. All his games and fantasies about power and strength and triumph against Evil, the fantasies of a person who feels weak and small and guilty. Another mother had said last year at a school parents' meeting, "I'm delighted they're using the tempera paints now, but is my kid going to stop with the monsters and weapons? It's *all* he draws," and all the other mothers of boys nodded and murmured.

"Oh, not only that," said the teacher, "but listen closely to them. At this age they all ask all the time about police, and jail, and if the police put kids in jail. They don't know if they identify with the heroes, or the victims, or the criminal, or all three."

"But what are they *thinking* about? What's going on in those heads? Noah seems to me to be this jolly well-adjusted five-year-old, and then he sits down to draw, and out comes blood and gore."

The teacher shrugged. "It's the age. They all go through it, and it doesn't do them any permanent harm."

SO, VERY OFTEN the kids never complain or blow the whistle on a guy who may live right in the neighborhood, and he'll get away with it for years. That's somewhat uncommon, but not really rare. More often, the men move around. They come to town for a few months and show up as camp counselors, or librarians, or athletics teachers. They get to know the kids and they get the kids dropping by their house. The curious thing is how often there seems to have been no force involved. Once the sex begins, the kid realizes that his fantasy has come true—

that he's in a position of power, he's got complete control of an adult. Older kids understand that the threat that they'll tell someone what's going on is a constant terror for the man, and they use it. But even very little kids understand on some level that they have some kind of control they never had before. It's incredible to see their bland little faces saying: He was very nice to me. He treated me fine.

THE CHICKEN-PORN MEN took pictures. They put movie cameras on tripods and made their little boys into stars, with themselves in the supporting roles. They passed the pictures on to other men like themselves, for a price. Sometimes they passed along the little boys. Hard to say if it was kidnapping exactly. On the rare occasions that the men were caught, or that the children got away or ran away, they were so amazingly sly about what had been going on that it was hard to tell. "He told me my mother and father had moved away and didn't want me anymore, and that I was supposed to live with him now." "He was very nice to me. I called him Dad." "No, he didn't lock me up or anything. Yes, I could have called home; there was a phone. Why didn't I?" Blank mild faces. Expressionless eyes, like marbles, under long childish lashes. Hiding what? Fear? Guilt? Confusion? A corrupt memory of power?

Then, there were the ones who did force. Perhaps by accident at first, perhaps by choice. The ones who drugged and tortured, and sometimes killed. Less likely to be part of any porn ring. If you catch them at all, you catch them for good. The candy man in Texas, with his dozens of pubescent male bodies buried along the beach. Gacy in Illinois, a man his ex-wife described as a kind and gentle lover. Who turned out to have murdered at least thirty-three young men and boys and buried them around his house and yard, in pits and trenches, covered over with quicklime to speed deterioration. Often he would have the pits dug by new young men. He also raped and tortured some and let them go. They were so appalled by what had happened that they never told anyone. A few told and were not believed. One, giving testimony more than two years later about the night Gacy kidnapped him, threw up on the witness stand.

Many parents of boys who were ultimately found in Gacy's

yard had reported their sons missing, and asked or begged the police for help. They claim nothing whatever was done to help them. When a child of seven or over disappears, in many states he is presumed, going by the books, a runaway. Many police departments would consider the child's history and the account the parents gave of him, and investigate the chance of crime or accident. On the other hand, many would not.

This information gave Susan quite a different perspective on what was meant when Menetti assured her they'd *never* had a child like Alex disappear without learning sooner or later what had happened. There were thousands of children missing, all right. They were carried on a different list. Two months older, and Alex could have been shrugged off too: a runaway.

"The police feel they have a real lead, as of two days ago," Susan had written. She had written instead of telephoned because she didn't want to answer her mother-in-law's joyous questions about what the lead was. She preferred for the moment to deal alone with the equivocal nature of the hope.

Menetti had had men combing their records for known child molesters, especially those who specialized in boys. They had checked the movements of everyone they knew about involved in chicken porn, although Menetti admitted to a despairing sense that there was a hidden underbelly that they didn't know about. Two days ago, they'd come up with three separate leads pointing to a man called Neil Mooney, twice convicted of particular kinds of sex offenses. Child molesters are the lowest scum in the prison pecking order, the first to be raped or brutalized. It causes the prison officials an extra problem, protecting them against other inmates. Neil Mooney had been given early parole after being nearly beaten to death in prison. After all, he was a model prisoner. He had been released in early May.

Mooney had come straight back to Boston, where he had a place to stay with a lawyer friend named Bolton, whom police suspected of trafficking in chicken porn. Bolton had been arrested twice but never convicted. The second time, officers actually found a stack of black-and-white pictures of teenage boys in seductive poses in the trunk of his car, but Bolton had the case dismissed because the officer hadn't sufficient cause to search his car without a warrant, since he'd only stopped

Bolton for running a red light. Bolton agreed that he'd let Neil Mooney sleep on his couch in the living room for about three weeks, but then Mooney found a room to rent. Bolton said he hadn't seen him since. Bolton lived on Clarendon Street, three blocks from Fremont. Two days after Alex disappeared, Mooney missed his meeting with his parole officer. That was the lead. Bolton himself failed a lie detector when he claimed he'd never seen Alex Selky before he vanished. Police were working as hard and as fast and as quietly as they could, trying to trace Mooney's movements without letting the news get around. A con with no money and very few friends would have trouble traveling far, especially if he had a small child with him. He might be underground someplace nearby, if only they could find him before he started to run.

THE END of the second week, at seven in the morning, one of the police came up to Susan's bedroom door to call her to the phone.

"Susan! Susan! It's Una Wright, you know, Una Smith!" (A girl Susan had liked very much in college.) "I'm so happy for you, I'm really . . . I'm trying not to cry. Oh, I feel stupid, but I had to call you the minute I saw the paper. Oh, Susan! I'm sorry I didn't call when your little boy disappeared. You can't imagine how people have felt for you; people just talk about it all the time. It's like it happened to all of us. Oh, that's a stupid thing to say after what you've gone through. I know I don't know how you feel. I couldn't just call and say, 'Hi, I haven't spoken to you for six years, but I'm sorry your son disappeared.' "

Susan said, "It's all right . . ."

"I didn't know what to say to you, but I've thought of you day and night, every time I look at Valerie and Simon. Oh, I have two now. Did you know that? Eight and three. Anyway, when I went out to pick up the paper five minutes ago, I saw the headline and burst into tears on the doorstep . . ." At this point, she burst into tears again.

"Una . . ." Susan tried to think of what to say. Nothing bizarre surprised her much, and she felt very little, except fatigue, but it was hard to know what to say. Oh, hell—if she sounded rude, people would just have to make allowances. "Una, it is good to hear your voice, but I just don't know what you're talking about."

"You . . . don't?" Una, in the grip of high emotion, took some time to get the words out.

"No . . . there's nothing to be happy for me about that I know of, unless I'm engaged or something. I wish there were."

"Oh, my . . ." said Una. "The headline in the New York *Herald* this morning says the case is solved."

"It says *what?*" Susan had a wild, irrational moment of hope. Maybe it was solved and she didn't know it. . . . No. "Una, exactly what does it say?"

Una was having trouble keeping from crying, and probably fighting a wish to hang up. "Well, the headline says, 'Selky Mystery Solved.' And then the story says something like . . . It says that police have . . ."

"Please read it to me. Do you have it there?"

"I'll get it." Her voice sounded chastened and scared. "Here. 'A source close to the family revealed tonight in New York that police are ready to announce a happy ending to the case of little Alex Selky, missing from his home in Boston now for fifteen days. Police do not wish to reveal details of the mystery until after they clean up some loose ends,' in quotes, 'but an announcement is expected later today. Indications are that the boy is unharmed. Alex Selky, aged six, disappeared from a street near his home on May 15 . . .' It just goes back into telling the story of the case."

"Oh, Jesus," said Susan. What was this going to mean? How could this happen? She felt overcome by a great wave of anxiety. "Thank you for letting me know about this, Una. It really *was* good to hear from you, and I wish it had been good news. Thank you . . . I have to get off now." She hung up.

By the time she dressed and got downstairs, the phones were ringing like banshees, and she could tell from the police response that it was media from all over the tri-state area calling to confirm the *Herald*'s story. Alice Pushkin called from New York for the fourth time that week wanting to book Susan on her talk show (this time wanting Alex too) and was told for the fourth time that Susan wouldn't go on her show for any reason. "I may go to the talk shows sometime, if I have to, but not that one. That woman's a cannibal." A half-hour later, Mrs. Pushkin called back to offer Susan $100,000 for the exclusive rights to her story. She wanted to make it a movie. When she was told that the story was false, that Alex hadn't been found, she said she'd offer $25,000 for the rights anyway, "just in case."

Menetti arrived at eight, and Susan could tell from his face that he was upset. "It's bad news," he said. "It's not going to help at all. We're going to have phones tied up all day undoing the damage, and we're going to lose a hell of a lot of momentum. . . ." He went to Susan's kitchen phone and put in a call to the New York *Herald*.

They wouldn't, of course, reveal their source. They said they hadn't checked the story with the police because the tip came in just as they were putting the paper to bed and there wasn't time. Their source was very reliable and they had no reason to doubt him.

Menetti was furious. The minute he put the phone back on the hook, it rang; it was Jocelyn.

"Honey, God bless," she said, her voice glowing. "I just got a call from my aunt in New York sayin' the police have found Alex. Baby, I'm so happy for you . . . I haven't had a minute to put on the radio or go out for the *Globe*. . . . Aunt Jo said the paper didn't give any details. When did it happen? When will he be home?"

"It didn't happen." Here was Jocelyn, her good friend. Jocelyn, who couldn't be bothered to stay out of bed with Graham, but who sounded just the same, Jocelyn on her case, Jocelyn, the kind of daily intimate who noticed if you changed the color of your nail polish, and in her lightminded way, actually cared.

Menetti was signaling her to get off the phone. His face was tired and red. Seeing him under the fluorescent light, Susan noticed that he had the large-pored skin of a man who worked too hard, ate cheap food, and drank too much. He seemed to be aging before her eyes.

"I can't talk now. I have to clear the line," she said.

Jocelyn cut herself off in mid-sentence ("It's not true? He's *not* found? Oh, honey . . .") and said, instantly businesslike, "I'll call you later." Click.

"This is a mess," said Menetti. "I want to get on to our public-relations office and see if they can get the Boston papers to run a story about the false story. Otherwise, we're going to lose pressure like you wouldn't believe, and I'll have trouble keeping the department on the case." He was dialing. "And you'll lose your volunteer corps," he said over his shoulder to her. "Yeah! Menetti! Get me Eleanor Mailman! . . . Eleanor, Al Menetti, glad you're in early. Look, we've got a big problem here with the Selky case . . ."

As Susan listened, her heart sank farther and farther. The media were her lifeline. She felt like a diver in an antique suit with lead weights on her feet and her life supports far away connected by one slender tube. They could murder her with one chop. Bad enough, the prospect of the media gradually losing interest and withdrawing their incredible power to enlist help in looking for Alex. But this . . .

She could hear from the next room that phones were swamped with congratulations. The rumor had spread with astounding speed. Many calls were from the New York area, but many were not. And exactly as Menetti had seen, many calls were from the volunteers of the Committee to Find Alex Selky. Those who called could be told, but what about those who did not? What about those who simply got the story third-hand, in the bank, at the supermarket, in the street? It's all over, he's found, thank God we can ease our minds. The grateful willingness to be excused, to forget it and return to their own concerns. Was there nothing in life that couldn't be turned to a danger to her?

Menetti came in. He was angry in a way she had never seen him before. "I want to know who the hell the 'reliable source' was, now. I can't work on a case that leaks like this. Did you tell someone something? Who do you know in New York that wants to hurt you? This is a mess."

"I don't know anyone in New York, except Robert. We've got a couple of friends there, but no one who would want to hurt us. Or, there are probably a dozen people from college who live around there, but not that we see anymore,

115

none who would hurt us.''

''Loose lips sink ships. They might not mean to hurt you, but people do all kinds of things they don't seem to mean to do. *I* told you not to tell anyone anything we were doing. Didn't I?''

''Yes.''

''And did you tell someone? Old friends? College roomie? Uncle Robert?''

''*No!* I wrote a note to my parents-in-law, and my father. All I said was, things weren't as bad as the papers would make them look, but we couldn't afford to have any details get out.''

''In other words, you hinted we had a lead.''

''I said there was a lead, yes. They're Alex's grandparents! They're worried sick . . . literally. You can't cut me off from everyone in my life!''

''Look, I can't make you do anything. I'm doing this for you. I'm just telling you for your own good . . .''

Susan sank onto a chair. He was absolutely right, of course. He told her he knew better than she did what was necessary, and she should have listened. ''I didn't see how it could hurt . . .''

''Well, you should have asked me. I asked you to check with me before you confide in anyone about anything. Now, didn't it occur to you that the first thing Mrs. Selky would do would be share the good news with Robert?''

''No. It actually didn't.''

''Well, tell me now, what do you think has happened?''

''I don't know! I still don't understand this!''

''Well, think about it! It's not my job to know what happened *before* I investigate, it's my job to look at possibilities and check them out. I'd say we got a leak in New York, and we've got Uncle Robert in New York, and I'd check it out.''

Susan stared at him. There was so much dislike in his voice when he spoke Robert's name. Why? She actually had opened her mouth to ask him, when she stopped herself. A cold new Susan realized first, for the first time, that there was no longer anything she wouldn't believe. There were no longer any questions you could ask if you weren't prepared for any filth to be the answer. She shut her mouth again. If it was something she had to know, Menetti would tell her. Otherwise she didn't want to hear it.

She went back to the kitchen phone and with perfect sang-froid put a call through to Robert.

He greeted her with concern. "Susan! How are you? Is there anything new?"

"There's a story in the morning *Herald*, Robert, that says that the case is solved. The case is not solved, Robert, the case is nowhere. I wonder if you can tell me anything about where the paper got that idea?"

"How should I know? Why are you asking me?" He went on the defensive so fast, without first expressing surprise or dismay or concern, that she knew in her heart that Menetti had guessed it in one.

"I'm asking you, Robert. Did your mother tell you we thought we had a lead?"

"I spoke to Mother yesterday, yes. I call every day to find out how Dad is."

"Fine, did she tell you there was a lead?"

"Well, she was so encouraged. Why, did you tell her not to tell me?"

"Of course not. I hardly told her anything except that I wanted her and Dad to be optimistic, but I didn't want anything about it to turn up in the goddamn papers!"

"Well, she didn't say anything about that."

"So what did you do, did you phone in the story to the *Herald*, or what?"

Robert's voice turned loud and angry. "Now, wait a minute. I know you're in a tough situation, Susan, but that doesn't mean you can ride roughshod over everybody. It happens I was at a dinner party last night and I happened to mention that there was going to be a break in the case. One of the gals at the party does book reviews for the *Herald*, which I had forgotten. Besides, it didn't occur to me that she'd tell."

"It didn't occur to you! If you couldn't keep your mouth shut, how did you expect her to, when it's her job? What *right* did you have, Robert . . .?" She started to cry.

"Now, just a minute, just a minute," Robert yelled into the phone. "You talk about rights! Let me ask you this, Susan, what right did you have to tell every flat-footed asshole in the police department all about my private life?"

"What do you mean?"

"I mean, Susan, what did you have in mind, telling the police that when Bobbie and I were married she shaved her pubic hair for my birthday present?" He sounded livid.

Susan stopped to think. *Had* she told them that? She *knew* about it . . . but had she mentioned it? Yes, that's right, she had. They were questioning her for the fifteenth time about Graham, Robert, Philippe, Mr. Berlin, everyone. The main thing she remembered about that particular conversation was Menetti asking how many people knew she was separated.

"I don't know. A lot."

"What do you mean, did you advertise it?"

"Well, no, but . . . a friend of mine, a psychologist, asked me to be on a panel show with her on Channel 38 to talk about how kids adjust to divorce."

Menetti looked as if he needed to spit. "*Jesus*," he said. "You went on a show where they did, 'This is Professor Susan Selky, she lives in Boston and her husband has left her'?"

"Well . . ."

"So basically you said to 10,000 people, or 50,000, whatever it is, 'I'm a pretty young woman, I earn a good salary, I live alone and you can find me by looking in the phone book'?"

Susan felt a cold nauseous twang in the pit of her stomach, followed by a flash of defensive anger. Did Menetti expect a normal person to monitor every decision in terms of the harm that could *conceivably* come of it, one chance in a thousand?

Yes, obviously. That's exactly what he did expect.

"Why?" she asked in a much smaller voice, already knowing what he was thinking.

He shook his head. "Never mind. Forget it. Now, can you remember anything more? Any little thing, no matter how small? It may not be significant to you, but we'd like you to tell us if you can think of anything."

It was so sad, so exhausting, so boring. She was upset that Menetti was upset. She wanted to offer him something he could use, and she remembered about Robert. It just sort of came to her. It had stuck in her mind because she had thought it was rather sweet of Bobbie. Bobbie and Robert married one year. Bobbie couldn't afford to buy him anything, so she shaved herself as a present ("Oooh, it itches growing back in!'').

"I just want to know how you presented it to him," Susan had asked her, and Bobbie giggled, "Guess." Bobbie hadn't had to figure out what to do for a follow-up; by the time Robert's birthday came again, they were divorced.

Well, Susan thought to herself. It was true that when she repeated that story she was thinking of herself and Alex. She didn't expect the police to repeat it to Robert; she hadn't thought about him at all. They said she could help find Alex by telling them everything she could think of. That's what she did. Well, she supposed she could see where Robert might not be too thrilled to have someone know about that, but just because it was private. She couldn't see it was really that big a deal. Certainly not compared to what it was going to do to her to have half the city believing the case was over.

"I've been given the third degree by every jerk-off cop in New York over whether I have a thing for prepubescent girls!" Robert was yelling. "You really could have given it some thought, Susan, how those assholes were going to twist a thing like that!"

Susan gave it some thought. "And do you?" she asked.

Wham. Robert slammed down the phone. Susan sat down and put her cold fingertips to her throbbing left eye.

The phone rang at once. It was Eleanor Mailman for Menetti. "They've caught all papers but one suburban one, and notified the radio and TV stations. They won't repeat the *Herald* story, but no one will run a story to stop the rumors, either. The news that there's no news doesn't interest them."

When Susan went out late in the afternoon to walk Taxi, she noticed that two of the posters in windows on her block, of Alex, with the headline "MISSING," had been taken down. The glad tidings were spreading.

IN THE MIDDLE of the third week, the police took out their bank of phones, folded their table, and left the house. The tax-payer is entitled to the expense of that kind of search effort for

119

only so long, and Susan had had her allotment. In the sudden quiet that fell on the house as they departed, Susan felt that she was experiencing Alex's death.

Menetti was still with her, and there were, he assured her, a dozen detectives still committed full-time to the case. But the house was still again, as still as it had not been since the afternoon she had sat in her chair by the window and waited for Alex to come home. That analogy kept recurring to her, and by midafternoon she went into the living room, placed the chair as it had been that day nineteen days ago, and sat down and began to wait.

Menetti came in to ask her a question. She looked at him, a long empty gaze, while she turned over in her mind this answer and that answer as if they were pieces of sea glass at the beach, and then she realized that she didn't want to bother to answer at all. A tiny smile twitched the corner of her mouth, and she looked at Menetti. He got tired of waiting and left the room. She turned back to the window and went back to waiting, her mind a smooth satin blank, like an empty cell precariously suspended in fluid.

She had felt a maniacal twinge of release at the moment she chose not to speak to Menetti. Of course it was deranged to refuse to speak, but if she did it, it would change the way everyone treated her. She could stop trying, and people would skirt around her, leaving a nervous arc of space, watching her covertly out of the corners of their eyes. She could nod, with her lips pressed together. Feel the ingrained impulse to speak, to act, to rise to the challenge. Instead of bringing up under it the hourly dwindling reserves of courage to carry through, she could let the impulse subside. Let it sink back into her weariness like a leaping fish sliding back into its pool. She actually could, if she chose to; no one could force her. Of course, if she stopped speaking, no one outside her could tell if she was actually nuts or as sane as ever but simply not speaking. Only she would know.

Did all crazy people think they were perfectly sane, but choosing to act crazy for their own good reasons?

THE PHONE rang. She looked at it obliquely, straining her eyes to the side, without turning her head. She pictured what she must look like, doing that, but she felt a great desire to be utterly physically still. In her stillness she felt a uniform warmth all over her body, like a fetus in the womb; any motion would destroy the illusion of peace.

. . . IT WAS the afternoon Alex disappeared, and the phone was ringing. If she answered it, her life would wind back, like a movie run backward, to a moment before she knew. It would start forward again, but sane this time, the world a sunlit idle place. On the phone would be the school nurse, or Jocelyn: "Hello, Mrs. Selky? Yes, I knew you'd be worried, but Alex was feeling sick at his tummy, so we thought he should lie down in the office until you could come for him. Yes. Oh, he's fine. Would you like to speak to him?"

". . . Hello . . . Mommy?"

"Hi, sweetie, it's Jocelyn. Justine and Alex just begged to come to our house; they're in the middle of acting out *Charlie's Angels* or something—yes. So why don't you leave him for supper; come over at six and we'll have a glass of wine. Want to speak to him? . . ."

And then Alex: "Hello, Mommy?"

OR SIMPLY Alex, with his dime, at the deli on the corner. He's stopped to read a comic and lost track of the time. Earnestly, solemnly, he has hoisted himself up to kneel on the seat in the phone booth, so he can dial.

"Hello," he says, quick and stern, ". . . Mommy?"

THE PHONE is not Menetti. It can't see her, it can't worry about her, it can't resolve to redouble its efforts to help her to bear what no one can bear. It just rings. The phone will not react if she acts crazy and doesn't answer. It will simply stop ringing, and she'll never know what it might have brought her.

"Hello, Mrs. Selky?"

"Yes . . . this is she," she said.

"This is Mrs. Feldman in the office of the English Department. Dr. Lynn asked me to call you, to tell you how sorry he is—"

"Thank you very much. That's kind of him." It was kind of him, and of hundreds of others. It just didn't happen to help.

121

"Tell him I thank him, and—"

"Oh, Mrs. Selky, wait," the secretary cut in, sensing that Susan was going to hang up. "I really called to say that, um, Dr. Lynn wants to know if you're planning to teach your summer courses this year, because . . ."

Because, um, you see, it's very sad for you, but not actually for us, and in fact we have a department to run. She thought: He could have called me himself, after all the friendly hugs at faculty parties and the accumulated hours of talk and department politics and sherry. . . .

"Oh," said Susan. "Yes. . . . Tell him that I am not planning to teach."

"I see," said Mrs. Feldman.

"Good," said Susan.

She didn't want to think. To stretch her mind, to wonder, to care. She wanted to sit very still.

"HAVE YOU talked to Susan today?" Jocelyn asked Martina, without preamble, when Martina answered the phone. "The police took out the special phone lines this morning—the house must feel like a tomb after what it's been like."

"Oh, I haven't . . . I forgot that was today. I've been having this damn root canal and it seems like I've . . ."

"I don't know, she seems so distant," Jocelyn went on. "She hasn't seemed like herself to me at all for a week or so. Do you think she's all right?"

"What do you mean, 'all right'? How 'all right' can she be?"

"Well, you know, Philippe was here yesterday. He said the police have searchd his apartment twice, and they got pretty rough with him the second time."

"Yes, he mentioned that," said Martina. "He said they even gave him a lie-detector test."

"Yes, he was in a total panic when he told me. But you know what he did? He took one look at Susan when he was over there for his day, and decided she was such a wreck, he never even mentioned it."

"Oh, I'm glad. He told me he was going to."

"I don't know how she can go on like this," said Jocelyn. She broke off, and Martina could hear her say to Justine,

"Sweetie, leave the cat alone . . . Justine, leave the cat alone, sweetie . . ." Then the cat screamed. Jocelyn sighed deeply. "Justine is just in such *pain* over this thing with Alex," she said to Martina. "This morning she said to me, 'They're never going to find him, Mommy. He's dead.' And no matter how you try to help them get their feelings out, it just gets blocked up in there and turned into something else. She said it just like that, flat. 'He's dead, Mommy.' God . . . a kid shouldn't have to *deal* this. My stress therapist said I've got a knot in my chest like *this*, all around my heart chakra. . . . My therapist is incredible, Martina; you really ought to see her."

"Why? I don't have a knot in my chest."

"We weren't allowed to feel anything when we were kids, and the pain is all *in* there. . . ." In the background there was another scream from the cat, then a bump, then Justine starting to cry.

"Justine," yelled Jocelyn. "Justine, sweetie, I know you're very upset, but try not to hurt yourself, will you? I know you hurt, honey, you don't have to bang your head." Martina heard her turn back and sigh into the receiver. "They're so incredible. She doesn't know how to say she's in agony, so she knocks her head on something; *then* she can cry. God, if six-year-olds are that knotted up, no wonder *we're* all a mess. Anyway, Philippe said he didn't want to upset Susan any more, but he didn't want to go hang around Menetti, either. 'I don't like the way he looooks at me,' " she mimicked Philippe. "So he spent the whole afternoon in the kitchen scrubbing the oven. Isn't that sweet?"

Martina said she was sorry she couldn't get away to see Susan before the weekend. She had dance performances Friday, Saturday, and Sunday, and she was in rehearsal wall to wall getting ready. "Do you think I should offer Susan a ticket? . . . No, of course not."

Jocelyn said she had stopped by to see her earlier in the week, but she had this look of absolute agony on her face when Justine went up to Alex's room and started playing with his toys, just the way she would have if he'd been there, so Jocelyn realized that seeing Justine was just more than Susan could handle. "What are you doing about Jorge, by the way? Do you let him go out by himself?" asked Jocelyn.

"Are you kidding?"

"Exactly—that's how I feel."

"Tuesday, he went out around the corner to the cookie cart without asking me. He's been allowed to go buy a cookie every Tuesday afternoon for his treat all year. I didn't know he was out of the house, and when he came back, he had this weird supercasual look on his face. He told me that two different people had stopped him on the street and asked him if he wasn't the little boy who had been missing."

"Oh, my God! What did you say to him?"

"Well, I just said that it was true he looked sort of like the picture of Alex, although he doesn't really look like Alex himself, and then I said that for the time being I'd rather he invite me along when he's going out."

"What'd he say?"

"Nothing."

"God. They just can't handle it. I mean, how could they? Justine's fantasy is that she's going to be the one to find Alex."

"Jorge too . . ."

"Whenever we go out, she's peeking into alleyways and down sewer grates as if he's going to be in there. I suppose I think the hero thing is good, but now Jorge is going to identify with the victim too. Can you imagine the crossed-up wires in their little heads? Friiits, friiits." She made a buzzing sound, like electrical wiring sparking, and Martina laughed. "I hate to think what this is going to come to in therapy bills for all these kids."

MIDMORNING, four weeks to the day since Alex disappeared. The mail continued to pour in for Susan and Graham, and the phone rang often. Susan was beginning to recover from her paralyzing fear that she had been cast adrift to search the world alone for the rest of her life for her son. Menetti was still constantly in and out of the house and around the neighborhood, and the Fourth District was now taking scores of calls on the Selky case. It seemed to be true that there were still a dozen etectives working on the case, though she saw them far less because they were no longer working out of her house.

She was opening the morning mail, sorting it into piles of notes from personal friends, well-wishes from strangers, dreams and visions from the Lord, lunatic abuse, and the ones that seemed to have information. She was surprised that she heard so much less from people she knew than from strangers, and continually astonished by the number of people who offered their visions with such utter confidence.

The filth—she didn't know yet how to field the attacks. She didn't seem to feel much about them except pity, and she dropped them into the wastebasket without reading more than a line, the way one hangs up on an obscene phone caller. But they swung their weight. They delivered their body blows, that leave no mark but cause hemorrhaging later. They gave her dreams, or they flocked around her like evil winged monkeys when she was too tired to knock them away, and they yammered at her with their malicious voices. You killed him yourself. Your husband killed him. You killed him together and you're pretending to be separated so the police won't think you're conspiring. You're guilty because you did it. You're guilty because you were negligent, careless, lazy, you endangered your own child's life to save yourself walking a block. You're an unfit mother who deserved to lose your child. If you loved him so much, why don't you have more than one? This could never have happened to you if God didn't want it to. You're selfish selfish selfish and guilty guilty guilty. Guilty. Imagine letting a six-year-old boy out alone. Imagine letting a child walk down the street by himself. Imagine letting him cross the street. Have you learned your lesson? Did it serve you right? Do you know how glad I am that you've been punished? I hate you, I hate your kind. People like you shouldn't be allowed to have children. God saw you were an unfit mother. God has done this to show you. And I'm so glad. I'm so happy you got what you deserved.

God could see that there was so much to forgive in the world that the weight of the pity alone could crush you before you got close to finding the strength to forgive. Not to mention the late nights alone, when she crossed the line and believed that she was guilty, that she had risked his life to save herself walking a block, that she did deserve to lose him and that perhaps she had killed him herself.

Menetti buzzed her from downstairs, and she let him in. "All alone?" was his first question. Yes, she was, today. Graham came over only when there was a really promising lead that looked as if it would turn to something. There had not been anything like that now for days.

Margaret Mayo was at work, and Susan's friends were very busy:

"I lost about four days, the first week, going around with the posters; now I have to really charette if I'm going to hang my show in a month."

"I've been having this damn root canal done, but I'm thinking about you . . . I'll try to get by on Sunday. . . ."

"As soon as I get the boys off to summer camp I'll be free again. . . ."

She could understand it. Their lives did have to go on. She only wished hers could. They *had* given tremendously of their time and their love, the first weeks. And of course there were a number who had simply dropped away from her, in tears, for their own reasons not able or willing to be around the pain. And the ones who, owing to one thing or another connected with the investigation, no longer considered themselves friends.

"Yes," she said to Menetti, "holding the fort by myself. Has anything happened?"

"Well . . . nothing good." He saw her blanch and hastened to add, "No, I don't mean that. Just, we found Neil Mooney."

"And?" Susan's heart was cold with fear.

"And it's a dead end. His parole officer called me last night at home to say Mooney had walked into his office at five in the afternoon. He's been in Belmont all this time and had no idea we were looking for him—he claimed he had gone to the bars, and got lucky. Picked up a dental student from Tufts who took him home for a sleepover, and Mooney was just having such a good time he couldn't tear himself away. We've checked the girl and her room-mates, we've checked at the Inn-Square, and we've talked to Mooney, and it looks like it all stands up."

"Oh," said Susan. Oh. Well, that was that. What was she

supposed to feel? What was she supposed to say? No news was good news. No news was bad news. All news was bad news.

"So," said Menetti. "Back to the drawing boards."

"Yes. I guess."

"Okay. Well . . . take care. I'll be in touch during the afternoon. And look, try to get some sleep, will you? I can't do anything without your help, you know?"

"I know. I'll try. I have trouble sleeping."

"Can't your doctor give you a pill or something?"

"I'd rather not get started with that, if I can help it."

"Well, it's up to you."

THE COMMITTEE to Find Alex Selky called a meeting at Susan's house for the following Wednesday. Susan called several of the television stations that had been most importunate in the beginning to tell them about the meeting to see if they'd like to cover it. The pressure was still on, the neighbors still cared, it was still essential that people remember Alex and that they see his face, that people keep looking for him. Are there new leads? the producers wanted to know. There were not. Oh, said the producers, then we'll pass. But people will forget, explained Susan. They'll think the case is over and they just missed it. Yeah, well, said the producers.

SUSAN WENT to the supermarket Saturday morning to do the week's shopping. The store was jammed as usual. As she worked her way past the produce she saw Alma Wein start up the other end of the aisle. She didn't know her well, but she liked her. Alma had twin daughters in Alex's class at NBS. Susan finished checking over the eggplants and chose one, meaning to push on down the aisle to speak to Alma, but she found that Alma had disappeared. Evidently she had turned her cart around and gone up a different aisle.

When she was ready to check out, she saw Alma near the head of her line, her head buried in *People* magazine. Susan never could manage to catch her eye.

THE MEETING of the volunteers attracted a smaller group than in the beginning. Jocelyn and Martina were there, of course, and perhaps two dozen others, including Graham, Margaret,

TJ, and Annie. It was an awkward hour. People came in in twos and threes, no longer in the stunned, frightened silence that had filled them all at the first news, but now chatting with each other about work, play, vacations, camp, and kids. Susan could hear their voices on the stairs, then she'd hear them suddenly hush themselves as they reached the landing, as if they'd caught themselves telling jokes at a funeral.

At the meeting, which Graham conducted, it was agreed that the main thing now was to keep people interested. "I heard a guy on the street the other day look at a poster as he passed and say, 'Oh yeah? Whatever happened about that kid? They must have found him by now.' "

People have short attention spans. Some thought dimly that they'd heard something. The kid was found in New York with an aunt? It was all a fraud? Others supposed that they had missed the conclusion of the Alex Selky story, possibly called away as the show was ending, or had skipped the issue of the paper that ran the last episode of the serial. A decade or two of television does not prepare the audience for plots without resolution.

"What we have to do," Graham said, "is demonstrate that the search is active. If people only see that first handbill in the same store windows where they've been for a month, they stop seeing it, or stop believing it."

Tiny Muriel Kopp spoke from the depths of the blue sofa. "Graham . . . if you'd like to go to a four-color poster, my office will donate the graphics. I can have my printer do the job at cost."

"Muriel . . . thank you." Graham looked at Susan, who was sitting in a chair behind him. "Can we afford?" he whispered. "Should we?"

"Absolutely." She nodded.

Jocelyn called across the room, "Graham, I'd like to help with that. I can afford some money toward the printing."

"So can we," said Martina quickly. Her husband, sitting beside her, nodded.

"I'll go in," said Ben, the chef. "Do you have a clue how much it will be?"

"Well, it depends on how many we print," said Muriel.

"Never mind . . . just let me know when you have the estimate. I'll be the sinking fund, Graham. Anyone who wants to donate, see me afterward." There was a rattle of assent from around the room.

"Thank you," said Graham. "Thank you all."

"You're welcome," said Ben.

"Well . . . until we can have new posters ready, Susan has an interim plan . . ." Graham looked around and then located a brown paper bag tucked on the floor near Susan's chair. "We had a dozen rubber stamps made up that say 'STILL.'" He reached into the bag and held up a stamp with a wooden handle. "And we've got a dozen red ink pads. If some of you would volunteer to be responsible, each for an area of the city, we could get around and stamp the handbills, and put up more where the old ones have been taken down, with the word 'STILL' stamped on them in red, by the word 'MISSING.' You don't have to do your whole area yourself, just be responsible for making sure someone does it."

"I'll do out around the Fen," said Jocelyn. "I have to go out there anyway, to my therapist."

"That's great, thank you. How much do you think you can cover?"

"How about . . . Mass Ave up to the Med School? Between Huntington and the Riverway?"

"Great." He looked to Susan, who wrote this down on a pad of foolscap.

"I'll take Beacon Hill, Front and Back of the Hill from the South End," spoke up a painter whose son and Alex often used to be mistaken for brothers when they were at day-care together.

"John," said Graham, and relayed the area to Susan, because John had spoken softly. "That's a big area, John—can you cover that?"

"My colorful garb deceives you. I grew up on Pinckney Street. I still have a mother and two sisters living up there, and I shall press my nieces and nephoos into service."

"Why, John," said Ben. "A closet preppie . . . and all this time I thought you got nosebleeds if you had to go above the Common."

"The power to cloud men's minds," said John, waving his fingers.

Martina and her husband volunteered to do the South End, and Muriel Kopp volunteered for the Harvard Square area around her office. Graham said that donating the new poster was enough, but Muriel insisted. Section by section they accounted for the whole map except Roxbury; Graham said he would feel better if they let the police cover that area. If nothing had happened in two weeks, they agreed they would meet again to deploy the new color poster.

The meeting ended soberly, but as the group descended the stairs, Susan and Graham heard them pick up their normal preoccupations like so many briefcases checked at the door, which was apparently where daily life resumed. Susan heard a small group of them decide to go over to Mass Ave for Thai food.

IT WAS already stifling hot out in Saugus that third week in June. Pat Menetti was keeping the air-conditioning off except in the bedroom, to do her part to help with the energy crisis. Al had been late getting home from work again tonight and had had to eat a plate of stiff food she'd kept for him in the oven. She couldn't hold dinner past 6:30; it was too late for the kids, and in this heat, she wasn't going to cook dinner twice. At least this time he wasn't late because he was with Susan. He'd had to sit in a line for an hour and a half trying to get gas for the car.

"Look at you," she said to him when he laid his fork down in his pile of rice and said he was finished. "Your clothes are hanging on you. You must have lost ten pounds!"

"Good," he said. "I needed to." That was true, he had, but still his cheeks looked sort of sunken. Losing had left him drawn-looking.

Now he was upstairs in the bedroom going over reports from the Selky case. There were over seven hundred now, some short, some ten pages long, of interviews, phone conversations, polygraph tests, and so on and so on. He'd spent so many hours reading them, you'd think he had them memorized. She said as much.

"I have," he said, pressing his lips together and looking lost in thought. He went over and over them anyway, in a process that would be called methodical, except that what he was waiting for couldn't be achieved through method, any more than you could fall asleep by being determined to. He was having trouble doing that also.

As soon as she had the youngest three kids tucked in, Pat went to their room and invited him to come out onto the patio with her to have some Sanka and cake.

"Maybe in a little while," he said vaguely.

"I want a divorce," said Pat.

"You do?" He turned the page.

"I'm going down now to call an attorney."

"Look, find a cheap one, will you? I can't support you and the kids and a lawyer too."

"I'll give you another half-hour," she said.

"Yeah . . . okay."

The kind of connection he needed had to make itself. You couldn't make it happen by working just a little harder or trying just a little more. All you could do was be there, so your head would be a place for it to happen in. When it hit you, it was magic, and when it didn't, you felt like a cold turd. At the beginning of any case, the magic was all around you. You were full of hope and high on the chance of breaking through, pulling it off, putting together the pieces. There was no bigger high in the world than doing that.

When the trails began to get old, and the scent was gone, and the challenge changed from possible magic to a swamp you had to slog through, you had a much different kind of job. The pile stopped steaming and it stiffened up. Then it began to take another kind of courage to keep rubbing your nose in it.

The night was warm, moist, and starry. Pat handed him a delicate cup with a gold rim, containing watery instant Sanka. He set the cup on the wooden arm of the patio chair so he could accept the plate of pound cake with toasted coconut she was handing him. He really didn't want it, but he knew all hell would break loose if he said so. If there was one thing his placid wife disliked, it was feeling fat by herself.

"So," he said after a long drink of the night's sweet quiet. The lawn chirped with crickets, and faintly, very faintly, the

131

sound of a Kiss record floated from his teenage sons' bedroom window. He hadn't taken an hour to relax with Pat for a good long time. "How've you been?"

"Oh, pretty good, thanks. The hens have stopped laying and the horse died, but it looks like we'll have a good harvest."

"Oh," said Al, "that's sad. I always liked that horse."

"Want to hear about Eugene wetting his bed?"

"Yes. He's wetting his bed again?"

"Well, he did once."

"I don't like the sound of that—is something wrong with him?"

"Who knows? The doctor said just to be very patient and wait for him to grow out of it."

"Yeah, well, let's hope so, because that kind of thing can embarrass a guy at college. Really turns off your sleepover dates."

"Well, he's got a little leeway on that. Anyway, if it's still going on in a month or two, there's a thing you can buy that will buzz and wake him up as soon as it feels him wetting."

Al drank his coffee and looked at the stars, and in seconds was back on Fremont Street. He could see that morning as if he had been there. He could see that little boy wave to his mother and turn the corner. He could see him walk down the street, giving a little skip now and then, the way Eugene did. He just couldn't—somehow—see him disappear.

"So, Al," said Pat, going up, "I read a story in the *Sun-Gazette* about the Selkys."

"That rag," said Al, leaning his head back and closing his eyes.

"Well, I just glance through it at the checkout. I don't buy it. Anyway, they said the case had been solved. Something about the boy being with his uncle."

"Is that what they said? I wondered what they would come up with."

"Well, that was about all. It was mostly pictures. But now I have to keep explaining to people—you'd be amazed at who reads the *Sun-Gazette*; either that or an awful lot of people spend an awful lot of time exchanging the latest on Alex Selky."

"Both."

132

"Did that hurt you much, when the rumor went that it was all over?"

"Yeah, it did. . . . I don't think Susan realized how much it did . . . or else it didn't. The last day or two, the more I go over those reports, the more I have a creeping suspicion I've been on the wrong track since the beginning."

"Really? Meaning what? Have you come up with something?"

"I made what I thought was a real dumb move the first day. I was going by the book, and the book says you smell for a custody fight. You look for the father, which in this case wouldn't be kidnapping, because they have a joint-custody decree. So I went for the father, especially since he couldn't be located. I didn't call for bloodhounds right away. . . . Oh, you know, blah-blah. I've told you."

"But you did what would have been right ninety percent of the time."

He waved her remark away. "It was a mistake. I should have done both things, suspected her and believed her. So I went all the way the other way after that. I didn't want to keep making the same mistake, so I said, 'Okay, it's a stranger. It's no one these people know. It's a psycho killer, it's a child molester, it's a poor deranged woman who wants a kid.' . . . I've even found myself very seriously listening to these psychics. They all tell us something different, but it's interesting. Just about all of them believe the boy is alive."

"But last week you said you were dragging the South Bay for him."

"Yeah, we were. Thank God Susan never heard about that. We dragged for two days. Of course, he wasn't there. But we got the kind of tip that was a little too complete to ignore even though you know that it's rhubarb."

Pat shook her head in the dark. For the millionth time, for the familiar certainty of not hearing an answer, she asked, "Why do people do things like that?" The luxury of not understanding those who are Not Our Kind.

"Oh, Christ. Actually, this time I know why; it was somebody's idea of a good joke to see the police wasting all that equipment and time and money. It's the ones who truly believe what they're telling you that scare me. I had one today. She

133

swore that her next-door neighbor had the boy locked in her attic. She could hear him crying at night.''

''And did you check it out?''

''Oh, sure. You have to.''

''And?''

''*Nada.* Bonkers. That's what it's been like.''

''And you don't believe in the psychics?''

''Oh, at this point I believe in anything that keeps the mother's hopes up.''

Pat knew what that meant. She herself had her chart read by a woman she thought was absolutely incredible, the things she could sense about Pat and her past lives, but she knew better than to get into it with Al. ''So you were going to tell me about your new theory.''

''Oh, yes, so Susan is convinced that the boy is alive somewhere and that the media are her hope. She feels that if she keeps the faith and she keeps looking for Alex and waiting for him to come home, sooner or later someone will recognize him somewhere, and it will happen. It was a real threat to her when the word got out that the hunt was over.''

''Does she really believe it?''

Al thought. ''I just don't know. She's one very determined lady. . . . It's like asking the pope if he believes in God. It's beside the point; the subject doesn't come up. The pope's job is whatever it is, and Susan's job is being Alex's mother.

''Anyway, I've been going right down the line with her. I've checked records, I've combed the books, I've checked into every possible effing thing you can trace about perverts and child molesters and pornography rings and kidnappers. It's dead as a mackerel. Lately I've begun to suspect I've led myself down the garden path.''

''Oh, yes?'' Pat had just realized that another very small slice of cake wasn't going to kill her.

''I don't know that I'm looking for a stranger, and I don't know I'm looking for a live boy. Most murders are committed by people who know the victim. This was a very bright kid, and his mother had talked to him about going with strangers. That's the thing I kept pushing out of my head. The little warning bell I kept ignoring. Why would he go with someone he didn't know? If he was forced, how come nobody saw him struggle or heard him scream? The street was full of people; we know that.'' He fell silent.

"Are you saying you think it was done by one of them?"

Al shrugged. "It's possible. I *want* to believe what the mother believes . . . but I can't let it get in my way. The other thing is very, very possible, and I can't do my job right if I don't check it out. That is, if it isn't already too late."

"Does Mrs. Selky know what you're thinking?"

"Oh, jeez, no.'' He was silent again. "Jeez, no, that's the last thing I want."

"Do you suspect someone in particular?" asked Pat. She suddenly developed several strong and exciting suspicions of her own.

Menetti didn't answer. He shrugged, looked at the sky, looked at his fingernails.

Uh-huh, she said to herself. She knew she wouldn't hear any more tonight.

--◄┤ ├►--

ON THE MONDAY of the first week of July, the producer of *A.M. Boston* called Susan. "We talked several times about a month ago, Mrs. Selky," he said. "We've just gotten word that another child, a little five-year-old girl, has disappeared from her playground in a neighborhood in South Boston. The little girl's mother has agreed to appear with us tomorrow morning, and we have a psychologist with us to talk about this phenomenon, of what happens to a family when a little child disappears. Our producer wondered if you'd be willing to join us?"

"If you will show Alex's picture on the air, and if you'll make it very clear that the case is active and we want the viewers to look for him."

"Fine," he said. "Makeup call is at 6:30 and we're on the air live from eight to nine. We won't know until tomorrow which segment you'll be scheduled for, so please plan to be with us for the whole show. Here's the address. Do you have a pencil?"

Susan had left the house so little since Alex disappeared that for a moment she had a reflex thought that she'd have to somehow manage to find a baby-sitter for that hour.

SUSAN AND the other mother sat side by side in the makeup room. The makeup artists were husband and wife, their identical black kits set up on the counter, full of jars and bottles and paint pots and swabs. The kits were hinged and could unfold to reveal several layers, like a tackle box. Susan watched in the mirror as the makeup woman silently worked on her, nodding when Susan said she would like as little as possible, please, since she rarely wore makeup herself. On went the mascara and scarlet lipstick anyway. This was a soft-news show, or more truthfully, an entertainment show. They were concerned with the viewers' comfort, not Susan's, and the viewers were not entertained by guests who looked chronically ill under the lights. Susan, seeing her own face tricked out in unfamiliar high color, thought she looked as if she'd been embalmed.

Simultaneously, the husband was chattering to the missing girl's mother, a light-skinned black woman named Jannette. Her round face was yellow with worry, but she was excited about being in a TV station. "You're lucky you got me, darling," babbled the makeup man. "I can blend something special for this golden skin color. . . . It's a very unusual color, though. . . . Do you usually wear eye shadow? No? Well, this gray color on the upper lid blending to blue, like this, is just right for you for daytime. . . . Just watch how I do it, and always remember to blend well . . . like this. Now. How are we going to give you some cheekbones? Now, when you're at home, remember this. You take a little highlighter, and just dab it on the cheekbones, right here, and here."

Susan wondered if she could listen to much more of this without shouting, "Hey, buster, this woman has just lost a child!" But Jannette seemed distracted in spite of herself. "Here?" she asked, pointing to her cheek. There was something dull and simple about her speech and the slow flatness of her gaze.

"*No*, no, *here*," said the makeup man, daubing on light cream. "Then you put the cheek color here, and here." He brushed powdered rouge of a purple tone on to create the impression of hollows. "And *voilà!* Cheekbones! Aren't you gorgeous?"

Jannette looked at herself intently, as if she were a child too old for magic tricks who had just fallen for one anyway. She seemed almost reluctant to yield her chair to the Chinese actor who was going to demonstrate his recipe for omelets on the segment after theirs.

The producer's assistant showed them to the greenroom, where they were to wait. "Of course, it isn't really green," said the assistant. "That's just a show-business term. The waiting room is always called the greenroom." Susan already knew that, but Jannette did not, and she seemed quite interested. "I heard them say that on *Johnny Carson*," she remarked.

The room was bare and tacky. They sat side by side on plastic chairs and looked at a print of a clown on the opposite wall. Susan didn't want to talk to her about losing children. She would do it on camera when she had to, but she didn't want to get into a chat about it. Jannette seemed a little intimidated by her, and the only conversation she offered was to ask if Susan were nervous. "I am," said Jannette. "I'm real nervous—I hope I don't sweat."

Five minutes before the show was to begin, two policemen were shown into the greenroom. "Mrs. Smith?" one asked. Jannette identified herself. Susan realized later that she was surprised that they didn't even ask to see her privately. "We've found your little girl, Mrs. Smith," said the officer. "She's dead. The hatch was partly open on your neighbor's cistern. She fell in and drowned." Jannette simply stared up at them with a puzzled expression until she was led away, and Susan was left to stare at the Chinese actor in stunned silence.

A few minutes before her segment, the producer's assistant came in and bent over Susan. Though she must have been all of twenty-two, she talked to Susan as a nurse speaks to a sick child. "You going to be all right, dear? That's a good girl. Would you like a cup of water? Okay, what we're going to do then is send you on with the psychologist by yourself. Do you think you feel up to it? Good girl!" Susan wanted very badly to slap her face.

In the studio, Susan and the psychologist were introduced.

137

They stood in the relative darkness behind the tangle of lights and cameras, watching the show's host finish up a segment with a state senator. Susan couldn't help remarking to herself that the host was wearing a wig. "It's not fake anything, it's real Dynel," went through her head; the wig was an unnatural glistening gray-blond color. On the monitor she could see that the host looked blond and tan. From where she stood, his makeup was bright orange.

The orange man smiled warmly into the camera, thanked the senator, and cued a commercial. The two men stood, and the production assistant gaily rushed Susan and the psychologist into the blue-white bath of light on the set, like children hurrying in from a summer shower.

"We've given you eleven minutes, because we thought there were going to be three of you," the assistant was burbling. "Eleven minutes can be a really long time when you're up there under these lights—they're hot, aren't they? But don't be nervous. I know you'll both be great." She made a winding motion with her finger—"and that just means things like 'stretch it out,' or 'finish up.' Don't you pay any attention to Mike, our floor manager. Valerie Scott, who's interviewing you, will be watching, and she'll take care of the timing. Oh, here's our Valerie. You've probably seen her on TV. Valerie, this is Mrs. Selky, and this is Mr. Mandelbaum. *Doctor!* Dr. Mandelbaum!" She laughed gaily and laid one hand warmly on his arm, as if they were old friends sharing a joke. "*Excuse* me! Okay, all set? Everybody ready? Now, don't be nervous, Mrs. Selky. This is your first time on TV? I know Dr. Mandelbaum is an old pro!" And she tapped his arm again.

Susan and Dr. Mandelbaum sat in low armchairs across a Formica-topped coffee table from Valerie Scott, who looked over at her video image in the monitor and made last-minute adjustments to her hair as if she were in private looking in a mirror. The cameraman obligingly wheeled his huge camera in so she'd see a closer picture of herself.

"Don't look into the monitor once we start," was all she said to Susan. "Watch Mike and he'll tell you which camera to look at. Or else, look at me."

The segment began. Valerie Scott explained that Mrs. Smith, whose presence on the show had been announced earlier, was no longer with them because her little girl had, tragically, been found. She retold the story of Alex's disappearance six weeks before, and while she talked, Susan saw in the monitor that they were broadcasting Alex's picture. For a moment she remembered with vivid, piercing clarity why she was there; she got lost in that laughing face—there he was. There was Alex, in a freeze-action frame. In a moment he would start moving, finish his laugh.

"Mrs. Selky, you were in the greenroom with Mrs. Smith just a few minutes ago when police came to tell her that her little girl had been found, dead. Can you tell us what your feelings were at that moment?"

"Why, yes," said Susan. "I thought, when you have a little baby, you look forward to protecting him and teaching him and guiding him in gentle stages through all the hard things about growing up. And now suddenly her little girl has gone on ahead of her into the experience that we all fear the most."

Valerie Scott looked at Susan as if she expected her to say more. "It must have been a very *sad* moment," she prompted, after a beat.

Susan looked back pleasantly, as if she were not sure what the word meant. "Well . . . yes," she agreed. Valerie turned to Dr. Mandelbaum, who delivered what was expected of him. Death of a child, deeply disorienting, psychologists feel, deepest grief known, parental love, natural order, reversed expectations. It flowed over Susan like a stream flowing over a rock.

"Now, Mrs. Selky's position is different from Mrs. Smith's in that her little boy has disappeared and she has no way of knowing if he's dead or not. Tell me, Mrs. Selky, how do you feel about the case now that six weeks have gone by. Are there any new leads?"

Obediently Susan described the situation. No leads at the moment. Many similar cases, every reason to hope that someone had Alex who was taking good care of him. Essential for viewers to memorize his face, to watch for him, and report anything they saw.

"Well, your confidence is inspiring, as I'm sure our viewers will agree. But there must be times when you fear that knock on the door, bringing you the same news that Mrs. Smith heard

139

this morning?'' Susan looked at the sleek polished face that asked her the question. Tell us you're afraid, Mrs. Selky. Break down and cry. Let us feel that warm wet wash of pity, that prurient grief, that thrills because it's happened to you and not us. Give it to us, Mrs. Selky.

Fine, thought Susan to herself, still pleasantly. Her interests aren't mine, but then, whose are? She wondered if Menetti were watching. She'd learned a lot from him. She said, ''Yes, of course, but fears are different from faith. I have faith that my son is alive. I believe that if he were gone from the earth, I would know it. Having faith is different from saying the odds are two-to-one or you think something or know something. Faith is a power in itself, and it happens to be the only one I have left. If we care about children like Alex, if we all remember them and look for them, then there is hope that they will be recognized and returned. If we don't, then, alive or not, there's no hope.''

''Are you saying that if you give up hope, the police will stop searching for Alex?''

''Not only the police. Your viewers. Everyone. If Alex is alive, sooner or later someone may see him. If I keep faith that he's alive, if I keep looking for him and asking for help to look for him, there's a chance that he will be brought home. If I don't, there isn't. Therefore, I believe he is alive.''

''Isn't that a non sequitur, Mrs. Selky?''

''No.''

''Mrs. Selky is describing a very interesting phenomenon,'' Dr. Mandelbaum volunteered briskly, to Valerie's obvious relief.

''She is in a very unusual situation from a psychologist's point of view, because in a normal mourning situation, there comes a point when the mourner *must* begin to put away thoughts of the loved one and pick up the pieces of her life and go on. To fail to do so at some point becomes neurotic. But in the case of an unknown fate, the normal rhythm is interrupted, the person is prevented from going on to the healing stage of grief. To do so would be seen as a betrayal of the loved one, so the mourner is frozen in the most painful moment of human experience. Her situation becomes like a metaphor for unchanging grief. And yet everything must change, in some way, as time passes; we saw this phenomenon during the Vietnam war, with the families of soldiers missing in action. I call it the Niobe syndrome . . . Niobe, as you remember, was punished by the gods for being too proud of her children, by having to watch every one of them slain. Then she turned to stone at that first moment of anguish, to weep forever. . . ."

Susan listened gratefully as Dr. Mandelbaum droned on until the end of the statement. When she got the thirty-second sign from Mike the floor man, Valerie broke in and cued the picture of Alex again, and that was all Susan wanted. In the corner, the stagehands were silently preparing the kitchen-counter set, and the Chinese actor stood ready to plug his series and demonstrate his omelets.

—◄❙ ❙►—

IN THE NEXT three days, Susan was startled by the growing numbers of a new kind of phone call. Phone calls from all over the country from other parents who had lost children. There had been letters of sympathy since the beginning. She had read partway into the stack of them, but it took the heart out of her, and she had put the bulk of them aside to read when she was more ready. Still, the number of heartbreaking stories she had heard already was legion.

But these calls were different. They weren't sympathy calls so much as calls from recruiters. The conversations were variations of this:

"Mrs. Selky?"

"Yes?"

"This is Andrea Detweiler in Colorado. We recently learned of your loss . . ."

"We?"

"My husband and I subscribe to a clipping service, anything that has to do with lost children. The Denver paper ran a story about you and Alex . . ."

"I didn't know that."

"Well, it was a wire story, they picked it up from the Boston *Globe*. Anyway, we want to tell you from the bottom of our hearts how sorry we are. We lost our little girl, our youngest, three years ago.''

"Yes," said Susan. "I'm sorry."

"Well," said Andrea Detweiler, "I want to acquaint you with some work my husband and I are doing. We feel that there's a great need to establish a sort of national clearing-house of information about these children who disappear. . . .''

"A national clearinghouse."

"I won't go into it, but for instance, we have very good reason to believe that our little girl is alive, and that by now she's probably been enrolled in school somewhere, probably in the West. Now, if there was some central bank of information, every school could automatically receive information, with pictures and descriptions of missing children at the start of every term.''

"I see," said Susan, for lack of any other response. Something inside her wanted to scream resistance to this new demand. Could it be that she was going to have to find the heart to care as much about another lost child as about her own? A hundred others? A thousand?

"Another thing it would do, the clearinghouse, it would provide information to all airports and customs places about runaways and missing children, to prevent them going out of the country. Think of the wives whose husbands can afford to simply flout a custody ruling, steal their own kids, and leave the jurisdiction—''

"I know," said Susan weakly.

"Our congressman is very interested in trying to support a bill to help us, but we need a lot more than that. Now, we understand you just did the *A.M. Boston* show . . ."

There was work to be done. If Susan had lost a child, she was one of them. If she had access to the media, she could help them all. The consensus was that she not only could, she must.

She agreed to a visit from members of a group from Rhode Island called Parents Remember! They arrived one afternoon at teatime, damp with heat. There was Sonia, a tiny woman with jet-black hair and plucked eyebrows; Marjorie, who was heavy and had brought her nursing baby with her; and Marjorie's husband, Bob. Bob had a crew cut and saddle shoes. Bob did most of the talking.

Parents Remember! thought of itself primarily as an educational organization, its main aim to make the public aware of how many children disappeared forever, how many others were kidnapped and abused before they were finally found, alive or dead. Their goal—or, as Susan gradually realized, their obsession—was to alert parents and children to danger and to educate the public on the plight of parents like Sonia and Marjorie and Bob and Susan. Sonia's nine-year-old son had vanished from his schoolyard four years ago; nothing whatever had ever been learned of his fate. Bob and Marjorie's little five-year-old girl was kidnapped from their front yard where she was playing with a neighborhood child.

"She had just had her fifth birthday," said Bob. "We still had some of the balloons up on the patio. She was playing in the sandbox in the front yard with Barbara . . ."

"The little girl next door," said Marjorie.

"She was seven at that time, Barbara."

"Allison was wearing her new sundress she got for her birthday," Marjorie suddenly interrupted again, appealing to Susan. Susan realized that Allison was the name of the daughter.

"Barbara told us exactly what happened," Bob went on. "A man in a new blue car, a nice-looking fellow in a suit, about the same age as her Uncle Dave, she says. He stopped the car by the curb there, he called to the girls, would one of them come over, please, so Allison got up and went right over . . ."

"Her white sandals were still in the sandbox . . ." said Marjorie.

"And when Allison got close, he just opened the car door and pulled her in and drove off."

"I heard Barbie scream," said Marjorie.

The neighbor child had given the police a vivid description of the kidnapper, but the man was never found. After four months the little girl's body was discovered half-buried in a nearby wood. There was enough left of her to determine she had been raped.

As they told her their stories, Susan realized that though their stated purpose was to establish the community of this shared experience, they were demonstrating the opposite. As

Bob talked, and Marjorie sat beside him looking at the floor while he talked, she saw their eyes grow glazed with the knowledge that there was no pain like their pain, no story as devastating as their story. She saw them isolated by their anguish, not only from her, but from each other. Shared or not, the horror was malignantly private. It seemed to her that, when it was Sonia's turn to tell her story, the mechanics of shifting Susan's attention from one to the other left all three slightly aggrieved. And yet they truly shared the need to join each other, because only in numbers could they make the rest of the world feel their grief.

"Parents Remember! offers a service to the community," said Bob. "We've had two film strips developed by professional psychologists, which we make available to schools—one's for elementary, one's for junior high—that explain to the children that not all grown-ups are safe; some are sick and dangerous. They tell about what kinds of people there are, the molesters and perverts as well as kidnappers and they explain, you know, about how even little children can be careful about these people. Things like, if they're walking along and they think someone might be following them, to find a lady and walk right next to her, and act like she's your mother. Or, a lot of kids, they say if they were kidnapped, they would never tell their right name and address?"

"Really?" said Susan softly.

"Yes. Boys especially. They've seen about big ransoms on TV and they say, 'Well, I'd save my parents all that money, I just wouldn't tell my name, and then they'd have to let me go.' The film strips explain what would really happen if they did that.

"Also, we have members who volunteer to go to these schools and talk and answer questions about safety. We have a pamphlet we prepared with the help of the police. Sometimes the police will send someone from public relations to do a program for us . . ."

The more Susan listened, the more uncomfortable she became. No matter what happened to Alex, she didn't believe a film strip could have saved him. This program could only have robbed him of his vibrant trust in life. "So what we'd like you to do," Bob was saying, "when you do talk shows or interviews, whatever—you done the *Donahue* show yet? Try to do *Donahue*. We did him last year. Anyway, when you go on, be sure to have them hold up one of our fliers and explain the program just briefly. Or else just be sure the viewers know how to get in touch with us."

"Another thing the public needs to know about—the police." Here Sonia interrupted him. She spoke with a very slight accent and a great intensity, shaking her head with feeling every few words. She never, Susan noticed, called her son by name.

"When my son disappeared," she said, "I went to the police, and the sergeant at the desk, he actually laughed at me. 'Lady,' he said to me, 'I know your kid. I picked him up for throwing crab apples at your neighbor's car; the first time, he was six years old. That boy ran away, Mrs. Silva.' When I demanded to see his commanding officer, he got mad. He said I had to wait twenty-four hours, and then, if my boy was not home, they would file a runaway report. Well, I waited twenty-four hours. It's four years, and I'm still waiting. The police don't know how I feel. They don't care."

Bob and Marjorie both crowded in with their own complaints of the way their case was handled, or not handled. "They never even tried to get an artist to make a portrait of the kidnapper!" said Marjorie fiercely. "They said, 'That child's too young to be a reliable witness.' "

"They said, 'Oh, a child that age can't give a useful description.' And this is a bright girl, she skipped second grade . . ."

"They kept on asking if Allison had ever wandered off *before!*" How Bob and Marjorie roared that word.

"And later," added Bob, "when the policemen came to say they had her body in a drawer down in the morgue, they never even said that they were sorry."

Well, Susan was sorry. She was appallingly sorry that those things had happened to these poor anguished people. "But the police have been very good to me," she said quietly. "I couldn't have asked for more. I believe they're doing everything that can be done in Alex's case, and more."

The other three looked at her stonily. "Well, you've been lucky," said Bob bitterly. Susan didn't know how to say that the visit had made her feel many things, but that in no way did she feel lucky. Sonia and Bob and Marjorie went on their way, incompletely satisfied. Susan's first reaction was that she never had been a joiner, and this was the last club in the world she wanted to belong to. But their faces stayed with her.

Over the coming weeks, more stories poured in, in calls and letters. She would come to feel that she had in fact a responsibility to all of these parents alone in their separate nightmares, to help, if her situation could help anybody else. It was one of the thoughts that kept her facing the media over and over again in the weeks to come. Every time she thought of stopping, she would hear one more story, of parents who had almost given up when some local newspaper ran one last squib about their plight, and their child was recognized and brought home.

SUSAN FELL into the habit of beginning her days by sitting at the window from eight to nine, drinking a cup of tea, and watching the sidewalk below. Once she would have been bored to sit still that long. Now she wanted to be still. Still in the body and still in the mind. She gazed down at the steaming neighborhood street, nearly immobile, except for her watchful eyes. Boston was having one of the hottest summers on record, and by 8:30 the heat was often already heavy enough to stifle the breath. And by 8:30 nearly every morning, she would see Menetti's car pull up in the street below. Menetti would get out and start from her doorstep to walk down the street exactly as Alex had. When he got to the corner he stopped and looked back up the street, as Alex had. Then he turned the corner and disappeared, as Alex had.

Any morning Menetti didn't come, Susan got depressed.

IN MID-JULY, Susan relented and agreed to let her father and stepmother come east for the weekend. They would be careful not to be any bother. They would stay at a hotel, as they always had when they came over to spend Christmas with Graham and

Susan and Alex. Susan dreaded it. For years, the safest and happiest topic of conversation they shared had been Alex.

They made it very easy for her. Her father was a tall, thin, quiet man in his mid-seventies. At home he kept to himself and played a lot of golf. Since his retirement, he'd developed the habit—was more like a hobby, really—of getting decorously drunk each night before dinner. His peaceful eyes would grow watery with the second double martini, and he smiled quietly to himself as he pretended to follow the conversation, murmuring, "Mmm? Oh? Oh, yes!" at times that seemed to have more to do with his inner rhythms than with anything that might be said. He looked content and happy in there, behind his glasses and his glazed eyes. Susan liked to cover his escape by pretending he was playing a lively part in the conversation.

Susan's stepmother, Connie, looked twenty years younger than her husband, having been plucked and dyed and face-lifted within an inch of her life. She was not a silly woman, but she was made very anxious by silences. This anxiety led her often to chatter when she had nothing to say. But sometimes she did have something to say, and when she did, she was well worth listening to. She ran a small decorating business in the suburb where they lived, selling gilt mirrors and flowered wall-paper to her friends. The business was quietly subsidized by Susan's father, who was proud that Connie took the trouble to do something besides playing bridge. They reminded Susan of a pair of birds, one brightly colored, alert and preening, darting eyes scanning the distance, the other tranquil, dun-colored, myopic and blinking, the two perched companionably side by side on a sheltered branch.

The first night for a special extravagance they took her to dinner at Locke-Ober's. Susan was touched to note that her father as well as Connie worked hard at maintaining a flow of conversation. They talked about the flavor of everything and ordered expensive wine, knowing those things had once been great treats to Susan. Neither remarked that she was eating none of her lobster soufflé.

Connie talked in detail about their renovations at home. Business was slow, so she was redoing her downstairs. She'd brought fabric and wallpaper samples for Susan to advise her on, and the three of them got through nearly an hour choosing

147

combinations, changing their minds, making substitutions, and returning to their first choices. When that topic was exhausted, Susan's father began to tell stories of his boyhood in Kansas that neither Connie nor Susan had heard.

"Why, Andrew," Connie would exclaim, as if she had just heard a riveting analysis of the oil crisis or how to stabilize the dollar, "why, I never realized the school was five miles from your house! How did you get there, did you walk, or was there a school bus?"

"Oh, there were two school buses," said Andrew. "A one-horse bus, and a two-horse bus. In the winter, we had a bus with sled runners."

When the evening was over, they insisted on getting into the taxi with her and driving her to her door. "Good night, dearie, lovely to see you. Sleep well," they said, kissing her good night as if she were a little girl and they were tucking her in.

The next day they labored through the Gardner Museum and then went to the Ritz Carlton for tea. "Isn't it just *sinful?*" said Connie. "I always wanted to come to Boston and just be a tourist, and now . . ." And now, this is all we can think of to do for you, Susan. Please be pleased.

She was not pleased in the sense of feeling pleasure. She felt so dull and heavy and sad that it was a great effort to try to seem happy. But she was pleased at what they wanted to do. In the evening they went to see the road company of *Annie.*

"We're so lucky it's here, it's the one play Andrew really wanted to see," Connie confided. There was no way they could have known that Alex had asked for the cast album of *Annie* for Christmas and played it noon and night till he could sing every song. (Alex in the tub, draping himself with suds from his bubblebath, belting obliviously "*Lucky* me , *Lucky* me, Look at what I'm dripping with . . . LIDDLE GIRLS!")

When it was over, Susan's father said, "Why don't you come back to the hotel for a nightcap, since we won't see you in the morning?" She wanted so much to go home and be alone that she made herself say she'd love to.

Andrew had a glass of brandy, which Connie and Susan declined. Susan sat uncomfortably in the armchair while they sat on their beds. It was odd to be in their bedroom. She wondered how long she should stay.

"Susan," said her father, looking down at his fingernails. "I'm very proud of the way you're handling this." Susan froze in her chair. If he said any more, she would cry. But he didn't.

Connie said softly, "I don't know if you remember old Mrs. Gable. . . . Years ago, her daughter left, and left her a note that said, 'I'm going away, and don't try to find me because you never will.' She *never* got over it."

Susan did remember old Mrs. Gable. She remembered seeing her drunk at the country club at lunch.

"Well," said her father, standing up. "It was lovely to see you, honey. Thank you for coming. . . ."

"Thank you for a lovely time, Daddy. I hadn't been to the Gardner in years, even though it's right there. . . ."

"We're proud of Graham, too . . . please give him our best wishes."

"I will, Daddy."

"And here's a little something . . ." He took from his dresser drawer a large gaily wrapped package and handed it to her. The card said, To My Grandson on His Birthday . . . "just in case . . ."

SUSAN FOUND herself haunted with the fear that when people left her she'd never see them again. When she'd said good-bye to her father, she felt as if she were really saying good-bye to him forever. She slept badly and left the radio on all the next day so she'd know if the plane they took home had crashed. She was increasingly preoccupied when she was with other people. If she found herself relaxing into an hour of forgetfulness, she snapped back, like someone trying to doze sitting up in a chair. She was never wholeheartedly present even at moments of ease, because a part of her mind was fearing the moment passing. Every minute of health and safety seemed so precious that she spoiled it by caring too much.

"I don't know what to say to her," Martina told Jocelyn. "What are you supposed to say? 'How's it going?' 'How've you been?' 'How are you?' I'm ashamed of myself, but I find myself putting off calling her."

"It's *really* hard," said Jocelyn.

"Maybe she needs to be alone for a while. . . ."

"Maybe."

SUSAN'S PHONE rang. It was Menetti. It was late on a Monday afternoon in July. He hadn't been near the neighborhood all day, and she'd been feeling very low. She knew it was irrational to fear that if he wasn't hunting for Alex where she could see him, no one was hunting at all, but she felt it.

"Susan. I just wanted to see if you were home."

"I'm home. You didn't come by this morning."

"I'm afraid I was waiting on some news. I'm still expecting a call any minute, but in case it doesn't come in right away, I wanted to be sure I knew where to reach you this evening."

"What's happened?" She already knew from his voice it wasn't good.

"Well . . . I got a call from Philadelphia PD today. Some kids early this morning, they found a plastic bag in the woods down there, with a body. With the heat we've had for a month, it's not in very good shape . . ."

She felt a deep wallop of pain, as if everything inside her had just cracked up the middle.

"You think it's Alex."

"Susan, it's a small body. They didn't even know when they called me if it was male or female. We're waiting for the coroner's report. . . . It's taking a while. Apparently the head's missing."

"Okay," she said. "I'll be here."

"They promised to call me this afternoon or tonight, as soon as the autopsy's finished."

"Okay," she said.

She sat a moment by herself in the afternoon light and then called Graham. He wasn't home. She told Naomi, and Naomi said she'd find him right away. Graham arrived in less than an hour. "Did he call back yet?" was all he said as he burst in the door. She shook her head.

"Is it evil for me to pray it's not Alex?" she asked.

They sat down together on the couch, and Graham took her hand. He shook his head. "But it *could* be Alex," he said. "We always knew it might be this."

"I know," she whispered.

The call came at eight o'clock. By that time dusk had fallen in the room, but they hadn't turned on the lights. Graham leaped to answer it.

"It's a female," said Menetti. "The body was incomplete; that's why it took so long. But they make her four or five inches taller than Alex, probably nine years old." As he listened, Graham's face telegraphed the news to Susan, an expression of awesome relief.

"The head wasn't with the body," Menetti was saying, "to make it hard to identify. No dental records, no face. A kid that age has hardly ever been fingerprinted. So far, the details don't correlate with any kid who's been reported missing anywhere near here."

"You mean a nine-year-old girl could disappear and no one would report it?"

"Oh, yeah."

"How could that happen?"

"Hey, Graham, tell Susan good night for me. Tell her I'm glad."

"I will, Al. Thank you."

"Okay. See you later."

Graham went back and took Susan in his arms. "What are these tears?" he said, holding her.

"I'm so relieved . . ." Her voice was trembling. "It's disgusting, but I thank God. I feel like celebrating."

"Me too! Let's go out and eat something spicy, and drink champagne."

"Cold beer!"

"Cold beer!"

"Let's call TJ and Annie!"

"I'll call them right now."

"No . . . let's just be together."

"Okay. Let's go!"

BY HALFWAY through dinner, the mood was spoiled. Susan

151

couldn't eat. Her lethargy had returned and she felt choked at the thought of happiness, as if that alone was a betrayal of Alex. Just because he hadn't been found yet, it didn't mean he wasn't rotting in a garbage bag somewhere too.

Graham felt helpless and disappointed. "Susan," he said tentatively, "you know it could have been Alex."

"I know that—don't you think I know that?"

"I think you know it in your head, but I don't see you doing anything to prepare yourself for it."

"What do you mean?"

"What I said—you put everything into this police stuff, going through the mail, dealing with the calls, answering the cranks, calling Missing Persons five times a day with suggestions."

"Yes? So?"

"Please don't get defensive. I'm with you, I'm not attacking you."

"That's not what it sounds like."

Graham counted to ten, then began again, gently. "Honey, if that call tonight had gone the other way . . . or even worse, if we just don't ever hear anything again . . ."

"Yes?" she said coldly.

"What I'm trying to say is, there may come a time when you will have to consider . . . accepting . . ."

"Accepting what? That it's too painful to go on hoping, so I should give up on him? I should cut him off to save myself the inconvenience of missing him?"

"Not of missing him, Susan—we'll miss him for the rest of our lives. Of trying to save him if he can't be saved. . . . For your own good . . ."

"For *my* own good! What about *our* own? Am I in this by myself now? Isn't he your son too?"

Graham looked down at the table and sighed. Her face had a dark flush and her eyes gleamed with an anger he dreaded because it seemed to come from somebody else who now and then woke up inside her.

"Of course he's my son too. I just wanted to talk about you because you worry me."

"And you don't, eh? I'm in trouble over this, but you're perfectly fine, eh? That again? Crazy Susan, can't cope? Well,

152

I'm coping, Graham. And don't tell me I haven't had plenty to cope with."

"Please, Susan. I didn't mean anything like that, and in your heart you know I didn't. Of course I'm having trouble; I'm having more trouble than I ever thought I could bear."

She glared at him across the table. She knew he was right, that she was trembling with fury and he was in fact much more stable than she at this moment.

"Well, maybe you're bearing up so well because you didn't care so much in the first place. You didn't care enough to resist fucking around and fucking up his home when he was still with us, did you?"

Graham's face fell. When he looked up, he looked awful, but his voice was still soft as he said, "Susan, when you get like this, you say some things that are very hard to forgive."

And she knew it was true, and she knew it was precisely her ruthless rage when she was hurt that she had contributed to the crash of the marriage. "I want to go home," she said. And the two people inside her, the sane one and the hurt one, fought all the way home, trying to say to Graham that she knew how wrong she was, that she'd take it back if she could. But her eyes and throat were still dry with anger—at what, she wasn't even sure—when they parted in silence. It wasn't until the door closed behind him that she started to cry.

SHE DIDN'T HEAR from Graham for almost a week. In fact, she didn't hear from anybody not connected with the case. *Boston* magazine sent a reporter to do a story with her. Susan found it a real relief to have someone to talk to, who listened with intelligence and attention, who wouldn't then go away in pain and never call again.

Susan knew now for certain that people she'd known for years were crossing the street when they saw her, so they wouldn't have to chat. She didn't blame them, but she could have used the contact. She could have used the dailiness of a smile, and a "Hello, how are you?"

But then, what could she answer?

Still, the acquaintances disappearing around corners didn't hurt as much as the man who stopped her on the street with a warm smile. "Aren't you Susan Selky?"

"Yes?" . . . Who are you? Do you know something about Alex?

"Mrs. Selky," he said, his voice sincere, his mouth still smiling, "I want to tell you that I think you were grossly irresponsible to let a six-year-old child out on the street by himself. I know you've had a hard time, but I just felt you ought to know that you really showed poor judgment. That's what I think, grossly irresponsible . . ." His voice followed her down the street as she walked away, still seeing his pleasant smile beneath remorseless eyes.

People saw you on television. They listened to you tell how you felt. They thought it only fair you should hear how they felt.

Susan was sure that Graham would at least come back on Alex's birthday. He wouldn't let her spend Alex's birthday alone.

The phones were especially busy all that muggy rainy day that Alex Selky turned seven. The Boston papers ran his picture and a recap of his disappearance for the occasion, and Susan appeared on a new talk show called *Live at Noon*. Sometimes now, when she talked to strangers in such an artificial setting about Alex, she was dry and matter-of-fact, even to the point of being slightly ironic, as people are when they are deeply immersed in a topic and explaining it for the hundredth time to novices. Her control surprised her, since sometimes she seemed to weep all day. It occurred to her as she explained to the camera with a calm smile that, as far as she was concerned, Alex was alive and that someday he would be coming home, that she must seem oddly aloof to people hearing her story for the first time. If the impact was new to them, they would expect to see her first grief. In the greenroom after her segment, as she was putting on her rainboots, she heard two of the light-crew men taking a cigarette break in the hall.

"I've been covering news for twenty-three years," one said, "but that's one of the toughest cookies I've ever seen."

"Yeah, she's tight. Even weird."

"Very tough lady . . ." They went on down the hall.

Really, thought Susan. Compared to what? How many mothers have you known whose sons have been missing for seventy-three days?

Martina called in the middle of the afternoon.

"Hi, Susan," she said in a worried voice. "How are you?"

"Fine. I'm just back from doing this *Life at Noon* show."

"How was it?"

"It went pretty well."

". . . Foul weather," said Martina.

"Yes," said Susan. Alex had wanted to go to Crane's Beach for his birthday this year. He was planning to invite his friends and take a picnic. ("Can we take fried chicken, Mom? Can we go to Chucky Fried?") The rain would have spoiled it.

"I've had better days, actually. This is Alex's birthday."

"Oh, I know," said Martina. She seemed embarrassed. Well, it was true that she hadn't called in a while. Susan should have known it was a birthday call.

"Thank you," she said softly. "I'm glad you remembered."

"Is there anything I can do for you?" Martina asked. Yes, you can come over for tea, or invite me to have a drink, instead of asking. "No, thank you. Just thank you for calling."

After a while, Susan tried to call Jocelyn. She thought she would like to see Jocelyn. She would even like to see Justine. Maybe they would come for tea—she'd go out and get little cakes. She would like to do something happy for Alex today.

There was no answer at Jocelyn's. She tried again a couple of times.

It wasn't until nearly suppertime that it occurred to her that Graham might not come. He always came back and stroked her hair and said, "Honey, I'm sorry"—especially when she was wrong. He couldn't really be meaning to stay away today.

What had she said to him? Was it possible she had finally said something so vicious that he didn't forgive her?

She tried to remember. She remembered the conviction that he had, unforgivably, patronized her. She remembered the rage as being a black envelope lined with scarlet, rather than being made of words. She remembered that when she felt that deranged sense of abandonment and wrongful loss, her rules

155

were that she said whatever would hurt. She didn't attach any moral or cognitive meaning to the weapon at all, as a connoisseur might say, "Ah, a Florentine dagger, early Renaissance, unusual filigree." She just reached for whatever was going to cut to the bone.

Graham understood that. He had always understood that.

By nightfall, when he had still not called, she was as paralyzed with leaden depression as ever in her life.

AT NINE O'CLOCK she heard steps on the stairs. Graham? No, not his step. Who? She couldn't bring herself to care. Maybe someone was coming to kill her. She hoped it wouldn't hurt too much.

TJ stopped at the dark inside the hall.

"Susan? Susan? Are you here?" He started up the stairs and called her again. Then he walked into the living room and stood for a minute before he turned on a lamp. He walked over to where she sat by the window, scooped her up, and sat down again, cradling her against his chest.

"Happy birthday," he whispered, and she nodded against his chest and began to cry, and went on for a long time.

When she felt emptied of tears at last, she took a deep breath and asked politely, "Where's Annie?"

"She's playing at Passim tonight. She sent you her love and said to tell you she's going to sing the lullaby for Alex." Susan nodded. Alex loved to listen to Annie sing. Last year on his birthday, TJ and Annie had come at bedtime as a surprise and serenaded Alex under his window.

Hushaby . . . Don't you cry
Go to sleep, Little Baby.
When you wake, you will find
All the pretty little horses.

"Where's Graham?" TJ asked softly.

Susan shrugged and shook her head. TJ didn't press it.

"Today," said TJ, "I thought about the day Alex was born. I got to see him through the window in the nursery in the evening. He was red with black hair. A little straight nose that looked just like Graham's. Graham and I could see one of his

156

little fists outside the blanket. I remember feeling I was seeing a miracle when he moved his fingers, like this. . . . You were asleep, but I sneaked in and left you the flowers, remember? . . . Graham was so proud of you. He said you had been so strong and brave. . . . Your hair was all wet across your forehead. You looked like you were having the sweetest dream.''

"I was." There had been no Alex, and then all in one day he was in their lives. And now there was no Alex again. Who could have dreamed the time between that day and this one would be short?

"Remember the day he was christened? He yelled when the minister put the water on his head. He looked furious to wake up like that, and we all had trouble not to laugh. I was afraid I'd drop him, when you handed him to me, in that long christening robe. . . .''

"And Connie said it was good when babies cried at their christening. It meant the devil was being driven out,'' said Susan.

"I was proud that day. It felt good to stand up holding Alex, with you and Graham beside me. It felt like we were all the family, the four of us.''

TJ reached into his pocket and took out a jeweler's box, which he handed to Susan. She opened it, and in it found a small Swiss wristwatch on a child's band; it was engraved on the back. "To AGS from TJF, July 27, 1980.''

"I had it done in the spring . . .'' whispered TJ.

Susan realized it was the first time in all the years she had known him she'd seen TJ crying. "He gave us so much joy,'' she said. "We didn't know we weren't going to have time to give him all the things he deserved. . . .''

Out of words, joined in one warmth but in their heads each deeply alone with their griefs, they leaned together in silence for a long half-hour. Presently TJ stood up, with Susan still in his arms, walked up the stairs in the dark, and without giving it much above animal thought, they made love. They exchanged their old friendship with the brainless simplicity of flesh when all words and thoughts had become more than they could bear. Afterward, as they lay silently wrapped around each other, Susan felt grateful that TJ, arm's-length Yankee that he was, had been willing to comfort her in the one way that said his

157

feeling for her was really for her, and not just an adjunct of his older love for Graham. How simple it seemed now that it had happened to her, to see that feeling could be shared with bodies that in no way touched or compromised their love for absent others. Oh, Graham.

TJ and Susan were downstairs sitting together over a cup of tea when they saw from the living-room window a bright light from a car driving slowly down the street. The light careened around the walls, vanished, circled in again. TJ went to the window and leaned out.

"Police car . . ." he said over his shoulder. The light went out and the motor sound died. Susan, sitting at the table frozen, heard him say, "They've got Graham. They're holding him up." TJ and Susan looked at each other. Her eyes were wide, her expression bewildered. TJ set down his cup and leaped down the stairs. It seemed to Susan to take forever for them to get Graham up. She could hear him coming one step at a time. One or the other of the policemen kept saying, "Easy. Easy. *Don't rush.*" Then TJ said, "You're okay." And a voice that might have been Graham's, if he had rags in his mouth, said something. When she saw him come through the door, she knew it was a measure of how much she had changed that she didn't make a sound.

Graham's face was battered, as if it had been stamped on. One eye was swollen shut. The distended skin over it shone where it was stretched, like a pregnant woman's belly. It was a mottled purplish blue. His lips too were swollen and bloody from where they'd been sliced through by his own teeth, and there was another huge purple bruise across his right cheekbone and cheek. He moved his lips so little when he tried to speak that it was very hard to understand him. He held one arm stiffly at his side, but when she looked at it fearfully, he said, " 'S bruised. Not broken."

TJ helped him to a chair as one of the policemen said, "He wouldn't let us take him to a hospital, missus. He oughta have that X-rayed."

"He oughta have everything X-rayed," said the other one.

"I'll go tomorrow," Graham enunciated with great care. She saw him wince as he filled his lungs after speech.

"Ordinarily we would have called an ambulance, or taken

im to the station house and let him make a call, but when we found out who he was and what happened, we decided to bring him home.''

"He wouldn't let us take him to a hospital," said the other one. "He said he had to get here."

"And what did happen? Where did you find him?" asked Susan.

"North Cambridge. That's where we're from. He wasn't making much sense when we found him, but from what we gather, he got some kind of a ransom call."

"What he thought was a ransom call," put in the second one.

"Yesterday morning. Instead of calling the police, like he'd been told to do, he decided to walk into an alley by himself at ten o'clock at night carrying ten thousand dollars in cash."

Susan's heart nearly stopped. "Jesus!" said TJ. They both stared at Graham.

"I . . . got this call from some woman," Graham said, as clearly as he could. It hurt him to breathe, so the words came out in brief gasps. Again the swollen lips made him sound as if he had rags in his mouth, and it was all Susan could do to listen without clamping her hand over her own mouth. "She said she had . . . Alex. She said he . . . got sick. So she was scared. She didn't dare . . . call . . . a doctor for him. She said he had a fever. She said she'd sell him back . . . to me . . . for ten thousand dollars."

"Didn't you ask to speak to him?" Susan asked in a tiny voice.

Graham nodded. "I heard . . . this little voice say . . . 'Hi, Daddy.' " Here Susan saw his one open eye fill with tears. "I told her . . . it wasn't enough . . . I couldn't tell if it was Alex. She said he had a fever and . . . and had . . . to go back to bed."

"But *why* didn't you call the police?" asked TJ.

"She said . . . if I did . . . she'd leave him alone and he might die. She said she had a boyfriend on . . . the police and she would know if . . . I called . . . them. . . . "

"Oh, Graham!" TJ looked at his friend's battered face.

"She said . . . ten thousand wasn't enough . . . to risk getting . . . caught for. She was only doing . . . it

159

because he got sick.''

"But where did you get ten thousand?" asked Susan. It was true it wasn't much to risk being charged with kidnapping for, but it was much more money than she and Graham had ever had at one time, except for the down payment on this house.

"Borrowed it . . . two thousand from Dad . . . eight thousand from Robert.''

"Who?" said Susan. It had come out sounding like "Bobberd.''

"Roberd," said Graham, trying again.

"Robert lent you eight thousand dollars?"

"Did you tell them you were acting on your own?" TJ demanded.

"Not Dad.''

"And Robert didn't try to talk you out of it?"

Graham shrugged.

"We gotta be getting back across the river," said the first policeman. "We'll explain what happened and send a report over to your team. Who's your man, I read in the paper, Menetti?''

Susan nodded. "Thank you for bringing him home." She offered her hand. "Thank you very much.''

"I'd rather have taken him to a hospital," said the second policeman, shaking her hand in turn. "You be darn sure he goes first thing in the morning. We'll be in touch, Mr. Selky, to see if you can give us a better description . . ." But Graham shook his head.

The first policeman looked at Susan and said, "I wish he'd of called us first, Mrs. Selky." She nodded as if to say, "I know.''

"Do you want us to help you get him into bed?"

"Yes . . . thank you.''

The two gently hoisted Graham to his feet, and he put his good arm around one pair of blue shoulders. The first policeman put his arm around Graham and hooked a strong hand into his belt, while the second supported his back from behind, with his hands gripping his shoulder blades. Susan went up before them, turning on the lights, while the two officers half-pushed, half-lifted Graham up the stairs. In the bedroom she saw Graham for one moment look at the rumpled bedclothes, then glance at her and then at TJ. Then the officers said their goodnights.

"I'll go out with them and lock up," said TJ. Gently he put his arms around Graham and held him briefly. "You dumb shit," he whispered. Graham tapped TJ's shoulder with his palm and nodded. Susan could see that the shock was wearing off faster and faster, and his courage was seeping away, leaving a face dense with pain. When they were alone, she set about wordlessly helping him to undress and painstakingly inched his body into bed.

"Light out?" she whispered. He nodded. At a twist of her hand, the light died. She stood in the darkness and in a moment she sensed, rather than saw, him reach his hand toward her.

She knelt beside the bed. With his good arm, he stroked her hair, and then he drew her against him and held her hard; through the tears and the swollen mouth she could hardly hear what he whispered.

"I wanted . . . so much . . to bring him home to you."

Later, she slipped into bed beside him in the dark, trying not to make the mattress bobble, and spent the night, half-awake, half-sitting, with his mauled face supported against her shoulder. The breath in his mangled nose made a thin rasping sound, as if wheezing and fluttering through something torn deep inside him.

GRAHAM HAD cracked ribs where he had been kicked, and multiple bruises on his arms and face. The doctors strapped the ribs in place with wide bands of adhesive tape to heal, and gave him a wide cloth belt with many buckles to support his lower rib cage once he got out of bed. They kept him in the hospital for two days to be sure he had no more internal bleeding.

Susan went in to visit him. His room was narrow and bare except for a nightstand with a bedpan on it, a rack for IV bottles, and electronic monitoring equipment. It was very hot; the window was open and there was soot around the windowsill. The first evening, Graham seemed very low. He looked over at the door when she came in, as if he'd been waiting for her, and held out his hand. She stood by his bed for about ten minutes holding it; then the nurse came in and told her he had to go to sleep. The second evening, his color was better and she could tell he was breathing more easily.

"I can leave tomorrow," he said.

"I know . . . I just saw the doctor. She said you'll have to be still, though."

Graham nodded. "I'd like to come home," he said. She was silent, looking at him as if she were seeing something behind his eyes.

"Okay," she said. He gave her his hand again, and again she stood quietly, holding it.

A lock of hair had slipped across his forehead to the fringe of dark lashes of his one good eye. She reached to lift it away with a fingertip.

"Do you want me to come back for you?"

He shook his head. "TJ will bring me. He'll go over to Naomi's first, and get my stuff."

"Okay. I'll see you tomorrow, then."

"Okay." She studied his face for a moment more, and felt in it a strange quality of peace, as if in coming to rest he'd already forgotten she was there. But as she turned to leave, he pressed her hand before he let it go.

On the way to the elevator, walking bare-legged in wooden clogs that clicked against the linoleum, she met Naomi. Their eyes met as they approached each other; neither smiled. Susan said hello, and Naomi nodded twice, as if answering yes to a question. They were poised face to face for a moment, each holding an orange visitor's pass. Then they passed each other.

Al Menetti had been to see Graham in the hospital twice, and now he came in every day to hear the story over and over of the false ransom call, looking for the one detail that Graham had failed to mention, something that would tell him where to start looking. But it was useless. The call could have come from anywhere, the two men who beat him could have been anyone. The night had been dark, and the men had worn ski masks. They'd appeared so softly and swiftly from behind him that Graham couldn't even say how tall they were. They set about the beating with cool, silent efficiency. Graham had only seen their cheerful woolen faces from the ground as the attackers bent over him administering the final kicks to the head that would leave him unconscious. Menetti's reaction seemed to be a mixture of respect and disgust. He asked over and over again why it was Graham hadn't called him the minute he got the ransom demand, but no matter how often he heard it, the explanation didn't seem to satisfy him.

Philippe was delighted to find Graham home again in Susan's bed when he came to clean. He sat on the edge of the bed by Graham's feet and demanded to hear all about each injury, its diagnosis and treatment. Then he told Graham in generous detail about the time he had broken his leg in two places while skiing. When he'd finished his cleaning, he laid a tea tray for himself, Graham, and Susan and carried it up to Graham's room.

"You're lucky you're not very hairy on the chest," he said to Graham, eyeing the adhesive tape that braced the left side of his torso. "That's going to hurt when they take it off. I used to scream when I had to change a Band-Aid." He took a sip of his tea. "No, of course I didn't really.

"Susan, did Jocelyn tell you I have a new client? Yes, I have this new client, a friend of hers, and he's a channel."

"A channel?" asked Susan and Graham together.

"Jinx!" said Philippe. "That's what *I* said, a channel? Like Channel Two? Or like the English? But he said no, no, a channel from the other side, you know, like a medium. They call themselves channels now because people think a medium is a person with gold bangle earrings. But this fellow is being studied by this team of psychologists from Yale. He showed me a videotape of one of his sessions."

"What was it like?"

"Oh, it was weird. He rolled his eyes up in his head, like this, and his mouth dropped open, and then he began to talk in this odd sort of voice like a chipmunk record, so you couldn't tell if he was supposed to be a man or a woman." Philippe rolled his eyes back so you could see only the whites and recited nonsense syllables in a high electronic whine.

"For God's sake, Philippe, just don't make me laugh," said Graham with his hand against his sore ribs.

"Oh, sorry. Shall I go on?"

"Yes, please, just don't be funny."

"Well, it works like this. He's a channel for this spirit called Yasha or Masha. They can't quite be sure. The spirit isn't a ghost; it's a thing that hasn't ever been a person. I gather being a person is considered rather gross in spirit circles. Yasha is a high-class being.

"So I asked Ray, what's it for? I *know* we have no idea what's really going on in the universe, and I'm perfectly sure there are spirits all over the place. I'm fairly sure there's one in my apartment that keeps hiding my *TV Guide*."

Graham made a sound between a hoot and a groan.

"Oh, sorry, Graham. No, really, I don't have any trouble believing this Yasha or Masha, but there's only so many hours in a day, and if you're going to put in the time being a channel, I'd want to know what it's good for, wouldn't you? I mean, does it heal, or tell the future, or make you a better person, or what?"

"And what's the answer?" asked Susan.

"Well, Ray seemed to think it was a peculiar question. 'I'm in touch with the beyond!' he said. 'I can prove there's intelligence in the universe greater than man's.' I said, 'I never doubted that for a minute. I know house cats with greater intelligence than man's.' " Susan laughed.

"But don't you think so?" said Philippe. "I said to him, 'So what, that doesn't surprise me a bit!' He got very annoooyed. He said I could come to a session if I wanted, and ask Yasha a question. They're every Friday. I'm going to ask him about Alex."

"Thank you, Philippe."

"You're welcome. I doubt if he can tell me any more than the cards, but there's no point not trying."

Graham was watching Susan. He saw in her face that beginning query: Could this be it? Could this help? Wanting to distract her, he said to Philippe, "Oh, do the cards for me, Philippe. Find out how long it will be before I can turn over in bed by myself without yelling."

"You can't just ask them a question like that," said Philippe seriously. "They'll answer whatever question they want to, you know. Once I was doing the cards for my neighbor and her husband. She wanted to know if her husband was going to get a raise or something, but I laid out the cards three times, and every time I got the same thing showing some kind of trouble with the two men in her life. It was so embarrassing. Her husband got suspicious, and, sure enough, he found out she was sleeping with her dentist. They got divorced. I felt so responsible!"

"That's okay, Philippe, I'll take my chances," said Graham. Philippe went to get a deck of cards from the living room. Graham smiled at Susan. "See," he said softly, "a few swift kicks in the head, and even I believe in fortune-tellers."

"I see," she said. "If he tells you you're sleeping with your dentist, we'll know he has a one-track mind."

Philippe bustled in and cleared away the teacups. He smoothed the sheet on the bed beside Graham to make a place to lay out the cards.

"I'll shuffle them," he said to Graham, "and you cut. Good. Now, cut again. It's a good thing it hurts you to laugh, because this is very serious. Okay, now, watch. I lay them out in this pattern." He was swiftly setting out the cards in elaborate design as they came from the top of the deck. "And then I interpret the way they lie in relationship to one another. For instance, this here means house, or home, and now . . . oh, the black man . . . now, that could be the devil or the hangman, or a dark handsome stranger, depending . . ." He let the sentence hang as he finished laying out the pattern. Then he sat looking at the cards with a puzzled expression that gradually deepened to a look of distress.

"Okay, Philippe," said Graham. "Let's have it. There's the house and the black man, and there's the queen of hearts right beside it, which is Susan, of course—the devil is going to break into the house and steal the silverware and then Susan is going to run away with him."

"Well, you may think it's funny," said Philippe, "but if that card is the hangman, then someone in this house is going to be arrested." He scooped up the cards and put them back in their box.

"SUSAN, WHEN was the last time you had your period?" Graham was standing at the door of the bathroom watching Susan brush her teeth. Except for the rib belt and neck brace he still wore to keep him from reinjuring his cracked ribs and healing muscles, he was nearly back to normal, at least physically. It was true, however, that he no longer believed Alex was alive. Not that being beaten up proved anything one way or another. To believe or not believe was based on something other than proof, but in the month's work of healing his body, the enforced stillness of it, the gingerly caution and the slowly diminishing ache, he had imperceptibly healed over the source of his hope. Although this had not been stated between him and Susan, she knew it, and he knew she knew it. It made her edgy, as if he were a cuckoo in her nest.

Susan shrugged, her mouth full of toothpaste.

"No, really," he said, "when?"

She rinsed her mouth and her brush and put the brush away. "I don't know." She didn't. "Why do you ask? Have you been rooting around under the sink? Did you find cobwebs on the Tampax box?"

"I just thought about it this morning. I've been back home a month . . . I thought month . . . moon . . . I just wanted to be sure if you were okay."

"Oh. Well . . . really, I don't know."

"Since Alex disappeared?"

"I guess not."

"Don't you think you ought to have it checked out?"

She shrugged.

"Are you sure?"

"Yes," she said, and walked past him into the bedroom to finish dressing. He followed her and again stood watching from the doorway. She had her blue jeans on and was search-

166

ing for something in one of her drawers. He came up behind her and with a finger lightly traced the long line of her naked backbone. She ignored him. She pulled a shirt from the drawer and straightened, and he stepped closer to her. With the fingertips of both hands he reached to stroke the back of her neck, from the hairline down and around the throat to the collarbone. He stood still, with his hands on her shoulders, as if waiting for a sign that he might slide them down to her breasts. She was a statue, giving none. As the moment lengthened, her resentment against him for asking grew.

"Could you be pregnant?" he asked softly. She would have been touched at the wistfulness in his tone, except she was angry at having been made to identify with her own numbness. It had been a dead spot, unfeeling, unfelt. He made her feel it as damage. He seemed to have damaged her.

"No," she said. "I couldn't." And she shook off his hands and finished dressing.

"Oh," he said. "Well. I'd feel better if you saw a doctor, anyway. Maybe he'll give you some vitamoons."

Oh, okay, Graham. Patienter than thou. I know you hate to be turned off. Well, I'm sorry, I can't feel what I can't feel. She brushed crossly past him, out of the room, without answering.

ON THE SUBWAY on her way to the doctor the next day, she found herself praying, but without being able to identify what she was praying for. She could picture the doctor with his gleaming bald head and his hand-tinted pictures of his children on his desk saying, "It's very early to be sure, Mrs. Selky, but my guess is you're about six weeks along." And that meant TJ. . . . Oh, TJ, is the world so full of punishment? I needed a friend, not a baby. Supposing the doctor said that, would she have a baby?

Could she let the doctor wash his soft pink hands and sterilize curettes and spoon it out of her?

A baby, with blind eyes and tiny grasping fingers, and a little pointed chin that trembled when he yawned, as she wondered him wrapped in her arms. A baby's milky mouth with its sweet hot sploosh against her neck, burping after nursing. The big head wobbling on its tiny neck, like a tulip bobbing. The endless hours of watching the funniness of a baby.

She could say nothing, but TJ would know.

She pictured the doctor saying, "I'd say you're about ten weeks along now, and I imagine you're anemic again, so I want you to get some of these . . ." Scribbling. Well, Graham . . . do we have the courage to really begin again? Do you? Do I? If I don't, do I have the courage to have a baby alone?

Do I have the courage to have another baby at all?

Another hostage to fortune?

Indeed.

And then she pictured what she pictured every morning, every evening, every night—the phone ringing. "Hello, Susan? Al. I've finally got some good news for you."

Then the voice on the other end, so sweet and small. "Hello, Mommy?"

What if Alex came home and there she was with her new baby?

WHAT THE DOCTOR actually said, when he had finished his examination and she sat in his office looking at his bald head and the tinted photographs of his daughter with her white lace collar and his son with the Brylcreem, was, "Mrs. Selky, have you been under a lot of stress lately?"

She stared at him. In the last three months she'd been talked to, interviewed, ignored, advised, written to, harassed, and ogled, but this was the first time she'd heard anyone ask her with a straight face if she'd been under any stress lately.

He didn't apparently care much whether she answered. He looked at the large index card full of scribbles he held in front of him. "You say you haven't had a period since the first of May, you're not pregnant, and I see no recurrence of that little cyst on your left ovary two years ago . . ." He looked up and gave her a hearty smile. "So I'd say that whatever you've been doing to yourself lately, you ought to stop doing it."

He was serious. He assumed he was talking to a normal woman, maybe a little high-strung, with a husband and a job and a seven-year-old son at home with the baby-sitter. This was the man who had delivered Alex.

"I see," she said. The doctor rose and walked around the desk to open the door. "You could put on a little weight while you're at it; not that it'll hurt you. I wish all my patients had

168

your weight problem!" He was speaking loudly, a little joke for the benefit of the women in the waiting room as he ushered her out. "The old pumps will start up again by themselves as soon as you relax a little—nothing to worry about. All right, nurse . . ." and he went back into his office.

She felt such a weariness by the time she reached the street that she took a taxi home. She couldn't tell what was ripping her, relief or disappointment, and it took much too much energy to analyze. Besides, it was hardly connected with her real self. She knew about it without really feeling it at all, like a very distant detonation somewhere underground. After the first death, there is no other. Life appeared to her as a bright tedious jamming of the passages that led through birth and death to the same vast darkness.

Graham was in the living room doing his back exercises when she got home. "Been out?" he asked.

"I went to the doctor."

Graham never said "I told you to" or "I told you so."

"Oh, that's good. And?"

"He asked me if I'd been under any stress lately."

Graham looked astonished. "Dr. *Anderson?* Has he been under a rock?"

Susan shrugged, smiling. "Well, he may not read newspapers . . . or it may have just slipped his mind."

"Jesus! You people aren't kidding about your gynecologists."

"So we've been saying. . . . It was kind of a relief, actually."

-◄≡ ⊫►-

NOBODY EVER SAID, exactly, that the police department was giving up on Alex. In mid-July there had still been five or six detectives who were in fairly constant touch with Susan. But one by one they were unavailable when she called, because of vacations. They somehow never returned to the case. By the end of August, there was only Menetti and a sergeant named Laughlin who kept her informed of the number of tips or leads they were getting. These were down to a few dozen a week, from hundreds a day in the beginning. The number would triple anytime there was a news or television item about Alex, or anytime Susan appeared on a talk show.

Susan had been down to the Fourth District headquarters once in August to try in person to ask them to increase the manpower in her search. The building, incongruous on desolate Warren Avenue, had a massive gray cut-stone face at the street level, with Federalist brickwork on the upper stories. Inside, uniformed policemen loitered in the reception office. They eyed her skeptically as she asked to be directed to the chief of detectives. Why skeptically? What could she be concealing? And yet their manner filled her with such a sense of their casual presumption of guilt that she couldn't help but understand that here, the victims, the suspects, and the police were all in the same business. It was like a seedy little corporation of crime.

Susan recalled a news story she read once about a jewel thief who confessed to a hotel robbery after being unsuspected for two and a half years. "You want the respect of your peers," he'd explained. "The only people who could really appreciate the beauty of what I did were on the burglary squad." Crime as a performance medium. The jail term as finite measure of the artist's need for his audience. William James would have been enthralled.

The detectives' offices lined the narrow hallway that ran the length of the second floor. Susan found Menetti's office first at the top of the stairs. It was the corner office with two desks, a lot of scarred wooden office chairs, and posters of Alex on every wall. There it became concrete again for Susan what crime was. It was disgusting, aberrant, evil.

Menetti's office was empty. At heavy desks in small cheerless rooms on either side of the hall as she passed, detectives smoked cigarettes and plied their trade. She doubted if they could even hear in their voices the subtle undertone when they answered their phones that expressed the belief that whoever was on the other end was either nuts or guilty of something. She recognized many of the officers. One by one they would speak to her or give a nod of recognition and concern as they went about their business. She waited nearly a half-hour before she got to speak to the head of the department.

Lieutenant Bennet was a tall man, gray-haired, with receding gums. He asked what he could do for her.

"Well," she said, "there doesn't seem to be anyone working on my case. I haven't even seen Al Menetti all week."

"Your case is very important to us," he said. "It's very important to every man in this department. Every man in that room out there is ready to drop what he's doing and follow any lead we get if there's any chance he can help find that little boy. Now, believe me, I know how you feel."

"If I shoot the next person who says he knows how I feel, would it be justifiable homicide?"

"Okay, okay," said Bennet, unperturbed. He shifted his weight in his chair and gazed at her paternally. "I've been in this business a long time, dear, and I do know how you feel. . . ."

"Being in the business is not the same thing as losing your son!"

Bennet glanced past her through the open door to the hall beyond, as if daring anyone out there to look up or take notice of the woman yelling in his office. "Maybe not," he said blandly. "Maybe it's not the same as losing a son, but I still know more about this business than you do. I am doing the best job for you that I can. We are following every lead we get. If we have any reason, any reason at all, to assign more men to track down something promising, you will have this whole department at your service."

Susan was sitting very straight on her chair before him. She had fine blue eyes and faultless oval fingernails. He happened to know that she pronounced as *har*assment a word he'd always thought was ha*rass*ment.

"And who is the judge of what could turn into something really promising?" Susan's voice trembled.

Bennet stood and smiled. "I know how you feel," he repeated deliberately, "and we will continue to bend all our efforts to solve this case. It has our very top priority—you'll have to take my word for that. I'll see that Lieutenant Menetti stays in close touch with you."

Oh, they are right, she thought as she left the office. We *are* all nuts, or guilty. Quivering with emotion, she walked the

171

whole way home, sometimes actually talking to herself.

Menetti called her early in the afternoon.

"He as much as said they have no one looking for Alex because there are no leads at all, so let's give up!" she yelled at him.

"I'm sorry if it sounded that way," said Al. "It's not true. Look, I swear to you. There are two of us assigned to Alex full-time and six others who spend part of every day on it."

"But I haven't even seen you for a week!"

"I was checking on some things. Believe me, nothing has changed. We're looking for him the best we know how."

"Well, then, Al . . . tell me what I can do. What should I be doing now, to keep up the pressure? Do the talk shows help? Should I let this magazine do this article?"

He paused before answering. "It's pretty hard to say. We get a lot more calls when there's publicity, but none of them have been adding up to anything. But you never know."

"I see," she said, and surprised herself with the sneering tone in her voice. It was becoming a habit, the impulse to shoot the messenger who bears the bad news. "Meaning," she said, correcting her tone, "that it makes more work without actually helping."

"But you just never know what it will stir up tomorrow," he said. "Look . . . don't worry about it. You do whatever you feel you can handle, and whatever it stirs up, we'll deal with it."

For a week after this conversation Menetti was there every morning at 8:30, walking the street from Susan's door around the corner onto Beacon. He'd look up at her window as he got out of the car. If she was there, he'd nod.

SUSAN NOW HAD her public manner pat. She was calm, cheerful, and firm, so that you could neither get past her nor run through her. When she saw an acquaintance on the street, she made a point of speaking. She took control of the situation so there was no awkwardness.

"Alma," she'd call, "hello. I haven't seen you in a couple of weeks. Isn't the weather filthy? Poor Taxi's nearly cooked, aren't you, fur-person? Have a good afternoon." And off she'd go with a smile. She made it easy, and she kept it shallow.

172

She became a master at forty-five seconds of small talk that never included the question "How are you?" or "What have you been doing?"

She called the English Department and arranged her course schedule for the coming year. The general full-term lecture course in the American novel, with four sections, one of which she'd teach herself, an honors seminar in Cather, and another on twentieth-century Southern fiction, concentrating on Faulkner, Welty, and Flannery O'Connor.

She agreed to give a long interview to a New York writer from one of the ladies' magazines, for a story to be published nationally that would ask the readers to join the hunt for Alex. She spent several evenings arranging all her photographs of Alex from his birth to the time he disappeared. She planned for the magazine to use a couple of pages of them, arranged to look like the pages of a family album, which would give the readers a sense of Alex as a normal, happy child in an ordinary family. You had to remove the bizarre clack of crime publicity and police procedure that surrounded Alex for them to recognize that he was a regular child like theirs. It could have happened to any of them. It still might. She explained her thoughts to Graham while she worked on the pictures, and he said it was a good idea, she was perfectly right. He didn't offer to help.

She had taken to rising very early. She had trouble sleeping more than four or five hours a night, and besides, they often got crank calls in the early hours of the morning. At seven A.M. along the river in late August you could feel the cold beginning of autumn in the heavy air, like a chill rinse of water over sun-heated skin. One morning when Susan came in from an early walk she went up to Alex's room, taking care not to creak the steps and wake Graham. She caught some of the thick minty smell of sleep as she passed his door. In Alex's room she quietly placed one of his baby chairs at the closet so she could step up and reach the shelf where she had put most of his sweaters in a plastic case with mothballs when the weather turned hot in the spring. These she brought down. On a hanger on a back hook she found Alex's favorite jacket, made of silky blue cotton and lined with soft flannel, with elastic black knit ribbing at the waist and cuffs like a baseball jacket. When she slipped her hand into one of its pockets, she touched a squash ball and a

173

little nest of rubber bands, and stood tingling with the most intense recall of her son she had felt in months. It was like holding his hand.

"Are you putting his clothes away?" Graham stood in the doorway in his shorts. His hair was rumpled from sleeping, but his eyes were alert. Though his voice, almost a whisper, seemed to reach out to support her, she had started when he spoke.

"No," she said, "getting out his fall things."

"Oh," said Graham after a long pause. He went into the bathroom and shut the door.

ROBERT HAD RENTED a house in Nantucket for August, and he invited his parents and Susan and Graham to come for Labor Day. Graham wanted them to go.

"It's the big party weekend . . . Robert will want us all to go to a yacht-club dance dressed as chickens," said Susan.

"Well, we won't," said Graham, putting his arms around her. "We'll go sailing by ourselves, and we'll eat a lot of steamer clams, and we'll sleep in the sun."

"Do you really want to go?" she asked.

"I think Mother and Dad would like to see us . . ."

"I know. They would."

"And I hate to turn Robert down—I owe him a hell of a lot of money." He smiled. "Anyway, he sounded lonely."

"Well," she said.

"And I think it might make you feel good."

She didn't answer.

"And I'm lonely too." She immediately felt this remark as from his whole body, warm against her, and she felt a twinge of panic that turned to resentment as it reached her consciousness, as the first snow turns to rain when it strikes the gritty, not-yet-cold-enough pavement, coldness being relative.

"Okay," she said, turning away from him. "I guess it will be okay."

THE EVENING before they were to leave, the phone rang while

Susan was packing. Graham answered it.

"Who is this?" she heard him say. She put down the clothes she was folding and went to the top of the stairs to listen.

"Where in Toronto? . . . Why didn't you call us before? . . . When was the last time you saw them? . . . How can you be so sure?" She went quickly into the bedroom and picked up the extension.

"I'm on the upstairs phone, Graham. This is Mrs. Selky."

The voice on the other end, young, husky, and nervous, said, "Oh, hello," and started again.

It was a woman living in Toronto; her married sister, she said, lived down the hall from a young couple who'd been trying for years to adopt a baby. This June they had suddenly turned up with a nice bright little six-year-old boy. The boy, the caller said, bore a powerful resemblance to Alex.

"Did you call the Toronto police?" Graham asked. No, she hadn't. She only visited her sister now and then, and she didn't always happen to see the boy. She'd actually seen him only three times, and her sister said, "Don't be ridiculous. They got tired of waiting for an infant and adopted an older child, they're a lovely couple." But if he's such a nice bright child, why wouldn't he have been adopted before? It's the retards or children with harelips or something who knock around foster homes all their lives—that's what she'd understood. Her sister had said maybe he had a harelip and they got it fixed. Healthy white children were in great demand, weren't they?

"How do you know he's so healthy and bright?" asked Susan.

She had talked to him. She stopped him in the hall one day last week and had a long interesting talk with him. "He was bright as a button, and not a bit shy. He said his name was Ronny. I asked him if he'd ever lived in Boston, but he said he didn't think so. Then the mother came along and she didn't look at all pleased. She rushed him off into the apartment and she gave me a strange look. I've seen you on television, Mrs. Selky."

"But why did you wait so long?" Graham asked again. "Why didn't you call us the first time you saw him?"

"My sister mentioned on the phone tonight that the family is moving. The couple with the little boy. The mother mentioned that her husband got a better job in California, and they were leaving right away. I didn't tell my sister I was going to call you. I hung up and thought about it a long time. But I just felt there was nothing else I could do.'' Would she talk to the police? Would she give her name and address? She would rather not. She gave the name, address, and apartment number of the couple with the little boy, then she said she was terribly sorry and hung up.

Susan ran down the stairs. Graham was sitting on a stool in the kitchen, leaning heavily forward on his elbows with his chin on his hand, staring at the phone.

"What do you think?" she asked.

He didn't look up. "I don't know. . . . What do you think?"

"Well, I thought she sounded *compos mentis*."

"*She* believes what she's saying."

"Yes, she believes it."

Graham closed his eyes for a minute, as if overcome with fatigue.

"I think I ought to call Al."

"That's what I thought you were going to say."

She looked at Graham sharply, but he wasn't looking at her.

PAT AND THE CHILDREN were already in the car when the phone rang. Al heard it only because he'd gone back to the carport for some clothesline with which to tie his suitcase to the roof. The kids got restless sitting in the hot car for so long, waiting for him to come back; it was a steaming-hot evening. When he finally walked back out to the car without the clothesline and walked around to Pat's window on the passenger side, she said, "Let me guess. That was Susan Selky on the phone, and we're not going."

"I'm sorry," he said. "Listen, you go ahead. I'll join you as soon as I can—maybe I can get there for tomorrow night." In the backseat the kids had stopped chattering and shoving each other, and now Eugene wailed, "Daddy!"

"And how the heck are you going to get to the Cape without a car? Swim? Let me unpack your water wings."

"Oh, jeez." He'd forgotten he'd left his car at his brother-in-law's service station to have the brakes fixed.

"So I'll have to rent a car."

"On Labor Day weekend? Good luck."

"Pat, I'm sorry. Something came up, and that's life, okay? Tell Sam and Sandra I'm sorry, I'll be there as soon as I can."

"Al, how long is this going to go on?"

"I don't know! Look, you've got to get moving or you won't get there until midnight. I'll see you as soon as I can."

Pat slid over to the driver's side. She started the car. "Al? I would seriously like this to be the last time this happens for a while. This has not been a lovely summer."

"One way or the other . . . I don't think it will be much longer."

"Okay," she said to the backseat, "who gets to ride up here with me? I'm thinking of a number from one to ten . . ."

He watched how she backed out of the driveway, and hoped she'd slow down once she was out of sight.

WHEN SUSAN hung up from calling Al, Graham was still not looking at her. "Well?" he said.

"Well? Well. He's going to have to get authorization, he's going to get in touch with Toronto police, and he's going to have it checked out."

"I bet it wasn't his first choice for how to spend the weekend."

"He didn't say. He just agreed that we couldn't not check it out and he'd get right to work."

"And what about us?" asked Graham.

"What about us?"

"Yes, what about us? I notice you didn't give him Robert's number in Nantucket. Does that mean we're not going?"

"Well, Graham, what if they need us to identify him very quickly? What if he could be on his way home? Should we be somewhere fogged in where it could take us days to get back?"

"Susan, what did Al think the odds were that this will be Alex? How many leads like this have they tracked down so far?"

"He didn't say anything about odds—the odds are fifty-fifty. Either it is Alex or it isn't."

"The odds aren't fifty-fifty, Susan."

She looked at him stubbornly.

"I think we should go to Nantucket," he said.

"And do what? Sit by the phone all weekend out there?"

"I think we should go to Nantucket, Susan, and go sailing and eat steamers and sleep in the sun. I think we should decide to live."

"As in 'live it up'? Goodness, Graham, don't let me keep you. Maybe Robert has party streamers and funny hats."

He looked at her hard. "If not now, then when? If you don't come this time, will you next time?"

"I don't know."

"If we don't go this time and the phone rings next time, will we unpack our bags and sit back down?"

"I don't know."

"How long will we let it go on, Susan? The rest of our lives?"

"*I don't know!*"

"Well, I'm going to go to Nantucket tomorrow morning. I'd like you to go with me."

"And if I don't?"

"There's no 'if you don't.' That wasn't a threat, I just would like you to go with me."

"But if I don't? Not this time *or* next time or next time? When does it become a threat, Graham?"

They looked at each other with long steady stares.

"I don't know," he said finally.

"Well, I guess we'll see," she said.

SO HE WENT to Nantucket by himself and she spent a long, nearly silent weekend in the deserted city. The sidewalks and even the leaves in the trees out her window seemed to glitter with the heat and the brilliance of the sun. Even Margaret was out of town for the weekend. Susan sat quietly in the house, dark by contrast to the light outside, waiting for the phone to ring. It took until Saturday for Al to cope with the holiday absences and international red tape and arrange to have the Toronto police go to investigate the report, armed with specially expressed photographs of Alex, all the most recent ones she had.

It wasn't until twilight Saturday that Al called her back. "I'm sorry," he said. "It looks legit. The couple haven't been

178

out of Canada since last summer, and they have the boy's birth certificate and all the adoption papers in order. On Monday we'll talk to the agency that arranged the adoption, but from here it looks pretty cut-and-dried. Toronto says he does look like Alex. Does Alex speak any French?"

"No."

"This boy is bilingual."

Something beneath her rib cage leaped and tore. These slams of pain were so physically felt, she wondered if it were possible to go on taking them without the inner fibers beginning to actually shiver apart, like the creak and scream of a wooden boat breaking up in a storm.

"Oh," she said. "Well . . . I suppose I should be getting used to this." Did she suppose that? Should she be? Not only was she not getting used to it, it was getting worse instead of better.

"Yes," said Menetti.

"Sorry about your weekend. Will you be able to join your family now?"

"I think I'd better. If I get down tonight, I can at least spend half a day on the beach before it's time to drive back."

"I'm sorry."

"Comes with the territory. Well . . . I better get on the road. You take care, now."

"Yes, I will. Drive carefully."

She tried to reach Graham in Nantucket, but the phone in Robert's house rang and rang and rang with that particular high tinny overtone, a summer-house sound.

On Sunday afternoon, on the spur of the moment, she dialed Philippe's number. He answered after the third ring and he sounded very absent.

"Oh . . . I'm sorry, did I wake you? It's Susan."

"Susan. Oh, no, that's all right. Is anything the matter?"

"No, not at all. I'm sorry if I disturbed you. . . . No, I was just thinking, and it occurred to me you never said if you went to that channel person to ask the spirit about Alex."

"Oh," Philippe said. "Didn't I? Yes, I went. It was peculiar."

"Do you have a minute to tell me about it?"

"Sure, Susan. Just hold on a minute." After a brief silence, he was back. "Well, it was in this big apartment over in the Fenway; the elevator was broken and we had to walk up. There's an enormous living room, with lots of furniture, but we all sat on cushions on a rug in the middle of the floor. Ray lit candles, and he had a big vase of fresh flowers on the floor beside him. We meditated for a little while, and then they started asking questions."

"What kind of questions did they ask?"

"Oh, the first girl was the most interesting. She said her neighbors had this sick little baby and the doctors said it had colic. Yasha Masha thought about the baby and said it was constipated and they should feed it apple juice, but first they should put a rubber glove on and cover a finger with Vaseline and reach in and unplug its little hole."

"You're making this up, Philippe."

"I'm not. I asked the girl if she thought this would save the baby, but she said, oh, no, her neighbors didn't believe in Yasha, they only believed in doctors. I've worried ever since about whether that poor little plugged-up baby popped."

"And then what?"

"Well, then some other people asked questions, and then I asked if he knew anything that had happened to Alex, and he thought about it awhile and then he said, 'The earth weeps.' That's all he would say."

"Oh," said Susan.

"But don't be depressed, he said that all the time. He isn't very interested in human affairs, although he's a little interested in babies. He's interested in us as a species and what a mess we're making of the planet, so when you ask him a question that he thinks is too specific or something, he just says, 'The earth weeps.' He's been like that since Three Mile Island."

"I see," said Susan. "Well, I just suddenly remembered you hadn't told me how that came out. I'm sorry if I interrupted something."

"No, that's all right. I'm sorry I forgot to tell you about it. I'll see you on Tuesday."

SHE DID NOT, however, see him on Tuesday. Monday evening of Labor Day weekend, Philippe had a date with an old friend who lived over a bar on Boylston Street. They were going to try a new Hunan restaurant in Central Square, and after that, "Who knows?" as his friend had worded the invitation. But Philippe arrived early and got no answer when he rang the buzzer in the narrow entryway to the staircase. He wished his friends could afford his professional services. The tiny white tiles of the floor inside the street door were black with grime, and while he stood before the bank of tin-faced mailboxes, he saw an enormous cockroach appear from a crack at the floor line and stroll brazenly into the open. Philippe squashed it with his boot and went quickly outside to the summer evening. It had been a warm day, but the warmth was fading with the glow of light. Fortunately Philippe had caught up his jacket from the closet when he left the house early that morning. Jacket time again, the first sure sign of fall, he'd thought. He sat down on a bench across the street and settled himself to watch the twilight and wait.

He noticed the boy walk past him the second time, if such an idle observation could be called noticing. He thought dimly that the boy had already cruised him once. When he came by a third time, slowly, sauntering, and looked at Philippe, Philippe glanced up. The boy was very slight, with dark hair and eyes, and long black eyelashes that seemed to cast deep bluish shadow beneath his eyes. "Mister," said the boy very softly, "do you have a match?" And he took a cigarette from his pocket and held it up for a moment before he placed it slowly and deliberately between his lips, his eyes firmly on Philippe as he did so.

"No, I doooon't," said Philippe. "I don't smoke. And you shouldn't either, you're much too young!"

181

The boy laughed. "No, I'm not," he said. He put the cigarette back in his shirt pocket and sat down on the bench beside Philippe.

"Besides, it's not good for you."

"I'm sixteen," said the boy, turning to look at Philippe. Philippe took in the slender small body and the smooth face without a shadow of beard, and sincerely doubted it. "It doesn't matter," said the boy. "I don't need to smoke." And he settled himself contentedly and began to gaze at the violet sky to the west, as Philippe had been doing. Philippe was extremely conscious of the boy's utter childlike relaxation. He seemed to have settled at once into a sort of concentrated trance, aware only of what he was looking at. As the minutes passed, however, Philippe felt, in a disquieting tumescence in his trousers and the raising of the hair along his arms, extremely aware of the languorous presence of the boy.

After a while the boy began to hum to himself, as if he'd forgotten he wasn't alone. He shifted and dropped his hands onto his lap and sat there humming. He seemed so innocently at home in his skin, Philippe was convinced that he gave no thought to what was beneath his own hands in his own little groin. But Philippe couldn't help noticing.

The boy went on humming. He began to keep time with his tune with a gentle brushing of his index finger, and it happened that it brushed again and again over the soft suggestion of flesh just beneath his zipper. Philippe stirred inadvertently and suddenly crossed his legs. The boy went on humming and tapping himself and staring at the sky. Philippe stole a glance sideways at the dreamy profile and then at the little hand and its tapping. He tried to see if there was any hint of stiffening flesh. Guiltily he glanced back at the dreaming black eyes and found himself caught. The boy had turned his face to Philippe, and the wide, direct innocence of his look seemed to reach directly to his heart.

"Feel like a walk?" the boy asked softly.

Philippe looked up and down the street. As the light deepened, there were more and more sleek young men cruising idly along the sidewalks. He saw no sign of his friend.

"Why not?" he said, standing. He had to give his trousers a hitch. The boy rose too, sauntered off up the strip in the direction of Herbie's Ramrod Room, and Philippe walked along a little behind him, noticing the light, athletic assurance of the boy's stride. They made no attempt at conversation.

After a block or two, the boy turned down a deserted street. Philippe followed him to a big Dodge van, newly painted a metallic bronze color. Along the side of the driver's door it said in curly white letters, "Le Machine." The boy opened the back door and climbed in, beckoning Philippe to follow. He pulled the doors shut behind them.

Then he stretched out on his back on the mattress that filled the entire floor of the van and gazed at Philippe from under his long eyelashes. His eyelids dropped, and in the dim light Philippe watched the smooth face in fascination as it relaxed into the apparent innocence of a little child going to sleep.

"Are you drowsy, little man?" Philippe whispered softly. The boy nodded. The eyelids fluttered closed. The boy began to breathe deeply, and with dreamy abandon slipped one hand onto his groin and began to stroke himself. Philippe, greatly stirred, looked away. In a net hammock hanging against the side of the van he noticed a nest of objects—a belt, some soft cotton rope, a large kerchief.

"What are these?" he asked softly, swinging the hammock so it bumped against the wall. The boy didn't open his eyes.

"Sometimes I'm bad," he whispered in a voice that sounded high and shy and young.

"You are?" whispered Philippe.

"Yes," said the little voice sadly. The boy was stroking himself firmly, and Philippe could see for sure that his young flesh was swelling with each caress.

"I'm being bad now," he added.

"You are?" Philippe repeated stupidly. He was dazed, in a dream of watching the little hand.

"Yes. Very bad." A tiny soft groan escaped his throat. "I'm not allowed . . . it gets me all hard . . . see?" he asked appealingly. "Feel. Feel." Philippe felt, and indeed, what he felt was stiff and straining with life. The boy moaned and began to rotate his hips very slightly as Philippe stroked him through the cloth of his jeans.

"Sometimes," the boy whispered, "my hands need to be tied . . . to keep me from being bad."

"Oh . . . you are a bad boy."

"Very bad . . . I have to be tied," he moaned sorrowfully. He held his slender hands out before him, his eyes now open and fixed pleadingly on Philippe.

Philippe took the rope from the hammock and used it to tie the boy's hands together at the wrists. "Such a bad boy."

"Yes," the boy said, and rolled over, as if overcome with guilt. He pressed his face into the pillow and his groin urgently against the mattress. "I get so hard. . . . Don't spank me. Please don't spank me."

Philippe was on his knees, his eyes and then his hands on the perfect squirming round buttocks. "I'm afraid I'll have to spank you," he whispered.

"No, no," moaned the boy, squirming. Philippe pulled him to his hands and knees, and kneeling behind him, reached around to unfasten the boy's pants and slide them down. The boy's white hips gleamed like ivory in the dim light.

Philippe reached into the hammock for the broad leather belt and folded it in his hand. "I'm afraid I'll have to spank you."

"Oh, please," moaned the boy. The folded belt slapped against the white buttocks, making a loud sound, nearly all leather on leather. "Oh, don't hurt me," the boy cried, and Philippe reached around to fold his big hand over the small stiff phallus and hairless balls, like little walnuts. Both groaned loudly at the same moment, and the boy pushed and thrust his penis against Philippe's cupped hand. It was so like touching his young self.

"I'll be good. Don't hurt me," the boy begged, and the belt slapped again with a loud stingless smack. The boy cried out, and Philippe stroked him harder. Philippe, panting with passion, could feel the hot tip of the boy's penis as he raced to contain the boy with one hand while he freed his own swollen member with the other. He was just at the point of entering the little buttocks, while the boy, hands bound and head bowed, whimpered and squirmed against his big hand, when the door of the van crashed open and they became a tableau, silhouettes in shrieking white light.

"Oh, Jesus," whispered Philippe. He dropped the belt in his hand and sat down hard.

184

The boy, only momentarily frightened, yelled, "You sons of bitches!" with a ferocity that startled Philippe.

"Police! Shut up, you little whore," the voice roared, seeming to vibrate off the walls as if shouting into a barrel at vermin trapped in the bottom. "Now, get the hell down out of there!" Philippe turned to see in the doorway a pair of men in standard vice-squad undercover issue. The short one wore a long black mustache and a denim jacket with the sleeves cut off. The other, the one holding the flashlight, wore baggy shorts with many pockets, and running shoes. With a sinking heart Philippe realized he'd seen him before. Two nights ago, he'd thought with a twinge of excitement, that this same fellow was following him home.

"Now, button up and get the hell out of there, you dumb faggot," snarled the one in shorts.

Dumb faggot is right, thought Philippe. He had to stand on his knees in the cramped space, struggling to stuff his shirttail and himself back into his pants. He quickly scrambled out of the van, and before he could even see it happen, Mustache had him in handcuffs.

"Boy, when you decide you're tired of keeping your nose clean, you go for broke, don't you, big boy? Beating and sodomizing a twelve-year-old—"

"I'm fourteen," snapped the boy, who had squirmed out of the van feet first and was standing holding his pants up with his hands still tied.

"Oh, look, how thoughtful—already tied up. See, Jerry? We won't need the junior handcuffs."

"He said he was sixteen!" said Philippe.

"And you believed him, didn't you, you dumb shit pansy? Jesus, you disappoint me. You really do. Get your hands up on the side of that truck."

The cop whirled Philippe around, knocked his joined hands upward, gave him a shove so that he caught himself leaning against the truck, and a kick on the inside of the ankle to make him spread his legs. Philippe felt him roughly and quickly slapping along his back and sides and down his legs. He had to make an effort not to wince, the hands pounded so hard.

"Christ, I wouldn't be surprised if you get off on this . . . What's this?" He pulled a ball of cloth out of Philippe's jacket pocket. "What the hell is this?" he heard the cop say again, and the tone in the voice caused a cold frightened sweat to begin at Philippe's scalp. What on earth was it? What did he have in the pocket? He hadn't had the jacket on since spring.

"Jerry, hold the flashlight over here, will you?"

There was a long silence, during which Philippe could tell by the movement of the light on the ground that the two were standing side by side staring at whatever it was. Finally one of them said, "You better turn around, you fucking creep."

Philippe turned, his cuffed wrists dropped before him, and he stood impotently staring. In the white glare of the flashlight, they held up a pair of small boy's underpants for him to see. The leg holes had been cut up the sides so that the garment opened out like a diaper. It was soaked with stiff brown dried blood. In the waistband, beside the label, Philippe knew without having to read it that the name tape said Alex Selky.

The two cops were staring at him with icy murder in their eyes. "You filthy shit!" snarled the tall one suddenly, and launched a kick at Philippe's groin.

"Hey, cool it." Mustache grabbed his partner as Philippe doubled over soundlessly. "I want this bust clean enough to eat off of."

"You're just lucky I was wearing sneakers, you screaming prick," said Shorts. He spat at his shoe as if his mouth were full of evil slime. He glared at Philippe, quivering. Then quickly he gathered a second mouthful of slime and spit it at Philippe's face. "You are under arrest. You have the right to remain silent." He spat the words as if they too were slime in his mouth.

"I'm calling a squad car," said Mustache. He stopped to handcuff the boy, now flattened of bravado and staring at Philippe, to the handle of the van. "Listen good, Cinderella. These are your rights too." Then he jogged off toward the edge of civilization, the sidewalk along Boylston Street.

"If you choose to speak, you filthy faggot, anything you say may be used against you . . ."

In the black clammy shadow of the deserted alley Philippe watched the gays gathering, far up the street, in the circle of light in front of the Ramrod Room. Only the throbbing bass track of the music from inside could be heard, and the thick

186

crowd of patrons in the warm night outside seemed to stand or shift or thread among each other in near-silence.

THE PHONE on the nightstand by Susan's bed was an instrument, not a tool as a chisel is the tool of a sculptor, but as a prophet is an instrument of God. It was not within the realm of possibility that there be no shaping intelligence to determine what came out of the telephone. When she opened her heart to hope or pray, Susan often stared at the telephone. If it were a funnel through which all the news of the workings of the universe were compressed and piped to her, so also could her grain of faith press through the same wires to where it could expand outward and make itself felt, ticking and tripping and growing through the clockwork of the world until it found its heart. Bring my boy back. Bring my boy back.

On the morning of Tuesday, September 2, a little after dawn, the telephone elected to bring her the information that Henry Sullivan, known to her as Philippe Lucienne, had been arrested and formally charged with the crime of kidnapping in the first degree, for the theft and presumably the murder of her son, Alexander Graham Selky, Jr. The afternoon paper carried the fullest story. "POLICE BREAK SELKY CASE" ran the headline.

The story read:

Police announced in the small hours of the morning that after months of painstaking detective work, they have arrested a suspect in the case that has baffled the city, the disappearance of six-year-old Alexander Selky a block from his home in Back Bay on May 15 of this year. Arrested tonight is Henry Sullivan, 42, a self-confessed homosexual and a convicted child molester who has worked as a houseboy in the Selky home for over two years. Police say that although Mr. Sullivan, who calls himself Philippe Lucienne, passed a lie-detector test in the days just after the boy's disappearance, he has been under close observation for several weeks.

Detective Menetti, whose dedication to the solving of this mystery is likely to win him high commendation from the department, explained this morning:

"I suspected from the beginning that the kidnapper had to be someone the boy knew. Everything about the case pointed to that, but it was only after weeks of checking police records from all over the country pertaining to this type of crime did we happen to discover Mr. Sullivan's true identity and previous record. At that time we began to recheck his alibi for the day of May 15 and those following, and when we found a number of serious discrepancies, the decision was made to put him under surveillance."

The trail that eventually led to Mr. Sullivan's arrest began with the discovery here that Mr. Sullivan had served eighteen months in prison in the state of Utah following his conviction in Salt Lake City in 1959 for sodomy, homosexual rape, and impairing the morals of a minor.

Evidence began to mount when police discovered that a neighbor of John Murchison, a wealthy art dealer who also used Mr. Sullivan's services as a housecleaner, repeatedly saw Mr. Sullivan enter Mr. Murchison's lavish duplex apartment on Beacon Hill during the days immediately following the Selky boy's disappearance. She was aware that Mr. Murchison was away in Europe for the week.

The neighbor, whose information has been corroborated by others on the block, said that at one point Mr. Sullivan arrived carrying groceries and that during the nights in question there were sometimes loud noises coming from the apartment that could have been part of a scuffle or struggle. On one occasion a youth of about seventeen was seen leaving the apartment with Mr. Sullivan. Police are attempting to locate this youth as a possible accomplice in the kidnapping.

Questioned more than a month after the event, Mr. Murchison was able to remember that although his apartment seemed to be in order when he returned home, he had shortly after that discovered that one of his bath towels had been neatly folded and placed in his linen closet in such a way as to conceal several large brown stains. At the time he

...umed that one of his girlfriends had stained the towel and ...n reluctant to admit it.

On the night before Mr. Murchison was to return, the ...eighbor, whom police have not identified, apparently ...eard screams and loud noises coming from the master-...athroom area, where Mr. Murchison has a large Jacuzzi ...ath. The noises were followed by sounds of the Jacuzzi bath being filled and refilled, which police explain can be heard in the pipes which run up through the building from one apartment to the next. Late that evening, Mr. Sullivan was seen leaving the apartment carrying two large plastic garbage bags.

Police say that a court-authorized wiretap on Mr. Sullivan's phone has turned up ample evidence that Mr. Sullivan's sexual tastes are frequently violent, but have produced only veiled references to the Selky boy specifically. Friends have testified, however, that he was "distraught" over the boy's disappearance, and indeed one went so far as to say he was "obsessed" about it. Mr. Sullivan was apparently keeping a file containing clippings of all the press reports on the case, although police say that a search of his apartment has not turned up either the clippings or any of the boy's personal effects except for a pair of little socks and a collection of Spiderman comics, known to be Alex Selky's favorite. The search did reveal an extensive collection of photographs of naked boys and men and a wide range of products, including a whip, a lariat, and two sets of handcuffs, apparently purchased over a period of years from shops specializing in erotic paraphernalia related to sado-masochistic and bondage practices.

Police admit that up until last night their case against Mr. Sullivan seemed to be at a stalemate. Detective Menetti explained: "I have two witnesses who put him at the scene of the abduction the morning Alex disappeared, although he has sworn he was somewhere else. It would have been a simple matter for Mr. Sullivan to persuade the boy to accompany him, since Alex knew and trusted him. The teenage boy later seen with Mr. Sullivan may have been involved as a driver. The Murchison apartment provided a perfect hideout, but at the end of the weekend, when Mr.

189

Murchison was due to return, I believe the suspect realiz[e]
that he could neither release the boy nor continue to ho[ld]
him. At that time, I believe that he murdered him, draine[d]
his body of blood in the Jacuzzi bath, and divided his bod[y]
between two plastic bags so that neither bag would break
when he carried it down the stairs. The bloodstained towel
would have provided further physical evidence, but since
that has been destroyed, we have been concentrating our
efforts on finding the accomplice. We just got lucky.''

Detective Menetti referred to the fact that Monday night
two undercover investigators observed the suspect in the
company of a teenage homosexual prostitute. At the time of
his arrest the suspect had bound the frightened boy with a
rope and was beating him preparatory to committing
deviate sexual intercourse. In searching the suspect for addi-
tional weapons, the arresting officers found in his pocket a
slashed and bloodstained pair of underpants bearing the
name tag of the missing little boy.

"I'm just glad it's all over," said the exhausted Detective
Menetti, who had spent most of his Labor Day weekend
investigating one of the thousands of leads and clues that
have come in since the boy disappeared, this time a rumor
that he was living with a couple in Toronto. "I've thought
for a long time we knew our man, but we needed help to
make our case, and now someone gave it to us. I thought if it
ever came, it would be from the Almighty, not the suspect
himself."

The district attorney's office says that they plan to fore-
stall a preliminary hearing and proceed directly to the grand
jury, asking for an indictment on first-degree kidnapping as
well as the lesser offenses relating to the suspect's assault on
the boy with whom he was found Monday night. Under the
state penal code, kidnapping in the first degree includes a
case in which the person abducted dies during the abduction
or before he is able to return or to be returned to safety.
Death is presumed, when the kidnapped person was less
than sixteen years old, from the fact that his parents, or
guardians, did not see or hear from him following the
abduction and received no reliable information during this
period indicating that he was alive. The penalties for the

crime of first-degree kidnapping are the same as for first-degree murder.

AFTER THE FIRST DEATH, there is no other. But Graham and Susan had lost their child so many times. Graham's mourning was ferocious, like a man who walks deliberately into the heart of a storm and opens his coat to it and uncovers his head. Susan's grieving instead seemed to be held inside her, as slow-burning hardwood holds the heat, or a well-tempered carbon knife holds an edge. She had lost her son; she had lost her own youth. Within her, as if in every cell, was something that would never cease to ache. That anguish was all that remained of her son's life. Her grief, closed within her, was all the grave her son would ever have.

And God gave his only begotten Son. Yes. Because if the world could not understand God's love as love, it could at least understand the loss of a child, which even to God is the worst the heart can suffer.

The first night, Susan dreamed of Alex, the first time in a long while. She had been afraid of losing him. She had tried to remember exactly the way his hair fell across his forehead and to picture what he'd been playing with the last night they were together as he sat on the floor of his bedroom in pajamas while she read to him, but she could not. But he was there in her, deep beneath the rind of her consciousness, and he was walking between her and Graham in the dream, holding both their hands. It was spring, and they walked through a park that was mounded high with pink and white azaleas blooming on high green bushes. The park was full of people who were dressed up. Susan felt the luxurious liberty of her jeans and her sneakers as other women tripped along in high heels, and she felt that she and Graham and Alex were the only ones who hadn't been to church. Over the vault of treeline the sky was a cathedral. She felt Alex's hand in hers, and her heart glowed in her chest, as if it were full of sunlight.

Sometime during the second day she said to Graham,

"When he disappeared, there was a place in me that was thrilled. 'All right,' I said, 'this is what you waited for all your life. Now you'll find out what life is really like. You'll find out what real pain is, and then you won't have to be afraid of what you're missing.' But life is what I lost. Now I'm afraid of everything."

Graham nodded.

Later she added, "I never thought I'd admit that I felt that, the first day. I think that's the worst thing I ever admitted."

Graham nodded again.

Once, after long silence, Graham looked up at her with an expression almost of surprise and said, "This is going to go on forever, isn't it?"

They were both dry-eyed almost the whole time through those first three nights and days, walled up in their house, while a high storm streamed outside. They were both almost silent themselves. Once, late at night, Susan tried reading the Bible. A ribbon between the tissue-thin, gilt-edged pages, probably there since Sunday school, marked a chapter in Deuteronomy. "I have set before you life and death, blessing and cursing; therefore, choose life, that both thou and thy seed may live. . . ."

"My seed," said Susan.

TJ and Annie came, Susan's father and Connie came, Robert and Graham's parents came. Then, once they got there, nobody knew what to do. The press was encamped on the front steps so that neither Graham nor Susan could leave the house. They kept the phone off the hook. Margaret Mayo went in and out for food for them all, and took messages for Susan on her phone downstairs. She brought in the newspapers, and on the fourth day she insisted that Susan read them. By then Philippe had been indicted and arraigned and was being held at the Charles Street jail.

Everyone sat around the house and tried not to talk about what they were thinking about. There was little to distinguish night from day, since the clamor of reporters kept them trapped inside, and there were no set mealtimes, just a clutter of platters of cold food on the dining-room table that Margaret refilled from time to time. The gathering had the air of a wake without a funeral.

Graham's father grew restless and uncomfortable without television the longer he was there. He kept getting up and walking around the room as if he were looking for something. He tried reading the book Susan had written on Willa Cather but couldn't seem to get past the introduction. He tried to get Susan to explain to him what was meant by a "narrative of place," but she said that was in the book.

"I know it is," he said. "I just thought since we have the authoress . . ." Finally he got up, slapping his hands together as if he'd just had a fine idea, and strode over and turned the set on. He watched a rerun of *Hollywood Squares*, and then came the noon newsbreak.

"Good afternoon," said the announcer. "Cleanup efforts continue around the metropolitan area in the wake of high winds and record-breaking rains. Although winds were below hurricane force by the time the center reached us, damage has been estimated in the millions of dollars, with heavy flooding and parts of Massachusetts and Rhode Island still without electricity."

"We drove through that," said Graham's father.

"Oh, is it noon?" said Graham's mother, noticing the news.

Graham said to Susan, "Nature rages . . . the Pathetic Fallacy, ten points on the mid-term."

"The earth weeps," she said back bleakly. Then she remembered that Graham didn't know the joke. Who did? Philippe.

Philippe appeared on the screen, walking calmly between two huge uniformed policemen. His hands were handcuffed in front of him. He made no attempt to duck or hide his head from the cameras; rather, at one point Susan had the vivid impression that he had looked straight into the camera, and through it, at her. As he appeared, a swarm of reporters with microphones and cameras surged toward him like bugs on a cake crumb, and you could hear the reporters shouting, five, ten, twenty at a time, in overlapping layers of demanding sounds: "Mr. Sullivan, Mr. Sullivan! How do you feel? We understand that you pleaded innocent? Is it true that you refused to see a psychiatrist about a plea of insanity? Are you going to consider Mrs. Pushkin's offer for the exclusive rights to your story? What are you going to say to Mrs. Selky? . . ."

Philippe made his way through them without looking to

right or left and without saying a word. As he got into the waiting police car, she had the impression for the second time that he had looked up into the camera and straight at her.

The announcer's voice was saying, "This was the scene a few minutes ago on the steps of the Suffolk County Courthouse, where Henry Sullivan, the alleged torture murderer of little Alexander Selky, has just been arraigned on a charge of first-degree kidnapping, plus a number of lesser charges stemming from his arrest Monday night in the company of a young homosexual prostitute. Mr. Sullivan pleaded guilty to the lesser charges but not guilty to the charge of kidnapping. As you can see, he would not speak to the reporters who have been waiting here hoping to get a word with him. There was a near-riot here after his departure, as angry demonstrators attacked a small group of gay activists, whom you can see here in the corner of your screen, carrying signs saying, 'Philippe Lucienne is a political prisoner.' There's another one saying, 'No witch hunts.' No one knows exactly what set off the melee . . . here you can see police stepping in to break it up."

At that moment the picture took several zags and pointed toward the sky as the announcer explained that the cameraman had been knocked down, and a voice could be heard shouting, "No pictures of faggots," or perhaps, "No pictures, you faggots." As he fell, the cameraman got one clear shot of a uniformed policeman hitting one of the gay demonstrators with his nightstick. The shot changed to a view of Susan's front door, apparently being taken live about twenty feet from where they sat, giving them the most intense sensation of being beleaguered. The Selkys and Philippe each walled up alone while the vandals howled and hammered around them on the outside.

The announcer was saying, "And at the house where little Alex Selky lived, the scene is unchanged, the family still in seclusion. The boy's grandparents arrived last night, but the only statement so far has come from a friend of the family, Margaret Mayo." Now the door on the screen opened, and they watched a rerun of Margaret's image step out and stop on the front step. She was on her way to work. Her straight iron-colored hair sat on her head like a helmet, and she faced into the lights and waited calmly for the clack of questions to stop being flung at her: "Mrs. Mayo, are you going to give us a statement? How is the family? Have they spoken to Henry Sullivan? Are they surprised? Are you surprised? What kind of person is Mr. Sullivan? Did you have any idea he was under suspicion? Did Mrs. Selky? Are they going to give a statement?"

"Well," she said when there was a lull, "I have something to share with you, but I have no intention of shouting." There was a sudden relative quiet although no pause in the flashing of camera bulbs from the print media. She said, "Two hundred years ago, when a family suffered as this one has, there would be straw put down in front of the house to deaden the sounds of wheels, and horses' hooves would be muffled before they entered the streets. No one expects such a show of civility now, but this family has lost enough. It would be good of you to allow them to mourn in private." There was a brief silence during which Margaret wisely made her way off down the steps before the questions could start again.

"Wish I'd done that," said Susan's father. Susan was obscurely pleased. When she thanked her for it that evening, Margaret smiled her remarkable smile and said, "Yes, sometimes there's comfort in a really fruitless gesture."

SUSAN HAD to go out sometime. She physically shrank from it, as if the lights and questions were birds that would fly at her, scratching and flapping with venomous wings. She was afraid she would be photographed holding her hands before her eyes. At last she made herself walk out the door by pretending she was Margaret. She tried to hold herself as Margaret had, and to wear Margaret's imperturbable expression. When she opened the door, there was a leaping and a clamor of surprise. She stood on the top of the steps, quite silent. The reporters evidently thought she was waiting for quiet so she could speak, but as soon as they stopped shoving at her, she started down the steps. The howl of questions began again. One reporter actually caught her by the arm as he shouted something at her.

She looked at him with patient eyes. She looked down at the hand on her arm; she looked back at him. The hand dropped. She walked on down the steps and gained the sidewalk. Then she walked away. After two days of this, the group thinned out, then gave up and finally disappeared.

SHE SPOKE to no one about how deeply she dreaded her first day of teaching again. Every step she took in the direction of a normal life was a step away from her lost child. In the early morning of the first day of classes she had a waking dream that she was walking to the podium in the lecture hall with hundreds of eyes turned on her like lenses. Then, when she started to speak, she couldn't hear her own voice. Instead she heard Alex crying. Only she would hear him, ever again.

Graham's first lecture of the term was the same morning as hers. She knew he hadn't slept well either. But when he had finished dressing and had his coffee, he said, "I'm glad it's here. I'm glad to have something I have to do." He kissed her on the cheek and wished her luck.

She was looking over her notes from the opening lecture for last year when TJ appeared in the living room.

"Oh," she said, "Graham's already left . . ."

"I know. This is the neighborhood escort service."

"Ah." She went through the notes one more time while TJ sat down at the edge of a chair and waited. He kept his car keys dangling in his hand.

"I just look at one of these headings," she said, nodding at the card she was holding, "and the tape in my brain where I stored the lecture starts to roll. I see 'Christ-haunted South,' and out that all comes."

"That's good." He looked at his watch. She didn't get up.

"TJ, I really don't want to do this."

"But you're going to," he said.

"At least you can't say I should do it because Alex would have wanted me to. Alex would have wanted me home."

"You're going to do it for yourself," he said.

"Oh, TJ . . . imagine having no reason but myself to do anything."

He saw the panic begin to tremble in her. "Come on," he said. "Move."

SINCE PHILIPPE'S arrest, a wave of homophobia had swept the city. A total of seventeen men had been set upon and savagely beaten on successive dark nights by a gang of teenagers in the park around the Fen. The papers identified this as a "well-known place of assignation for gay men." The papers expressed a pious shock at learning that several of those hospitalized were prominent businessmen with wives and families, and a professional ice-hockey player had been clubbed so badly that he eventually lost one eye.

The papers kept the story alive for days by discovering or inventing fresh details that would allow them to reprint the whole story. "Witness remembers: They were shouting 'Queers kill kids!' " Or, "Police say they have no clue to the identity of the gang of pipe-wielding youths who . . ." Or, "Key witness in gay beatings refuses to press charges. Prominent socialite financier pleads, 'It would ruin me.' "

The man-in-the-street interviews on the evening news were illuminating. Crowds of people smiling and waving at the camera gathered eagerly around Mike Bogan, whom they recognized from TV. "Well, Mike, I think it's sick, it's a crime against God."

"The beatings were a crime against God?"

"No, the homosexuals."

"Mike . . . Mike . . . I think they shouldn't have beat them up, but I think the homosexuals should do it inside in their own houses. I don't care if you're green or blue or polka-dotted or what your preference is, but they shouldn't be having sex in the park, where there are children."

"But there aren't any children in the park at eleven o'clock at night."

"There could be!" cried the woman.

"Mike, Mike! Hi, Mike, I'm from Melrose and . . ."

197

"Mike! I believe the homosexual has his rights, but we have to protect our children . . ."

"Did you know that according to statistics a homosexual is far less likely to molest a child of either sex than a heterosexual?"

Blank look. Voice from the back: "But look at the Selky kid!"

"Yeah, yeah!" Shouts of agreement.

ONE AFTERNOON about a week after classes had begun, Susan found a man waiting for her in the hall outside the room where she met her seminar. "Mrs. Selky," he said, jumping up to walk beside her as she started down the hall. "I'm sorry I didn't make any appointment. I've tried hard to reach you at home, but the line is always busy. Henry gave me your number." He was a tall, soft man with an astoundingly round head. He dipped it shyly when he talked, and she saw that the small round bald spot on top was covered with freckles. "I'm not from the press," he added as she strode down the hall. "I'm Lesley George. I'm Henry's attorney."

"Henry?" She stopped.

"Philippe," he said.

"Oh." She felt a quake of embattled loathing grip her insides, followed by a real fear that she might throw up. This passed quickly. The man's eyes swam behind round wire-rimmed glasses like goldfishes peering out at her from twin bowls. His appearance seemed to give the impression of a series of circles, a soothing infinite form.

"Can I buy you some coffee?" he asked.

"I guess," she said.

"The point is," said the attorney when they were seated over mugs of tea in a booth in the coffee shop, "Henry wants to see you."

"God. Why?"

"To tell you he's not guilty." The round eyes behind their round shields were remarkably ingenuous. Susan found his expression impossible to read. "You're the only one he will see, as a matter of fact. He wouldn't talk to the court's psychiatrist. He tried to fire me the first day I met him because I mentioned the idea of an insanity plea."

198

"I take it you think he did it." She was astounded at the nauseating impact she felt at the same time as she tripped this phrase off her tongue. "Killed my son" was what "did it" meant.

Lesley George carefully placed the fingertips of each hand together and sat looking thoughtfully at the shape these mirror images made when they joined together. He had pushed his lips far out while he was thinking, making a face that looked something like a grouper's.

"I believe he's entitled to the best possible defense. And I believe he stands a very good chance of being acquitted. In spite of all the papers are making of it, the prosecution's case is very weak. I'm not surprised they went straight for the grand-jury indictment; I think if I'd had a preliminary hearing I could have gotten the case thrown out to start with. . . ."

Susan's mouth was dry with fear. Her insides felt as if the acid of her tea had tanned them. The soft tubes and organs were tight as chafed leather. She simply did not believe she could endure to entertain any more ambiguity than she had up to now. The worst had happened. At least the worst was over.

"If I can keep his Utah conviction out of the record—and I ought to be able to—all of a sudden, what have you got left? There's the testimony of the boy they arrested him with. I've talked to the kid, but so have the police, and he'll say that Henry was beating the hell out of him. Henry claims it was just a little slap and tickle, and the kid wasn't bruised . . . so there's testimony but no physical evidence. They've got witnesses that put Henry on Beacon Street the morning your boy disappeared, and that's bad, because he lied to the police about that. The odd thing is, he passed the lie-detector test they gave him in the beginning. He just failed two in a row since he was arrested, but I can keep all that out of the record. Frightened subject. Prejudiced interpretation of the test. That sort of thing."

"What about motive?" Susan whispered.

The lawyer waved his hand. "Don't need a motive in a sex case. Sex is a universal motive. Of course, in Henry's case, his . . . um, particular predilections, which are unfortunately pretty well documented, are going to weigh heavily with a jury. He might even be better off with a court trial . . . but I don't

199

like the odds there. If the one judge you've got happens to hate homosexuals, you're down the tubes. With a jury you have twelve chances to find someone on your side. Against that, a jury doesn't understand the fine points of the law. This trial isn't going to be about kidnapping, it's going to be about rules of evidence.''

"And what about the . . . Alex's . . . in his pocket?"

This time Lesley George looked at her directly. He looked as if he were writing his brief in his mind; his head bobbed slightly as if he had decided to agree with himself. "Henry can explain that," he said. "The blood type on the pants is O-positive. Very common. It's your son's type, and it's also Henry's. He can explain a lot of things. Well enough to create reasonable doubt. . . ."

Susan felt a creeping horror, like a sick chill, as the ambiguity made itself part of her. Was he telling her that Alex was alive, and an innocent man was going to be tried for doing something that might not have happened at all? Or was he saying that the man who murdered her son stood a very good chance of going free?

"I'll see him," she said.

"Well, good. I'll arrange it."

THE ROOM in which Susan waited for Henry Sullivan was walled with large turquoise tiles, like a school cafeteria. There were high bare windows covered with heavy wire like schoolyard fencing, through which slanted bright bars of light jailed behind crisscrossed shadows. A guard sat at a big bare desk with a telephone on it. He wore a pistol in a holster on his hip. An air conditioner whined in the window.

Philippe was led in between two guards, each wearing blue shirts and pistols on their hips. He was wearing bright brown dacron pants, like pajama pants, and an orange shirt of the same material. He sat down at the table across from her with his elbows on the table. They looked into each other's eyes for what seemed a long time.

"*Hypocrite, mon semblable, mon frère*" is what came into her head. Hypocrite, my likeness, my brother. His eyes were bald blue, with gray radial glints around the pupil like spokes on a wheel. Do you not flinch because you are innocent? she asked the eyes, or because you are so guilty?

"Shall I call you Philippe or Henry?" She spoke first.

"Henry."

That surprised her. She also caught, a beat later, that he hadn't pulled the vowel the way Philippe would have: Heeenry. "You wanted to see me?"

He nodded. For a moment he put his hand up, a half-closed fist, and covered his mouth. Then he put it down again quickly, as if he had resolved to conduct this interview without defense.

"Susan," he said, "I am guilty of a great many things. I am, as my stepfather would say, a screaming queer. But I have never in my life knowingly hurt another person who didn't want me to, and I did not, ever, in any way hurt Alex."

Their faces were matched in blankness as they faced each other across the table, like Man and Death playing chess.

"You went to jail for raping a little boy in Utah."

She saw, rather than heard, him sigh.

"Little boy," he said. "When I was in college in Salt Lake City, I had an affair with a freshman. He was a music prodigy. He didn't tell me he was fifteen. His parents found out about it; his father was a leader of the church, and they persuaded him to claim rape. I guess they thought if they changed what it was called, they were changing what it was."

"But you pleaded guilty."

"If you have to ask why, you know nothing about Mormons. Or Utah."

"You lied about being on Beacon Street the morning Alex disappeared."

"No," he said, "I didn't."

"You failed a lie-detector test about it. Twice."

"Susan, I was scared."

"How do you explain two people who say they saw you there?"

"Error. Mistaken identity. I can't. Take your pick."

"What were you doing at Murchison's that weekend if you

didn't have Alex hidden there?"

"If you met somebody you liked and you lived in a fourth-floor walk-up but you had the keys to a duplex apartment with a king-size bed and an owner in Europe, what would you do?"

She looked at him levelly. "You didn't exactly answer the question."

He shrugged. "You understood me. The belief has to come from you, not me."

Susan dropped her eyes before he did. She finally made herself ask, "All right . . . what about what you had in your pocket?" She didn't want to hear the answer. She was afraid she would not believe him and afraid that she would. Resisting, she felt the old hope stir painfully within her, as if someone were inching a huge rock away from the mouth of a cave.

He held up his right hand with his palm facing her, fingers spread. He pointed to the web of flesh that curved from his index knuckle to his thumb. There was a scar an inch long from a cut that must have bitten deep into the thumb muscle.

"At your house. Last spring. I reached into a sinkful of sudsy water and cut my thumb halfway off on a broken glass. I keep rags for dusting under the sink, and I grabbed one. A pair of Alex's underpants. I cut them with the poultry shears and tied the cloth around my hand. I was bleeding all over the place. I started home with my arm above my head and this pair of underpants on my hand, and by the time I got to the subway the bleeding had stopped so I took the bandage off and put it in my pocket and went home."

She looked at him a long time. The truth, whatever it was, was all in his eyes, and she groped in them as if trying to learn some spiritual Braille that would help her to read what was hidden in front of her.

"Did you go somewhere for stitches?"

"I told you . . . the bleeding stopped."

"I see," she said, although she saw nothing. She was feeling.

WITHOUT A PLAN, in a suspension of belief and disbelief, Susan found herself again on Warren Avenue on her way to Menetti's office. She walked up the stairs to the second floor slowly; everything held the rank odor of cigarette smoke. A young black man with the elaborate dusty braids of a Rastafarian paused in his animated talk with a colleague in uniform to stare at Susan, as if it were taking him a moment to place her. She could see him pick her out of his memory bank, then return to his conversation. Before she turned the corner into Menetti's office, she had a sudden intuition of what she would see, and she was right.

Inside, the posters of Alex were all gone. On the bulletin board immediately inside the door was a new poster with a police sketch of a young man who had raped two young girls. "WANTED," said the poster. "HAVE YOU SEEN THIS MAN?"

It was the first time Susan had seen Menetti since Philippe's arrest, though they had talked on the phone. He looked better rested, but he met her with a look of very great sorrow in his eyes. "Come in," he said, and led her into his office. He sat down at the desk and she sat on a straight-backed chair facing him, with her back to the open door. Behind her, at other desks in offices up the hall, the police continued to search for other lost humans.

"How are you?" he asked sympathetically.

"I've been to see Philippe," she said.

Menetti nodded. He sighed. "Never in my life," he said, "have I hoped so much that I was wrong about a case."

"I think you are," said Susan.

"Excuse me?" Menetti had a pretty good idea that he was about to be promoted. He'd been on the news every day for a week. He'd gotten in the rhythm of modestly dismissing his contribution to solving the mystery.

"I think you made a mistake, Al. I don't think he did it."

Al stared at her. His eyes were pale and permanently red-rimmed. Pockets of flesh at his eyes and jowls hung from his face as if they were weighted with sand.

He lit a cigarette. "I see," he said gently. "Well . . . I guess I can understand that. He is very persuasive. I'm afraid that's part of the DA's case against him."

"Al, have you talked to him? You knew him . . . did you give him a chance to explain—?"

"Now, let me explain, let me explain something to you," Al interrupted, still soothing. "Now, it's only a Missing Persons case up till the time that we discover for certain that a crime has been committed, do you understand? He was arrested by Vice, and the case against him, that's handled by Homicide. Of course they keep me informed."

"Al, have you talked to him?"

"Of course I've talked to him."

"Well, did you give him a chance to explain?"

He stubbed out his cigarette impatiently. "Look, you're not following me. The case is out of my hands. Homicide—"

'If I'm not following you, it's because you're not being clear. *Have you heard his explanation?* I'm asking you as a man for your personal opinion."

"Just a minute," said Al. "Just wait here a minute. I'll be right back." He strode out, looking annoyed. Susan did not turn to watch him go. In a minute he strode back into her unshifted field of vision and sat back down in his chair. He dropped a sheaf of papers on the desk in front of him.

"Now," he said, "I want you to follow me carefully. First, this case is not going to be tried in the newspapers. We've got a very strong case against Sullivan, believe me, and you're not going to read the whole prosecution in the *Globe* before they empanel a jury, so—"

"What evidence do you have? Besides the underpants?"

Menetti looked exasperated. "I'm sorry," he said, "but that's just none of your business."

"Oh, really."

"Excuse me . . . I'm sorry. What I meant to say was, the prisoner has a right to a fair trial, and the people have a right to a fair trial against him. There's a gag order on the department, and I'm not going to tell you any more and I'm not going to tell the press. But look, now, here's something I want you to hear. This is a copy of the psychiatrist's record from the court in Utah. This is something I've had in my desk for six weeks. He pleaded guilty to raping a young kid, did you know that?''

"I know that," she said.

"All right, listen to this. 'Herewith is the report of my examination of Henry Sullivan at the county jail on April 3, 1959. Present difficulty. Prisoner gives very sketchy account of why he is in jail. He agrees that on March 19 of this year in the dormitory bedroom of the boy who has brought the charges that he performed an act of deviate intercourse, that he penetrated the boy's rectum with his penis, and that the boy performed two acts of fellatio on him, the accused. He denies that he threatened the boy or that force was involved. . . .

" 'Personal history, nothing unusual; medical history, ordinary childhood diseases, denies venereal disease, denies alcohol or drugs. Family history. Prisoner states that his parents separated when he was eight. That he has three sisters and a half-brother. He has not seen his father since the separation. He clearly remembers being beaten with a curtain rod by his father, once to unconsciousness. Denies knowledge of hereditary mental illness in family.

" 'Arrests. At age twelve, prisoner claims that his stepfather forced him to have homosexual relations with him. His mother refused to believe his account of the event; shortly after that, he was arrested in the company of several other youths and charged with stealing a car in which they were joyriding. He spent one month in the juvenile hall. Two years later he was again arrested for car stealing. He admits to extensive homosexual activity with other inmates while in the juvenile home; he further admits that he has had no normal sexual intercourse with females.

" 'He sees his mother infrequently; he is on poor terms with his mother owing to his hostile relationship with his stepfather. He claims that at one point his stepfather had him arrested on charges of setting the garage on fire, which the prisoner claimed he had not done.

" 'Psychiatric examination. The prisoner answers questions relevantly except on the subject of force or violence, when he becomes evasive. He denies delusions and hallucinations. His memory and mental grasp and capacity are within normal limits. Insight and judgment fair to poor.

" 'Conclusion: Prisoner, who has pleaded guilty to lewd and lascivious conduct, to sodomy and to forcible rape of a fifteen-year-old boy, has shown poor judgment, is rebellious and resentful, and has displayed poor social adjustment since age twelve. Concerning the present offense, he readily admits to the act but is evasive and vague on the subject of premeditation or force, although extensive bruises were found on the victim's back and throat. He denies having had pathological urges prior to this crime.

" 'It is the examiner's opinion that the prisoner is a psychopathic personality. He has clear homosexual drives and a predisposition to commit sexual crimes that make him a menace to society. It is further the examiner's opinion that he is unable to distinguish when and whether he has used physical force and that as this dysfunction alone constitutes a menace to the health and safety of others, it is recommended that he be confined in an institution suitable for the care and treatment of his disorder, namely, sexual psychopath.' "

Menetti finished reading, laid down the papers, and looked at Susan. She appeared lost in thought. "Well?" he said.

"Well . . . was the psychiatrist a Mormon?"

Menetti slapped his hand on the pile of papers and glared at her. "I don't know if he was a Mormon, and I don't care. What do you want from me? Why are you looking at me like that?"

"Like what?" Susan's face was mild, but her eyes were fixed on Menetti's as if they were boring tools.

"Now, *listen*," he said, losing his temper. "I didn't kill your son. All I did was find out who did. *I have done all I can for you* . . . it's over. It's the end of my job. You'll just have to accept that."

"If you're wrong, and I'm right, then there's still a missing person."

He stood up. "You'll have to talk to Homicide, and I've already told you, they can't tell you any more than I have."

"Who are the witnesses who saw Philippe the morning Alex disappeared?"

"I'm sorry . . . there is nothing more I can do for you."

Susan stared at him steadily for a long moment. He glanced out to the hall once—she could feel him weighing the possibility that she was going to refuse to leave the office. When he looked uncomfortable enough that she thought the moment would stay with him, she rose slowly and left of her own accord.

THE CLOCK on the mantel over the fireplace ticked softly in the living room. Outside, the evening sky was streaked with pink. Susan looked ahead in the cold mauve light of it to the long evening ahead, with nothing to do but suit herself. Graham sat at his desk in the corner, working quietly on his Milton book. He had his papers in one pile, and ranged along the back of the desk against the wall, a series of stacked index cards in different colors, containing notes from different sources for different chapters of the book. The lamplight shone on his thick blond hair. She noticed how he sat. No twitching, no twisting a lock of hair, no tapping a pencil. His grief seemed to have coursed through him in one galling dose, leaving behind only this rather frightening, fiercely determined stillness. Somewhere upstairs, at the evening bathtime, bedtime, story time, an idle creak reminded her that there was nothing human up there moving.

"Graham," she said. He held up a hand, without turning, to indicate that he wanted a moment more before being interrupted. Oh, the stillness. No more drilling clamor of the telephone. No meandering friendly chat between them. As much of the future as they cared to contemplate was tomorrow, and they had more than enough reason to avoid the past. The present, without inflection or implication, was all, and they floated in it quietly, side by side.

"Okay," said Graham. He turned his head to her without turning in his chair.

"I went to see Philippe today," she told him.

Now he put down his pen and turned to face her. He

moved reluctantly. "You did?"

"His lawyer asked me to."

"Well," he said. He wasn't asking, but he was going to have to hear.

"He wanted to tell me that he didn't kill Alex."

"Yes, I'm sure he wanted to tell you that." Graham looked at her stolidly. It occurred to her that he had somehow mastered a trick of making no speculations whatsoever, as if the future ceased to exist the moment he finished speaking. Instead of forming an expectation about what was coming next, he subsided.

"I think it's true," said Susan.

Graham just looked at her. He looked a little adrift, as if, like Proust with his madeleine, this remark had set off a chain of absorbing ideas and memories and he was pursuing one and then another. She could see his eyes flick over her, up, inward, out at the night, and back to her.

He said, "No."

"What do you mean, 'no'?"

He stood up from his desk, stretched, hitched his pants, and carefully pushed in his chair. Towering over her, he said, much louder, "No . . . no . . . no! No more." He left the room and went upstairs, and she sat looking after him, stunned. No? No? No conversation even?

She sat for some time listening to him move around upstairs. What was he doing? Not getting ready for bed. Looking for something? What? She listened for a while longer to the rhythm of it, as he crossed to the dresser, walked to the bed, crossed to the closet, and returned to the bed. Finally she recognized it. He was packing.

Cleaning out the nest. Leaving the cell.

She listened then as a lip-reader watches a conversation. There he went into the bathroom for his shaving things; there he was moving the stool to reach the upper shelf of the closet. For what? His running shoes. Feeling well enough to start jogging again. He had been saying so. There he was checking the dresser drawers to see what he forgot, there he was closing the suitcase. There he was walking into Alex's room and standing there in the darkness for a long time.

She heard him bump the suitcase against the banister as he

came down the stairs. He set it down in the kitchen and came into the living room. He looked at her once, with an unreadable expression; then he went over to his desk, picked up and opened his briefcase and set it on his chair, and began packing his cards and papers. What was he challenging her to say? Yes? Yes I want you, yes I believe it's over, yes I want to forget I had a son? Have a son? Yes I surrender Alex so I can love you?

No.

She watched his face while he packed the briefcase, and she could feel that all the while, deliberately holding his eyes away from her, he was having a vivid conversation with her. His heart was so full of needs, of things his mind was saying to her, that he had to keep his lips pressed together to keep them inside his mouth.

At last he snapped the briefcase closed and turned to look at her. He looked slightly flushed. His eyes were filled with a dense, beaten, challenging stare, and as she returned it, the exchange between them was so empty of excuse, blame, hope, or forgiveness that it was loving only in being left unsaid.

As he reached the top of the stairs she said only, "Where would I reach you, if I needed to?"

He said, harshly, as if addressing a child who has deliberately and mischievously hurt herself, "At Naomi's."

He was almost out the door when she suddenly ran to the landing and called down after him, "Wait a minute . . . don't you even have to call her to tell her you're coming?" He just stared at her. Then he shook his head, glaring, and she could see him holding his down-curved lips together to keep in the tears.

SHE HAD CALLED the office of the Gay Activist Alliance and explained that she had a friend who was in jail and she felt that he was innocent; she wanted the name of a lawyer who would be willing to take on a criminal case involving a man being prosecuted for his sexual preferences.

"Why, yes," said the man on the phone enthusiastically.

"Now, here's a name. He's called Auberon Levy. He's very good, he's been looking for a test case like this, too. Tell me, are you related to the fellow in jail, or are you one of our members?"

"No, neither," she said. "Just a friend."

"Are you sure that your friend will permit a defense like this? You'd be surprised, when it comes to publicity."

"I'm not perfectly sure," said Susan, "but I think if I found the right attorney, he would consider it."

"Well, that is just *fine*. Now, please let us know if we can help. What is the nature of the case, by the way?"

"It's a man named Henry Sullivan. He's accused . . ."

But the voice on the other end had issued a resounding "Oh." She stopped. There was a brief silence. "Could you hold on a minute, please?" said her man, and she could hear him talking to someone nearby, through the muffling squeak of his hand over the mouthpiece.

"Is something wrong?" she asked when he came back on the line.

"No," he said. "Go ahead and call Auberon. And we'd be grateful if you'd keep in touch with us about it."

"I will."

"Good luck."

AUBERON LEVY'S office was a stylishly converted store-front off Copley Square, only a ten-minute walk from Susan's house. The entire front of the office was a plate-glass window. At eye level, in large typewriter-style letters, was the legend "Attorney-at-Law." Inside for all to see were a clean white desk and two red plastic Italian folding chairs. Against one wall stood the High-Tech chrome-wire industrial shelving, holding rows of leather-bound law books. In one corner of the bright white room a five-foot-high plastic pencil and a five-foot-long plastic paper clip hung from the ceiling. In one of the plastic chairs, at the desk, typing on the small tidy portable Olivetti, was the lawyer. "Attorney as theater," Jocelyn used to say when they passed it.

Now Susan sat in the second chair, with her back to the audience, and Auberon Levy sat in his chair facing her and the street. He had tufts of curly red hair surrounding the barren field of the top of his head, and cold reddish-brown eyes that went very well with the exposed brick wall behind his desk. Today Mr. Levy was dressed in an imaginative version of an English country lawyer's costume, in tweeds, a yellow vest, and a pair of jodhpur boots that showed off the smallness of his feet. There was a slight undertone of comic fantasy in the way he presented himself, and it was clear to Susan that the tableau was very much for his own enjoyment. Anyone who thought Auberon Levy was the butt of this performance had almost certainly missed the joke.

He had listened with attention, and almost without interruption, to Susan. She had repeated to him everything Philippe had said, and given her impressions of the meeting. She had told him that she had serious doubts as to whether his court-appointed lawyer believed in the innocence of his client.

"I believe he'll do his best, because he's an honorable man," said Susan, "but I also feel sure that if you were interested in joining the defense, or even in taking it over, that he would be relieved. I think that may be part of the reason he came to me."

Levy shifted in his chair. He waited a moment as if to be sure that she had said everything that was on her mind. Then he crossed his arms, looked at her intently, and said, "Well. . . . Well, Mrs. Selky. First, I must say that I hope I haven't wasted your time in agreeing to see you today. I must say, I was curious to meet you. Like everyone else in Boston, I've followed your story with great sympathy, and I was a little piqued to know if you were the woman you appeared to be. Of course, I've seen you on television, and I've been struck by your . . . presence."

Susan didn't know what to say.

"Now. The next thing I want to say is that I know Lesley George, and I think you're quite wrong about him—oh, I don't doubt that he may be unsure of his client's innocence, but I'm quite sure that he would resent my horning in on the case. He's an experienced and committed attorney, and he will certainly give Sullivan the best defense he knows how . . . and that's pretty good. You're probably a lot better off with Lesley than you would be with some passionate *pro bono* straight out of Harvard Law who can quote all of Oliver Wendell Holmes

211

and doesn't know how to find the courthouse.''

"But better off than with you?"

"Ah . . . well. Perhaps not, but aside from the fact that professional courtesy prevents my interfering, unless of course Lesley George asks for me, is the fact I wouldn't touch this with a barge pole.''

A lance of old despair impaled Susan under the breast-bone. It was as if she could see its long shaft quivering between them in the air.

"I'm sorry if I shocked you . . . I didn't mean to sound so rude, but I must say, I intend to make this point with a certain . . . force. The unfortunate truth here is that I am far too old and unromantic to act on an ideal, if I can see clearly that the practical outcome will endanger my cause. 'The greatest good for the greatest number' is a pretty heartless dictum, unfortunately. Do you know Shaw's play *Major Barbara*?''

"Of course," said Susan in a weak voice.

"Do you remember when Barbara confronts her father over the fact that she dedicates her life to pious causes, while his money comes from the evil manufacture of munitions, and he points out that his money is necessary to fund her pious works? The confrontation of Romance and Pragmatism. She cries, 'Who cares if it's true if it's wrong?' and he answers, 'Who cares if it's wrong . . . if it's true?' You notice, Shaw gives him the last word. Good works are expensive.

"Well, that's a roundabout way of saying this: Gay rights are in their infancy; for all practical purposes, they're in the womb, in constant danger of miscarriage. If there is one issue that is a red flag—not just to the fag-baiters, but to the nicest people—it's pederasty. We have some sympathizers who would call it 'boy love,' but as far as I know, it's been called 'child molesting' since the fall of ancient Greece, and we are a very long way from a world or an age that's going to call it anything else.

"You may know, and I know, that by far the majority of child molesters are heterosexual men, and that a homosexual is no more likely to lust after little boys than your Aunt Mabel— but we also know that once in a while Aunt Mabel will surprise you. Once in a long while. Well, no one can keep Aunt Mabel from teaching school, or being a camp counselor, or getting a

212

civil-service job or an apartment, or letting her join the country club, but they sure as hell can stop gays. All we need, Mrs. Selky, is a big splashy nationwide murder case about a swell guy who beats up his lovers and screws teenage boys but who may be innocent of this particular crime, and gay rights go back to the Dark Ages. For one thing, imagine if we mounted a defense identifying Sullivan with gay rights and *lost?* Can you imagine if we came out and said he's a sweet boy being persecuted for being a little funny in the bedroom—and he's convicted?

"I'm sorry if I've been harsh. There are those in the gay community who will not agree with me, of course. But my personal feeling is that this case will be a disaster for gays and that we should do everything in our power to keep from being identified with it."

During this long speech Susan had felt herself growing colder and colder. She felt a deep nauseous fear in the pit of her stomach, and she realized that the wide, unflinching stare in her eyes had to be very like the expression in Philippe's when he walked down the steps to the police car and looked for that one moment directly into the camera. That mingled resignation and disbelief, as if to say, "But this is me we're talking about, a person. Look at who I am, and this will all go away."

"But . . . if he's innocent?"

"Then," said Levy, "I am very, very sorry this is happening to him."

"And my son? If my son is alive? But no one ever again except me will believe it, or keep looking?"

"Then I am very, very sorry for him, and for you. And that is the truth."

Susan rose and shook hands with him. Throughout the meeting she had never doubted that Levy was sincere in his sympathy, and she had no trouble seeing his position. She thought, given his goals, that he was right.

The trouble was, who would understand her position?

And Alex's?

‐‐❦ ❦‐‐

SUSAN PUT in a call to Charlotte Mayhew at *Mother's Day* in New York.

"She's in a meeting," said the secretary at nine in the morning. "Can I tell her what this is in reference to?" Charlotte Mayhew had spent some ten hours in Susan's house less than a month ago, taping interviews and preparing an article on Alex to be entitled "Have You Seen This Child?" She had with her the scrapbook Susan had made up, containing almost all of her photographs of Alex.

"It's in reference to an article she's writing," said Susan. She had to keep calling for three days before Charlotte called her back.

"Susan," said the arch maternal voice. "Oh, I have been praying for you . . . I'm sorry I haven't had a minute to call you back, you have *been on my mind* . . . how *are* you?"

"Fine," said Susan.

"Now, I'm sure you're wanting the photographs back. I'll send them airmail special . . . Give me the address again."

"Charlotte, I want to talk to you about the article. Could we meet? I'd be glad to take the Shuttle down."

"Oh, *yes*, let's do lunch, let me just have my girl check my calendar . . . oh, you know what? Isn't this just disgusting . . . do you know, I don't have a lunch open for the next two weeks?"

"I don't care about lunch, just tell me when would be a good time for us to talk?"

"But I want to *see* you . . . now, what about lunch the second of October, that's a Thursday. There's a restaurant I'm in love with called Hakubai, in a Japanese hotel on Park Avenue South. How's 12:30?"

"But, Charlotte, I'd like to just talk to you sooner about the article."

214

"Well . . . but, honey . . . I'm afraid the thrust of the article was the inspirational approach, your faith and your courage . . . plus the appeal to the readers themselves, the idea that they could *help*. Well, that's how I sold it to the editorial board in the first place, and even then I met a lot of resistance—you know, crime stories are not at all our material . . ."

Susan thought of the weeks of phone calls from this woman last July, to the effect that the editors of *Mother's Day* were unanimous in their feeling that Susan's story was the *Mother's Day* story of the decade.

"But, Charlotte . . ." Susan heard an undertone of pleading in her voice and stopped for a moment. Don't show need, you'll lose her. "But, Charlotte, I don't feel that the nature of the story has changed except that now the magazine itself is in a more heroic role. I'm convinced that the police have made a mistake." She paused to hear Charlotte's reaction to this bombshell, but there was judicious silence at the other end of the line.

"Yes," Susan said. "I've talked to Philippe and I've talked to lawyers and to police, and I believe that in all good faith they have made a mistake. A tragic mistake," she added, suddenly seeing the headline as *Mother's Day* would write it. "Don't you see? Nothing has changed. Alex may still be out there, missing me, but because the police have made this terrible mistake, not only is an innocent man in grave danger . . . but so is Alex and so am I and so are all our hopes. It's nobody's fault, I wouldn't think of slanting the story that way . . . it's just one of those tragic errors. Charlotte, if I'm right . . . don't you see? Don't you see what it means?"

Susan finally stopped talking. A silent beat or two.

"I *do* see," said Charlotte emphatically. "I see exactly. But I have to be honest with you. I know what I went through to get approval for 'Have You Seen,' and this just isn't a *Mother's Day* story. Understand"—here her voice dropped to a conspiratorial hush—"understand, our readership is about half in the Bible Belt, and we have to be so careful about editorial content that smacks of anything to do with . . . well, we actually have a list of no-nos, and I'm afraid that anything about homosexuals . . . you understand, as far as we're concerned we don't know it exists. Pathetic, isn't it? But I have to be honest with you, that's what I'm up against. There just isn't any way I could write the story that would make it right for *Mother's Day*. But I'm sure somebody will do a bang-up job of it for you. I'm sorry it won't be us. Now, lambie . . . I'll see you on the second, all right, now I'm looking forward to that!"

"Good-bye Charlotte," said Susan. When she wrote to cancel the lunch date, she hoped she would have the rudeness to say, "Sorry, I just had my girl check my calendar, and I'm all booked up."

Susan had originally chosen to work with *Mother's Day* almost entirely because of the size of their circulation. Now she called back, one by one, the editors from the more prestigious magazines who had shown interest. They fell over themselves getting to the phone. One of them offered her $25,000 for the exclusive rights to her reaction to Philippe's trial, but when she said that she wasn't interested in selling them a story of the likelihood that Alex was still alive, she met a perceptible frost. One editor even asked her point-blank if she had considered seeking psychiatric help.

"If money's a problem, I'm sure there are therapists who would see you for free, under the circumstances. . . ."

"Thanks," said Susan. "I'll be sure to think that over."

SUSAN CONTINUED to teach her classes, working mechanically from last year's notes. She reminded herself of the famous professor where she did her undergraduate work who gave the same lectures year after year in the same order, even to making the same joke every April about the appearance of the first fly in the classroom, whether a fly had appeared or not.

There were times, more and more often, when she thought of giving up out of sheer loneliness. One night a new faculty couple on a one-year fellowship from Israel invited her on the spur of the moment to join them and a few friends for dinner. The talk over drinks was lively and trivial. One of their friends, a writer, had recently been to a formal dinner at the home of his accountant.

"They're people our age and they live the way my mother and father do . . . they have water goblets and doilies and all they talked about was money. If Betty admired something in their house, they would launch into this long description of where they got it and what it cost, and where they saw the same thing the next week for ten percent more."

"Their life is so filled with drama, I don't know how they take the pace," said Betty, the writer's wife. "All day long, the intrepid adventures of superconsumer."

"I think it's a moral fable on the perils of life without Art."

"No, it's a case of hardening of the expectations . . ."

Susan, quietly listening and sipping her wine, was keenly aware of how long it had been since she'd been with people who were just enjoying themselves and each other and being alive. It was a golden evening for her, an escape back into the lost world of the ordinary, until just before the supper was served, when the hostess brought in her little six-month-old daughter in her pink terry-cloth stretch suit to be kissed good night.

"Oh, here," said Betty, "let me try on that baby, will you?" The women each took a turn holding her, and for Susan the warm fragrant weight of the baby against her breast brought back a deeply held memory that gave her profound pleasure.

"She's a real dream," said Betty to the young mother when she came back from putting the baby in her crib.

The mother nodded shyly. "I worry about her all day long. Simca claims I wake her up at night to see if she was sleeping. So many things can happen to them, crib death, accidents . . . I won't leave her outside in the sun in her carriage, I'm afraid someone will steal her."

Here her husband joined in. "Ten thousand little babies in New York alone, but ours is so perfect, gangs of criminals are plotting at this minute to steal her away from us." He laughed at his wife.

The little wife said softly and earnestly to Betty, "But things do happen to babies. . . . If something did, I know I would kill myself."

"Why do you say that?" asked Susan sharply. "Is that what you think you *should* do?"

The young woman looked at her in surprise.

"Do you have children?" Betty interrupted to ask Susan.

"Yes," said Susan vehemently, and then, immediately realizing that she could not answer any specific questions about her child without killing what natural ease there still might be in the evening, contradicted herself and said, "No."

By that time it was clear to everyone that Susan was reacting to a rather ordinary situation with uncommon emotion. When conversation resumed, it had lost its spontaneous drift, the quality that had made it so precious to Susan. She apologized and excused herself early.

For the first time that night she understood why some of the parents in Parents Remember! talked about having to move and start a new life among strangers in order to find their way back to what they had lost besides a child. If people expect you to be ordinary and you behave as if you're ordinary, from time to time in five or ten years do you begin to have stretches of being released back into an unexamined life? Staying here was like having a chronic illness—knowing that every day for the rest of your life you would wake up with mortal pain for which there is no hope of cure.

But how could they go away? How could she, ever? This was where Alex knew to find her. This was where he would try to come home.

THE POSTERS of Alex, the ones that said "STILL MISSING," had nearly all been taken down. Susan had new ones printed, using a different photograph, another way of seeing his face, and in the evenings and on weekends she would walk around the neighborhood asking permission to post them. She preferred to put them in storefronts where they could be seen through the glass but not harmed by the weather or defaced. Recently on the subway she had seen one of the old posters with Alex's face overdrawn with felt-tip pen to look like a minstrel-show pickaninny. In a balloon like a cartoon character's he was saying, "I'm chocolate! Eat me!"

Often now when she showed a store owner the new poster he would look at her oddly and say, "I heard they solved that, the kid was murdered by some gay guy."

"No, it was a mistake," she'd say.

"Oh . . . I guess, go ahead," they said usually.

But one owner of a deli in Kenmore Square, thinking she was another of the volunteers, said, "Hey, honey, give me a break . . . it pisses off the customers, you know what I mean? The kid stares at them . . . MISSING! Boom! You know? They say, 'All right, already, what do you want me to do about it?' People want to come in here and eat without feeling like they should lose their appetite from sympathy. Somebody should tell the parents, enough is enough."

"Thank you so much," said Susan.

ONE CHILLY FRAGRANT Sunday morning in mid-October Jocelyn appeared at Susan's front door carrying a bag of fresh bagels and a copy of the Sunday *Globe*. "Justine's out for the night, and I woke up early this morning and said to myself, this is *too* nice a morning to be having breakfast alone. So here I am. Besides, I wanted to show you my new down vest."

"I'm delighted," said Susan. She found some real coffee beans in the refrigerator, knowing Jocelyn would complain if she made her instant, and produced orange juice, butter, and from the back of the shelf a jar of jam.

"Uh-oh. Here's some antique jelly. It seems to have fur on it," she said.

"Looks to have been there since Alex's regime," said Jocelyn.

Susan looked at her in surprise. "Yes, probably," she agreed warily.

When the coffee was ready, they sat at the small round table in the sunlight overlooking Fremont Street and read the paper. It was like old times, except that in old times the children would have been playing upstairs.

"Feel like taking a walk?" asked Susan. "It's a beautiful morning."

"No, thanks," said Jocelyn. "You know you don't take walks, honey, you go on hunts."

Susan stopped between the table and the kitchen, her hands

219

full of dishes. "Now, what do you mean by that?"

"Just what I said," answered Jocelyn. "You never go out anymore but what you're studying every little child to see if it's Alex. You look down every alley and peek into people's windows. . . . I can't sit by any longer and watch you do this to yourself."

Susan went slowly into the kitchen and set down the dishes she was carrying; then she returned to the table and set herself down with equal care, and with a deep breath said, "Okay, Jocelyn. Get it off your chest."

"All right, honey." Jocelyn reached across the table and touched Susan's arm. "You're a brave lady," she said. "You've been through a whole lot of pain and you've carried it like a warrior. But . . . it's time to let go. You've been so brave, you don't know how to admit the fight is over. But going on this way, you're not doing anyone any good and you're only hurting yourself. Now, I know it's none of my business, but your friends are worried about you."

"Really?" said Susan dryly. "Where are they?"

"Look, Susan. There was a time in my life when I was just so unhappy I was making myself and everyone else miserable, and it took someone I loved, getting real tough with me, to help me get off my butt and pull out of it. So, lady, I don't care if it makes you mad, or sad, or what, I have to say this because I love you. . . . It's time for you to face facts. Alex is gone, and he's not coming back, and the way you're taking it makes me afraid for you."

"Believe me," said Susan, "I'm sorry if it's inconvenienced you."

"That's all right," said Jocelyn. "Be angry at me, it's a start. My therapist says that's part of why you haven't started to heal yourself, you're carrying all that anger about what Philippe did inside of you. Susan . . . you must want to *kill* him."

"I not only don't want to kill him, I want to clear him. I don't think he did anything."

"Now, see . . . that's just what I'm talking about. You've been denying your anger so long, you're denying that the whole thing even happened. . . . It scares me to say this, honey, but you're just out of touch with reality. If you don't face what's really happened to you, there's going to be no pulling you back."

"If I don't believe what you believe, I'm out of touch with reality?"

"Now, listen . . . I just want you to listen. Honey, we're so much alike . . . I know you're angry, but I'm trying to help. I just wish you would come with me to see my stress therapist."

"This therapist who diagnoses me without having met me?"

"Susan, she's a fabulous woman. You wouldn't believe this woman. She does a little Jung, a little Reich, a little bio-feedback . . . she's *brilliant*."

"Jocelyn, I don't know how to break this to you, but there is a difference between neurotic pain and real pain. There's a difference between stress over whether the bags are bigger under your eyes and what you feel when your only child has been stolen."

"Pain is pain," said Jocelyn patiently. "Do you know that with bio-feedback, people can learn to reduce their heart rates and their temperatures, and they can unconstrict their blood vessels and cure migraine headaches?"

"Yes, I do know that. The point is that I do not have high blood pressure, or an anxiety attack, or a migraine headache."

"Loss and fear happen to all of us, honey," said Jocelyn. "You shouldn't be ashamed to ask for help to cope with it."

"Jocelyn," said Susan, "did anyone ever tell you you're incredibly full of shit?"

After Jocelyn left, she threw and smashed the moldy jar of jam against the kitchen wall and cried hot tears of annoyance and loneliness as the red clotted mess dripped down the wall.

THE ONLY PERSON during all those weeks who seemed to preserve a sense of Susan as a normal person was Margaret. She had a knack for being supportive without passing judgment, sympathetic without being sentimental. She made it clear that laughing once in a while didn't mean giving up one's faith, and if Susan needed to cry, she knew the difference between comforting her and demanding that she stop.

That Sunday evening, she let herself into Susan's apartment, calling, "Susan! Susan!" She walked into the living room and found Susan sitting in the twilight watching the color of the sky change. Margaret was wearing an embroidered evening skirt and a frilly blouse and an apron, and she demanded, "Have you got any lettuce? Any spinach? Watercress? I don't want to have to go to the store at this hour."

"Don't know," said Susan, getting up sluggishly. "I'll see."

Margaret followed her into the kitchen, talking. "I'm having some of my daughter's friends in for supper, and I thought I'd make a big salad. Do you have one of those lettuce dryers where you put the leaves in and pull a cord and it spins them dry? Well, I don't . . . my daughter told me you could do the same thing in the clothes dryer, if you put the lettuce in a pillow case and set it on cool air . . . but mine came undone." Her gray eyes glinted with irritation, but slowly her wide smile took over her unwilling face so she found herself smiling through a fierce scowl. Susan pictured the present condition of the dryer and began to laugh as she sorted through the refrigerator drawers. "I don't think it's a bit funny!" cried Margaret, laughing loudly. "Thank you . . ."

"Sorry if it's wilted," said Susan, handing her a bag of Bibb lettuce.

"*If*," said Margaret, studying it. "You've got an optimistic way of looking at things! Listen, would you like to join us?"

"No, thanks," said Susan. "I'm still sulking over a fight I had with Jocelyn this morning."

"I see. Nothing serious?"

"Oh, I'm afraid so . . . she finds me monotonous company and wants me to see a therapist so I'll cheer up."

"Uh-huh," said Margaret thoughtfully. She stood, studying Susan, in case she was planning to say anything more.

"I'm not the only mother ever to lose a child," Susan said, defending Jocelyn.

"No, you're not."

"There are some people, though, who can never believe there's a problem they don't have the answer to," explaining herself.

"I lost a child," said Margaret.

"Margaret!"

"She'd be thirty-two now, if she'd lived."

"Margaret . . ."

"I don't talk about it," said Margaret.

"Even now?"

"My daughters always remember me on her birthday—that's enough."

They shared a silence. "I am lousy company," said Susan.

Margaret paused, following her train of thought. "Why, yes
. . . you are, but I don't think it matters."

Susan smiled. She was afraid everything mattered.

"Would a hug help?" asked Margaret.

"Don't think so." Susan shook her head. Her lips were a thin strained line.

"Well, then . . . I'll be downstairs. Thanks for the lettuce."

NOVEMBER 3.

It was a small story in the Boston *Globe*, not even carried in the first section. A man named Albert Lipscomb was found living in a cabin in a small town in the mountains of West Virginia with two young boys. One was nine and one was twelve; the one who was twelve had never even been reported missing. The other one had disappeared from a park near his home in Philadelphia over a year ago and had been written off as a runaway. According to the brief news report, the boys had been calling the man Dad, and even attended school. The nearest neighbors considered them nice quiet kids, both loners. The whole family kept to themselves, it was said. What had led the police in a desultory way to investigate the "family" was the curiosity of a country schoolteacher who was puzzled by the fact that the boys claimed to be brothers although one of them was black.

Albert Lipscomb, the paper noted, was a convicted sex offender and a sometime member of a ring that produced pictures of little boys in pornographic poses. He was known to have been in the Boston area in the spring gathering money on the pretext of running a fresh-air fund. He had been questioned at the time in the disappearance of Boston's Alex Selky, which was the principal reason the story even made the Boston papers.

To Susan, it was a sign. The local media woke up and remembered her name. One news show asked if they could send down a mini-cam and get a scene of her phoning the mother in Philadelphia whose little boy had been found, giving congratulations. Would they run pictures of Alex? Would they let her explain that she still believed he too would be found? They talked it over with the producers. They agreed they would.

"How would you feel, Mrs. Selky," the reporters asked her eagerly, "if you got the news those parents got today? How would you feel knowing your son had been living for months with a known sex criminal . . . ?"

"I would feel overjoyed that he was living."

"Yes, but I mean . . ."

"Everything depends on how adults react to him now," she repeated steadily. "How does a young child know for sure what behavior is inappropriate when it's completely outside his experience? Unless adults get overwrought. He may know he doesn't like it. But who's to say what's the worst thing in the world to a child?"

She didn't care that they thought she was deranged. She suited their purposes; they suited hers. Hope coursed through her like a cleansing fire, and she was full of energy and fierce conviction.

She called Menetti. Yes, he said, he'd seen it. No, it didn't make any difference . . . what kind of difference was it supposed to make? They had already questioned Lipscomb at the time, there was no point in doing it again.

In the evening, she called Naomi's apartment and asked to speak to Graham. "Did you see?" she asked Naomi. Yes, Naomi said, they had seen. They had seen Susan on the news, making that phone call. Yes, she said, she'd have Graham call her back. Susan could tell it hadn't reached his heart, as it had hers, but she wanted to hear his voice anyway.

ANOTHER PERSON who saw her on the news was Menetti. He'd been in a bar up the street from police headquarters. On the black-and-white set above the bar, she had seemed a little thinner than the last time he saw her. He sipped his draft and watched the deep steady look in her eyes as she called the woman whose child had come home. The smile on her face, so like the little boy's on the poster, came straight from her heart, and nearly broke his. Where was she getting the courage from? How long was she going to keep it up?

The traffic was heavy on the expressway when he started for Saugus. It was nearly at a standstill by the time he reached the Mystic River Bridge. Some kind of accident, probably. He could turn on the radio and listen to one of those helicopter guys who told you where the tie-ups were and how long the delay was, but tonight he didn't want the distraction. He felt gathered and intent. His eyes moved ceaselessly: he was scanning the traffic. Presently he allowed himself to recognize what he was doing: he was looking for the blue car. Blue '63 or '64 Oldsmobile sedan; rust spots on the doors; one whitewall, on the right front. Systematically he scanned the slowly moving lanes and asked himself for the thousandth time, just for the record, how it could happen that that car was never seen again.

IN THE AFTERMATH of the brief flurry of excitement over the missing boy's return, Susan felt desperately depressed, as if the burst of hope had stripped her nerves of some vital insulation, so that now she felt the return of agonizing loss, such as she hadn't felt in months.

After a day or two, when she began to be able to talk again without crying, she called information in Rhode Island and got the number for Parents Remember! She no longer had any choice, she saw. She was part of their abandoned sorrowing fraternity, whether she wanted to be or not. She looked forward to being in a roomful of her own kind, as a wounded animal looks forward to the smelly, muddy dark of its own lair. She had lived too long in her own isolation. She finally recognized the isolation itself as another enemy.

Bob picked her up at the station to drive her to the meeting. He apologized briefly for the battered condition of his car. Why? she wondered. Had she been so proud? Other than his remarks about the car, he drove in silence.

It was a small group this afternoon. They met in a church basement, in a room with two pianos and a stack of hymnals left from choir practice. They sat around a large table on gray metal folding chairs that squeaked when they shifted their bottoms, and listened to Mrs. Karakys read the minutes of the last meeting. Mrs. Karakys was a large blonde in a pantsuit who wore glasses hanging on a ribbon around her neck. The glasses were draped onto her bosom whenever she wasn't reading. Every adult in the room had lost a child in essentially the same grotesque way.

There was a treasurer's report, having to do with the revenues realized from the group's two film strips, then a discussion of how to make the most of the recent incident, the rescue of the two little boys. Mrs. Karakys had been in touch with the mother of the boy from Philadelphia. "She was a very nice woman, but she said her agent had told her not to give out any information till they see if they can sell the story to the movies." Everyone around the table groaned.

"I hope they understand it'll be X-rated," said Bob.

"Maybe we can get Mrs. Schumway on the talk shows again."

"Who is Mrs. Schumway?" asked Susan shyly. They all looked at her.

Bob said, "This is Susan Selky, the mother of the little boy who was kidnapped and murdered."

There were murmurs of sympathy around the table, and Mrs. Karakys said, "Sylvia Schumway, about four years ago, had her son disappear, and he was gone for—what was it, Bob —nine months? They found him living with some guy in a trailer park. Poor woman. Her son was eleven years old. He never called her or made any attempt to escape. When the police brought him home he stayed in his bedroom for a week. He couldn't believe that he wasn't going to be beaten—that's what the guy had convinced him of, that his parents were so mad at him that if he ever went home they'd beat him up. Sylvia says the boy's dad—he's dead now, God rest him—his dad had given him a spanking for stealing some pocket money the day before he disappeared. Sylvia says it killed him when the boy came home and he realized . . . The boy just cowered around the house for months, but when the parents weren't looking, he beat up on the younger children. They think he'd been given drugs to keep him quiet while he was gone, and it changed his personality. He never completely trusted his parents again, and when he got into junior high they suspected he was taking drugs. Then he started to get arrested for dealing drugs . . . they caught him trying to get his little sister, seven years old, to smoke marijuana.''

Susan felt utterly sick. "Where is he now?" she asked, with her hand to her mouth.

Mrs. Karakys shrugged. "He was in reform school for a while . . . I think he's out right now. It's worse for his mother when he's out." There was a long silence following this.

"Well," said Susan.

"We spoke to Susan about a month after her little boy disappeared," Bob volunteered to the group, who appeared already to know it. "Of course," he said to her, "we're all sorry about the way it turned out for you."

"Well," said Susan again. "That's really why I'm here. I need your help, and you're the only place left for me to turn. I believe the police have made a mistake about Henry Sullivan . . ." She began her explanation of her faith that Alex was alive, her need to revive interest in the possibility that he too would be recognized living somewhere . . . like the two boys who were just found. When she had finished, she found the ring of faces around the table looking at her in distant appraisal. The feeling was too cold to be called sympathy; it was more a sort of familiarity.

"I see," said Bob carefully. He spoke with a certain percussive finality, like someone setting nails with a hammer. "I'm sorry . . . there's so little we can do. I guess most of us here know how it feels to believe the police have made a mistake," he said, looking straight at her. "But we're an educational group, as you know, and we don't have any money. We have to depend on the generosity of people with access to the media to get our message across. If we can think of some way to let people know that you think your boy's alive . . ."

"Thank you," said Susan, with a cold, sick feeling of *déjà vu*. "I appreciate it." It was intensely uncomfortable to have to sit returning their flat gazes until the meeting was over and Bob could return her to the train station.

IN EARLY NOVEMBER Philippe tried to kill himself. He was cut

227

down from a bar in his cell from which he had hanged himself with a torn bedsheet. Nobody knew how long he'd been there, and the hospital couldn't determine for days whether or not there had been brain damage. Susan tried to go to the hospital to see him, but she was refused.

Late one evening she called Graham. "He's not here," said Naomi.

"Naomi," said Susan through tears, "I need to talk to him. I feel like I'm drowning . . . I don't know what it means, Philippe trying to die. Does it mean he lied to me? What can't he live with—his guilt? Or his innocence? I don't know who else to talk to. No one else has lost Alex except Graham. . . ."

There was a long silence. Finally Naomi said, "All right, Susan. I'll give him the message. But we're trying hard to make a life together here, and I resent you using this situation all the time to get to Graham."

Graham called her back the next morning, but by that time the urge to speak to him had passed.

AS THE DAYS grew shorter and the chill in the autumn air deepened, the long uneven panes of glass in the living-room windows were gray with thin frost when Susan went with her coffeecup in the early mornings to sit looking down at the street. From the lush gold and blue, deep as an overturned bowl, of the last morning on earth that she saw her son, the light had changed to the flat gray brightness of impending winter.

He would be so cold now, if by some prayer-answering overlay of transparent time she could see him once more on this morning's streets as she saw him the last morning. If she looked down as she did every morning as if she were a normal mother and there he simply was, striding out into the new summer day. She could see him so clearly some mornings. The lilt of his walk, the plump baby's curve of his cheek, his fragile, sturdy bare neck and arms, and the flash of sunlight on his dark hair, soon to be streaked with copper by the summer sun. And every morning, every morning of her life, she saw him reach the corner, turn, and smiling, wave good-bye.

These long, even, empty days now, she rarely felt anger or fear or sadness. What she felt, with simplicity too profound to express, was a brimming love for him and no way to give it. There was a dim sense memory that haunted her nights, of flesh on flesh, the intense multiple impact of the smell of his skin, and the sight of his head pressed against her cheek so close that its outline became the curve of the earth, and the angular feel of limbs, all knees and elbows—that gave a pleasure too complex to recover or yet ever to give up, the deep unremarkable joy of hugging her child.

IT WAS a slushy gray-bright morning the week after Thanksgiving. Menetti was forty-five minutes late to work because the battery in his car had gone dead. He had had to have Pat drive him over to her brother's service station with the battery in his lap to have it recharged.

When he finally got to the office, he just happened, as he stopped to hang up his coat and pull off his rubbers, to overhear Sergeant Pollard saying into the phone, "I see . . . I see . . . Yes, well, as I told you, we've closed the file on that case. Yes. It was in all the papers, Mrs. Robbins. . . . No . . . no, I'm sorry, my superior officer is away from his desk . . ." He glanced at Menetti. Menetti mouthed at him silently, "Which case?"

"Selky," Pollard mouthed back.

Menetti reached for the phone. "This is Lieutenant Menetti," he said. "Can I help you?"

"Of course not, I'm calling to help you," said the woman. "I know where that little Selky child is and I've called twice now to tell you about it. If I were a Massachusetts resident, I'd be pretty concerned about what the police are doing all day, you can't bring home one sad little child. Write my congressman." She had a rich confident voice with a southern slur, dropping most final consonants.

"Yes, I understand," said Menetti. "Could you give me your name and address, please?"

"I told you already, two times."

"My fault. . . . Please give it to me again."

"Malvina Robbins, 4429 Baily Street, Willimantic, Connecticut." As he wrote this down, Menetti saw Pollard look up at the ceiling and sink his chin in his hands. "I can see the child out my window this minute marching around in that mush by himself. Now, why isn't he in school? Tell me that."

"I can't, Mrs. Robbins. You tell me."

"Because he's that stolen child. I did tell you. Saw when they moved in, the man didn't have no toys for him like a real daddy would."

Menetti waited, but Mrs. Robbins had apparently delivered her most telling point.

"Well, how do you know he doesn't have any toys?" he asked eventually.

"I watched them move in! They only got the one suitcase. When I used to go someplace with my kids, take a wheelbarrow to bring the toys in."

"Maybe they can't afford toys. Maybe they're poor, Mrs. Robbins."

"Poor! Tell me poor. He's no more a daddy than the man in the moon."

"And how do you know that, Mrs. Robbins?"

"I know it because I know this is that little stolen child. I got the picture of him from the paper, and also I saw his mother on the TV and she showed us another picture. But what happened was, when I was reading the paper about this little Boston boy that disappeared, I looked up and there was Jesus, and he said to me, 'Malvina, you better clip that picture. My father moves in mysterious ways, as you know, Malvina, and it may be that you will be the instrument that will bring that lost little lamb home to his grieving mommy.' And I said to Jesus . . ."

At this point Menetti picked up an eraser from the desk and threw it at Sergeant Pollard. "I see, Mrs. Robbins," he was saying as Sergeant Pollard, laughing soundlessly, went on about his deskwork.

MALVINA ROBBINS no longer would talk to Pollard or any other duty officer who happened to answer the phone. She had Menetti's name and she believed in dealing with the man in charge. She talked to Menetti an average of twice a week. He sometimes wondered how she found time to work him in between conversations with Jesus. Two times in the week after Christmas he'd had to listen to a complete rendition of what the Lord had said to Malvina when he sat down to share her Thanksgiving turkey. (Would you believe that that dear Christ baby had never tasted turkey before in all his life?)

This morning, it had taken close to three minutes by the clock for her to pause long enough for Menetti to say into the phone, "Happy New Year to you too, Malvina."

"I want to know when you'll be coming down here," she was saying, "because after you pick up that little lost child, I want you to bring him by here for milk and cookies. I offered him a plate of my Christmas cookies just the other day, but that man took that child off by the arm like I was the devil. Won't let the child talk to me at all . . . he's seen the Lord knocking at my door, that's why. I said to him, 'Suffer the little child to come unto me,' but that man just looked at me with the one straight eye he's got, he looked at me like I was a crazy woman. That's the devil's way, you know . . . the devil has a walleye too, that's what we called 'em when I was a child, a walleye, 'cause one eye's looking at you while th'other one's rolled out staring at the wall. Devil looks just like that, my Redeemer told me . . ."

"Malvina," said Menetti, "thank you for calling. I appreciate your help very much, and I have to go now and make arrangements to come down there. Yes. That's right. Yes, I'll be in touch very soon about when we're coming, and I'll let you know. Yes, it takes time to line up all the squad cars and so on.

231

Yes, Malvina. Yes, Malvina. Thank you . . . I'll pray for you, too."

Menetti hung up the phone and sank his head in his hands. I'll pray, all right, he thought. I'll pray that the phone company takes your phone out by the roots. I'll pray that my Redeemer drops by here and gives Jerry Pollard a walleye for letting me talk to you in the first place, you poor nut case.

And in Willimantic, Connecticut, Malvina Robbins hung up her phone and went back to the kitchen window to look out into the next backyard again. No way she was going to rest until somebody came to rescue that child. She'd take him herself if she didn't know how dangerous that devil was, that walleye. Goodness, the Lord was going to be pleased with her for saving one of his little lambs, just like the Good Shepherd.

There he was, poor little boy. He was sitting on the concrete step by himself, just staring into the empty yard. There was a layer of gray snow on the ground. In the corner of the yard a broken canvas chair lay against the fence, and in the center, nearly filling the small dismal square, was a circular revolving clothesline tilting on its scarred aluminum pole. The little boy wore no mittens, because, Malvina knew, the ones he had were too big for him and prevented his using his hands for anything. He had laid out a row of little squares of bread, white against the dirty snow, in a neat line. Malvina watched him stare at them until at last a mangy sparrow dropped down, ate one of the chunks, hopped around for a while, then flew off again. After a long pause, the boy got up and replaced the sparrow's bread with another little piece; then he sat back down again.

IT WAS the Friday evening of the long Washington's Birthday weekend, and Menetti had gotten home late. Dinner was already over. Pat was angrily washing dishes. Eugene had just rushed upstairs crying and slammed the bedroom door. Before Al could take off his overcoat and find out from Pat what was going on, the phone rang.

"Hello, Al?"

He could hardly hear her. "Yes, Susan," he said. Pat suddenly took her hands out of the soapy water and whirled around and glared at him. Menetti pulled a chair out from the kitchen table, deliberately turned it so it would place his back to his wife, and sat down in his overcoat. "How are you?" he said into the phone. He had felt an odd quiver when he heard her voice again after so many weeks.

"Fine. Al, I just got a phone call, and I wanted to talk to you about it."

"Just a minute, I can hardly hear you."

He went to the kitchen door. "Kids! Eugene! Marco! Keep it down to a dull roar, will you?" Upstairs the volume was lowered on the record player. "Okay, I'm back."

"Can you hear me now?"

"Yes, I can hear you. How are you, you doing okay?"

"Yes, I'm fine. How are you?"

"Fine."

"Al, this woman called me today . . . she's called me twice, actually . . ."

Dammit, Menetti said to himself. Malvina. This was the place where he stopped feeling sorry for the loons out there and started wishing he could just have them rounded up and fitted with straitjackets. It was annoying enough having her on his back, but now Malvina was going to cause real pain.

"A woman in Willimantic, Connecticut," Susan was saying. "I've written down the address . . . but she said she'd been in touch with you."

"Malvina Robbins, right?"

"Yes."

"Now, Susan—"

"Al." She spoke softly, but something in her voice effectively stopped him. It seemed to flood him with awful sadness.

"Susan," he said wearily, "did she tell you about Jesus coming to Christmas dinner? Or how he takes his tea every afternoon? Did she tell you how he used to take two lumps, Susan, but now he just takes cream?"

There was a long silence, and he tried to remember how it was he got into the position of adding to the hurt of this woman. He knew from her pause that she had heard enough from Malvina to doubt her.

Susan started again. "But that doesn't prove there's no boy there. Why isn't a child that age in school, Al? *Why* is he there by himself all afternoon?"

Menetti stretched and shook his head. "If there really was a child there, I could still give you a dozen reasons. He could be retarded, he could have a handicap . . ."

"Or he could be Alex."

Menetti sighed. He tried to think of what to say, but he couldn't, so he didn't say anything.

"Couldn't he, Al?" she persisted. "Are you so sure that there is not *one* chance left under heaven that it is Alex, that you can't even give one afternoon of your time to checking it out? Can't you just have the police in Willimantic drive by and *look?*"

"No," he said, "I can't. This case is closed and there is no investigation, so there's no way I could justify an action like that. Besides, I am under very specific orders not to spend any more time on this matter, for the very good reason that we have a trial coming up, probably by the end of the month, if Henry Sullivan's lawyer is finally out of maneuvers to postpone it. It's going to attract a lot of press, and like any lengthy jury trial it's going to cost the taxpayers a lot of money, and if it comes out that any member of my department, let alone me, is muddying the waters by looking for the child Henry Sullivan killed, I'd be very surprised if we didn't see the indictment thrown out, and I'd be lucky if I wound up directing traffic. Got it?" He realized by the end of this sudden burst of anger that he was shouting at her. The volume of his voice alone made him understand how torn with guilt and pity he felt.

Susan was silent for a long moment, during which he dreaded her reaction. When it came, her voice sounded softer, a little frightened, but firm.

"I guess I could borrow the car from Graham and go myself," she said.

Menetti put his hand to his forehead. "Oh, Jesus, Susan," he said angrily. He pictured her going to Malvina's door and felt a spasm of fear. He knew so much better than she how many different kinds of weird a person like Malvina might be. "Look, don't do that, all right?"

"What else can I do?"

234

"Just think it over a little while, will you? Sort out what you want to believe from what's happening. You might give me a little credit for having learned something about this type of situation after thirty years, okay? It's a long weekend, anyway. Just give yourself the time off, and we'll talk about it Tuesday."

"Give myself time off from what?"

"Susan, I'll talk to you Tuesday."

He hung up the phone, and turned wearily to share his sorrow with Pat, only to find from the way she was staring at him that she clearly had a few things she intended to share with him first.

"Susan Selky?" she said coldly.

He shrugged and nodded.

"Not only did you miss dinner again for the fifth time in two weeks, we're going to start with Susan Selky again? We're going to have a whole instant replay of last summer, when the kids forgot what you looked like? Honest to God, they were going up to strange men in the supermarket, saying, 'Is that you, Daddy?' "

"It's the first time I've talked to her in two months," said Al.

"Did you happen to notice your youngest son, that's the one called Eugene, bawling up the stairs as you graced us with your presence this evening?"

"Yes."

"Did it cross your mind to wonder what was going on before you dived for the telephone? You've spent more time in the last year worrying about a kid who's been dead since May than you have about your own children, you know that?" Menetti just stared at her. She was in full cry, all right. Jesus, what a day.

"For your information," stormed Pat, "Eugene is crying because I promised he could sleep over at Sean and Willy's house this weekend and now he can't because he wet his bed again, and he knows if it happened anymore he'd have to be kept home."

"I see. And I made him pee in his bed."

"Oh, very funny, Al. Did you bother to read that article I gave you? Did you?"

Brother. Al dimly remembered her putting one of those

235

women's magazines on his night table and telling him som
thing about it, but he hated those magazines, they were a
about Jell-O molds and breast cancer.

"No, you didn't, because if you had, you might be able t
figure out that when a kid with no medical problem continue
to wet his bed, he's probably trying to get attention. Like fo
instance the attention of his father, who hasn't spent on
whole day with his family since Christmas. You haven't prob
ably spent one whole day alone with Eugene since I brough
him home from the hospital. Just because he's the younges
and you've already been through this six times before doesn'
mean Eugene has. Remember Angela? Remember when sh
was Eugene's age? You used to spend all day Saturday wit
her, just . . . and I'm the one who winds up washing piss
sheets the whole time!"

Al knew better than to interrupt when she was in overdrive
especially since it was true, he hardly ever spent time wit
Eugene, the way he had with the first kids.

". . . and don't think it doesn't screw up my life to have t
keep him home, because it does. Maryann and the twins ar
coming in the morning, and now I don't have anywhere fo
little George to sleep."

"Wait a minute, your sister's coming? Why?"

"Because it's the long weekend, that's why! I told you I wa
inviting her, so don't give me any grief, I was embarrassed
enough not asking them to spend Christmas."

"Now, wait a minute," Al said back, loud enough to startle
her into momentary quiet. "You can't have it both ways here.
On one hand I'm making Eugene wet his bed because I don't
spend any time with him, and now I've got a long weekend off I
can't spend any time with him because I have to entertain
Maryann and big George instead!"

"No you don't, because big George isn't coming," said Pat
triumphantly.

"Good," said Al. "Then you won't need me. I'll take
Eugene and we'll go off for the day, and you and Maryann can
spend the whole day complaining about your mother, and
when you're done, you can start in on mine."

"Well, *that's* just great. And what am I supposed to say to her, 'Oh, hi, Maryann, Al heard you were coming, so he left town'?"

"Yes. Fine. Say that."

Al got up and marched up the stairs and hammered on Eugene's door. "Eugene! Eugene!"

Eugene, who expected to be spanked for wetting his bed, didn't answer.

"Eugene," yelled Al through the door, "how'd you like to spend the day with me tomorrow? What do you say, buddy, we'll go off somewhere and leave the ladies and the babies to themselves, okay?"

Downstairs, Pat was glaring up at him with hands on her hips, furious and stymied.

Eugene opened his door and came out, his face still puffy from crying. "Gee, Dad," he said. "Okay."

THEY DROVE OUT right after breakfast. Pat had not addressed Al directly since the night before, but at least Eugene, who was glowing with pleasure, didn't notice. They drove for a while before Eugene asked, "Where we going, Dad?"

It was a bitterly cold day, and though the roads were clear, the yards and sidewalks were piled with snow.

"Gee, I don't know. How about the amusement park—Wonderland?"

"I don't think it's open in the winter, Dad. How about a movie?"

"At nine in the morning? How about the Aquarium?"

"We went there with Mommy last week."

"You did?"

"Yeah."

"Oh . . . how was it?"

"Great."

Menetti thought awhile. "How about Boston Common?"

Eugene looked doubtful. "What would we do there?"

237

"You know. Walk around. You could have a swan-boat ride."

Eugene looked at him sympathetically. "I'm too big for swan-boat rides, Dad."

"Oh. Are you?"

"Yeah."

"Oh. Well . . . what do you want to do?"

"Well, I'd like to see your office."

"You've seen my office."

"No, I haven't."

"You haven't?"

"No, never. I haven't."

Menetti thought about it. He was probably right. He'd taken a lot of his kids into the office, but come to think of it, he couldn't remember ever taking Eugene.

"But, Eugene, your mother would kill me if I went to the office today. Even to show you."

"She would?"

"Yes, she's very mad at me for spending too much time there."

"You're right," said Eugene philosophically. Uh-oh, thought Menetti. "It's okay, though, Dad," added Eugene. "I just like driving with you."

"You do?"

"Yeah. When I drive with Mom, I never get to sit in the front seat."

"Well, fine. I'll tell you what, you can be my deputy, and we'll pretend we're going to do a mission."

"Hey, great! Can I have a gun?"

"Sure," said Menetti. "Here." He cocked his thumb and stuck out his index finger to make a pistol and handed it to Eugene. Eugene took it solemnly and pretended to tuck a pistol into his belt.

"Where's your gun, Dad?"

"Right here." He patted his pocket.

"Can I see it?"

Menetti hesitated. It was very much against his policy for the kids to know anything about his firearms, let alone where he kept or carried them, but this seemed like a time to make an exception. He reached into his pocket and took out the small automatic pistol he carried there, having first checked with his thumb to be sure the safety was on. Eugene said, "Wow!" and reached for it.

"Don't touch!" Eugene's hand jumped back. "But you can look at it." Eugene did. Then the gun went back to the pocket and Eugene settled back in his seat. They drove for several miles in silence, both feeling highly satisfied.

What the hell, thought Menetti after a while. Maybe I can kill two birds with one stone here. After all, I have to go somewhere. I could let him know what police work is really like. Maybe it would help him understand better where his daddy is when he can't be home for dinner.

"Say, deputy . . ."

"Sir," said Eugene. Eugene watched a lot of World War II movies with Marco on the 4:30 movie.

"I've got a mission you can help me out with. But it's a very delicate mission and it must be an absolute secret. Nobody else can help me but you, and it will have to be just between us. No talking about it down at headquarters."

"Honestly, Dad?" asked Eugene.

"Honestly who?"

"Honestly, sir?"

"Absolutely. Do you accept?"

"Yes, sir."

"Okay. Now, remember, you have to do exactly what I say."

"Yes, sir."

"Okay, first, open the glove compartment and find me the road map marked Southern New England." Eugene did this. "Okay, now open it up." Eugene did. It seemed to unfold endlessly and threaten to envelop him. Menetti kept glancing over, trying to check the map without taking his eye from the road. "I think what we're looking for is on the other side," he told Eugene, and then Eugene had to wrestle the large creased sheet around till he was looking at the second side.

"Okay, next. You can read, can't you?"

"Yes, sir," said Eugene crisply.

"Good. See the legend on the side of the map—the list of names over there?"

"Yes, sir," said Eugene, holding the map up with both

arms stretched wide.

"Good. See if you can find a town called Willimantic, under Connecticut. The list is in alphabetical order . . . do you know how to find something in alphabetical order?"

"I don't think so, sir."

"Well, the W's are near the end. Look at the end of the list till you find the W's and then find Wil-li-man-tic."

There was a long silence while the deputy held the small print quite close to his face and studied it. "Found it!" he cried finally.

"Good man. Now, do you see a number and a letter beside it?" Eugene nodded. "What are they?"

"F-eight."

"Good. Now, do you see the letters running down the left side of the map? And do you see the numbers running across the top? Well, if you ran your fingers straight down from eight and straight across from F, where would they meet?"

Eugene tried to do this with his fingers and the map collapsed on his head.

"Do it with your eyes, but keep holding the map up," said Menetti. This time Eugene found it. He turned the map to his father and pointed quickly to Willimantic.

"Route 6 to 84, that's what I thought," said Menetti. "Good man!"

Eugene refolded the map with some difficulty, and they drove on in silence.

"What do I do next, sir?" he asked after fifteen minutes.

"You sit."

"How much longer?"

"Probably another hour."

A while later Eugene said, "Couldn't we do a closer mission, Dad? I'm getting bored."

"Police work is often boring, deputy."

"Why do we have to go so far?"

"We are doing one of the jobs that we do the most here in Missing Persons, and that is checking out a crank call. You know what a crank is?" Eugene shook his head. "It's the thing you used to crank up and start an old Model-T car with." He held up his fist beside his head and made a circular cranking motion. Eugene laughed. "Sometimes we ask for information, and a lot of cuckoos call us up and tell us wild stories. We have to check them out, because a person can be crazy but still know a little piece of the truth. Unfortunately, that doesn't happen very often, which is what makes checking them out so boring.''

"Do you think it will be dangerous, Dad?"

Menetti sighed. "No. I don't think so. I think it will just be sad. But you're right to ask. Everything we do in police work that deals with the public could be dangerous, and it's just when we get bored and sloppy that it can catch us off guard. That's why good investigators like us are always on our guard. And for that reason, deputy, I think you ought to learn to clean your gun."

Eugene promptly produced his thumb and finger from his belt. Menetti began to describe, step by step, how you dismantle and oil a revolver, which was what Eugene decided he was carrying.

After that they listened to the police band on Menetti's two-way radio, but Menetti wouldn't let Eugene broadcast on it. "Only real police business," he said. "You know about the boy who cried wolf, don't you?" Eugene did.

After another long hour which included a stop at Howard Johnson's for milkshakes, they reached Willimantic. Menetti gave his deputy his orders. "The first thing is, no one must know we're here or that we ever came here, even when the mission is over. For that reason, I prefer not to discuss the nature of the case with you, but I will tell you this. You must not talk to me at all while I try to find Baily Street, because being talked to while I'm getting lost in a strange city makes me very jumpy. Understood?"

The deputy nodded.

Willimantic is a small city on the Hop River east of Hartford. From the highway you can see a cluster of turn-of-the-century brick manufacturing buildings, like the abandoned textile mills that stare with glassless eyes along the rivers of eastern Massachusetts. Once down into the warren of streets of the town, Menetti found his way to a grimy neighborhood of frame houses, the sort of neighborhood with a launderette on every second block and a tavern on every corner that you find in factory towns from Pittsburgh to Fall River. At first, on a street of sooty two-family houses he asked a man in khakis and a lumber jacket for Baily Street, and got a blank stare.

"You live around here?" asked Menetti. Still he got a mumble and a stare. Menetti asked him the question in Italian, and this time learned that the man had lived on this block for a year and a half, but that he'd never heard of Baily Street. Menetti pushed on. After four or five blocks on a street of brick-and-stucco bungalows, he stopped a woman coming in from her backyard with a basket of wash stiff from the clothesline. She had lived in Willimantic all her life and was pretty sure Baily Street was somewhere on the North Side.

"Why don't we stop at a gas station, sir?" asked Eugene. "That's what Mom always does."

Menetti had to suppress irritation. He hated asking directions and he hated not knowing where he was going even more, and he hated to be reminded that there was a witness to his confusion.

"Because, deputy, this is a secret mission. Asking at a gas station is just what *they* expect you to do. This way if *they* ever try to trace our movements, *they'll* have a hard time finding out where we were going."

The deputy nodded. No need to explain to a seven-year-old who *they* are. He doesn't care.

As Menetti felt his way from one street to the next, following some instinct about how mill towns grow and what kind of neighborhood he was looking for, a sad black ball of embarrassment began to grow inside him. This was a truly dumb-ass thing to be doing. If the DA's office ever found out . . . if the press got one whiff of it . . . he would find his behind in a sling, and the next thing that would happen after that was he'd find his marriage down the tubes. For that matter, if Eugene told Pat how they spent the day and she figured out what he'd been up to . . . Menetti glanced over at the deputy, who was sitting erect, studying the passing neighborhood with his pistol at the ready. Well, he'd have to find some way to cool Eugene. He could do this much for Susan, keep the ripest nuts off her back. Besides, after this they could have lunch, then the drive back would take two more hours, and by then they could go to a movie and kill the rest of the day. What do people do with kids all day?

242

He drove slowly through a small section of shops and bodegas, and found his way into another residential neighborhood. The houses were poor, small frame buildings, and several still had Christmas lights on in the windows. He had to stop the car for a group of black children who were playing Frisbee in the street because dirty mounds of snow pushed to the sides of the street by a snowplow blocked the front yards. On the corner, a dog had torn open a paper bag with the foolish face of Colonel Sanders on it. Lying on the snow beside an overflowing garbage can, the dog was eating the bones from some fried chicken.

"Look, Daddy—that dog's got some chicken bones. He could choke. Should we stop?"

"No, honey. I've got a feeling that dog can take care of himself." What am I doing here? Did I really need to have my nose rubbed in this case one more time? Pat must be right. I'm not using my head, I'm obsessing. She's probably right, I've got Type-A behavior and the next thing is I'll have a heart attack. Taipei Behavior.

Maybe I'm just getting too old to get creamed as hard as I did this year. It's not so easy anymore, to say, "You win some, you lose some." It used to be easier, when you still had fifteen years and thousands of cases ahead of you. It's not very easy at all anymore. God, and people gripe about cops retiring at fifty.

Point Street. Canal Street. Baily Street. Well . . . I found it.

"Baily Street, sir!"

"Yes, I see, deputy." Here they were. At least it wouldn't take long. He was glad he'd have Eugene for company on the way back. Then he wouldn't have to spend two hours driving alone with that sour restless feeling. Which way do the numbers go? Try on the right first.

The first numbers on the block were in the 3300's and they were going down. Swell, Al, he said to himself as he pulled into a driveway to turn around. Another choice move by the old pro.

"Are we almost there, Dad?" Eugene whispered. He was sitting tensely forward on the car seat, peering over the dashboard.

"Almost there, pal. Now . . ." He paused, peering to find a house number as he drove slowly down the street. Found one.

243

3812. Good. "Now, when we get there, deputy, your job will be to guard the car. I won't be inside long, and I'll give you a full report when I'm done. You cover me from outside, okay?"

"Okay, sir." Another block.

"What number are we looking for, sir?"

"It's 4429. Sorry, deputy, I should have told you sooner."

"Okay . . . we just passed 4018."

"Good looking. Keep it up."

More dreary blocks to reach the 4400's. Okay, Malvina, thought Menetti. You win. Here's your big chance to show me where Jesus sits and drinks tea with you. And, of course, you lose, because after we sort out whatever nubbin of fact has accreted all these pearly fantasies, you won't have anyone to call three times a week anymore, will you? And then what will you do? 4421. 4423 . . . 4429. There you are, Malvina.

The car drifted to a stop. Menetti had switched off the ignition and turned to unlock his door before he saw it. Eugene watched his father freeze. He waited patiently, but nothing happened. What part of procedure was this? Why doesn't he get out of the car? Eugene glanced up at his father's face and was astonished to see that his eyes were glazed with tears. Eugene looked back at the street, following his father's gaze. He wasn't looking at 4429. He was looking at the house next door, a gray house with peeling paint and a torn screen door on the front door. In front of the house was parked an old blue car with rust spots all over the doors, and on the front-right wheel, a whitewall tire.

"Daddy?" whispered Eugene after a minute.

"Oh, Jesus," said his father. "Susan . . . Jesus." He put up both hands to cover his nose and mouth, and for a second or two, he really cried.

MENETTI dried his eyes and nose with his big handkerchief. He told Eugene to stay in the car, head low, and watch the house next to 4429. If anyone came out, Eugene was to lean on the horn. "I'll be right back," he said.

Menetti walked up to 4429 and rang the bell. He was still not very far from tears. He hoped he'd have a grip on himself when he had to speak again.

The door was opened by a tiny black woman with cloud-white hair. She was wearing glasses and an apron, and she greeted Menetti with a look of annoyance. "Well, you certainly took your time, Lieutenant," she said with perfect mad confidence. "Now, come in here, before he sees you." She tipped her head left in the direction of the house next door. Menetti stepped into her living room, which was dark and tidy except for the stacks of magazines and newspapers that rimmed the walls and were gradually taking over the remaining floor space.

"Thank you," he said. "May I use your phone?"

"Right there," said Malvina, pointing. He dialed 0 and said to the operator, "Get me the police, please, this is an emergency."

Malvina was looking out the window at the street. "I don't see no squad cars," she said suspiciously. "You don't have much time, he goes out to work in the hospital, afternoons, you know."

"Hello, who am I speaking to, please?" said Menetti into the phone. "Could I speak to your captain?"

"What child is that you got in your car out there?" Malvina demanded suddenly. "What *you* got a child with you for? I would like to see your badge, please."

Menetti, about to answer her, reached into his pockets instead and began to rummage for his badge, as he said into the phone, "Captain Lugo. This is Detective Albert Menetti, Boston PD . . . Yes. Yes. I'm on 4429 Baily Street. It looks like a long shot just paid off for me here, but I'm here without any backup. . . . Yes, a missing child. Alex Selky. . . . That's right. . . . Yes, I know. . . . I haven't actually seen him, but I'm pretty sure. Could I have two cars, please, as fast as you can. No sirens. Unmarked cars, or approach on foot. . . . Yes. I'll wait for your men in my car across the street. A gray Plymouth."

And then, ten minutes later, with four policemen with drawn guns covering them from the street, Menetti stood with two plainclothes detectives on the porch of 4431. He rang the bell. Silence. An eternal wait. And then the door was opened by Alex Selky.

Menetti felt the breath lock in his lungs, as it collided once again with a painful urge toward tears—this small, very thin boy with the perfect round head, and eyes that blinked in the bright winter sunlight, as if he were not used to leaving the dank of the house. His hair was cut ragged and short, a flat orangy-corn color. The nails on his small hands were gnawed to the quick. As he stood in the cold air holding the door open, Menetti could see a lavender bruise on the inside of his left forearm.

A man came to the door right behind Alex. He was dressed in a white Dacron pantsuit and white canvas shoes, the uniform of a male nurse. He had a plump pink face and was nearly bald. One brown eye looked wide to the right into space. He was carrying a can of diet Seven-Up in his hand and in the living room behind him as he stood in the front doorway, Menetti could see the fluorescent-blue flicker of the television.

"Yes?" he said, putting a fleshy hand on Alex's head. "What is it?"

Menetti heard the echo of a thousand rehearsals of the words he had ceased to believe he would ever say. "You are under arrest for the kidnapping of Alexander Selky. You have the right to remain silent. . . ." The man never moved as he was given his rights. He just stared mildly at the men on his porch as if he half-wondered what had taken them so long. When the handcuffs appeared, Alex, looking bewildered, shrank back and began to whimper, but the man with the walleye said only, "Allen . . . would you please turn off the TV?" And Alex immediately turned back into the living room to do so, and so missed seeing the man with the walleye being taken away.

Menetti, fighting an urge to scoop the boy up and hold him, followed Alex inside. Alex whirled around when Menetti entered the room, and edged away from him. Menetti opened his mouth to speak, but closed it again. He went into the kitchen, where against a counter littered with open boxes of cereal, jars of jelly, a half-eaten can of cold cooked potatoes, and a container of milk, he found a phone and dialed Susan's number. It rang ten times. He hung up and asked an operator to dial it for him. Again, no answer. He went back out onto the porch where the remaining policemen with the second squad car were waiting for him openmouthed with excitement.

"Alex Selky! No shit! Didn't you arrest a guy for killing him?"

Menetti nodded. His throat ached with joy . . . rage. It had been all he could do, in the moment his gaze met the mild, skewed one in the plump babyish face, to keep from lunging at the man's throat and battering that stringy bald head against the doorframe.

"Look," he said, "I can't reach the mother. What I want to do is just take this boy home the fastest way I can. Can I get an escort?"

The two officers looked at each other. They hitched at their belts. "I'll call headquarters," said one. He went down the steps to his car, now pulled up in front of the house, and leaning in the driver's side, made a call on the radio. He was back in a moment. "You got it," he said. "They just arrived with our man, and the place is going nuts down there."

"Okay, good," said Menetti, but inwardly he was thinking: Shit . . . the media. They'll be next. He went back in to Alex and knelt to talk to him eye to eye.

"Well, Alex . . . I've been looking for you a long time. I'm glad I found you."

Alex's face was blank and wary.

"My name is Detective Menetti, and I'm going to take you home to your mommy now."

Alex just stared at him. Menetti held out his hand, and Alex looked at it, then drew back.

Menetti stood up. "Just come on, now, Alex," he commanded, and he walked outside. God, it was cold, he suddenly noticed. Where in the body were the feelings? The heart? The pancreas? Did a mauling of the feelings show up in an autopsy? He suddenly pictured himself on a slab in the morgue, his chest cavity standing open like a woman's pocketbook, and the coroner taking out of it something that looked like a mass of chopped liver.

Alex had put on a cheap blue parka and followed Menetti onto the porch.

"A team is on its way over to search the house," said one of the waiting policemen. "We can go as soon as they get here."

"Good." The policemen stared at Alex, and smiled at him. He stared back at them. Menetti suddenly wondered if his pupils were unnaturally constricted. Drugged? His heart groaned. He thought of the nurse's uniform. That gutless shit . . . it must have been so easy for him. "I'm glad I don't have to do it," he said.

"Do what?" asked the policeman.

"Search the house. I don't want to know any more just at the moment."

"Oh, yeah," they said.

--❆ ❈--

ALEX STOOD on the porch, utterly alone. Walter was gone. He was supposed to keep the door locked all the time whenever Walter was gone. He knew what happened if Walter came home and found it open. What he didn't know was what happened if Walter didn't come home. He'd wondered that a lot. He wondered about it every time Walter locked him in and drove away. He had a pretty good idea that Walter wasn't coming back this time.

And now there was this one. My-name-is-Detective-Miniddy-I'm-going-to-take-you-to-your-mommy. Uh-huh. Walter wasn't a detective. Why should this one be? Walter didn't take him to his daddy. Why should this one? Why was taking him to Mommy a good idea, all of a sudden, after all this time? She changed her mind again?

Here comes another car, up the street, and it stops at our house. Out get four more men. Here they all come up the steps. They all stare at me and buzz and ogle. Ogle ogle. They don't know I can stare back, without blinking, longer than anybody.

If they take me somewhere else, what will happen to my birds?

I hope where they take me next there's a TV. Whenever you're locked in alone, it's bad when there's no TV.

This one that came up first is squatting down again talking.

If I don't listen to what he says, he can't fool me. He can *make* me; but he can't fool me.

He has things under his eyes like pockets. What would happen if I put bird bread in them?

He's squatting down talking to my face. The way we had to squat in the back to make BM's in the last place. It was so dark when I had to go at night without Walter. And no TV. It was good when Walter got tired of freezing his bum, because here is better.

Come, Alex. Well . . . here I go with my-name-is-Detective-Miniddy. He has a better car than ours . . . gee, he even already has a boy. Maybe this one will be with me at the next place. It would be good to have another kid.

MENETTI, HOLDING the front door of his car open, found that he could hardly bear to look at his own son. He didn't know whether he wanted to hug him or ignore him. He didn't know if he wanted to give all his attention to Alex or if he wanted to never have to look at that blank stare again in his life. He had an overwhelming desire to stop everything for a minute and sit down and pray. Eugene, who had been kneeling at the steering wheel watching the whole scene across the street, was agog.

"Dad . . ." he breathed. "We found Alex . . . didn't we? You're Alex, right? Dad, how did you know? Are we going to be famous?"

"Alex," said Menetti, "this is my son Eugene. Eugene, this is Alex. Do you want to ride up here with us, Alex?"

Alex said nothing. Eugene slid across the seat to the passenger side, his glowing eyes darting back and forth from Alex to his father, and gestured excitedly for Alex to get in beside him. Alex, looking at neither of them, climbed obediently into the car and sat down, facing straight ahead.

Eugene knew absolutely that something of stunning importance had happened. If he hadn't been able to figure it out, he could certainly have read it in the faces of the local police who had come to help his father. But he was both boy and deputy, and he took his cues instantly. His father was for some reason choosing to cork his sense of triumph up inside himself, as if he and Eugene solved famous crimes together every day, so Eugene tried to stop his own mouth and confine himself to wondrous staring. **This was the best game he had ever played,** and he was going to play it just like Daddy.

On the other hand, he was a little boy. When his father started the car and pulled out into the street, one of the police cars fell in behind them. From the radio came crackling instructions. "Left at the second light. Okay, stay in the right lane, and take your first right after the Mobile station."

"That's a police radio," Eugene whispered to Alex. Alex was studying it. He glanced up and eyed Eugene. He looked back at the radio.

"That's our microphone," said Eugene, pointing. Alex looked at it. "Dad," said Eugene quickly, "could I show him the microphone?"

Menetti said, "That's a good idea. Tell the escort we read them."

Eugene had long since mastered how it was done. "We copy," he said sternly into the microphone. "Do you read me?"

"Loud and clear," said the following car. "Take your next right on Barrow Street, and you'll pick up the signs for Route 6."

"Do you want to try it?" Eugene whispered to Alex.

Only Alex's eyes moved, from Eugene to the microphone.

"Here . . . you do it." Eugene handed him the mike, and after a moment, Alex said into it, "We copy," and then handed it quickly back to Eugene.

"Ten-four," said the car behind them. Alex looked at the radio, then at Eugene.

When they reached the highway, Menetti clamped his foot down on the gas and picked up to eighty. That was as fast as he dared go without endangering other motorists. The police car behind them picked up speed right with him and stayed on his tail. Menetti knew that in the car behind him the police would be alerting Connecticut Highway Patrol of their approach.

"Unmarked gray Plymouth with police escort proceeding east on Route 6, on urgent police business. . . . Yeah, that's right, we found the little boy that disappeared in Boston last summer, the Selky kid. That's right. Yes, alive. Willimantic PD. No, thank you, no assistance needed. Just keep the lanes clear and pass the word."

250

Eugene nudged Alex and pointed to the speedometer. The needle quivered above eighty. Alex looked at it, then back at Eugene. Eugene gave him a wide-eyed important nod. They both looked up at Menetti.

"Won't we get arrested, Dad?" whispered Eugene.

Menetti shook his head. "They'll have the news by radio. They'll know we're coming."

"Are we going to go this fast all the way to Boston, Dad?"

"Yes . . . unless it scares you."

"No way!" cried Eugene.

"Alex?"

Alex looked up.

"Are we going too fast for you?"

Alex shook his head.

"Does his mom know we're coming, Dad?"

"No, she doesn't. I tried to call her, but she must be out."

"She's always out," said Alex suddenly.

"What do you mean?" Menetti turned to him and spoke in a soft voice as if to him alone. But Alex had clamped his lips shut.

"Boy . . . is your mom going to be excited," Eugene whispered to Alex. Alex glanced over, a look that said that Eugene knew nothing about other people's family affairs.

"I've seen your mom on television about fifty times, telling everyone to keep looking for you. Would you say fifty times, Dad?"

"Maybe not fifty. But many."

"And my dad's been looking for you for about a year. You should have *seen* it on the news. Helicopters, and about a thousand policemen . . . didn't you see it?"

Alex shook his head. Jesus, thought Menetti, I wouldn't want to play poker with this kid.

"It was *neat*, and they had these posters with pictures of you all over the place; we had one in the window of our car everywhere we went. Didn't you see those?" Eugene went on. "And my dad was in charge of looking for you, it was all he did for months. Weren't you looking for him, Dad?"

"Yes," said Menetti softly. "I was."

Alex looked from one to the other. He wasn't surprised. Walter told him the police would be looking for him.

Their car sped through the countryside, and the police car stayed right on its tail.

"How much longer is it going to be, Dad?" asked Eugene. He was sitting tense with excitement on the edge of the seat.

"I think about another forty minutes." Menetti smiled at him. "Faster than the trip down, eh?"

"Boy, we should do it like this all the time." Eugene gave Alex a nudge, and Alex returned him a look of resignation. He supposed they thought they were fooling him.

He knew where he was going, and he didn't see why he should pretend he didn't. He didn't want them to think he was scared, though.

"Hey," Eugene whispered after a while. He guessed that his father had some reason for not asking Alex questions, but Eugene couldn't contain himself. "Did he keep you tied up?"

"What?"

"The guy who kidnapped you."

Menetti gave no sign that he was listening. The two small bodies on the passenger side seemed to him to take less room on the seat than one full-sized adult. He had always marveled at how kids could slip into a childworld where they seemed to assume that the adult driving the car had been struck deaf.

Alex looked perturbed. "My daddy hired Walter to pick me up. It was a secret from Mommy. She wanted me to go to school instead of seeing Daddy."

"You mean you were with your daddy all that time?"

"No," said Alex impatiently. "We went to this room and waited for a few days, but Daddy never came. He forgot."

Eugene was horrified. "I bet you cried a lot."

"I did." His impassivity slipped a little. For a moment his face was congested with the memory of those first days.

"Well, then, why didn't you go back home?"

"Mommy told Walter not to bother. She was mad at me for going with Walter, and she couldn't afford me anymore anyway. I eat a lot. Walter called her around Christmas because I thought she might want me for Christmas, but she told him that was all right, she'd got another little boy now."

Menetti couldn't keep silent for more of this. "Alex, he just told you those things . . . they're not true. Your father didn't hire him and your mother has been looking for you every minute since you disappeared. She missed you very much and she never gave up wanting you back."

Alex studied him with a face that was shrewd and thoughtful. He said, "But if I'm so much trouble, why would Walter lie?"

"If you're . . ." It took Menetti a moment to follow his train of thought. "Oh honey . . . Alex . . . just tell me one thing. Did he hurt you? Walter? Did he do things to you that hurt you?" He was painfully aware that Eugene was looking from him to Alex with a face confused and unhappy.

There was a long pause, during which Menetti began to regret having asked. "Walter took care of me," Alex said finally, without inflection. From the way he clamped his mouth shut it was clear that for him the conversation had ended.

They sped to the end of the Massachusetts Turnpike, they went north to the Mass Pike Extension and started into town. There, city traffic hemmed them in, and the police car behind them had trouble staying with them.

"Will his mommy be there when we get to his house?"

"I don't know, Eugene. They've probably found her by now. We could stop and telephone her and see. Alex?" Alex didn't answer. Menetti could see him perch forward on the seat studying the passing city sights, deep in a concentration of his own. "Is it getting familiar, Alex?"

No answer.

They reached the Copley Square exit, where the Willimantic police car caught up with them at the traffic light. Now it was Menetti's city, and he would have to be sure not to lose his escort. Together the two cars drove across Dartmouth Street. Alex was watchful and silent, Eugene was beginning to tense with excitement, and Menetti was numb, wondering what he was heading for.

"She's going to be so *excited*," Eugene whispered to Alex with dramatic earnestness. "She's gonna be *so* excited. We're almost there, Dad, right? Aren't we almost there? I came here with my dad last summer and helped put up posters of you. I think it was right around here."

Alex's gaze flicked warily from one to another. It *was* his neighborhood. Maybe they could be taking him to his mommy.

253

But probably they were taking him to jail.

They stopped at the corner of Marlborough. He could almost see Justine's house from here. He sat up straighter and craned his neck as if he might see someone he knew. What an odd feeling. The feeling of something familiar. He let something flicker inside him like the shadow of a high-flying bird flashing across a patch of sunlight. Was it possible he could be allowed to go home?

"Hey, look," yelled Eugene, "there's one! Hey, Alex, see it? In the window of that house! That might be one of the ones I put there, right, Dad?" Eugene pointed, and Alex looked, and there in the window of a secretarial school was a poster. MISSING. And under the word, the smiling face. Alex looked at it. "See? Asking *everyone* to look for you." Alex studied. Missing. They were missing him? He almost let himself give away a smile, but then he caught on to the trick. Missing. WANTED. He'd seen Wanted posters of other bad people in a post office once. Walter pointed them out. "And they know all about you, too," Walter had said. "So . . ." Alex didn't have to be told so *what*. He never made a peep if he ever went anywhere with Walter. He kept his head down.

Menetti, his face set and bitter, stepped on the gas hard. The car leaped toward Beacon Street. He'd had all of this he could take. He wanted to get to Susan. Behind him the Willimantic police car hesitated, then pulled through the intersection right behind him and turned on its siren. In the holiday-empty streets, the sudden urgent howl of it seemed to echo and reecho from the walls, a sound that filled Alex with cold certainty.

SUSAN HAD TAKEN Taxi with her to lunch in the South End with two of her section leaders, and afterward she walked him the long way home. She was just coming up Marlborough Street when she heard the siren. She thought, pushing her hands deeper into her pockets and breathing a cloud into the bitter frost of the February air: Another accident, or another crime. Ah, poor souls. Poor hurt souls.

It was only when the noise kept growing louder and louder as if it were coming for her that she began to feel afraid. It was more instinctive than specific. She was here, Taxi was here, they'd never again bring Graham home to her, what else did she have to lose? That didn't prevent her from hearing the siren scream closer and closer and knowing in her heart that there was simply no end to what the world could teach you to fear.

When she turned the corner into Fremont Street as the siren died, she saw so many cars and trucks and people crowded into the street that her heart lurched. She felt herself go cold with dread and forced herself to keep walking, one foot before the other, so that whatever it was, flames or not, she could never be said to have either hurried its coming or run away.

There were so many people milling up and down her steps, pointing to her, pointing to the street, pointing to each other, that she didn't know where to look first. There was much brightness, but no smoke that she could see; there were police and news vans, but no fire trucks. Surprise and fear seemed to freeze the scene before her, so she took it in slow motion. It seemed to be happening in a silent bubble world out of time and feeling. There was a car pulling up that looked just like Menetti's. The two front doors of the car opened at the same time. Menetti emerged from the driver's side and stood there in the street looking at her, an intense beseeching look, as if he were trying to say something to her but couldn't open his mouth. His presence made no sense to her at all.

From the scurry through the crowd to the sidewalk she saw that some of Menetti's kids were with him. There was Eugene and another kid, not Marco, more Eugene's age. Judging every small boy as she always did, she dismissed this one as older and taller than Alex, with dull, short, dun-colored hair. She moved forward. Now she knew: her father was dead. No, she'd left the iron on, the house was burning. . . . Margaret. Margaret was hurt, or trapped . . .

It wasn't until Taxi bolted away from her down the sidewalk, barking with lunatic joy, that she stopped cold and looked at the two children again. Taxi leaped at the blue parka. She looked again, and this time really saw the face. She actually saw the child who for so many months she had carried alive inside her. Right there. He was a dozen paces away from her. Her brain seemed to disconnect from her vision, as if she could see, but not understand what she saw. She watched Alex glance around and then subtly move his hands, then feet, apart and then together again, as if testing to see if they were restrained in any way.

Menetti was there with the boys now, and she looked back to him, with mildness and wonder. It was all so incredibly queer. What was the name for the look on Menetti's face? Contrition.

She was a lake of puzzled feeling dammed up behind the thinnest membrane. How could this be so confusing? How could there be so much to absorb? This was the simplest moment of her life.

It all broke open inside her as she looked back to Alex, and opened her arms to him, and in that moment, got past the Alex of the missing months to her own boy. She saw him smile. And then he cried, "Mommy!" And she was on her knees on the frozen sidewalk blind with tears when her son flung himself into her arms.